D1563424

DATE DUE

Maroon Arts

SALLY PRICE AND RICHARD PRICE

Maroon Arts

Cultural Vitality
in the African Diaspora

BEACON PRESS · BOSTON

Beacon Press
25 Beacon Street
Boston, Massachusetts 02108-2892
www.beacon.org

Beacon Press books
are published under the auspices of
the Unitarian Universalist Association of Congregations.

03 02 01 00 99   8 7 6 5 4 3 2 1

Text design by Scott-Martin Kosofsky at The Philidor Company, Cambridge

Library of Congress Cataloging-in-Publication Data

Price, Sally.
    Maroon arts : cultural vitality in the African diaspora / Sally
  Price and Richard Price.
        p.   cm.
    Includes bibliographical references.
    ISBN: 0-8070-8550-2 (cloth)
    ISBN: 0-8070-8551-0 (paper)
    1. Arts, Maroon.   2. Maroons—Suriname—Social life and customs.
  I. Price, Richard, 1941–   .   II. Title.
  NX537.2.A1P76   1999
  704.03'969883—dc21   98-29572

Contents

1.1. Armadillo in purpleheart, carved 1997 in French Guiana for the tourist trade by Djam (Elefina), one of the first Saramaka women to practice this quintessentially men's art.

Souvenirs

ON THE WALL of an upscale boutique in Cayenne hangs a handsome blond-wood paddle. "Quality reproduction—2500 francs," says the tag. Next to it, wired to the wall for security, hangs the dark-wood original, an antique studded with brass tacks. The French shopkeeper declares he wouldn't sell it for all the tea in China.

Several thousand miles to the north, in a dusty museum storeroom on Seventy-ninth Street and Central Park West, lies another carving of identical design. It has been there since the late 1920s.

The shopkeeper obligingly detaches both paddles from the wall so the Saramaka woodcarver who has come in with us can pose for our camera with one in each hand. (The artist has told us that he's the one who carved the "original," following a drawing provided by a schoolteacher from France. That Frenchman, we've realized, must have copied the design from a photograph of the New York museum paddle that was published in a 1970 art book.) The Saramaka carver whispers that the blond-wood reproduction was made by one of his nephews, a young man who provides objects for the boutique on a regular basis. The shopkeeper looks on, unable to understand the language being spoken but clearly pleased that we seem to be admiring his paddles. And then he turns to his next customer, a German rocket scientist employed at the European Space Center at the edge of the rainforest, an hour's drive away, who's interested in purchasing a framed butterfly.

Thirty years ago, when we began writing about Saramaka Maroons, such a scene would have been unimaginable. Then, Maroons' lives and concerns were securely anchored in the Suriname rainforest, where, a full century before Emancipation in that Dutch colony, their ancestors had wrested their freedom from their masters after a long guerrilla war and had forged vibrant new Afro-American cultures. In the 1960s, the six Maroon peoples were still being referred to by anthropologists as "tribes" and described as "states within a state." Running their own political and judicial affairs, they were known for such exotic practices as polygyny, oracular divination, spirit possession, body scarification, and ancestor worship, as well as distinctive styles of music, dance, and plastic arts, and countless other aspects of daily life that served as reminders of their uncompromised heritage of independence. Maroons' dealings with the outside world remained largely limited to men's wage-labor trips, aimed at accumulating enough cash to buy soap, salt, tools, cloth, kerosene, kitchenware, and other necessities for life back in the villages of the rainforest. Maroons felt tremendous pride in the accomplishments of their heroic ancestors, and on the whole they remained masters of their forest realm.

Over the past three decades, the world of Saramakas and other Maroon peoples has undergone enormous transformations and their arts have traveled in new directions. While woodcarvings, textiles, and other products of Maroon artistic creativity are still a part of everyday life in villages strung along the rivers of the rainforest, they now also appear in souvenir shops serving European clienteles, at crafts fairs in the United States, on festival stages in Amsterdam, Berlin, and Washington, in commercial videos, in museum gift shops, and in the living room decors of made-for-TV movies. Recently we helped a Saramaka carver set up a homepage on the Internet.[1]

During the same period, the discipline of anthropology and the questions its practitioners ask about art and aesthetics have also changed dramatically. Gone are the days of describing discrete, "authentic" traditions. Welcome, instead, to the exploration of change, movement, hybridization, creolization, negotiated identities, borderlands, and unstable authenticities. And, needless to say, the present authors are not quite the same as the two adventuresome anthropologists, then in their early twenties, who canoed up the Suriname River in 1966, deep into the heart of the rainforest, seeking ethnographic knowledge of these proud descendants of rebel slaves (fig. 1.2).

1.2. The two adventuresome anthropologists, 1968.

In retrospect, it is not difficult to see how our 1960s fieldwork and the writings based on it reflected the conventions of the day. Our professional training, which encouraged a panoptical, encyclopedic mode of fieldwork in the Malinowskian vein, may have had its merits. But the preferred modes of analysis (which tended to see small-scale societies as cultural isolates living outside history) and reportage (which systematically erased the ethnographers themselves and their relations with the people they studied) also led us to underplay what we now consider some of the more significant aspects of life in the rainforest—the nature of individual variation (in knowledge, skills, beliefs), the extent of Maroons' imbrication in the global economy, the depth of their historical consciousness, and other cultural phenomena that today seem central to an understanding of those societies.[2]

In this context, our 1980 book, *Afro-American Arts of the Suriname Rain Forest*, might be seen as an endpoint. Produced as an exhibition catalogue, it was our last real attempt to commit the impossible act of writing encyclopedic ethnography, trying to represent Maroon culture in the voice of omniscient (and, for the most part, textually absent) observers. By the time it was published, we—along with classmates who seem to have been experiencing similar tensions between the regnant anthropological models and what they had encountered "in the field"[3]—had already begun serious engagement with the notion of "partial truths" (Clifford 1986:7–8). And we had begun writing ethnography in which individual, historicized Saramaka voices took center stage—in which people who had traditionally been viewed by scholars as mythic heroes or as objects of study began to take their places as teachers, collaborators, and historians in their own right.[4]

1980 also marked an endpoint for Suriname. In February the army seized power in a coup d'état, and the country, just five years into its independence from the Netherlands, began a downward spiral from which it has not yet emerged. Crime, drugs, civil war, a plummeting economy, and massive deforestation have torn at the physical, social, and moral landscape. And thousands of Maroons have taken refuge, most clandestinely, in neighboring French Guiana, where they attempt to reconstitute the life they knew along the rivers of the Suriname rainforest. For many of these Maroon "illegals," the quality of life rises and falls with immigration policy decisions made in Paris—at the time of our 1997 visit, a number of men had sent their wives and daughters back to Suriname because they couldn't run fast enough when teams of gendarmes raided their woodcarving stalls and set fire to their houses.

Writing today, even on the subject of the arts, we must bear special witness to the devastating effects of the fighting that raged from 1986 to 1992, pitting Maroons against the national army of Suriname and bringing back to life many of the horrors of the eighteenth-century colonial struggles. African medicine bundles that had lain buried for two hundred years were unearthed and carried into battle (along with, apparently, copies of R. Price 1983a, which recounts the Saramakas' eighteenth-century fight for freedom). Ndyuka and Saramaka warriors, often armed with shotguns, confronted automatic weapons, tanks, and helicopter gunships dropping napalm. Whole villages were razed, particularly among the Cottica Ndyuka, as soldiers killed hundreds of women and children with machetes and bullets (see Polimé and Thoden van Velzen 1988, R. Price 1995). Some 10,000 Ndyuka refugees were forced to flee their devastated territory for refugee camps in French Guiana, where many remained for years.

On the home front, Ndyuka and Saramaka life has been changed, perhaps irreversibly, with rampant poverty and malnutrition, degradation of educational and medical resources, and the arrival of AIDS and prostitution. The restoration of peace in 1992 came at a price, as the Maroons were pushed into signing a treaty largely focused on the ownership of rights to land, minerals, and other natural resources—all of which are now claimed by the Suriname state. That document leaves no doubt that the government has embarked on a rigorous program aimed at the legal unification, the uniformization, and ultimately the appropriation of its Maroon and Amerindian minorities. Much of the forest for which the ancestors of the Saramakas and Ndyukas spilled their blood two hundred years ago is being auctioned off by the national government to Indonesian, Malaysian, Chinese, Australian, and Brazilian timber corporations (Colchester 1995). Concerned outsiders are still expressing the hope that the desperately poor government of Suriname will somehow work out ways to preserve the Maroons' forest resources, encourage economic development, and provide much-needed hospitals and schools, while respecting the Maroons' autonomy and their right to a separate identity. But as this book goes to press in 1998, the latest news is grim. Representatives of Chinese logging companies and Canadian mining enterprises are being flown by Suriname military helicopters into Saramaka and Ndyuka villages and telling inhabitants that if they venture into the newly granted concessions—which cover most of traditional Saramaka and Ndyuka territory—they will be shot on sight (see, for example Forest Peoples Programme 1998a, 1998b; R. Price 1998).

Meanwhile, those Maroons who are officially French citizens by virtue of having been born east of the Marowijne and Lawa Rivers have been adapting to a pervasive program of *"francisation,"* which disseminates the language and culture of the Hexagon, provides generous welfare benefits, redefines the nature of Maroon political leadership and land ownership, encourages consumerism both in the stores of French Guiana and through

European mail order catalogues, and promotes Maroon visual and performative arts as part of the cultural patrimony of Overseas France.

During the past dozen years, we have had opportunities to become acquainted firsthand with Maroons living in eastern Suriname and in French Guiana. Beginning in 1986, when military police subjected us to a midnight expulsion from Suriname in the initial stages of the civil war, our trips to the area have been through Cayenne, French Guiana, rather than Paramaribo (the capital of Suriname), our travel to the interior has been along the Marowijne River rather than up the Suriname, and our continuing research on Maroon culture in central Suriname has depended on the reports of Saramakas resettled in French Guiana. Thanks in part to the Bureau du Patrimoine Ethnologique in Cayenne (which has now become the Musée des Cultures Guyanaises), we have made several "expeditions" to Aluku, Ndyuka, and Paramaka villages (see R. and S. Price 1992a), bringing up to date the understandings of eastern Maroon art we had earlier constructed on the basis of the literature. And the adaptations that Saramaka workers have long made during periods spent away from their home villages are now something we've seen at first hand rather than through reports from afar.

Exposure to Maroons along the Marowijne and in French Guiana has, however, been meager consolation for the break in our trips to Suriname. Although the U.S. embassy was officially informed that our 1986 expulsion was "an administrative error" and that we were welcome to return to Suriname whenever we wished, acquaintances in Paramaribo have counseled caution—initially for reasons tied to our close association with the populations who opposed the military government during the civil war, and subsequently because of our participation in the prosecution of human rights abuses committed by the Suriname military, particularly R. P.'s testimony at a 1992 trial before the Inter-American Court of Human Rights, in San José, Costa Rica. Charged with assessing reparations to the dependents of seven Saramakas tortured and murdered by soldiers on New Year's Eve 1987, the international panel of judges ordered the government of Suriname (which had reluctantly acknowledged guilt for the massacre) to pay damages totaling U.S.$453,102 to the victims' families (R. Price 1995).

Our sense of loss at not being able to return to the villages of the Suriname interior came to a head ten years ago, when Saramakas honored the memory of their longtime leader, Agbago Aboikoni. Paramount chief between 1951 and his death in 1989, Agbago was the person who first granted us permission to conduct research in Saramaka, suggesting that we have a house built in his natal village a few yards from that of his older sister, Naai, then in her nineties, and within shouting distance of his younger brother, Kala, a formidable presence who held one of the eighteenth-century headman's staffs dating from the original peace treaties. Our 1980 art book was dedicated to these three siblings, each of whom was a central figure in our life in Suriname.

Agbago was a revered, deeply knowledgeable elder and leader, balancing an insistence on respect for the traditional values of his predecessors with the need for diplomacy during a period of increasing contact between Sara-makas and coastal society. Tenaciously holding on to life during the civil war, asserting that it was his duty not to die while arms were still being carried, he finally relinquished his grip at the age of 102. His exceptional stature was celebrated by an exceptional funeral, which lasted for many months and was attended by thousands of mourners. These events were covered by print and television journalists, and documented in books.[5] The next year we viewed selected scenes on a VCR in a ramshackle house in the Saramaka workers' quarters of Kourou, in the shadow of the Ariane launch pad. (The fourth chapter of this book opens with a scene from 1978 in which Agbago reminisced with us about his youth, and looked ahead to his funeral.)

MAROON ARTS is intended to introduce a new generation of readers to the arts of the Maroons, one of the richest, most creative bodies of cultural expression evolved by the descendants of Africans in the Americas. Building on our research of the past thirty-three years, it attempts to convey the artistic spirit that remains alive among Maroons despite the hardships they have been experiencing as individuals and as communities.

Our presentation of these arts is colored not only by changes in the world of the Maroons and general developments within our own academic milieu, but also by specific shifts in anthropological approaches to the study of art and history.[6]

A diminished focus on cultural isolates has reoriented understandings about the arts of non-Western societies over the past two decades. Where scholars once strained to discern the stylistic essences of particular arts in particular cultures, they are now directing their gaze more frequently toward the doorways where artistic and aesthetic ideas jostle each other in their passage from one cultural setting to the next. Where the emphasis was once on abstracting back from an overlay of modernity to discover uncorrupted artistic traditions, modernization now lies at the heart of the enterprise, providing a springboard for explorations of cultural creativity and self-affirmation. Where the site of artistic production was once located in lineages of convention within bounded communities, it now spreads into the global arena, pulling in players from every corner of the world, from

1.3. Chief Agbago's coffin on the final journey from village to cemetery. Gravediggers returning to the village, 1989.

every kind of society, and from every chamber of the art world's vast honey-comb. The hierarchies that assigned distinct roles (and value) to fine and folk, art and craft, primitive and modern, high and low are giving way to investigations of these categories' interpenetrations and an insistent deconstruction of the categories themselves. And sacred territories of art historical scholarship, where original works framed by erudite connoisseur-ship once held pride of place, are being quietly invaded by a growing interest in copies, fakes, appropriations, and derivative forms.

These shifts have been accompanied by a marked, if gradual, rapproche-ment between anthropologists and art historians. In the museum world, the most visible evidence has been an explosion, over the past decade or two, of exhibitions integrating anthropological and art historical issues and scholar-ship, juxtaposing arts from previously segregated categories, and calling attention to the defining (and redefining) power of display context. Concern with the ethics of cultural ownership is also moving to center stage, thanks largely to the rising number and volume of voices coming from third- and fourth-world populations, cultural studies programs, and spectators of the postmodern scene from the fields of literature, history, philosophy, econom-ics, and political science. Rights of interpretation are under lively discus-sion; cultural authority is being renegotiated; the privileged status of long established canons is under attack; and museum acquisition policies designed to maximize the preservation of data and the growth of scientific knowledge are being contested by more ethically focused debates aimed at responsible de-accessioning and repatriation.[7]

Our current perspectives on Maroon art follow in the footsteps of S. Price's *Primitive Art in Civilized Places* (1989). Setting Western ideas concerning "primitive art" in the broader context of art collecting, cultural politics, the legacies of colonialism, and the ideology of connoisseurship, that book argued for the critical reassessment of assumed across-the-board commonalities in the artistic and aesthetic lives of non-Western peoples. In terms of Maroon arts, this has meant that received wisdom about the sexual symbolism of Maroon motifs, the view of woodcarving as a tradition-bound art, the collapsing of individuals into a generic Maroon artist, and even the definition of Maroon art as a primarily male domain need to be replaced, one by one, with insights and observations that emerge from the specific context of the Maroon case rather than being built on the backs of truisms about "the primitive artist."

One tired notion we have disputed is the idea that discovering the "meaning" of art in nonliterate societies is a matter of deciphering a symbolic code, typically imagined as one in which sex, fertility, and the supernatural loom large. For many years, the literature on Maroons was dominated by an obsessive attempt to unravel the hidden secrets behind artistic motifs (particularly in woodcarving), each of which was thought to carry a specific "meaning" which could be "read" by those who learned the system. A chapter of our 1980 book called "Iconography and Social Meaning" attacked this assertion head-on and argued for alternative understandings of the nature of Maroon art. Citing examples from the ample supply of cases in which outsiders had cajoled their Maroon informants into an acceptance of iconographic interpretations, we attempted to show that the resulting studies reflected Western stereotypes of "primitive art" more than the meanings that operated within the artists' communities.

Even today, the vision of Maroon woodcarving as a readable symbolic system has not completely disappeared from the popular Western imagination. As recently as 1995, an urban Guyanais claimed to have unlocked the secrets of "this unknown art" in a lavishly (if garishly) illustrated coffee-table book which offers (for $70) "authoritative" readings of woodcarving motifs:

> The symmetrical scrolls are the abstract representation of the body of a pregnant woman, thus symbolizing fertility. (Bruné 1995:42–43)

> The motifs convey the desire to maintain sentimental harmony within the couple . . . and others depict the tongue, a reference to the importance of communication. (Ibid., 32–33)

> The "ants' trail" motif symbolizes agility and pugnacity in the context of work, almost like the [European] fable of the ant. (Ibid., 27)

In short, woodcarving is seen as "the rebus of sexual relations, which the man gives to the woman to decipher . . . a symbolic language intended to amuse and seduce her" (Bruné 1995:ix).

But serious scholarship on Maroon art has by now shed its insistence on uncovering meanings of this sort, which frees us to focus attention more exclusively on the kinds of meaning that Maroons themselves consider important. As a result, the tie-ins between art and social life become central to our task—whether we're looking at the sentimental associations of woodcarvings that men present to women as gifts of love, the (often biting) social commentary implicit in the naming of particular cloth patterns, or the practice of men setting aside a decoratively sewn textile made by each of their sexual partners as a token of these relationships to be displayed at their funeral. Maroons also view the arts as a canvas for the confirmation of gender differences, finding significance in distinctions between the men's tendency to excel at rigidly symmetrical geometric designs and the women's to produce free-form, off-center compositions (see S. Price 1993 [1984]).

Our determined pursuit of the art *history* of the Maroons goes hand in hand with recent attacks on the popular image of "timeless primitives" who perpetuate the "age-old traditions" of their ancestors. And our insistence on recognizing the individuality of Maroon artists, which has emerged directly from our understanding of Maroon priorities, is closely bound to the more general argument that the "anonymity" of the "primitive" artist emerges, more often than not, in the course of the process by which Westerners take physical and conceptual possession of the creative output of identifiable individuals.

A rapprochement between history and anthropology—the flowering of what might be called ethnographic history—has also altered the intellectual landscape. At the time we began our work in Suriname, most scholars believed that the early history of Maroons (like those of most nonliterate peoples—"the people without history" in Eric Wolf's [1982] ironizing phrase) was largely irretrievable and unknowable. Since then, it has been shown that oral traditions in these largely nonliterate societies, when combined with archival resources, can yield striking pictures of their formative years. Many historical processes that had hitherto been merely hypothesized could now be demonstrated. A great deal about the ways enslaved Africans coming from diverse Old World societies and cultures were able to form new African-American communities has became clear. The development in the Americas of new languages, religions, arts, and social and political institutions, all based in part on complex amalgams of diverse African heritages, has begun to become visible. And in this fashion, the study of maroon societies has helped pioneer the recovery of the ways African-American cultures more generally came to be.

A programmatic essay by S. W. Mintz and R. Price, first written in the early 1970s and published in 1992 as *The Birth of African-American Culture,* argued for acknowledgment of the cultural heterogeneity of enslaved Africans who arrived in the New World, for the importance of inter-African cultural exchange as a creative force in the building of new societies, for an attention to processes of cultural formation that occurred during the early years of colonization, and for a recognition of the crucial role played by underlying cultural principles and assumptions shared by Africans of diverse ethnic origins. It insisted that Africans and their descendants in the New World, far from being mere victims, played active and dynamic roles— despite unspeakably oppressive conditions—in forging their own destinies. Since that essay first appeared, its proposed scenarios have been much debated but only infrequently explored empirically (see Mintz and Price

1992 [1976]:vii–xiv). Because our own research over the past three decades has turned Maroon history and historical consciousness into one of the most fully documented cases in the literature on nonliterate societies, and because we have cast our ethnographic net over a wide range of cultural forms (from speech and music to dance and the plastic arts), it is now possible to trace foundational aesthetic undercurrents as they have passed from one site to another, producing dynamic, creative forms of expression on the shoulders of solidly pan-African aesthetic principles. In this way, the present book may be seen as a demonstration in a specific ethnographic context—Maroon art history—of some of the general suggestions about the study of African-American history first set forth in the Mintz and Price essay.

Two decades of additional encounters with Maroons and their arts, as well as changing perspectives in the academy, have put us in a better position to situate Maroon art history within processes of globalization (or, perhaps better, translocality—see Clifford 1997) than when we published *Afro-American Arts of the Suriname Rain Forest*. And we are now better able to locate the Maroons' remarkable cultural achievements within the broader history of the Atlantic world.

It is this combination of fresh perspectives and long-term ethnography that we draw on as we try to make sense of the often unpredictable twists and turns of Maroon cultural history, whether an armadillo carved for the tourist trade by a Saramaka woman living in French Guiana (fig. 1.1) or a Saramaka carver posing with a paddle that is a copy of a copy of a copy being sold to European rocket scientists passing through Cayenne.

"A Rebel Negro armed & on his guard." Engraving by Francesco Bartolozzi (Stedman 1988 [1790]:391).

Maroons of the Guianas 2

Ayako had a sister who lived on the same plantation. One day she was at work, with her baby tied to her back. The child began crying but the white man didn't want her to sit down to nurse. It kept crying. She kept working. The child still cried. Then the white man called her, "Bring the child and I'll hold it for you." So she took the baby off her back and handed it over and returned to work. He grasped the child by the legs, held it upside down, and lowered its head into a bucket of water until it was dead. Then he called the woman and said, "Take the child and tie it on your back." She tied it on and returned to work until nightfall when they released the slaves from work. The child was dead, stiff as a board.

Well, Ayako saw this and said, "What sadness! My family is finished. My sister has but one child left and when she goes to work tomorrow, if the child cries, the white man will do the same thing. I'll be witness to the annihilation of my family. Now, when I was in Africa, I wasn't a nobody. I will make a special effort and see if I still have my powers intact." Then he got himself ready. And he escaped! He ran off with his sister and her baby daughter. It wasn't considered humanly possible to escape from that plantation, but he did it!

At the edge of the forest, he called out his praise name: "I'm the one. *Okúndo bi okúndo.* The largest of all the animals. I may not have tools but I can still take care of my family!" Then they entered the forest and continued on till nightfall. All he carried was the great Lámba gourd. Whenever they were hungry, they simply ate from that gourd. That was our food in those days.

—*Captain Kala of Dangogo*, 1978

For nearly five hundred years, societies formed by maroons (escaped slaves) have dotted the peripheries of plantation America. Ranging from tiny bands that survived for less than a year to powerful states encompassing thousands of members and surviving for generations or even centuries, these communities still form semi-independent enclaves in several parts of the hemisphere. They remain fiercely proud of their maroon origins and, in some cases at least, continue to carry forward unique cultural traditions

2.1, 2.2. "A Negro hung alive by the Ribs to a Gallows," and "The Execution of Breaking on the Rack." Engravings by William Blake (Stedman 1988 [1790]:105, 548).

MAROON ARTS

that were forged during the earliest days of Afro-American history (see R. Price 1996 [1973]).

Over the past three centuries, the classic setting for maroon communities has been the forested interior of Suriname, a Dutch colony in northeastern South America that gained its independence in 1975. The Suriname Maroons (formerly known as "Bush Negroes") have long been the hemisphere's largest maroon population, representing one extreme in the range of cultural adaptations that Afro-Americans have made in the New World. Between the mid-seventeenth and late eighteenth centuries, the ancestors of the present-day Maroons escaped from the coastal plantations on which they were enslaved, in many cases soon after their arrival from Africa, and fled into the forested interior, where they regrouped into small bands. Their hardships in forging an existence in a new and inhospitable environment were compounded by the persistent and massive efforts of the colonial government to eliminate this threat to the plantation colony.

The colonists reserved special punishments for recaptured slaves—hamstringing, amputation of limbs, and a variety of deaths by torture. For example, one recaptured town slave, "whose punishment shall serve as an example to others," was sentenced

> to be quartered alive, and the pieces thrown in the River. He
> was laid upon the ground, his head on a long beam. The first
> blow he was given, on the abdomen, burst open his bladder, yet
> he uttered not the least sound. The second blow with the axe he
> tried to deflect with his hand, but it gashed his hand and upper
> belly, again without his uttering a sound. The slave men and
> women laughed at this, saying to one another, "That is a man!"
> Finally, the third blow, to his chest, killed him. His head was cut
> off and the body cut in four pieces and dumped in the river.
> (Herlein 1718:117)

Several years later, two military expeditions against the nascent Saramaka people captured a number of villagers, and in 1730 the criminal court meted out the sentences:

> The Negro Joosie shall be hanged from the gibbet by an Iron
> Hook through his ribs, until dead; his head shall then be severed
> and displayed on a stake by the riverbank, remaining to be picked
> over by birds of prey. As for the Negroes Wierrie and Manbote,
> they shall be bound to a stake and roasted alive over a slow fire,
> while being tortured with glowing Tongs. The Negro girls, Lucre-
> tia, Ambira, Aga, Gomba, Marie, and Victoria will be tied to a
> Cross, to be broken alive, and then their heads severed, to be

exposed by the riverbank on stakes. The Negro girls Diana and Christina shall be beheaded with an axe, and their heads exposed on poles by the riverbank. (R. Price 1983a:85)

The organized pursuit of Maroons and expeditions to destroy their settlements date at least from the 1670s, when a citizens' militia was established for this purpose. During the late seventeenth and early eighteenth centuries, numerous small-scale military expeditions were mounted, sometimes at the personal expense of particular planters—but these rarely met with success, for the Maroons had established and protected their settlements with great ingenuity and had become expert at all aspects of guerrilla warfare. It was between the 1730s and 1750s, when "the colony had become the theater of a perpetual war" (Nassy 1788, I:87), that such expeditions reached their maximum size and frequency. Among those sent out in 1730, for example, was one that included 50 citizens and 200 slaves and claimed to have killed 16 Saramakas and captured 4 men, 12 women, and 10 children, including those whose executions are described above (Hartsinck 1770: 759-65). Other expeditions on this scale were mounted throughout the period: a force sent out in 1743 was composed of 27 civilians, 12 soldiers, 15 Indians, 165 slaves, and 60 canoes (Nassy 1788, I:93). Though the most successful military expeditions of the 1730s and 1740s returned with as many as "47 prisoners and six hands of those whom they had killed" (Nassy 1788, I: 92), most were fruitless. Indeed, by the late 1740s the colonists were finding the costs overwhelming, as typical expeditions were costing "more than 100,000 guilders each" and had to traverse "forty mountains and sixty creeks" before reaching the Maroons' hidden villages (Hartsinck 1770:766- 68). By this time it had also become clear to the colonists that the expeditions themselves were contributing to further marronage, by making known to the slaves both the escape routes from the plantations and the locations of Maroon villages.

The increasingly costly warfare between colonists and Maroons, which by the mid-eighteenth century had lasted nearly one hundred years, culminated in a decision by the whites, during the late 1740s, to sue their former slaves for permanent peace. But peace proved elusive, and in 1754-55, the colonists decided to mount yet another massive expedition, to consist of 500 men, against the Saramakas—"either to make one last attempt at a permanent Peace . . . or else search them out and completely destroy them" (R. Price 1983a:157). The story of this final expedition—as well as the whole saga of the hundred years leading to the peace treaties of the 1760s—is told in detail from a Saramaka perspective (and, separately, from a colonial one) in R. Price 1983a and 1983b. In 1760 and 1762 peace treaties were at last successfully concluded with the two largest Maroon peoples, the Ndyukas and the Saramakas, and in 1767 with the much smaller Matawai. New slave revolts and the large-scale war of subsequent decades, for which an army of mercenaries was imported from Europe (see Stedman 1988 [1790]), eventually led to the formation of the Aluku (Boni), as well as the smaller Paramaka and Kwinti groups.[1]

2.3. "March thro' a swamp or, Marsh in Terra firma." Engraving by William Blake (Stedman 1988 [1790]:403). Colonial troops and slaves searching for Maroon villages.

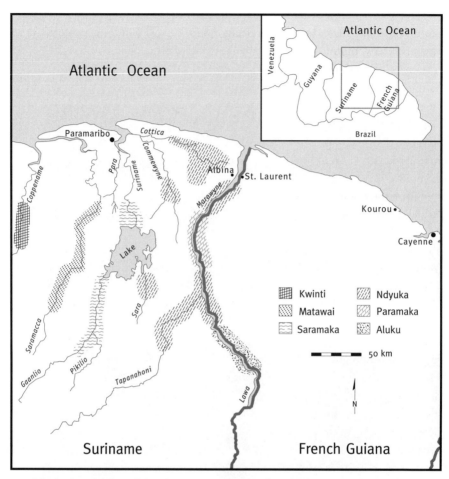

2.4. Principal territories of the six Maroon peoples. (For the locations of the villages mentioned in this book, see S. and R. Price 1980:16 and R. Price 1983a.)

TODAY THERE ARE SIX politically distinct Maroon peoples in Suriname and French Guiana—the Ndyuka and Saramaka each have a population of about 24,000, the Matawai, Aluku (Boni), and Paramaka are each closer to 2000, and the Kwinti number fewer than 500. Their territories are shown in the sketch map (fig. 2.4), though today large numbers of Maroons live outside of these areas, mainly in Paramaribo and the coastal towns of French Guiana. Although formed under broadly similar historical and ecological conditions, these societies display significant variation in everything from language, diet, and dress to patterns of marriage, residence, and migratory wage labor. From a cultural point of view, the greatest differences are between the Maroons of central Suriname (Saramaka, Matawai, and Kwinti), on the one hand, and those of eastern Suriname and western French Guiana (Ndyuka, Aluku, and Paramaka) on the other.[2]

Since the colonial government of Suriname signed treaties with the Ndyuka, Saramaka, and Matawai in the 1760s and later recognized the Aluku, Paramaka, and Kwinti, a loose framework of indirect rule has obtained. Except for the Kwinti, each group has a paramount chief (who from an internal perspective might better be described as a king), as well as a series of headmen and other village-based officials. Traditionally, the role of these people in political and social control has been exercised in a context replete with oracles, spirit possession, and other forms of divination. For the past two decades, the national government of Suriname and the regional French government in Cayenne have intervened increasingly in Maroon internal affairs—the government of Suriname as part of ongoing development schemes, a civil war that began in 1986, and subsequent mining and forestry projects, and the French government through its assimilationist program of *francisation* and its handling of Maroon refugees from Suriname's civil war.

Before these recent upheavals, Maroon villages—whether in Saramaka, Ndyuka, or other traditional territories—averaged 100–200 residents, mainly people related through the female line, but also some wives and children of lineage men. Although the relationships defined by such matrilineal ties have always been important in all aspects of life, from residence patterns to marriage prohibitions and succession to political office, men are very close to their children, often playing an active role in their upbringing and passing on ritual knowledge to their sons. Because many men have two or three (or, in rare cases, more) wives, and because principal responsibility for each child is entrusted to one adult rather than to a couple, "nuclear families" do not live together as households. Most children spend their first four to six years with their mother, after which they may be given to their father, an aunt or uncle, or some other relative, and at later ages there may be further shifts, in response, for example, to the child's developing needs and changes in the parents' marital status or residence patterns.

Maroons have always devoted massive amounts of time, energy, and resources to rituals of various sorts. Such decisions as where to clear a garden or build a house, whether to make a trip, or how to deal with theft or adultery are made in consultation with village deities, ancestors, forest spirits, snake gods, and other powers. The means of communicating with these entities vary, from spirit possession and the consultation of oracle bundles to the interpretation of dreams. Gods and spirits, who are a constant presence in daily life, are also honored through frequent prayers, libations, feasts, and dances. Birth, death, and other life crises are handled through extensive ritual, and much the same could be said of more mundane activities such as hunting a tapir or planting a rice field.

Because of the frequency of divorce and the variation in who raises children, social networks are highly individualized even for the very young. Each person's network of relatives is unique and extends over many villages (often as much as a full day away from one another by canoe), and the ability to come and go independently is crucial to the fulfillment of a whole range of social obligations. This, combined with the nature of their subsistence and marriage patterns, means that Maroons are accustomed to individual mobility and personal independence. All able-bodied adults have canoes of their own, which they use for trips to and from garden camps, visits to spouses and relatives, medical consultations at mission clinics, and attendance at funerals and other village rituals.

Houses belong to individual adults rather than to whole families, and many men and women have more than one. A woman might have a house in her own village (in an area shared largely with her matrilineal relatives), a house in her garden camp (which might be as much as a full day away by canoe), and a house that her husband has built for her in his village. And a man might divide the time he spends in his own village among three or four houses that he has built for himself and for past or current wives.

Since their earliest years in the forest, Maroons have both exploited the natural environment and drawn on the outside world for their material needs. Shifting-field horticulture, hunting, and fishing, together with some gathering (most importantly palm nuts for cooking oil) and the importation of a few essentials such as salt, provide the subsistence base. Production activities tend to be individualized—each adult works largely independently, and there is little specialization except by gender. Women take primary responsibility for the garden work, though men participate at the early stages after a site is chosen (in either virgin or secondary forest), cutting the underbrush and felling trees prior to burning. Gardens are planted most

2.5. A young Saramaka works in her mother-in-law's garden.

heavily in rice or cassava (depending on region), interspersed with other crops, from sweet potatoes, taro, plantains, and bananas to okra, maize, sugarcane, and tobacco. Peanuts are grown in separate spaces. Men do the hunting, an activity in which success carries strong gender-related prestige. Most hunting is done with shotguns, but traps are also used to hunt a variety of game animals. Fish, which are taken with hand-lines, poles, traps, bow and arrow, vegetable drugs, and, for the past few years, with ecologically destructive nets, contribute at least as much to the diet as does meat, and some kinds of fishing are practiced by women and children as well as men.

Maroons have always been dependent on coastal society for selected manufactured goods. The original escaped slaves often managed to take with them a gun, an axe, a pot, or some other object that would contribute to their chances for survival in the forest. All of the early groups, including those based as far as two weeks' travel from the plantation areas, sent out periodic raiding parties to recruit new personnel (especially women) and to replenish such supplies as guns, gunpowder, tools, pots, cloth, and salt. Indeed, a major incentive for the Maroons to accept the peace treaties of the 1760s was the guarantee of regular access to goods from the coast, and their concerns during the complex negotiations that surrounded these treaties focused sharply on the details of the "tribute" to be provided by the colonial government and its distribution among and within villages. Since the time of the treaties, the means by which Maroons have acquired manufactured goods have changed—first dependence on tribute and brief trading trips, then money-earning through logging, the bleeding of balata (wild rubber) trees, and the provision of river transport services, and, more recently, income from construction work, professional woodcarving for tourists, and regular employment, for example in the Suriname bauxite industry or at the European Space Center in French Guiana.

Since the mid-twentieth century, the pace of change in Maroon life has accelerated significantly. In the 1960s, the widespread use of outboard motors and the development of air service to the interior encouraged an increase in traffic of people and goods between Maroon villages and the coast. At the same time, the construction by Alcoa and the Suriname government of a giant hydroelectric project brought about a dramatic migration toward the coast, with some 6,000 people forced to abandon their homes as the project's artificial lake gradually flooded almost half of Saramaka territory. Two-thirds of these people were relocated in large government-built towns in the area between the lake and Paramaribo, where standpipes replaced the river water supply, standardized houses stood shoulder-to-shoulder in relentless rows (see fig. 2.6), and many kinds of fish and game, a variety of forest products, and other traditional subsistence resources were unavailable. Meanwhile, in French Guiana, beginning in the 1970s, the Aluku were subjected to intense pressures for *francisation*, which caused wrenching economic, cultural, and political transformations. Suriname's independence, in 1975, changed life for most Maroons less than for the coastal population, but the civil war of the late 1980s annihilated the Ndyuka villages along the Cottica River and sent some 10,000 Maroons fleeing to French Guiana, and continuing battles over the control of the valuable mining and timber rights in the interior affect every aspect of contemporary Maroon life in Suriname.

On the eve of these most recent transformations, we wrote a generalized sketch intended to characterize daily life for both eastern and central Maroons (S. and R. Price 1980:14–33). Judging from our visits in the 1980s and 1990s to Maroons in French Guiana and eastern Suriname, and from our discussions with Saramakas who travel back and forth between French Guiana and their home villages, that sketch still captures the distinctive flavor of life in the interior in terms of material culture, social relations, religious concerns, and other basic orientations. We present its main lines again here, but remind our readers that over the past two decades increasing numbers of Maroons have traveled and lived elsewhere, opening themselves to a much greater range of experiences than they had in the 1970s.

Maroons conceptualize villages and garden camps as contrasting environments. Life in the garden camps (fig. 2.7) is viewed romantically, especially by women. The atmosphere in camps is distinctly relaxed, despite long hours of hard physical work that contrast sharply with the less intense pace in villages. People are free to wear torn and faded clothes that would be less appropriate in the village, meals are less formally served and may even be eaten by men and women together, folktales (which are forbidden in the village except during funeral rites) may be told in the evenings, and, most important according to Maroons, the interpersonal conflicts and tensions inherent in village life are largely absent. Food is also more varied and abundant in the camps, since both forest and garden products are close at hand and it is during stays in the camps that women drug streams for fish and men do their most intensive hunting and fishing. Without doubt the most trying aspect of old age for both men and women is confinement to village life, the forced retirement from camp and forest.

For men, the forest itself is the focus of romantic associations. Days devoted to hunting are filled with the beauty, excitement, and dangers of lone forays into an environment populated not only by a wide variety of animals, from jaguars and peccary to scorpions and parrots, but also by a multitude of spirits who jealously guard their territories and may either aid

2.6. A row of houses constructed for Saramakas whose villages were flooded by the hydroelectric project.

or punish the human trespassers. The most animated stories told among men of an evening concern their experiences in the forest—adventures such as being seduced by a forest spirit who had assumed the form of a woman, being lost overnight after frantically chasing an animal, or rescuing a prized hunting dog from an anaconda.

In the villages (fig. 2.8), Maroons devote considerable time to social and ritual obligations. People come back to the village from the forest or their camp for funeral rites, for oracle sessions, and for rituals centered on possession gods. They also come to greet a kinsman who has returned from a trip to the coast, to attend a ceremony for a newborn baby, to visit a sick relative, or to bring food or firewood to a relative who is too old to leave the village. In addition, there are subsistence tasks: houses require periodic maintenance and rebuilding, grounds must be cared for, and food processing (winnowing rice, making palm nut oil) is sometimes carried out in the village. There is a great deal of both individual and seasonal variation in the pattern of alternation between village and camp, but in the area where we lived women spent on the average about half of their days in camps and men, aside from time spent on the coast, were there about twenty percent of the time.

2.7. A garden camp on the upper Pikilio which has three houses, four open-sided structures, and a menstrual hut (on the right in this photo).

2.8. A Ndyuka village near the confluence of the Tapanahoni and Lawa rivers.

2.9. An eastern Maroon woman and child paddle canoes on the upper Marowijne River, late nineteenth century.

The river not only provides the connecting link between villages, camps, and hunting grounds, but also constitutes a special environment of its own (figs. 2.9–2.12). People spend a great deal of time in canoes and at the water's edge, where they enjoy a respite from some of the constraints of village life—it is only there, for example, that Saramakas are free to whistle. In each village there are several landing places that serve as areas for tying canoes, bathing, laundering clothes, washing dishes, fishing, preparing fish and game, pounding and winnowing rice, building canoes, and catching up on local gossip. Women who are banned from most areas of the village because they are menstruating spend considerable time at the river, and children use it as a versatile playground.

2.10, 2.11, 2.12. The Pikilio River at Dangogo, 1968.

Maroon villages are irregular arrangements of small houses, open-sided structures, domesticated trees, an occasional chicken house, various shrines, and scattered patches of bushes (fig. 2.8). There are usually several paths leading into the village from the river, and other tiny paths providing access to gardens, to areas used as toilets, and sometimes to streams or neighboring villages. Most of the ground is scraped clear of vegetation, and all the trees have been planted by individual villagers for some usable fruit—oranges, mangos, bananas, coconuts, palm nuts, calabashes, or limes (these last being used for washing woodcarvings and calabashes). The bushes that interrupt the cleared ground mark divisions within the village, most frequently between areas inhabited by different groups of matrilineal relatives.

Most garden camps are set farther back from the river than villages, some at a several hours' walk into the forest, and always near a stream. Saramaka camps may have from one to as many as a few dozen different structures, and Ndyuka camps are often several times as large. Camps differ from villages in including more open-sided houses, more structures built by women, more single-room houses, and fewer made with wooden planks. The living area of a camp may be maintained over several decades, serving as a base for work in gardens that are cut in new sites in the surrounding forest each year or two.

Palm-leaf gateways mark the entrances to both villages and camps, and everyone (with the exception of menstruating women) must pass under them. Although most major shrines are located in villages (S. and R. Price 1980:fig. 18), both villages and camps carry the marks of specific minor ceremonies from the past, such as a bottle filled with a special leaf mixture and

2.13. Saramakas prepare food for a feast in honor of an ancestor.

partly buried in front of a house to appease a local god or a calabash set into a forked stick in the ground which was once used for purificatory ablutions (see again fig. 2.7).

The small size of most houses (just wide enough to accommodate a hammock and not much longer from front to back) and the absence of windows encourage a selective use of their interiors. Women take all their dishwashing and laundry to the river and prepare fish and game for cooking there, bake cassava cakes and pound and winnow their rice outdoors or in open-sided sheds, and do their informal visiting under the front overhang of the house rather than inside. Many women also prefer to cook meals in a small open-sided structure rather than in their houses (fig. 2.13; see also Kahn 1931:facing p. 64) and men's activities are similarly oriented toward outdoor settings. House interiors, then, are reserved chiefly for sleeping, sex, eating, some meal preparation, and visits of a private nature. (During large-scale community events, for example, guests from other villages are sometimes invited to sit inside, as a special gesture of hospitality and gratitude for their participation.)

In Saramaka villages, the door to a woman's house (and, if the interior is divided into front and back areas, the doorway between them as well) is usually off-center, which defines the house's "large" and "small" sides (fig. 2.14). There is a belief that people should sleep with their heads to the

2.14. A Saramaka woman's house. A basket, a cassava press, brooms, and protective medicines hang on the front wall. Horticultural products are stored in the bucket, basket, washtub, and sawed-off oil drum under the roof overhang.

"large" side, and a number of ritual procedures require attention to this distinction as well. The fire area, kept as immaculately swept as the rest of the floor, contains three hearthstones, which are made from clay by local specialists and should never be moved from their original sites (fig. 2.15). Above the fire area, supported by house beams, there is often a triangular shelf of wooden slats holding baskets, fire fans, brooms, salt barrels, and bottles of fat. Firewood is carefully stacked behind the front door, along with one or two "dustpans" cut from a local palm tree. In the third corner of the room, which may be covered with a layer of fine white sand from a creek for aesthetic effect, are buckets and gourds holding water. Utensils are stuck into the palm walls, hung from nails hammered into wooden planks, or placed in a wooden crate or specially made cabinet (see fig. 5.14). The owner's wrap-skirts, each one folded into a small packet, and other items of clothing are stored in brightly painted metal trunks imported from Paramaribo. If the house is divided by a partition, a cloth curtain hangs in the doorway; this may be decoratively embroidered or even replaced by a handsomely carved door (fig. 2.16). The space behind a partition is largely taken up by the woman's hammock, and a few other household items—typically a chamber pot, a tin lantern, a few crates, and a sack or two filled with calabash bowls—complete the furnishings. During the day, the hammocks in the front, where children sleep, are bundled up and hung from a side beam to make space. Women prefer houses with a "doorstep" (a massive wooden beam extending across the whole front), which they can use as a bench during informal visiting, and woven-palm walls, which they like for the storage of utensils. As we once overheard a woman remark to a friend, "I wouldn't ever want a plank-walled house. I'm not going to be put in a coffin more than once in my life!" (For schematizations of the interiors of Saramaka and Aluku women's houses, see S. and R. Price 1980:29 and Hurault 1970:46.)

One of the most variable features of the interiors of women's houses are the calabash, enamel, and aluminum wares stored along the walls (fig. 2.16). Figure 2.15 shows the back wall of an otherwise open-sided cooking house that is relatively typical in the number of utensils in wall storage. Figures 2.17 and 2.18 show how a particularly well-supplied woman from the lower Suriname River "dressed up" her house in her husband's village on the upper river. And figure 4.56 shows an equally lavish Ndyuka woman's house on the Tapanahoni River. These last two interiors, while more extensively furnished than many, illustrate how dishes and utensils are stored—stuck directly into the palm walls, wedged behind sticks stuck into the wall, and hung by ties from nails in wooden slats bordering the woven-palm area. Because items on display should be immaculate, many women keep only a small proportion of their calabashes on the walls, while many dozens of

2.15. Interior of a Saramaka cooking house.

2.16. The interior partition of a Maroon house, apparently Saramaka in the 1940s.

extras are stored in crates or in burlap sacks in the back room. Pots and pans are also kept sparkling clean, and the black covering that pots acquire from sitting on a wood fire is meticulously removed after each use. The sponge-like interior of the luffa gourd, together with bar soap imported from the coast and fine sand gathered from a creek, is used to scour each pot until it gleams, and a tiny rag may be used to remove the last traces of soot that hide behind handle joinings and other inaccessible crevices.[3]

A man's house is usually smaller than a woman's, is more likely to have a plank floor, and is furnished very differently (figs. 2.19, 2.20). As with women's houses, the ideal is to divide the back sleeping area from the front, even in a very tiny house. The hammock (or now, occasionally, a double bed imported from the coast) fills the entire back space. The front room, which serves as a parlor, is used for visiting, meals with other men, and the storage and display of personal wealth. Trunks filled with cloth and other coastal goods may be stacked high along the walls; a table and carved stools, or perhaps one or two imported folding chairs, are the main items of furniture. The table and walls are usually cluttered with such items as the owner's shotgun and hunting sack, a fishing bow and arrows, a flashlight, an umbrella, hats, a bottle of liquor, a few empty bottles, an alarm clock, some photographs, a jar of hair fat, a calendar, an assortment of machetes, knives, and shotgun cartridges, a tape recorder, and tapes or cassettes. Some men assemble collections of objects that rival the women's displays of plates illustrated above. A dozen or more differently shaped machetes, for example, may occupy pride of place (see S. and R. Price 1980:fig. 27).[4]

The several men who are in a neighborhood on a given day usually eat meals together in one of their houses. Each wife (or another female relative if a man's wives are all absent) brings a complete meal and set of dishes to the house and arranges them carefully on the floor. The bowls of rice have been mounded and smoothed with a wide calabash utensil, and several china and enamel bowls, each holding several pieces of meat or fish, as well as a plate with attractively arranged pieces of cassava cake complete the menu. Vegetable sauces made from okra, taro leaves, or other greens may be served, but meat and fish are very much preferred whenever available. In addition, a shiny aluminum teapot with cool water, a calabash or small aluminum pot for drinking it, another calabash for rinsing hands, a glass or enamel plate, and a metal spoon are provided by each woman.[5] The men share all the dishes, spitting bones onto the floor, and the youngest one sweeps the area clean after the meal. Women eat more informally in their own houses, with children and perhaps a sister or an aunt. Their rice is not mounded, and they often eat the accompanying foods (which are more frequently vegetable sauces than in men's meals) directly from the cooking

2.17, 2.18. Storage of dishes and utensils in a Saramaka woman's house. Plates and calabash bowls are supported by sticks inserted in the wall, porcelain bowls hang by strings tied around the base; pots are hung from nails by their handles, and calabash ladles, stirring sticks, and aluminum spoons are stuck into the wall.

2.19. A Saramaka "raised house." Relatively few men live in this type of house, which for over a century has been associated with age and seniority.

2.20. A two-story Ndyuka man's house (Jean Hurault, *Les Noirs Réfugiés Boni de la Guyane Française*).

MAROON ARTS

pot, adding water to soften the crusty rice that sticks to the bottom of the pot before scraping it out for the children or themselves.

The layout, use, and mode of construction of houses are basically similar among the various Maroon groups, but there are also recognizable differences in architectural detail and in the frequency of different types of housing. In the mid-twentieth century, notable features that distinguished many eastern Maroon houses from those in Saramaka were their elaborately painted facades, their larger doors, the triangular fronts of some houses (formed by a lower roof extension on the sides and a filling-in of the lower side area with planks), the absence of a "doorstep" beam across the front, and the optional use of vertical decorative posts placed at the very front of the roof overhang (fig. 2.21; see also fig. 2.20, and S. and R. Price 1980:fig. 28, plate V).[6] Since the 1970s, many of the new houses built by Maroons have been based on models seen on the coast, with shuttered windows, flatter roofs, full-size doors, cement floors, and complete plank (or sometimes cement) construction. Galvanized roofs, which had been introduced on the houses of particularly wealthy men in the 1960s, have become common, and the eastern Maroon art of painting house fronts has been for the most part abandoned.

2.21. A Ndyuka house (Jean Hurault, *Africains de Guyane*). Note the painting on the ends of the upper roof beams and the decorative tacks on the shotgun hanging under the roof.

3.1. Designs baked into Saramaka cassava cakes. *Top to bottom:* "dog's paws (in the sand)," "parallel stripes," "sieve," "curved fingers," and "kwenkwen-fish's belly"; *opposite,* "around the head."

MAROON ARTS

Art and Aesthetics

JULY 1976. Three Saramaka women were chatting together under the thatched roof of an open-sided structure. One had brought a supply of cassava flour and was baking large, round griddle cakes over a barely smoldering fire. The second woman sat on a small stool with a freshly washed calabash shell on her lap and a collection of broken bottle pieces in a scrap of cloth on the ground. The third woman, sitting with legs outstretched on an old cloth covering the earthen floor, was using a sharpened umbrella rib to fashion a pair of cotton calfbands for her husband, working the stitches around a bottle to create an evenly circular band.

The first woman spread her cassava flour deftly onto the dry griddle, drew her fingers over the entire surface to form a decorative pattern, and sifted a thin layer of flour on top (fig. 3.1). While each cake was baking, one by one, she used a wooden comb to produce a hairdo for the woman with the calabash, standing behind her companion to braid each section as part of an overall design: those around the face protruded forward and were secured with hairpins shaped out of aluminum wire, those in the back were linked in a pattern known as "insertions," and a long, tightly braided line of "ground hair" ran between (fig. 3.2). The woman with the calabash, well known in the village for her mastery of this decorative art, was marking several designs as a favor to the woman sitting next to her, who would later finish executing the carvings herself. As she worked, she rotated the bowl between her hands, adjusting it to the proper position for each curved line and trying to remember just how a particular design went. She discussed the design they had decided to replicate with the woman sitting beside her, and finally, when neither could remember exactly how the appendages were curved, settled on a new version, one which, she later concluded, came out even better than the original (fig. 3.3). The third woman, working steadily around the calfband, enlisted the advice of her friends concerning the width of the red and yellow stripes that formed its center. As the three of them worked, their conversation alternated between village gossip and discussion of their artistic activities.

Such scenes, which we witnessed in many variants during our time in the Suriname interior, reveal several striking features of the role of art in Maroon life—the pervasive influence of aesthetic considerations in everything from cooking to grooming, the active participation of all adults in a wide range of artistic activities, and the very real enjoyment of aesthetic discussions. Other outside observers have also been struck by how much "art" permeates Maroon life. Melville Herskovits, for example (referring less to the women's arts in our opening scene than to woodcarvings like the stool and comb these women were using), declared, "Bush-Negro art in all its ramifications is, in the final analysis, Bush-Negro life" (1930:167).

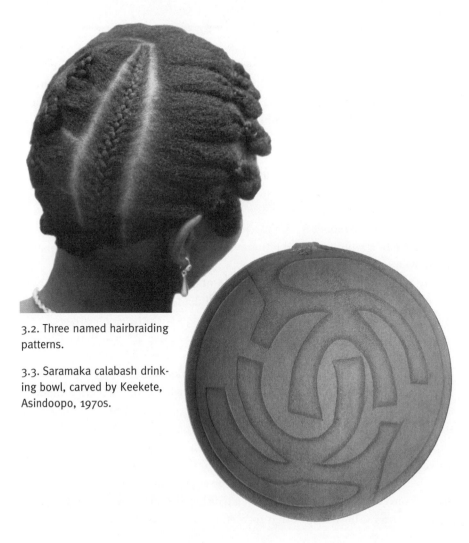

3.2. Three named hairbraiding patterns.

3.3. Saramaka calabash drinking bowl, carved by Keekete, Asindoopo, 1970s.

Maroons have elaborated a whole range of graphic and performing arts. Visual media include, for example, woodcarving and painting, interior and exterior calabash carving, patchwork, embroidery, appliqué, body cicatrization, hairdos, carving on scrap aluminum and aluminum kitchenware, decorative bead and yarn work, and culinary flourishes like the cassava cake decorations. Their performing arts are equally extensive. Specialized dance forms honor the mediums of each type of possession god, and there are many secular dances, each of which is enjoyed in a particular social context. Distinctive song styles are used in the whole range of Maroon ritual events (from complex funerary rites to the domestication of a new possession god), in communal labor such as felling trees or hauling logs, and in many casual and even solitary settings. We have rarely walked through a Maroon village without hearing someone singing. Drums are used singly or in various combinations to accompany secular dance forms, to announce, supervise, and comment on the proceedings of large public council meetings, and to communicate with each kind of possession god and with other deities, spirits, and ancestors. There are other musical instruments as well—from bells and wooden trumpets to a gourd stringed instrument and a "finger piano" (fig. 3.4). Finally, folktales, play languages, proverbs, oratory, possession speech, and prayer reflect the high value placed on verbal finesse and creativity, in both the languages of everyday speech and a number of esoteric languages associated with particular ritual contexts.

3.4. Mawoni Pansa posing with his finger piano, Dangogo, 1968.

The arts of the Maroons are unusual in the extent to which they have traditionally been practiced by the entire population. In contrast, for example, to many African societies in which certain individuals trained as "artists" produce objects and sell them to others (and in some of which even the role of critic is a recognized specialization—see, for example, Thompson 1973), Maroon expectations include the assumption that all adults will be active artists and assertive critics.

Within this pattern of generalized artistic production, some kinds of specialization are nonetheless present—most notably along gender lines. In terms of media, men are the woodcarvers and women compose patchwork textiles. And even in those media that are exploited by both women and men there are important stylistic differences according to gender. In embroidery, which is always sewn by women but sometimes on the basis of a design "marked out" by a man, the men's designs are geometric, angular, and rigorously symmetrical (fig. 3.5), while the women's designs tend to be more free-form and curvilinear (fig. 3.6). Calabash carvings, which may be designed by either men or women, follow the same stylistic division (figs. 3.7, 3.8).[1]

3.5, 3.6. Two Saramaka men's neckerchiefs from the 1960s. *Left,* marked in pencil by a man before being embroidered (in black, blue, yellow, pink, red, green, and orange) by a woman; *right,* marked and embroidered by a woman (in yellow, red, and blue).

Further specialization grows out of the recognition that people differ in both talent and interest in the arts. In all media, the work of certain individuals is generally considered especially beautiful. While these people have not traditionally taken on a special role as artists in their community and while there has not, until recently, been a local market for their work, they have always been rewarded by admiration within the community and occasionally asked to help sketch out a design that a friend or relative is preparing to execute. A woman may ask a man to pencil a geometric design onto a neckerchief and to advise her on the colors she should use to embroider each line segment. Or, as we saw earlier, one woman may ask another to carve a calabash for her or to mark the outline of a calabash design. But the enlisting of artistic talent has most often been confined to an advisory level, supplementing and enhancing but not substituting for the active production by every adult of objects in a wide range of media. Likewise, in the performing arts the recognition of special talent in no way diminishes the importance of generalized participation by all adults (and children) in the various forms of song, dance, and drumming appropriate to their gender. The performances of a well-known singer or dancer are accorded special attention at any communal event, but everyone is expected to dance and sing, since these activities are part of being an able-bodied human being.

3.7, 3.8. Saramaka calabashes. *Left,* drinking bowl made about 1960, with a design marked by a man and carved by a woman (Finuwomi and Keekete, both of Asindoopo). It is rare for a man to design the inside of a calabash. *Right,* handwashing bowl carved by a woman of the Pikilio in the 1940s or 1950s.

The tendency of Maroons to think in terms of an aesthetic dimension extends, in fact, to their entire environment, from gardens and postures to tin lanterns and outboard motors. Manufactured items (such as guns, buckets, trade cotton, bottles, and lanterns), which are imported by coastal stores from China, Japan, the Netherlands, the United States, and elsewhere, have contributed substantially to the material culture of Maroon societies since the very earliest days of their formation. The men who have usually bought these objects at the end of lengthy wage-labor expeditions outside of Maroon territories select their purchases carefully from the full range of products available. In addition to basic utilitarian features, the different perfumes of soaps, the slightly varying proportions and finishes of tin lanterns, the colors of different cloths, the fringed edgings on cotton hammocks, and the curve of the handles on aluminum pots are all subjected to scrutiny. Once brought back to the home villages and distributed to wives and relatives, articles that win approval are displayed with pride, serve as the inspiration for songs of admiration, and are understood to reflect the care and aesthetic taste of the man who bought them. Many are also given names reflecting their physical features, the circumstances of their first introduction into the region, or unrelated events that happened around the time of their arrival (see Chapters 4 and 8). These objects are often further embellished in the villages. For example, men may incise woodcarving designs on the metal spoons they buy in French Guiana, and pots are marked with simple carvings or red tape, both for identification and for embellishment (fig. 3.9).

Children participate in this world of artistic production, performance, and connoisseurship from an early age. As soon as babies can stand, they are frequently and enthusiastically encouraged to dance to the rhythm of handclapping or thigh-slapping (figs. 3.10, 3.11). Little girls begin to learn the principles of patchwork textiles by fashioning three-piece aprons out of scraps of cloth too small for other uses, and little boys carve crude wooden objects such as combs and small paddles.

3.10. Aluku girls perform an *awasa* dance (Jean Hurault, *Africains de Guyane*).

3.11. Saramaka girls dance to the song and rhythmic thigh-slapping of an older kinsman.

3.9. Aluminum spoons bought in coastal French Guiana and decorated (using wood-carving tools) in 1961 by three Ndyuka men from the village of Diitabiki—Ba Adan (*top*), Ti Asakon (*bottom*), and Ba Yesyintu (at end of this chapter).

The early learning of artistic skills and aesthetic judgments is achieved without systematic formal instruction, as an unstructured by-product of the communal settings in which adults engage in artistry. As the scene described at the beginning of this chapter illustrates, artistic production is generally a sociable affair, with advice and commentary flowing freely around it. Because children are never excluded from adult activities, they frequently overhear talk about art, and their own artistic attempts are greeted with the same kind of evaluative discussion, combined with selective ridiculing and reprimands. We once watched an elderly woman ask her nine-year-old great-granddaughter, sewing diligently on her fourth apron in two days, "What on earth do we have here?!" and playfully address her with a new nickname, Táku-naai ("Ugly-Sewing"). The girl's ten-year-old cousin, sewing with her, was then told that *her* apron was quite nice, though she should have known to turn all the seams toward the same side of the cloth.

The younger child apparently did not take her derogatory play name lightly; five months later our field notes record that while sewing a blue border onto a white apron, she defiantly showed her work to her great-grandmother and announced that as of *this* one, she was *not* Táku-naai. The old woman examined it critically, pointed out that the strips were slightly crooked, and asked the child why she hadn't asked for help in aligning them. The girl, looking hurt, said nothing, but returned with determination to her work. Five years later, when she was ready to marry for the first time, she would need to be an accomplished seamstress and to know the principles of the narrow-strip textiles then in fashion, since a narrow-strip cape of her own making would be just one of the many gifts required to cement the marriage. Likewise, although woodcarving skills are envisioned as being passed from father to son, there are no formal apprenticeships under chosen experts, and much of a boy's understanding of the aesthetic ideals behind carvings is derived from listening to adult conversations.

The pervasiveness of aesthetic commentary also shaped our own introduction to Maroon art. The frequency of casual visiting within the Saramaka villages where we lived and the amount of artistic production and discussion that took place in those settings combined to form an inexhaustible source of natural exegesis, spontaneous evaluative remarks, and unsolicited commentary on both aesthetic principles and technical details. These settings provided the basic framework for our vision of Saramaka aesthetic life, which was then supplemented through discussions with individual Saramakas and extended to other Maroon groups through further fieldwork, museum research, and reading of the comparative literature. Within the context of anthropological studies of art, this field situation would seem to lie at one extreme in terms of the degree to which it allowed observed artistic activity and overheard aesthetic discussion—rather than formal analysis of the finished artifacts or discussions structured by the anthropologists' questions—to determine the shape of our developing understandings.

The expectation that everyone would achieve a basic competence in a variety of media, combined with a recognition that individuals are not equally "gifted" in the various arts, extends to other aspects of Maroon life as well, and affected both our fieldwork methodology and our view of cultural processes in these societies on a daily level. In rituals, the recognition of "masters" of particular kinds of rites in no way tempers the idea that everyone may join in during the frequent and highly animated debates concerning the proper way to carry out particular details. In fact, almost any "traditional" activity is hotly debated, with people vying for the authoritative last word. When a man packs a wedding basket with gifts for a new wife, for example, others gather to watch his progress and add their own commentary, suggesting additions and criticizing his choices. Alternating between praise and ridicule, jokes and earnest comparative discussion, these backseat drivers exercise a significant influence on the way the wedding presentation, though it may be envisioned as being fully determined by "tradition," is composed for a particular bride.

These kinds of informal exchanges form the lowest level, the "mechanics," of the very important process of cultural perpetuation and change—a process that, as we will see, is crucial to the understanding of the nature of Maroon art and Maroon life in general. Such scenes embody the subtle confrontation between individual and community-wide notions of propriety and aesthetics, between innovation and tradition, and between the diverse cultural ideas of men and women, young and old, and the inhabitants of different villages and regions. The result is inevitably an ongoing negotiation, an opportunity for the participants to both confirm and modify established cultural patterns.

In matters of decorative artistry, such discussions are often phrased in terms of the aesthetic and artistic differences among individual artists, villages, and Maroon groups. Rather than noting how a given object fulfills general "classical" standards for its type, Maroons often devote their attention to the features that mark its particular position in time and space. Overheard discussions make it clear that very few details of artistry and performance are unanimously agreed upon, and that people are unusually tolerant of—and fascinated by—the features that mark generational, regional, and individual diversity.[2] This contrasts with discussions about rituals, in which issues tend to be conceived more as matters of right and wrong, and participants aggressively defend their knowledge of the details of traditional custom by making frequent reference to their sources of information—either observed precedents or the authority of older relatives (see R. Price 1983a).

IN DISCUSSING ART WITH US, Maroons very often concluded their explanations of the formal, symbolic, or technical features of a particular style or medium with comments on the social uses of the objects—most frequently an enumeration of the gift exchanges appropriate to situations such as the ceremonial presentation of a newborn, the ritual marking of social adulthood, or the celebratory welcoming of a man returning home from a stay on the coast. One woman whom we asked to talk about the components of women's formal dress, for example, phrased her response in terms of a particular situation for which formal dress would be required—a woman's first visit as an affine to her husband's village—and devoted the bulk of her response to a description of the foods, clothes, and other objects that she would bring in her basket as gifts to her husband's relatives. And people rarely talked about a particular woodcarving without referring not only to the artist but also to the woman for whom the carving had been made and details of the couple's relationship at the moment the piece was given. Just as dance, song, and drumming are conceptualized firmly in terms of the social events at which they are most frequently performed, the "meaning" of an artistically crafted object is closely bound up with the social context for which it was intended.

Together with fish and game, garden and forest products, and Western imports, artistic objects contribute to the fulfillment of a variety of social relationships, from voluntary formal friendships and ritual clientage to ties of kinship and marriage. Most important among these is the conjugal relationship. Woodcarving, calabash carving, textile arts, and bodily adornment all serve in the ongoing campaign of every adult to attract spouses and lovers and maintain their affection over time, and the complementary participation of men and women in subsistence tasks (including artistic production) contributes to the solidarity of a variety of male-female relationships. Although a man may carve a paddle or clear a field for his mother, and a woman may greet her brother upon his return from the coast with some rice she has grown and winnowed or a new pair of calfbands she has made, the great majority of such exchanges are those between spouses or prospective spouses. Furthermore, exchanges of goods and services between a husband and wife (and, at certain stages of the relationship, between affines) tend to be more formally acknowledged and more carefully reciprocated than others. Even when a man is on the coast for a several-year period of wage labor, he sends periodic gifts back to his wives (or to a girl who has been promised to him when she reaches marriageable age), and each woman in turn works on the "thanks" she will present formally upon his return. All conjugal exchanges, whether of goods or services, are conceptualized in terms of an etiquette of direct repayment referred to as "giving thanks." A man whose wife scrapes clear the ground around his house may "give thanks" to her with a carved comb or a new cloth, and a woman whose husband carves a food stirrer for her may offer him a bottle of palm oil that she has made. Even in very small exchanges, the person who receives the gift is careful to display it to many people and to discuss at length how "big" (generous) it is (see R. Price 1975b:58; S. Price 1978).

Something of the tone of conjugal gift exchanges may be seen in the description that one woman gave us of a husband's return from the coast—just one of the many institutionalized contexts in which gifts, including art, are presented.[3]

> The woman works on art while her husband is away on the coast. She does everything—gathers palm nuts [to make oil for him], makes calfbands, sews things, and on and on until her husband finally returns. The husband and wife sleep together for three nights. On the fourth day he gives her coastal goods. [On the third day] he loads up a trunk, maybe 100 cloths, maybe 70 or 60 or 50 or 30. He and his relatives will load up the trunk till it's full, then put it aside. Then they pull over the soap crate and the kerosene drum—just slide it right on over. Then they take buckets, machetes, cooking tripods, and set them there. Finally they take all those enamel and metal things from the coast—dishes, pots, spoons, knives, chamber pots—and they put those there too. They get them all together. Then everyone sleeps until morning. Then the man calls the woman and he says, "Well, wife, come look at some presents your sisters-in-law have for you." And his sisters arrive at his house. They pick up the trunk— *kidé kidé kidé* [the rhythm of their walking with a heavy load on their heads]—and carry it to the woman's house. They come back and get the kerosene drum—*kidé kidé kidé*—over to the woman's house. Now they get all the goods and load them up in the woman's house. [Here the speaker pantomimes the wife, coyly looking at the floor, fingering the hem of her skirt, and squirming, embarrassed, on her stool.] Well, they'll load up things until they're completely finished. Then they'll say, "Well, Sister-in-law . . . Well, woman, don't you see? Here's a little something for you, that we're giving you here, since your husband's gone and come back." Only the sisters-in-law are present; the husband is

back in his own house. The sisters-in-law will address the woman, "Woman!" She answers shyly, "Yes?" "Well, woman, the things here are really nothing. But here's just a little something for you. Here's a little salt for you, so you can boil some taro leaves for us to eat. We've brought some goods to give you." Then everyone really celebrates in that house! Then the woman says, "Listen to me!" and she jumps up. She'll load [into an enamel basin] some calfbands. She'll load some narrow-strip cloths. She'll load some cross-stitch cloths. She tells the others, "Take these to the man for me." And they'll set everything on their heads and carry it off to the man. The woman will stay in her own house, rejoicing over her presents while all the others go off to the man's house. Then the man will say, "Well, here's something for you to take over to the woman." This last present can be anything from the coast—any kind of dishware, maybe an aluminum water jug. . . . They bring it over and say, "Woman, don't you see? Here's something that your husband sent over for you." The wife will jump right up—*vúúúú!* She'll grab the one thing that she hasn't yet given him and, right there, she'll give it to her husband's lineage. She'll always have one thing held back, to give him separately. It could be some cross-stitch or an embroidered neckerchief, or whatever. "Take this thing here. Go drape the man with it for me" [a way of thanking his soul]. After the gift is presented, shouts will ring out—*wooooo!!* "My goodness! The woman has really pulled the goods to the ground!" That means that she hasn't been shamed by having too little to reciprocate his gifts. That's what's known as "pulling the goods to the ground."

The fact that most woodcarvings and decoratively sewn textiles are intended as gifts of courtship or marriage and that handsomely carved calabashes are used principally in the presentation of meals by a woman to her husband (in a setting often charged with co-wife rivalry) allows these arts to carry a generalized sexual significance. Both men and women think of many of their material possessions in terms of the relationships which they in a sense symbolize. Saramakas, who nearly always deny sexual symbolism on the level of particular motifs, sometimes suggest that *all* woodcarving and calabash art is alluding abstractly to the same thing—"husband and wife business," they say, "is what they're really all about." And eastern Maroons are said to conceptualize sexual symbolism, on the level of particular motifs, somewhat more explicitly.

During the 1970s in the upper river region of Saramaka, and somewhat earlier among other Maroons, the growing use of money within the villages themselves began to alter the place of art in social life. A few men began to carve in wood on a fairly full-time basis, selling their products to both Maroons and outsiders and using the money for their own subsistence needs.[4] When concentrated commercial artistic activity began to be possible in the villages, it not only created a specialized role for the artist, but also allowed his clients to narrow the range of their own artistic and subsistence activities. This trend toward specialization, a direct outgrowth of the introduction of the use of money into societies that previously had little internal money flow, exerted an influence not only on the sociology of artistic production, but also on subsistence patterns and social relations much more generally. While hunting, fishing, the clearing of forest gardens, woodcarving, and so on had long been performed on a regular basis by literally all able-bodied men, both opportunities and expectations began to change. In the late 1970s, for example, we noted that one man from the Pikilio had begun setting fish traps as a regular occupation; because of the new availability of cash for men and for some women, he was able to find customers and could use the money they paid him to buy goods and services that he had previously provided for himself.

In the late 1970s, we suggested that this development might well lead to the most fundamental social and cultural shifts these societies had felt since the beginning of widespread emigration of men to the coast in the last century. In terms of the commercialization of subsistence activities such as hunting, fishing, or garden clearing, the temptation to sell products and services for personal profit was beginning to compete with the traditionally unquestioned moral sanctions that had insured cooperation and sharing among kin. Women without husbands were the most acutely concerned with the potential consequences of this kind of shift in subsistence patterns, and in addition to resigning themselves to a lower standard of living, many of them were attempting to make up for their lost resources by entering the incipient monetary economy as well—selling garden products to the local mission hospital, charging money for favors that had always been exchanged more or less in kind, and sending decorated calabashes to the city to be sold rather than distributing them to friends and female relatives—thus confirming and accelerating the process. By the 1990s, such patterns had become the norm throughout Maroon territory. Today, except among the state-subsidized Aluku, the elderly and women without husbands quite generally find themselves in dire economic straits. The ethic of sharing that had permeated life in these societies for two centuries has been severely compromised.

In the realm of the arts, these trends toward specialization and commercialization have been further complicated and encouraged by the growing interest of outsiders in the "available culture" of the Maroons. Tourism has grown significantly. In the 1960s, the arrival of an outsider in the Saramaka paramount chief's village was an event of major local interest, but by the 1970s visitors were coming and going without causing a great deal of comment. By the 1990s, tour operators in Paramaribo and the Netherlands, in cooperation with Saramakas, were flying in adventurous tourists for several-day stays in specially built vacation villages in Saramaka. Needless to say, the objects these visitors buy to document their exotic adventures have been acquiring, through the bargaining process, monetary associations totally unrelated to the values that had been attached to them in the more isolated social and cultural setting of previous years.

Maroon art had, of course, been purchased on an occasional basis by outsiders long before the present day. We have no details concerning the field procedures of nineteenth-century collectors, but by the early twentieth century, commentators provided glimpses of the bargaining that surrounded their acquisitions. Melville and Frances Herskovits's description of their efforts to persuade one woman to sell them a peanut-grinding board (fig. 3.12) makes painfully clear the ultimate impotence of Maroon perceptions of value in the face of pressure from cash offers. After engaging a group of Saramakas in a lively discussion of the symbolism of the board's motifs, the Herskovitses suggested that they "might care to acquire the board."

> The woman became apprehensive. She took up the board, and excusing herself, disappeared with it inside her hut.
> "No, no," she called from the house, when her brother went to tell her of the offer we had made for it. "I don't want money for it. I like it. I will not sell it."
> The sum we offered was modest enough, but not inconsiderable for this deep interior. We increased

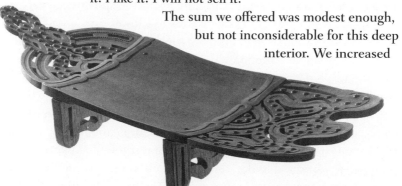

3.12. The Saramaka peanut-grinding board that the Herskovitses bought from an Asindoopo woman in 1929. For a detail of the carving, see fig. 8.1.

it, then doubled our original offer. There was still no wavering on the woman's part, but the offer began to interest her family. Such wealth should not be refused. Bassia [assistant headman] Anaisi began to urge her in our behalf.

"With this money you can buy from the white man's city a hammock, and several fine cloths. You should not refuse this."

The old woman took up the discussion, then another sister, and a brother. At last the bassia took us aside, and asked us to leave his sister alone with them.

"We will have a krutu [meeting], and tomorrow you will hear. She is foolish not to sell. But she cares for the board. It is good, too, when a woman loves what her man has carved for her. We will krutu about it, and you shall hear."

Three days passed before the woman's permission was given to dispose of the piece.

"When they see this, your people will know our men can carve!" she exclaimed in a voice which held as much regret as pride. (M. and F. Herskovits 1934:281)

Not only is the sale of Maroon artwork generally an exploitation of the Maroons' situation, but the rhetoric with which it is conducted often transgresses fundamental Maroon codes of etiquette. Many visitors insist on haggling over prices, perhaps because of stereotypes derived from such areas of the world as Mexico or the Middle East. But Maroons view bargaining as rude and offensive. In transactions among themselves, the seller calls the price on anything from a bunch of bananas to a new canoe, and differing opinions about the product's worth are discreetly avoided.

At issue in such confrontations is whose system of valuation will prevail, and the outsiders' insistence on imposing their own scales of value reflects an unselfconscious cultural arrogance. Many commentators have willingly described their tactics—both as a way of communicating what they considered the "childlike irrationality" of Maroons and as helpful advice to others who might wish to buy Maroon art. Morton Kahn, an American physician who made the great collection now at the American Museum of Natural History in New York, characterized the women with whom he had to deal in this way:

They laugh, giggle, put their finger coyly in their mouths, joke bashfully with bystanders, and cannot make up their minds as to the price. They never know how much to ask for a piece. Sometimes they will mention a preposterous figure, hoping like a naive child that the strange bahkra [outsider] will pay that much. But on such occasions a rebuke will make them more reasonable. Once an arrogant witch doctor intervened in a transaction with a Bush Negro woman, demanding angrily that she receive an exorbitant payment. His anger was squelched with a few sharp words, and, contrite, he sat up all night to carve an ornate implement to present to the bahkra as a peace-offering. Cunning Adjobo, the medicine man! (1931:196)

Within the context of life in their own villages, the sale of art represents one of the most unevenly balanced encounters between Maroons and outsiders. In the 1970s, Maroons were being relatively successful, we thought, at maintaining control over their own territory—setting minimal standards for the behavior of visitors, maintaining the prerogative to send visitors away, and rejecting interference in internal politics and social control. At the same time, we noted, the material poverty of most Maroons (from the perspective of the Western market economy), combined with the totally incomparable resources of outsiders, meant that pressures to sell personal belongings were often irresistible. Throughout Maroon history, women have been the most frequent victims of this imbalance, both because they are the ones who own the most woodcarvings and because they have few other sources of cash. The encounters described by the Herskovitses and Kahn have been repeated innumerable times by enthusiastic visitors to the interior. Maroon women have consistently fought not for higher prices, but for the right of possession and the right to define the meaning and value of a particular object in their own way. And they have generally lost.

It is worth noting that as Maroons began assigning monetary value to carvings and other art objects, they generally assumed that newly made pieces merited a higher monetary value than older ones, which they saw as "depreciating" through use. As outside collectors gradually made their own hierarchies of value clear, however, Maroons were exposed to the association of age with value that has fed into ethnographic collecting everywhere in the world. In logical response, Maroons began making claims of ancientness for given works of art, supported by creative genealogies of the original owners.

Cloths and Colors

4

"Quinze!"

Asindoopo, July 1978. Chief Agbago had offered to let us view the textiles from his storehouse, as many as we wished. Together, we selected seven of the heavy trunks and had them dragged outdoors to a shady spot where, with the help of Assistant Headman Takite, we could examine their contents. For us, the exercise promised to open up an ethnographic gold mine, rich in materials that would help flesh out our understanding of the development of the arts in Saramaka. For Agbago, it was to be an emotional journey into his personal past. Over the course of the three-day-long viewing, the two perspectives began to merge.

Takite helped open each carefully folded rectangle of cloth while S. P. scribbled in her notebook and R. P. manned the camera. Agbago reminisced: this embroidered kerchief had been sewn by his mother, that cape was made by the wife he'd had for many years in Santigoon, that other was from his inauguration as chief, and so forth. For many of the cloths, however, these details weren't possible for him to retrieve. As with other men who'd opened their trunks for us, he'd lost track of specific origins for much of his collection, and the individual gifts had merged, weaving a generalized testimony to a lifetime of relationships.

When he came to one small, round packet, however, his face lit up with a gentle smile. Taking it off by himself, he tenderly undid the knot in the kerchief and set aside the pieces of cloth it held one by one, counting softly in a language he had heard in French Guiana in the early years of the century. *Quinze!* Fifteen tiny adolescent aprons that had been cut from their waist ties with his knife and slipped into his hunting sack. Fifteen young girls who'd become women in his hammock. He recounted the aprons to make sure he'd got the number right. "*Dee ógi di mi du*," he remarked with a grin—"My little mischiefs."

Many of those youthful lovers' faces were now forgotten, but Apumba had been with him for more than seventy years. He had spoken for her even before her breasts were full, and when she died, earlier in 1978, she had been the senior of his three wives, withered and frail but still sharp-tongued and very much in charge.

As we asked Agbago for his associations with the various cloths he showed us, he asked us about our own interest in them, and we told him about the exhibition that would introduce Americans to the arts of the Saramakas and other Maroons. Then, he insisted, it was important for him to be properly represented. We should select four pieces to take back, textiles that would do honor to the Saramaka people. After a brief consultation, we put aside three patchwork capes (figs. 4.68, 4.69, 4.70) that had been sewn by a wife from Totikampu named Peepina, with whom he'd had many children, plus a beautifully embroidered cape with appliquéd borders that he'd identified as the work of either his mother or Apumba, he wasn't sure which (fig. 4.1). Agbago had no problem giving up the first three, since Peepina

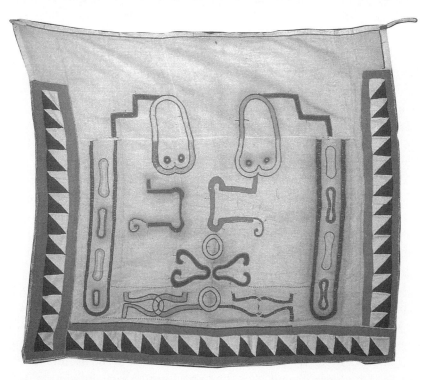

4.1 The cape we left behind . . .

had produced countless patchwork capes for him, but the fourth was special. That one would embellish his coffin some day, so we were free to photograph it, but would need to select an alternative for the exhibit (fig. 4.2).[1]

Because of his age and longtime position as paramount chief of the Saramakas, Agbago boasted an unusually large number of trunks, but other men also had extensive collections. Faanisonu, a senior headman from Dangogo whose three wives had been with him for decades, showed us many dozens of beautifully sewn textiles that spanned a half-century of embroidery and patchwork styles, representing six marriages and a healthy number of unformalized romantic encounters (4.37*left*, 4.66). And Dosili, a forty-year-old with a reputation as a ladies' man, invited us to choose virtually any textiles we wanted from his coffers as long as they weren't currently in style (4.59, 4.76, 4.77, 4.78). He would never wear those capes again, he said, and besides, he had more of them than he knew what to do with.

Years later, when we spent part of two summers among the eastern Maroons assembling artifacts for the Musée Regional de Guyane, we were astonished to find men's trunks containing collections of textiles that were if anything even richer than those we had seen in Saramaka. Although Aluku dress had come to be completely dominated by imported manufac-

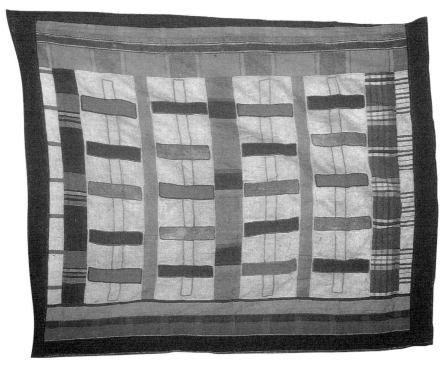

4.2 . . . and the one we took instead.

tured clothing (or perhaps precisely because of that trend), the storage trunks that were opened for our inspection were dazzling in their contents—breechcloths in patchwork, embroidery, and appliqué, elaborately tasseled men's bonnets, special "bibs" that men wore for dancing *awasa*, women's embroidered skirts, sewn hats embellished with buttons and fringes, a tiny cushion with a cloth strap carried purely as a fanciful accessory, composite textiles intended for decorating a coffin (fig. 4.3), and more (see R. and S. Price 1992a for additional illustrations).

The Saramaka men we worked with in the 1970s emphasized that they tried their best to keep one memento from each relationship for use in their funeral rites, but that with the fading of memories over time, this goal was only imperfectly realized. For our own purposes, this meant that the history of textile arts, which we reconstructed from Maroons' accounts of style

4.3. A coffin decoration. Tafanye, the elderly headman of the Aluku village of Papai-siton, opened his trunks for our inspection when we were collecting for the Cayenne museum. He told us that this object had been given to him when he was a young man by a lover whose name he could no longer remember.

sequences, research in archival documents and the literature, and examination of museum collections in Suriname, Europe, and the United States, had to be illustrated with work by women both remembered and forgotten.

Although they were no longer being worn, the capes and other garments that we took back from Saramaka, like the ones we left behind, had not yet run the full course of their life histories. Peepina's beautiful patchwork creations were, as Agbago wished, displayed in the art exhibition that opened in 1980 and admired by museum visitors in Los Angeles, Dallas, Baltimore, and New York. The image of one of them, featured on the catalogue cover, the exhibition poster, and invitations to each opening, and in newspaper ads (fig. 4.4), was seen by people too numerous to estimate, and has even been spotted several times in made-for-TV movies. The embroidered cape held back by Agbago contributed to his funeral rites when he died in 1989, but not before our field photo of it was reproduced in several books and articles

4.4. Publicity for "Afro-American Arts from the Suriname Rain Forest" in the *New York Times*.

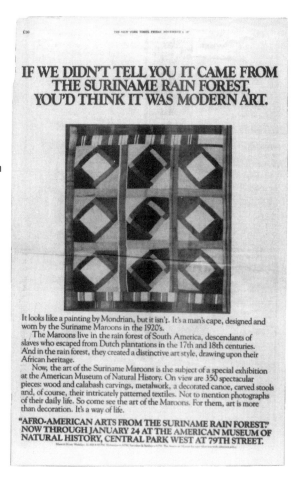

IF WE DIDN'T TELL YOU IT CAME FROM THE SURINAME RAIN FOREST, YOU'D THINK IT WAS MODERN ART.

It looks like a painting by Mondrian, but it isn't. It's a man's cape, designed and worn by the Suriname Maroons in the 1920's.
The Maroons live in the rain forest of South America, descendants of slaves who escaped from Dutch plantations in the 17th and 18th centuries. And in the rain forest, they created a distinctive art style, drawing upon their African heritage.
Now, the art of the Suriname Maroons is the subject of a special exhibition at the American Museum of Natural History. On view are 350 spectacular pieces: wood and calabash carvings, metalwork, a decorated canoe, carved stools and, of course, their intricately patterned textiles. Not to mention photographs of their daily life. So come see the art of the Maroons. For them, art is more than decoration. It's a way of life.
"AFRO-AMERICAN ARTS FROM THE SURINAME RAIN FOREST." NOW THROUGH JANUARY 24 AT THE AMERICAN MUSEUM OF NATURAL HISTORY, CENTRAL PARK WEST AT 79TH STREET.

and called into service to settle a publishing controversy centered on interpretations of political correctness (see R. and S. Price 1995:136–37). Faansisonu's textile collection lived on, too, some pieces contributing to his funeral rites in 1989 and others, distributed among surviving relatives after his death, showing up for sale at the 1992 Festival of American Folklife on the Mall in Washington, D.C. (fig. 4.5). The cloths Dosili offered us are now serving as teaching tools for anthropology students at the College of William and Mary.

4.5. One of the capes distributed to relatives of Faansisonu after he died. When his son Ayumbakaa came to dance on the Washington Mall, he deposited the cloth in the Museum Sales Shop, where we bought it for $100.

IN ORDER TO UNDERSTAND Maroon textile arts more fully, we need to view them within the broader domain of adornment, which in turn reflects fundamental Maroon understandings about human individuality in everything from aesthetic preferences to aptitudes, temperaments, and behavior.

One of the most striking features of Maroon life is the special pleasure people take in the subtle characteristics that contribute to the uniqueness of each individual. A strong and pervasive theme of Maroon understandings is the conviction that past events and actions condition the present in specific ways, for individuals as well as for the larger society. This means that each member of the community carries a unique social identity. At birth, such details as which gods were invoked to lend assistance during the pregnancy or whether it was a breech delivery establish ritual relationships and obligations that persist for the rest of the baby's life. But the molding of individuality is also an ongoing process that continues throughout life and even after death. Early in childhood, a person's social identity is distinguished from that of full brothers and sisters through formal recognition of a particular ancestor as a supernatural participant in the act of conception, and later through decisions about who will take on primary responsibility for the child's upbringing. At any point, life experiences may be commemorated by new personal names or nicknames (see R. and S. Price 1972b), and other events lead to individualized ritual prohibitions something along the lines of acquired allergies. Even long after death, people are honored with ancestral rites that reflect their special food preferences and other idiosyncrasies, and they are given a continuing role in daily life that fully recognizes the particularities for which they continue to be known.

It has been argued that this strong appreciation of individual distinctiveness, which is found to a variable extent everywhere in the African diaspora, and certainly grew in part out of pervasive African cultural ideas, may also have been a reaction to a system of plantation slavery in which personal identity came under fierce attack.

> While the greatest shock of enslavement was probably the fear of physical violence and of death itself, the psychological accompaniment of this trauma was the relentless assault on personal identity, the stripping away of status and rank, the treatment of people as nameless ciphers. Yet, by a peculiar irony, this most degrading of all aspects of slavery seems to have had the effect of encouraging the slaves to cultivate an enhanced appreciation for exactly those most personal, most human characteristics which differentiate one individual from another, perhaps the principal

4.6, 4.7, 4.8. Eastern Maroons in the early twentieth century. (For a full-length view of the men in fig. 4.8, see Kahn 1931: facing p. 98.)

qualities which the masters could not take away from them. Early on, then, the slaves were elaborating upon the ways in which they could be individuals—a particular sense of humor, a certain skill or type of knowledge, even a distinctive way of walking or talking, or some sartorial detail, like the cock of a hat or the use of a cane. (Mintz and Price 1992 [1976]:50–51)[2]

Within this context, the arts centering on the human body take on a special significance, since an important way of insisting on one's individuality is through postures, hairdos, cosmetics, clothes, and jewelry. John Gabriel Stedman described how, at the end of the nightmare of the Middle Passage,

> all the Slaves are led upon deck, . . . their hair shaved in different figures of Stars. half moons &c, /which they generally do the one to the other (having no Razors) by the help of a broken bottle and without Soap/ (Stedman 1988 [1790]:174)

And he remarked that rebel maroons distinguished themselves from slaves by their special braided hairdos. Although particular styles have come and gone over the years, pictorial documentation makes it clear that the hardships of life in the rainforest never suppressed the richness and creativity of these arts (figs. 4.6, 4.7, 4.8). German missionaries living among the Saramaka in the second half of the eighteenth century provide confirmation. Although these soldiers of the cross tended to minimize the aesthetic sensibilities of their hosts, occasional passages in their diaries bear inadvertent witness to the Maroons' strong interest in fashion. Brother Johann Riemer, for example, described his boatmen preparing for arrival at their home village after a trip to Paramaribo in 1779:

> Each of them opened his travel-basket, and in it were the different pieces of apparel which they wear when in Paramaribo or for ceremonial occasions. And they dressed themselves in the best manner they could. Our proud commodore, *Akra*, was particularly distinguished in the strange manner in which he dressed. By his bartering in Paramaribo, he had gotten a splendid colored nightshirt that had been made at Zitz, and for which he had been charged fifty guilders. He wore it tied together with a dagger, and he had a hat with tresses on it. In this ridiculous attire he ordered his comrades about, and I had a difficult time suppressing my laughter. When our muskets were finally charged with double loads [of powder without shot], the negroes, with pride in their splendorous dress, continued the trip in a most uncommon silence. (Riemer 1801, in R. Price 1990:189–90)

More generally, the accounts written by early observers show that although they tended to view Maroons largely as "naked savages," they were nevertheless struck by the attention these same people lavished on their personal attire. The German missionaries, for example, asserted that "all [the men] have as far as clothes are concerned is a small covering below the waist" (Staehelin 1913–19, III ii:141), and the engravings published with one of their accounts conform to this generalization (see S. and R. Price 1980:fig. 63). But these same missionaries also commented that men were sometimes "hung all over" with protective amulets (Staehelin 1913–19, III iii:131); they complained that Saramakas attended church "just to show off their finery" (Staehelin 1913–19, III iii:44); and in their dictionary of the Saramaka language they recorded names for multiple styles of breechcloths, skirts, hats, and rings, as well as a variety of terms for aprons, kerchiefs, fringed cloth, necklaces, and men's accessories such as umbrellas, hunting sacks, staffs, and walking sticks (Schumann 1778). John Gabriel Stedman's brief description of two Maroon warriors in the heat of battle alludes to wrist and ankle ornaments, a necklace with supernatural protective powers, a braided hairdo, and a gold-laced hat (Stedman 1988 [1790]:390–92, 405). And a long-term visitor to villages along the Marowijne River in the 1850s who describes Maroon clothing as "very simple," citing a single skirt for women and usually only a breechcloth for men, nevertheless mentions that "colored cloths are worn over the shoulders" for festive occasions (Coster 1866:26–28; see also S. and R. Price 1980:fig. 64) and enumerates a long list of accessories such as imported hats; necklaces made of jaguar or peccary teeth; calf- and anklebands hung with animal teeth, feathers, and tassels; strings of beads worn on the neck, wrist, and ankles; copper and iron bracelets; and copper rings worn up to ten at a time on fingers and thumbs. A mid-nineteenth-century government official assigned to a post among the Ndyuka Maroons confirmed this picture, describing men's dress as consisting of a breechcloth and large amounts of jewelry, and mentioning iron and copper anklets and bracelets, rings, and ritual jewelry incorporating glass beads, beetle antennae, jaguar teeth, parrot feathers, snails, and wooden "dolls" (Kappler 1854:124).

In addition to expressing individuality, fashion has served throughout Maroon history to mark membership in one or another of the six named groups and to reflect more specific regional identities. Among eastern Maroons, adolescent girls have always folded their aprons over the waist tie with the upper flap to the outside, but in Saramaka, the flap is put inside, toward the body (see fig. 4.7). Eastern breechcloths have always been narrower than those in Saramaka. Until the fashion changed in the 1970s, Ndyuka women tied their skirts with a red sash topped by a black (often tasseled) tie, while Saramakas have always used a folded kerchief with the point at the back (figs. 4.9, 4.10; see also S. and R. Price 1980:plate XIII). Saramaka men's capes more often incorporate special yarn or cloth ties at the upper corners than do those of the eastern Maroons. The hand-sewn caps that formed an optional item of men's dress until the mid-twentieth century also reflected regional variation, with Saramakas favoring the drawstring model illustrated in figure 4.38 and eastern Maroons using either that same style or the "bonnet" construction pictured in figure 4.6. And Saramaka women along the lower Suriname River, like women from the eastern groups, have sometimes embellished their skirts with elaborate embroidery designs, while women on the upper Suriname River have generally limited skirt embroidery to simple edging stitches.

4.9. A Ndyuka woman, early 1960s. Her yellow and blue skirt is tied with a red cotton sash topped by a black yarn belt. The patchwork bra was made on a hand-cranked sewing machine imported from the coast. The cape is a cotton aqua print.

4.10. A Saramaka woman, mid-1960s. Her predominantly orange skirt is tied with a navy waist kerchief and she wears a commercial terrycloth towel in place of the appliqué cape that her son has borrowed to dress up for the portrait. (See Chapter 5 for discussion of this boy's later development as a professional artist.)

Within such regionally defined conventions there is also considerable variability according to age, status, personal style, and social context, marking, for example, a state of mourning, the greater informality when people are in their own villages versus those of their affines, the behavior appropriate to, for example, casual settings, council meetings, and community celebrations. Public events such as funerals, rites for local gods, or large-scale council meetings are occasions for particular attention to personal adornment. Before leaving home, participants have their hair braided, scrape off unwanted facial hair around the neck and temples with a bare razor, and assemble clothes, jewelry, lanterns, umbrellas, and other accessories. Just before coming into sight of the village landing place where people are gathering, they stop their canoes at a boulder in the river, where they bathe, apply sweet-smelling lotions, change into clean clothes, adjust jewelry and accessories, and assume the special postures and tones of speech that reflect their role as visitors to an important community event. This ritual of personal preparation just prior to arrival in a village, which we witnessed countless times in the 1960s and 1970s, has apparently been practiced throughout Maroon history. The German missionary account quoted above documents it for eighteenth-century Saramaka, and a Dutch observer gives a similar description for Ndyuka in the early twentieth century (de Goeje 1908:1004).

Even children, often glossed in the literature as "naked," are not without special accessories, beginning with the essential waist tie made of a twisted piece of cotton cloth. Infants are often dressed in hand-sewn caps, and girls wear little rings in the ears, or at least a piece of string to maintain the holes pierced in early infancy. Into the 1970s it was customary in the area of Saramaka where we lived to mark children's readiness to begin walking by giving them their first pair of calfbands (known by a special term and "knitted" rather than crocheted),[3] as well as string anklets holding tiny rings cut from a gourd. And until very recently, when a young girl's nipples began to swell her father's matrilineage would formally present her with a pubic apron to be tucked over a waist tie, which she wore until it was cut by her first husband in the coming-of-age ritual alluded to earlier in this chapter (see figs. 4.7, 4.21).[4] Whatever their age, children enjoy getting dressed up in the kinds of clothes they will wear as they get older (figs. 4.11, 4.12).

The time considered most appropriate for experimentation in clothes and body ornamentation is young adulthood, beginning in the teens. This is when women have the largest number of cicatrization designs incised on their bodies and young men are expected to indulge in creative and (from their elders' perspective) "outrageous" new styles, using goods that they have bought during their first extended period of wage labor on the coast.

4.11. Saramaka girls dress up for a play visit to their husbands' village.

4.12. Three-year-old boys try out adult gear—a cape, a gun, and a hunting sack.

Cicatrization designs, a longtime cornerpost of beauty and eroticism for Maroon men and women, offer one example of this sort of generational change. Figure 4.13 depicts the designs that were widespread in Saramaka during the 1960s and 1970s, a time when it was unthinkable, for people on the Pikilio, that a woman would not have cicatrizations, at the very least in her "under-the-skirt" area, where the tactile dimension mattered most for love-making.[5] (See also figs. 4.14, 4.15, and S. Price 1993 [1984]:fig. 4; for two sketches of Aluku designs, see Hurault 1970:60.) Cicatrization designs were relatively standardized among peers, and although the patterns on a forty-year-old and a twenty-five-year-old might overlap in terms of design, it would be very unusual to see the duplication of a motif on women separated by more than three decades. The progression during this century has been toward reduction and simplification. In the late 1990s, Saramakas from the Pikilio still insisted on the importance of cicatrizations for women. One fifty-year-old man told us in 1997 that if he ever heard of a young woman in his lineage who didn't have any he would take her aside for a stern talk to bring her into line. (See fig. 4.29 and, for a history of Maroon cicatrization and a discussion of its precedents in Africa, S. and R. Price 1980:88–92.)

Men's necklaces in the Saramaka villages of the upper Suriname River and its tributaries offer another illustration of the kind of fads that charac-

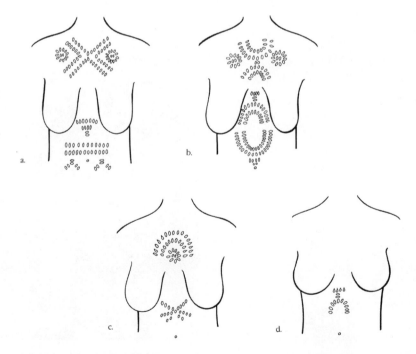

4.13. Cicatrization designs popular among Saramaka women born about (a) 1880, (b) 1915, (c) 1930, and (d) 1950.

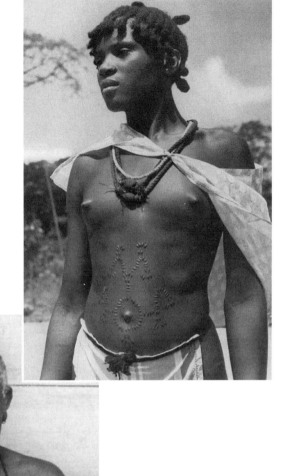

4.14, 4.15. A Ndyuka girl about 1950 and Kandamma, a renowned singer and storyteller from the Saramaka village of Dangogo, in 1978. (Kandamma's voice can be heard in R. and S. Price 1977, and a sample of her narrative gifts in R. and S. Price 1991.)

terize every aspect of personal attire. Stylish dress for young men at the turn of the century included bead necklaces that hung to the navel. Their sons' generation also made single strands of the same type of beads, but wore them over one shoulder and under the other arm. A decade later it became the fashion to wear a single-strand necklace of smaller beads that would hang all the way to the ground when the man was standing. If the necklace failed to reach the ground, the standard comment was that the wearer must have "picked it up off the ground," but if it was long enough people would compliment it as something "bought from a countertop on the coast." Around 1930, young men began wearing white over-the-shoulder beaded jewelry of up to seven strands, accompanied by a thin silver chain around the neck. Later, gold chains replaced the silver ones, and the all-white strands gave way to green, red, and transparent beads. During the 1960s the most popular necklace for men was a commercial gold chain with a cluster of three pendants—one of which could be used to clean the ears, the other two to pick the teeth (S. and R. Price 1980:fig. 47). (For more on Maroon jewelry, from earrings, watches, barrettes, decorative rubber bands, safety-pin pendants, and stacked aluminum anklets to protective amulets made from cowrie shells, parrot feathers, coins, and encased herbal bundles, see S. and R. Price 1980:86–87.)

Similar successions of fads could be described for any of the Maroon groups. Among the Ndyuka, for example, where breechcloths have traditionally been smaller than in Saramaka and Matawai, young men in the 1960s ostentatiously flaunted breechcloths that reached to the ground. The appropriate compliment for a woman to make about such a garment was that its owner's (sexual) potency must be "forty horsepower," like the most powerful outboard motors then being used on the river (fig. 4.16).[6] At the same time, Ndyuka women were wearing hand-sewn patchwork bras like that pictured in figure 4.9. By the mid-1970s, these fashions had disappeared and others had taken their place. Young men were experimenting with a variety of elements of Western dress, including thin plastic belts which they bought in Paramaribo and wore in clusters of three to five at a time, and young women had replaced their home-sewn bras, cotton wrap-skirts, red sashes, and black-cord waist ties with commercial bras from the city and a double layer of colorful bath towels which they tied at different sides and staggered heights on the body. In Matawai villages of the 1970s, women were sewing capes and breechcloths composed of red, white, and navy triangular patches, and this style was accompanied by the same suddenness of popularity and high-fashion excitement as the contemporaneous but completely different rages that were animating fashion trends in Saramaka and eastern Maroon villages (fig. 4.17).[7]

MAROON ARTS

4.16. Ndyuka teenagers wearing the long breechcloths popular in the early 1960s.

4.17. Matawai *bandja* dancers, village of Sukibaka, 1974.

Legbands also illustrate the kind of stylistic variation that Maroons enjoy in even narrowly limited artistic forms. We draw our examples from Saramaka (figs. 4.18, 4.19, 4.20), where they have always been a focus of sartorial attention.[8] Until the 1930s, both men and women often wore crocheted bands on their calves and ankles, and even on their upper arms. Although the expense of imported yarns meant that most of these were made of locally grown, undyed cotton, some also included red, white, and black commercial cotton crocheted into special designs that older Saramakas of the 1960s remembered from their childhood around the turn of the century (fig. 4.19a, b). Legbands were also embellished with protective charms well into the twentieth century, most commonly with a pendant made of cowrie shells and a raffia-like fiber from the Mauritius palm. By the mid-twentieth century, crocheted ankle- and armbands had largely dropped out of fashion, and calfbands were no longer made in plain white, but sported a single stripe of color in the center, a set of very thin center stripes (the "chicken stitch," fig. 4.19c), or a wider pair of off-center stripes (the "rainbow," fig. 4.19d). The edges were usually decorated with a thin line of color, added after the band was complete, and a small braided tie made from threads that had been pulled from scraps of colorful trade cotton. After about 1940 these braided ties were replaced by fluffy pompoms, which gradually increased in size after they were introduced (figs. 4.19e, f; 4.20b *left*). In the 1960s and 1970s, most Saramaka crocheted bands were white calfbands with yarn tassels and multiple colored stripes (fig. 4.21), but some villages retained selected styles from earlier generations. The rainbow stripe was still being made in the village of Guyaba, the wide stripes shown in figure 4.19g in the villages of the upper Gaanlio, and the chicken stitch in Pempe, and anklebands were sometimes worn in the village of Botopasi.[9] The occasions for which crocheted legbands were worn also varied by region. Saramakas from the upper river villages have always considered them most important for participation in funeral rites, but in many Saramaka villages of the lower river they were reserved principally for New Year's celebrations.

4.18. A Saramaka woman crochets calfbands around a bottle.

4.19. Calfband styles. All are Saramaka, except the last, which was made by Carib Indians in Suriname.

4.20a, b. Cylindrical forms used for crocheting calfbands. *Above, left to right:* a bottle with orange-and-white calfbands; a wooden form with Saramaka-style carving, collected 1932–38; *Below, left to right:* a Saramaka model made on the Gaanlio from industrial tubing with wooden top and bottom, and given to a young woman in the village of Asindoopo whose work was in progress when the object was collected in 1978; a wooden form with Saramaka-style carving.

MAROON ARTS

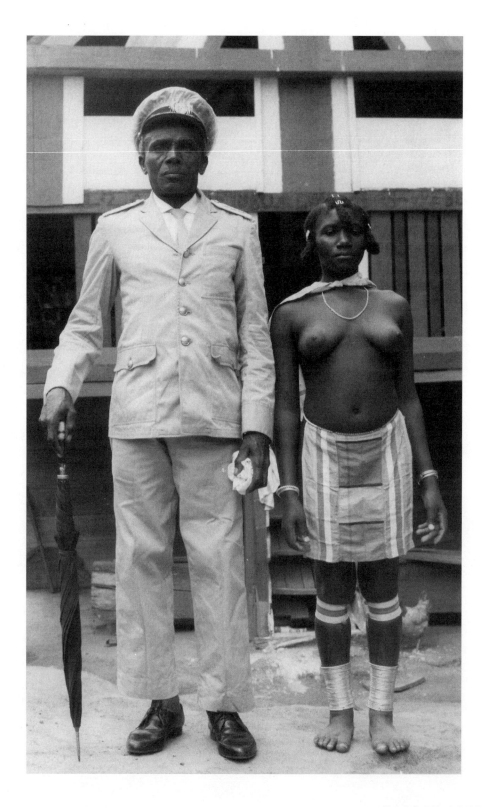

Calfbands illustrate both the tendency to associate styles with specific regions and the point we made at the beginning of this chapter about how hard it is to call the end of an object's active lifetime, even when it is "collected," documented, and laid to gather dust on the shelf of a museum storeroom. After our first year in Saramaka, we returned to New York for three months to assess our findings and make plans for our second year in the field. On a visit to the storeroom of the American Museum of Natural History, we came upon the calfbands illustrated in figure 4.19b, which were unlike any we had seen in Suriname. S. P. had already learned the basic stitch by that time, and by examining the new model she figured out how to produce a pair of calfbands with the same V-shaped pattern when we returned to Saramaka. Although our elderly neighbors recognized it and knew its names, the method of alternating colors had been forgotten, and young women were eager to be taught this "new" and, in their view, innovative technique. Returning to the same region ten years later, we overheard people discussing this style, unaware of its atypical history, as something that "belonged" to the village of Dangogo, where we had been based in the 1960s. And a collection made in 1991 by a Saramaka man from the Middle River, at the behest of museum planners in Cayenne, attests to the popularity of these patterned calfbands all along the Suriname River.

Small details of fashion not only shed light on cultural attitudes toward personal adornment and artistic innovation, but also provide important clues for the use of museum collections in the reconstruction of style sequences. It was often possible, for example, to establish the approximate age of a Saramaka man's shoulder cape by noting the form of the upper corners. On most early twentieth-century capes there were no ties; at most, the upper cloth was cut with a triangular extension to facilitate the shoulder attachment. In the 1930s-1950s, ties were made by folding strips of cotton cloth and sewing the edges together. Later they consisted of braided or twisted threads of several colors that had been pulled from the edges of cotton cloth. And that style was replaced in turn by ties made of commercial yarn twisted into a cord that ended in a large yarn tassel. Women's capes (which in Saramaka are worn over both shoulders and are smaller than men's capes) have also changed over time. Sewn without any ties during the early twentieth century, they were later fitted with short ties made from strips of cotton cloth. And in the late 1960s, that style was replaced by a single long tie, sewn in place at both ends, which positioned the cape over the lower back rather than at the shoulders.

4.21. Headman Kala (Dangasi) of Dangogo in his official uniform and his wife's teenage granddaughter, Maame, in cape, adolescent apron, calfbands, and aluminum bracelets and anklets.

Even the simple breechcloth has varied over time. Nineteenth-century illustrations suggest that breechcloths, at least in some cases, wrapped around the body rather than simply passing between the legs (see, for example, S. and R. Price 1980:fig. 69). And in discussing twentieth-century breechcloths, which may be either a long rectangular cloth draped over a separate waist string or a garment incorporating narrow cotton strips that are tied in front, Saramakas told us that the ties were introduced when men began providing river transport services, since breechcloths draped over a waist tie (see, for example, Kahn 1931:facing p. 110) tended to slip out of place when the job of handling the river pole became strenuous, and the ties were more successful at holding them where they belonged.

4.22. Aluku men, early 1900s.

4.23. A Maroon headman, 1928.

Western attire has always been used selectively by Maroon men and, to a lesser extent, by women. Throughout Maroon history, men have purchased varied kinds of hats, as well as shirts and pants made out of colorful trade cotton by coastal tailors (figs. 4.22, 4.23; see also fig. 4.8).[10] The "long shirt" (similar to the eighteenth-century "nightshirt" mentioned in the missionary account quoted above) was standard formal dress for Saramaka elders during the early twentieth century and for Ndyuka elders well into the 1960s (fig. 4.24). Even in the 1980s, Chief Agbago's everyday clothes were a modified version of the long shirt and matching trousers, made from colorfully patterned materials by Creole tailors in Paramaribo. During our fieldwork it was not unusual to see men wearing commercial thongs, sunglasses,

4.24. "Village elders on a ceremonial visit," 1929.

trousers, shorts, shirts, and hats (berets, golf caps, fedoras, stetsons, pith helmets, and more), not only during their trips to the coast but also back in their home villages.

Public office also contributes to the presence of Western clothes in Maroon villages, and has done so since the period immediately following the peace treaties. An eighteenth-century Moravian observer described one Saramaka village headman's uniform, provided by the colonial government, as

> a jacket, a vest, trousers of the finest striped linen, a hat with golden tassels, a lace shirt with cuffs, and a captain's staff made from cane and topped with a large silver and heavily-gilt knob. (Riemer 1801:370–71, in R. Price 1990:228)

"With all this finery," added the missionary, "he nonetheless went barefoot." Several decades later, another observer described a paramount chief's official uniform as

> a blue dress coat trimmed with wide gold braid on the collar and with cuffs on the sleeves; a three-cornered hat with gold braid, an orange cockade, and a black strap; and a gilt crescential breastplate, and a staff with a gilt knob on which are engraved the Government's coat of arms and the following inscription: "Paramount Chief of the Free Saramaka Bush Negroes, named Koffy." (van Eyck 1830:265)

Today, as in the past, all Maroon officials—which now means chiefs, village headmen, assistant headmen, and "women assistants"—own uniforms issued upon their installation to office in the capital, which they wear for council meetings and visits by outside dignitaries (figs. 4.25, 4.21).[11]

Women's ownership of manufactured clothing has varied considerably from one region to another. In the 1960s and 1970s, for example, many women in the villages of the Pikilio had to borrow a dress from a relative if they were taken to Paramaribo, and others wore a dress only when they were feeling ill. Closer to the coast, and in Christian villages, women some-times owned several dresses and wore them on an occasional basis in their own villages. In Ndyuka, women were wearing dresses, often folded down at the waist, as a nearly standard outfit. Kwinti women were wearing dresses every day and Matawai women were wearing them with a wrap-skirt tied on top (see fig. 4.17 and the illustrations in de Beet and Sterman 1981).

The Aluku Maroons seem always to have led the pack in adoptions of

Western clothing. Hurault, referring to clothing styles of the 1950s and 1960s, bemoaned the trend away from "traditional" dress:

> You see the men wearing shirts and shorts of yellow, red, purple or green. . . . Made with material of the lowest quality, these clothes rot and fall apart quickly in the humid climate, taking on a pathetic look that their bearers seem not to notice. And the women deck themselves out in halters, "mission dresses," multi-colored brassieres, etc. In recent years, hideous jockey caps were the thing on the Marowijne River, as well as jerseys adorned with ads for outboard motors and other motifs equally ugly, ridiculous, and vulgar. (1970:58–59)

Kenneth Bilby captured the flavor of Aluku style changes in the 1980s, fueled by a spirit of consumerism and an increased access to cash that flourished under the program of *francisation,* when he described

> small groups of villagers, as they take a break from the tedium of peeling or grating cassava tubers, huddled over the soiled pages of the latest offering from [the catalogue of] *La Redoute,* admir-

4.25. A paramount chief (in dark pants) and five headmen, early twentieth century.

ing the digital watches and bikinis, the patent leather belts and frilly party dresses. At night, and sometimes even during the day, they come out to sport their new booty, in a disconcerting pageant of alienated Frenchness. . . . An official government boatman, a man of means, shows off his newest acquisition: a bright blue pair of overall shorts, with cuffs at the thighs and a flaring collar, the *fantaisie* of an anonymous metropolitan beach-wear designer. A middle-aged mother of seven thinks nothing of parading about the village in a flouncy three-tiered miniskirt of the sort usually associated with clean-cut French teenagers. An elderly village chief wears a puffy pair of tinselly gold running shorts, three sizes too large, on top of ankle-high sneakers. The occasional passing boatloads of adventure-seeking French tourists from the coast keep an eye out for the few remaining loincloths and wonder about the *bouffonerie* being passed off as "les populations primitives." (1990:182–83)

The massive influx of mail-order clothing has not, however, wiped out Aluku women's enthusiasm for the art of decorative sewing. During a trip we took along the Lawa River in 1990, we attended a funeral celebration where young women were sporting lavishly patterned cross-stitch wrap-skirts, many of them elaborately fringed along the bottom, which they had been laboring over for the previous several days. The women were barefoot, and the skirts were secured by wide black elastic belts and topped with com-mercial cut-off blouses. A few hours later, at another stage of the ceremony, these same women reappeared decked out in European dresses, heavily sequined and ruffled, and high heels.

If we review the history of Maroon dress over the past three centuries, it is clear that a diversity of cultural models has come into play. We cite just a few examples. The basics of everyday clothing—women's wrap-skirts and men's breechcloths—are similar to the dress of early African Americans in many parts of the hemisphere. (For a striking example from Brazil, see Johnston 1910:plate 78.) On a more particularistic level, it has been sug-gested that a style of breechcloth known to eighteenth-century Saramakas as *abadjà* might well be related to the similar African garment that Ga speakers on the Gold Coast called *gbadsa* (Schumann 1778: s.v. *abadjà*). On the other hand, adolescent girls' aprons follow the model of Amerindian women's aprons, and the Maroon words that designate them (Sar. *koyó*, Ndy. *kwei*) derive from Suriname Indian languages (Galibi *kwai*, Trio *kwayu*). And two types of men's caps mentioned for eighteenth-century Saramaka reflect the diverse origins of the slave masters; knitted caps were known as *brae mussu*, from the Dutch words *breien* ("to knit") and *muts* ("cap"), and the cloth models were called *kwefa*, from the Portuguese term for cap (*coifa*) (or possibly the English word *coif*).

DURING THE SECOND HALF of the nineteenth century, Maroon clothing continued to be dominated by jewelry and other accessories, and a variety of reports lend support to the generalization made by Jules Brunetti that "while, on the one hand, clothing is treated as an accessory, [personal] ornaments play a central role in the Maroons' existence" (1890:172; figs. 4.26, 4.27, 4.28, 4.29).[12] At the same time, the social and economic conditions for a dramatic increase in attention to cloth and clothing were taking shape. Following the general emancipation of slaves in Suriname in 1863, travel between the interior and the coast was to a great extent freed from the constraints that had been in effect during the whole first century of the Maroons' independence. As a result, new opportunities opened up to them for earning money in coastal territory (particularly in logging and river transport), and the exodus of men soon led to a restructuring of many aspects of life back in their home villages, introducing changes in everything from marriage and residence patterns to the role of the arts in daily life.[13]

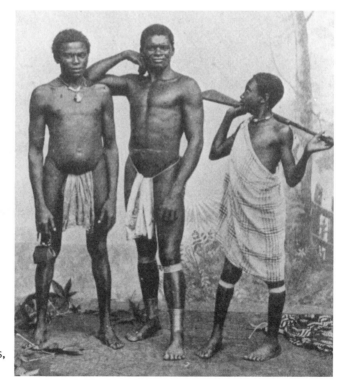

4.26. Ndyukas, about 1900.

In terms of gender relations, the balance of power shifted significantly in favor of men. The sudden drop in the ratio of men to women in Saramaka villages brought a reduction in the fierce competition for women that had characterized earlier male/female relations and led to a marked increase in polygyny, a conjugal arrangement that had always been ideologically acceptable. As a result, many aspects of the marriage system changed. The betrothal of young girls became rarer, and the related practice of promising an unborn child to a man—as a wife if it was a girl, as a "formal friend" if it was a boy—disappeared. So, too, did the "inheritance" of a deceased man's wife by his brother. And expectations that a man would spend significant amounts of time in his wife's village, performing a variety of services for her relatives, diminished perceptibly. Behavioral patterns between spouses were also affected. Men began expecting their wives to address them by respectful elliptical terms rather than their first names; divorces initiated by

4.27. A Saramaka, about 1900.

4.28. A Maroon wearing a dance apron over his breechcloth, early 1900s.

MAROON ARTS

women became rare; and certain domestic tasks, such as cutting and carrying firewood, shifted from men to women. Sexual competition among women, most viscerally between co-wives, became a central reality of daily life.[14]

It was in this situation of increased exposure to the outside world (directly by men, vicariously by women), of fundamental demographic shifts in the villages (significantly affecting the balance of power between men and women), and of dramatically expanding material resources (trade cotton in particular) that Maroons began exploring the artistic potential of cloth as they never had before.[15] Shoulder capes became an everyday element of men's dress rather than a rarity, and provided a stage where women could play out both their devotion to a lover or husband and their creative talents. We have been able to reconstruct the main lines of the style sequence that grew out of these developments, thanks to the help of older Maroons' memories from the turn of the century, drawings and photographs made by nineteenth-century visitors to the interior, objects in museum collections, and documents in Dutch and Suriname archives.

4.29. A Ndyuka from the Cottica River region, about 1930.

The initial experimentation produced an embroidery style executed on monochrome or subtly striped cotton cloth that lasted into the first decades of the twentieth century in much of Saramaka and somewhat later in other areas. Curvilinear designs placed more or less symmetrically around a vertical axis were outlined with linked stitches that sometimes shifted from one color to another. The interior areas were textured with a variety of dense "filler" stitches, and the dominant colors of the embroidery were black, red, white, and yellow. A nineteenth-century observer's description of this style shows that it drew on the cooperation of men and women in a division of labor that was carried on in subsequent forms of Maroon artmaking as well.

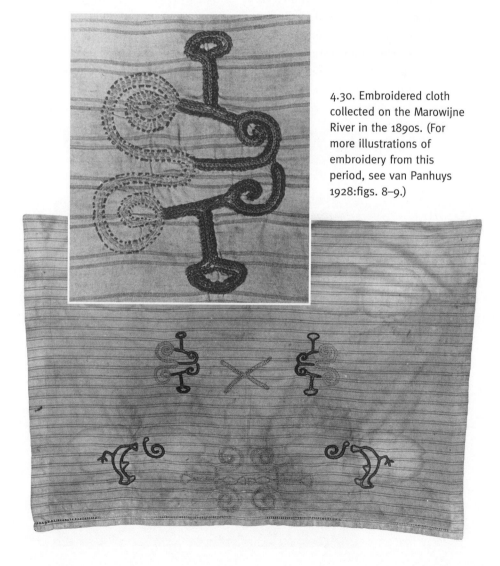

4.30. Embroidered cloth collected on the Marowijne River in the 1890s. (For more illustrations of embroidery from this period, see van Panhuys 1928:figs. 8–9.)

"On a piece of store-bought cotton destined for use as a skirt or shoulder cape, figures are drawn in charcoal by the men; these figures are embroidered by the women" (van Panhuys 1899:81). This style is illustrated in figures 4.30 and 4.31*left*; see also figures 4.5, 4.61, 4.62, 4.63, 4.64, as well as S. and R. Price 1980:figures 73–75. In the version of this arrangement that we witnessed often in Saramaka villages of the 1960s and 1970s, pencils had replaced charcoal, but the cultural rationale remained intact: a belief in the superior ability of men over women to plan out a properly symmetrical design.

4.31. A Dutch explorer with his Saramaka guides, 1908.

4.32. A man's shoulder cape embroidered by a Saramaka woman from Totikampu who included her husband's name and her own in the design. The original cape was later enlarged in response to changes in men's fashion.

4.33. Apron composed of four pieces of cloth, with appliqué and embroidery, collected 1932–38.

Even at this early stage, Maroon women were incorporating one feature into their sewing which for them seems to have arisen largely from practical considerations, but which their daughters and granddaughters would eventually transform into a vibrantly colorful, richly elaborated art. The joining of pieces of cloth to form a composite whole can be found on Maroon garments of almost every type and decorative style. The white background of the cape in figure 4.1, for example, consists of three pieces of white cloth of different sizes, discreetly sewn together to form a rectangle of the correct proportions (see also figs. 4.32, 4.33). Men's neckerchiefs and women's waist kerchiefs have often been similarly pieced together, using odds and ends left over from other sewing projects. Adolescent girls' aprons have almost always been patched from small pieces of cloth. A style of men's shoulder cape popular among Saramakas in the early twentieth century was created by segmenting a piece of striped cloth, repositioning the segments so that the stripes on the cape fall vertically rather than horizontally, and sewing them back together (fig. 4.34), producing a garment whose patchwork structure was barely noticeable. And in the 1960s, when Saramaka men were expressing a preference for breechcloths wide enough to wrap

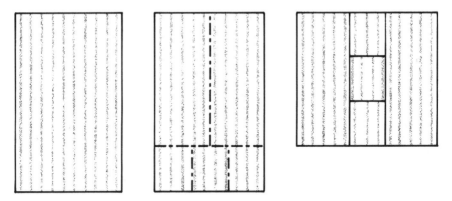

4.34. Cape construction based on realignment of a single piece of cloth (with cuts shown in dotted lines and seams in solid lines).

fully around their thighs, women would cut a length of striped cloth into two uneven pieces, reposition them, and enlarge the whole garment with supplementary strips of another pattern (fig. 4.35). Caps, cartridge sacks, hunting sack covers, and hammock sheets provide further evidence that patching, whether readily visible or carefully camouflaged, has long been an option in Maroon sewing. Close examination of figures 4.70 and 4.36 will reveal how "invisibly" this patching could be implemented.

At the very end of the nineteenth century, women began experimenting with the potential of patching for its visual effect, converting it from a discreet practical measure to a bold artistic statement. Embroidered textiles framed with appliquéd strips of colorful patchwork suggest that they may have first tried out this new style of decorative sewing in the margins of the earlier art of embroidery (see fig. 4.1), moving it more confidently to the center only as they achieved technical mastery and artistic definition. The basic elements of what came to be known as "bits-and-pieces" (or "red-and-black") patchwork were small squares, triangles, and rectangles cut from red, white, and black/navy cotton, but it also could include yellow, blue, green, pink, or even striped fabric (figs. 4.36, 4.2, 4.65, 4.67; see also S. and R. Price 1980:fig. 82). In most cases, the seams connecting the patches were meticulously tucked under and fixed in place with tiny stitches,[16] but in some (especially breechcloths), the patchwork panel was instead appliquéd

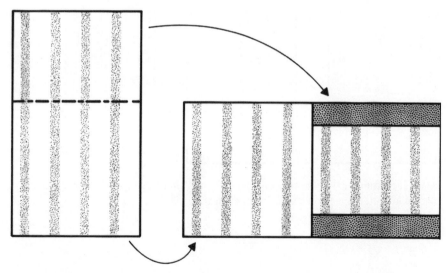

4.35. Breechcloth construction in which a length of trade cotton is cut into two sections and resewn with supplemental pieces of another cloth.

MAROON ARTS

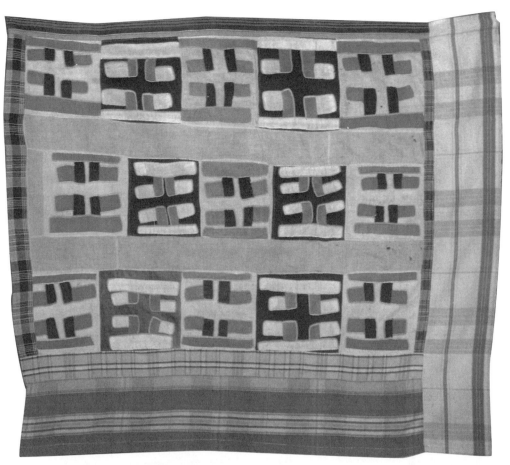

4.36. Man's shoulder cape in red, white, and black patchwork and appliqué, probably sewn in the early twentieth century.

onto a background cloth, often with a line of decorative embroidery (fig. 4.37). In a few cases, the curvilinear shapes characteristic of contemporaneous embroidery were executed as appliqués of solid-color cloth, edged with linked embroidery stitches (figs. 4.38, 4.39).

Almost as soon as bits-and-pieces compositions entered the mainstream, they began to foreshadow, in a variety of interesting ways, the next major fashion in Maroon textile arts, which was also a kind of patchwork but utilized long narrow strips of colorfully striped cloth rather than small pieces in solid colors. First, women often constructed bits-and-pieces panels in the form of long strips, inserting narrow strips of colorfully striped cotton between them (see, for example, fig. 4.69) and using multicolor strips to frame the whole composition. Other capes exhibit the compositional complexity of bits-and-pieces sewing, but were made largely with the striped cotton typical of the later narrow-strip style (see figs. 4.73 and 4.74). Finally, some compositions were meticulously pieced together out of small rectangles but arranged in such a way as to create the visual effect of a simple narrow-strip textile (fig. 4.76).

4.37. Breechcloths with patchwork appliqué in red, white, black, and yellow on rear flap

4.38. Saramaka cap with "bird's wings" motif in navy appliqué, sewn by Peepina for Chief Agbago, probably in the 1920s.

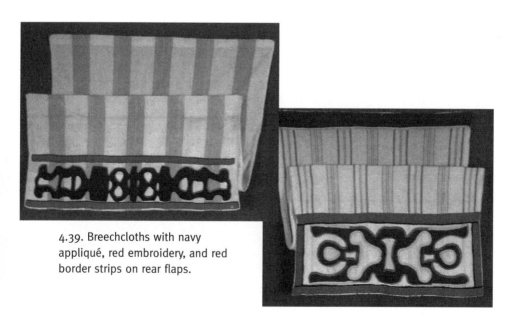

4.39. Breechcloths with navy appliqué, red embroidery, and red border strips on rear flaps.

The development of narrow-strip sewing out of bits-and-pieces compositions involved an important shift in chromatics. The tricolor aesthetic centered firmly on red, white, and black/navy gave way to an exploitation of the full color spectrum. As the principles of the new art were refined over the years, avoidance of a "dominating" color became a conscious aesthetic ideal, and textiles were admired for their success in juxtaposing a varied set of sharply contrasting hues.

Once textiles composed exclusively of narrow strips became popular, around 1920–30, they maintained their position as the epitome of a woman's artistic offerings to her husband and as the height of men's fashion for almost fifty years.[17] Throughout this period, the bulk of the cloth used by Maroons was colorfully striped trade cotton which men purchased in two-

4.40. Bolts of cloth in the "Jeruzalem Bazaar," Paramaribo.

4.41. Saramaka shrine to the ancestors, Dangogo.

MAROON ARTS

ell lengths on the coast (fig. 4.40) and brought back to the village (in quantities varying from tens to hundreds, depending on the economic climate), where they distributed about half of them to wives and female relatives, used some for ritual offerings (fig. 4.41), and kept others in reserve for future needs.[18] Women trimmed these lengths of cloth parallel to both the selvage (by ripping) and the end (with a knife), and saved the resulting strips for eventual use in their patchwork compositions. The vast majority of these were sewn as men's capes (figs. 4.42, 4.57, 4.59), but hammock sheets (fig. 4.79), caps for both men and infants, men's decorative dance aprons, adolescent girls' everyday aprons, and women's skirts have also been constructed in this way.

4.42. A Saramaka dressed for a visit to his wife's village.

The new cloth that was used for narrow-strip patchwork came in many color combinations, stripes and cross-stripes of different widths, and varying grades of cotton, providing a rich resource for artistic experimentation—and also for verbal play. From their very earliest days in the forest, Maroons had been enjoying the ongoing creative potential of language, including everything from personal names and secret play languages to whimsical turns of phrase and celebratory or derogatory labels for incoming or outgoing fads. Any item of material culture, whether locally made or imported, could be given a name (or several)—woodcarving "teeth," embroidery stitches, cicatrization designs, legband styles, the patterns traced onto cassava cakes, particular models of machetes, buckets, pots, and tin lanterns,[19] or even different arrangements of gold teeth ("tilted head" for a single gold tooth on one side, "city street" for one on each side) and ways of peeling an orange ("monkey's head" for a spiral cut perpendicular to the fruit's equator—see fig 4.43.) The colorfully striped trade cotton that first became available around the turn of the century provided a ready canvas for this sort of play, and various resources were quickly called into service as a way of referring to specific patterns. Although a few names have been made up by store owners in the city, most have been created by the Maroons themselves.[20] Some are straightforward descriptions—*alatjá balán* ("it goes rrrip!") for a cloth wide enough to split into two skirts, or *límbo muyêè* ("clean woman") for a yellow-on-white pattern that would show spots if it were not kept perfectly laundered. Some evoke an admired object or personality to produce indirect compliments—like *sitangáli* ("sky rocket")—and a few, such as *bómbo de a saáfu* ("cunt is in slavery"), are humorous comments on life.[21]

Current events have also fueled cloth naming—a visit by Princess Beatrix of the Netherlands to the interior, a meeting of the Saramaka and Ndyuka chiefs, an attempted assassination, or the first moon landing. Coastal experiences, from wage-labor opportunities to shortages of consumer goods, have been another source of inspiration—*kó gó a Lawa* ("let's go to the Lawa," a river in French Guiana where jobs were opening up) or *kónda kabá a kaise* ("they're out of necklaces at Kersten's," a department store). The great bulk of commemorative names, however, have been derived from local incidents (sexual scandals, petty theft, canoe accidents, quarrels and physical fights, run-ins with outsiders, and so forth)—*Agbago síngi a mòtê* ("Agbago sank with a motor," after the Saramaka chief's boat overturned in a rapids), *baáa kíi baáa* ("brother killed brother," after a man murdered his mother's sister's son), or *kambósa pêpè kambósa* ("co-wife peppered co-wife," after a woman crushed hot peppers and added them to the herbal bath her co-wife used to wash her genitals). In fact, Saramakas frequently turned gossip into potential cloth names, of which only a small proportion

MAROON ARTS

eventually made their way into general use. We often heard people reacting to a bit of news by saying they would use it to name the next new cloth pattern they saw, which meant that a particular pattern could have a number of potential names even before it made its first appearance in a Maroon village.[22]

4.43. Saramaka boys enjoy the aesthetic by-products of an orange snack.

At different times, and in different regions, women have made narrow-strip textiles in slightly varying compositions. For example, eastern Maroons have produced both more openwork and more textiles composed almost exclusively of strips taken from the weft (fig. 4.44; see also S. and R. Price 1980:figs. 61, 90, 91), while Saramakas have rarely incorporated openwork and have always preferred an alternation of warp and weft strips. The style

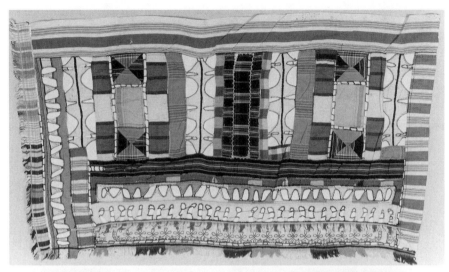

4.44. Ndyuka openwork textile for a woman to wear on top of her wrap-skirt for ceremonial dress. Sewn by Ma Losa, village of Fandaaki, probably about 1910–15.

of horizontal (rather than vertical) arrangements of strips (fig. 4.45) was also more common and more long-lived among eastern Maroons than it was in Saramaka. And within Saramaka, compositions in which the side strips extend further than those at the center (fig. 4.77) are more likely to have been sewn in the villages of the Gaanlio than on the Pikilio.

4.45. Paramaka man's shoulder cape, collected before 1938 in Langatabiki.

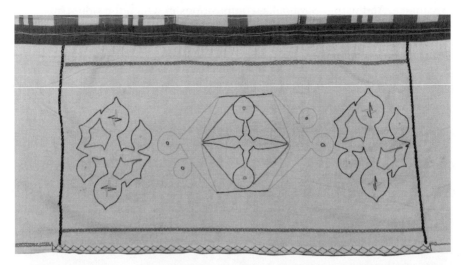

4.46. Embroidery on an Aluku breechcloth, sewn about 1960 by Ma Sokodon, from the village of Tabiki.

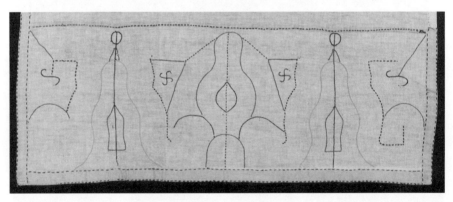

4.47. Embroidery on a Saramaka shoulder cape, probably sewn in the 1950s or 1960s.

4.48 (*opposite page*). Embroidery on a Ndyuka adolescent apron, sewn about 1940 by Atonseng, from the village of Tabiki.

During the same half-century that was dominated by narrow-strip patch-work, the art of embroidery continued, but with new stitches and changes in overall style. Women began executing their designs in single lines rather than filled-in forms, cut back sharply on their use of black thread, made fewer fringes of unraveled cloth, and incorporated overlays of eyelet, rick-rack, and ribbon (figs. 4.46, 4.47, 4.48; see also fig. 4.80 and S. and R. Price 1980:fig. 60). The option of asking a man to mark out a geometric design with straight edge and compass continued throughout this period, but women also embroidered more free-form designs of their own creation (see figs. 3.5, 3.6). During the 1960s and 1970s, the most popular style of capes for Saramaka women was a wide H-shaped overlay, often in several layers, on a monochrome cloth or "calico" print (see S. and R. Price 1980:fig. 95).

In the 1950s, when bits-and-pieces capes had long since gone out of fashion and narrow-strip patchwork capes had taken their place, women were devoting tremendous time, thought, and energy to assembling collections of cotton strips, arranging them in pleasing combinations, and sewing them in place with tiny, meticulous stitches.[23] Together with crocheted calfbands, these capes symbolized a woman's devotion to her husband, and all men wore them proudly. By the late 1960s, however, young girls from villages where there were mission schools had begun to learn the technique of cross-stitch embroidery and to pass it on to their older neighbors. Whenever one of these women came to visit a husband in another village, her sisters-in-law would watch with fascination as she copied a pattern from a needlework magazine. Although intimidated by the idea of calculating rows and stitches so exactly, they were acutely aware of the pride with which men wore the finished product. Older men continued to feel comfortable in their narrow-strip capes, but younger men were beginning to reject them, some declaring defiantly that they would never be caught dead in one. Capes of patterned cloth, embroidered cloth, or cloth decorated with overlays of ribbon and eyelet continued to provide an alternative, and women continued to apply themselves to the patchwork and embroidery they had learned as young girls. But the demise of narrow-strip capes was already well underway.

By the mid-1970s in Saramaka, all but the older men had packed their once-cherished narrow-strip capes in the bottoms of their trunks, and most

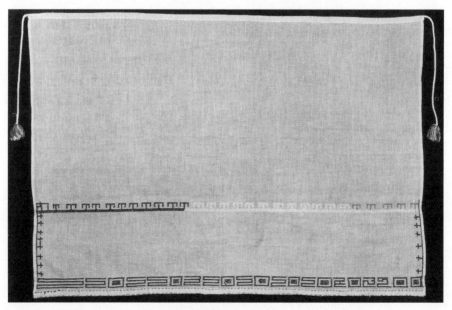

4.49. Saramaka man's cape with cross-stitch embroidery, sewn 1960–65.

women were diligently working to create cross-stitch designs that imitated the models in the foreign magazines.[24] The narrow-strip capes, like outgoing fashions before them, were subjected to newly coined, derogatory terms, becoming "motor covers" and "*apúku* cloths"—things better suited to shielding an outboard motor from the elements or paying off a debt to a forest spirit than donning for festive occasions. The women's strips were being hastily sewn into skirts or, more frequently, simply discarded. And the requirement for a woman to sew a narrow-strip cape as part of the gift exchange for her first marriage was being treated with leniency; older women, understanding that their young relative would probably never sew such a cloth again in her life and that her husband would never wear one, were either stepping in to help lay out the strips or accepting promises that the cape would be made "some day." By the time we spent the summer of 1978 in Saramaka, every kind of cloth object, from infants' caps to hammock sheets, was being decorated with cross-stitch designs, and the art had already passed through a sequence of stylistic and technical developments. Like earlier sewing fashions, it had begun in the margins, timidly bordering the edges of capes, before moving to center stage. For the earliest examples, threads were painstakingly pulled from lengths of thin trade cotton to set up a working grid in the area to be decorated (fig. 4.49). Later, a thicker cloth, with a built-in grid texture, made it possible to bypass this tedious preparation, and designs began to expand over larger areas (fig. 4.50). And this trade cloth in turn was replaced by an even bulkier fabric, which led to even more extensive designs (fig. 4.51).

4.50. Saramaka man's cape with cross-stitch embroidery, sewn 1968.

4.51. Saramaka breechcloth with cross-stitch embroidery, sewn in the 1970s. (See p. 113 for the matching shoulder cape.)

In the late 1970s it seemed possible that Maroon textile arts were about to disappear. The intricate embroidery designs, the magnificent appliqués, and the vibrant patchwork had given way to patterns taken from commercial needlework books, and we had even seen Maroon women in Paramaribo pouring their artistic efforts into macramé doilies made of purple and orange plastic yarn. A dozen years later, visiting Saramakas who had fled the civil war and settled on some unused land next to the St. Laurent–Cayenne road in French Guiana, we were reminded that the fat lady had not yet sung. Cross-stitch was still being made, but without the special cachet of a just-discovered phenomenon, and a new art was stirring up the same flurry of excitement that had greeted each one of the earlier styles. Constructed of decoratively cut overlays, it was being called *abena kamísa*, in recognition of the woman from the village of Abena-sitoonu who set off the craze by sewing a handsome appliqué panel on a breechcloth (*kamísa*) for her husband. Even as they honored its late twentieth-century inventor, women explicitly recognized that it pointed back, in both its technique and its aesthetic principles, to turn-of-the-century bits-and-pieces textiles (figs. 4.52, 4.53, 4.54). Relegating to the background the striped cotton that had given narrow-strip sewing its distinctive color scheme, and eschewing the heavily textured cloth that had provided a grid for cross-stitch compositions, the new technique was executed in thin monochrome trade cotton, most commonly red, white, and black or navy. Some of the appliqué was built up out of rectangular and triangular elements (see, for example, Scholtens et al. 1992:77), and other examples, known as *kóti fulá* ("cut and pierced") or *kóti peláki* ("cut and sewn down"), were curvilinear designs executed as reverse appliqué (cloth with cut-out shapes that exposed a contrasting cloth underneath), sewn in place with a running stitch which was then covered by a line of decorative embroidery. Our first encounter with this new style, in 1990, was a work in progress, in the lap of a woman named Norma who teased us for showing surprise: "Hey, you should know that Saramaka's just not the kind of place where you could come back after ten years and find people sitting around doing the same old thing!"

As this book goes to press, Maroon women are still producing cross-stitch textiles, and *abena-kamísa* appliqué retains its privileged status as "the new thing." But at the same time there are already rumblings of a potential successor. Women are beginning to use yarn to decorate cloth—

4.52, 4.53, 4.54. Three examples of Saramaka appliqué from the 1990s. *Top,* sewn 1991 in Botopasi (unfinished); *middle,* sewn 1997 by Malvina Edward, from the village of Futunakaba; *bottom,* sewn 1997 by Alma Amimba from the village of Pikiseei. (For an example from 1989, see Scholtens et al. 1992:156.)

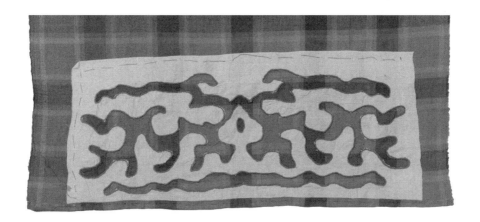

crocheting it into a colorful edging for skirts, tablecloths, and other items, or using it instead of embroidery thread in designs like that shown in figure 4.47. When we remember that bits-and-pieces patchwork began as borders for nineteenth-century embroidery, that narrow-strip art made its début at the edges of bits-and-pieces textiles, and that the earliest cross-stitch was executed as linear border designs, it seems likely that keeping an eye on those crocheted yarn perimeters will allow us to witness the blossoming of an early twenty-first-century art, as Maroon women continue to explore innovative aesthetic directions. (S. Price n.d., written before the recent yarn techniques entered the arena, offers a more detailed argument for the importance of borders in Maroon art history.)

In sewing fashions, as in other aspects of Maroon life, even a relatively straightforward replacement of one style by another involves a complex reworking of skills, perceptions, terminology, and patterns of use by different members of the community. The different perspectives of men and women are further nuanced by differences of generation, temperament, manual skills, and experience with other regions and coastal society. As a result, the relative merits of competing styles are worked into the larger idiom through which individuals express themselves and their place within the society. The designing of a cape, the giving of a cape, the owning of a cape, the wearing of a cape, the evaluative discussion of a cape, and even the final rejection of a cape and its relegation to the rag pile all become, in this context, part of the ongoing definition of cultural identity by individuals—and, over time, by the community as a whole.

FOR MOST OF THE MAROONS' THREE-CENTURY HISTORY, women's decorative sewing has been completely overshadowed by men's woodcarving as an art form considered worthy of attention in the literature. Our decision in 1980 to focus publicity for the exhibit "Afro-American Arts from the Suriname Rain Forest" on a textile rather than something in the more expectable medium of wood, was motivated by a desire to recognize and celebrate an art that had, for a variety of reasons, gone virtually unnoticed outside of its home setting. There was, for example, not a single textile illustrated in either of the two most widely diffused books on Maroon art—Dark's *Bush Negro Art* (1954), which pictured 200 woodcarvings as well as "obeah images," basketry, and calabashes, and Hurault's *Africains de Guyane* (1970), which offered lavish coverage of woodcarvings and architectural decoration and devoted five full-page plates to calabash art.[25] This neglect can be explained by a complex bundle of considerations which include stereotypes concerning the art of "primitive" peoples, gender ideologies espoused by both Maroons and the people who visited their villages, an imbalance in Maroon men's and women's access to coastal society, and the methodologies used to investigate and interpret Maroon art (see S. Price 1983, 1989). Once these textiles had basked in the spotlights of a traveling exhibit, however, their days of anonymity faded as quickly as their fragile dyes. Not only did they "enter the market" and begin to be noticed by art collectors, but they were also called into service for the first time in the context of broad intellectual debates concerning African-American culture history. We save for Chapter 8 our critique of the ways in which scholars have drawn on Maroon arts in these debates, but wish here to begin laying the groundwork for that discussion by introducing, for the realm of textile arts, the methodological position upon which it will pivot.

We note, first of all, that the début of Maroon textiles in the Western art world came at a time when interest in African roots was exploding in the United States. From the flowering of black studies programs to the TV serialization of Alex Haley's *Roots*, a tidal wave of interest in the African contribution to American culture was sweeping the country. In the field of art history, Robert Farris Thompson led a crusade for aesthetic connections, devoting his considerable energies to the discovery of what he was calling the transatlantic tradition, and inspiring others to join the enterprise. It was in this particular climate that outsiders redefined the range of Maroon textile arts (which, as we have seen, included at least five aesthetically and technically distinct styles), focusing attention virtually exclusively on the narrow-strip art that fell chronologically between bits-and-pieces patchwork and cross-stitch embroidery. The choice, though unacknowledged as such, made a certain kind of sense—narrow-strip textiles bore a striking visual resemblance to the well-known *kente* cloth of West Africa, and hence played well in the reconstruction of transatlantic tie-ins. Other forms of decorative sewing practiced by the Maroons receded into the background, and narrow-strip patchwork was offered up as *the* Maroon textile art with the same assurance that men's woodcarving had been presented as *the* art of the Maroons by earlier generations. Set next to edge-sewn textiles from West Africa, the narrow-strip compositions were presented as if they spoke for themselves, testifying to the power of African sensibilities to survive the Middle Passage, slavery, and three centuries of life in the Americas.

Indeed, looking at the Maroons' colorful narrow-strip cloths (especially in a photograph or behind the glass of a museum case), it is hard not to be struck by their visual resemblance to many West African edge-sewn textiles (see fig. 8.3). The parallels in overall form and color contrasts, the "syncopated" effect, in both cases, of subtle modifications to a dominantly symmetrical grid pattern, and the use of small motifs as occasional accents within the strip construction (silk inlays in West African cloths, embroidered designs in those of the Maroons) all might be taken to suggest, on grounds of formal similarity, that the textiles of the Suriname Maroons represent a direct inheritance from their seventeenth-century African ancestors. Once we realize, however, that Maroons began composing narrow-strip patchwork only in the twentieth century, it becomes clear that we have some further homework to do before we can responsibly analyze the African connections.[26]

This is where we would argue for the importance of comprehensive investigation of Maroon art, material culture, and aesthetic ideas as an essential prerequisite to the contemplation of formal similarities if the goal is to determine cultural connections across continents and over centuries. We need to dot the i's and cross the t's, and to respect the power of detailed ethnography for confirming or invalidating the hypotheses that are raised by visual contemplation, global comparisons, and decontextualized interviews.[27]

With textiles, for example, we need to know where Maroons get their thread, what they use to tuck under the raw edges in preparation for hemming, and how close their stitches are. What words do they use to label cloth as it passes from men's coastal purchases to conjugal presents, to women's skirts, to sacks of edge trimmings, to unsewn patterns on the ground and then back to conjugal presents, men's formal wear, pieces of laundry, and finally threadbare rags? Why do Saramakas use a single word for "cloth," "skirt," and "guilder"? What roles do textiles play in marriages, in worship, in political investitures, in popular songs, in legal disputes, in funerals? Do people talk among themselves about aesthetic principles? What, if anything, do they have to say about symbolism? Why do they always fold clothes wrong side out, into little wallet-size packets? Why do seamstresses sometimes lather up a newly sewn textile with bar soap and leave it in the sun before rinsing out the suds? Why, after carefully concealing the tiny stitches used to make a seam, do they lead the thread onto a part of the cloth where it shows clearly before cutting it off? How do they deal with slips, errors, and botched designs? What features of a textile inspire praise—from men, from women—and what features are disparaged? Are clothes mended when they tear, and if so, how? What tone do people adopt when they critique a child's first attempt to sew a patchwork apron? How do they talk about the obsolete arts of their grandmothers? What parts of a garment do women use to test out new ideas and how do their experiments affect fashion trends? Do they cut the cloth with scissors, knife, or razor—or is it ripped?

We have addressed these specific questions at various points in this book and in other writings. Here we offer a consideration of two windows on textile composition in support of our position that a defensible reading of

Maroon art history must be built on an ethnographic foundation that is ambitiously comprehensive and rigorously detailed. We will argue first for the need to look at the aesthetic principles driving all aspects of material culture and the ways that these might feed into the development of a particular artistic domain such as decorative sewing. Secondly we will argue for the need to take the technology of production fully into account. Chapter 8 will draw on these materials to reconsider the processes by which Maroon artists have combined their strong and multifaceted African heritage with the fresh creativity of each succeeding generation in the Americas.

If we view the range of settings and activities that constitute the life of Maroons, it becomes clear that certain preferences run through pretty much the whole fabric of their culture. Many of the aesthetic principles that lend a distinctive character to Maroon personal adornment influence other aspects of their life as well, and the pervasiveness of these "fundamentals" not only helps bring Maroon culture into focus, but also contributes to an understanding of the dynamic process by which it emerged from cultural models in West and Central Africa without directly recapitulating them. One of the most important of these considerations involves the aesthetics of color, where sharp contrast has been a consistent aesthetic goal, whether in the designing of embroidery, the composition of patchwork, or the choice of garments to wear together (S. and R. Price 1980:plate XIII and the numerous color plates in Scholtens et al. 1992, illustrating outfits worn by Saramakas to Chief Agbago's funeral in 1989).[28]

Women executing the lines of an embroidery design frequently change colors in midstream and carry the ends of the thread into the background cloth before knotting it, as a way, they explain, of embellishing the cloth with extra color contrast (fig. 4.55). In a narrow-strip textile, they say, each strip should "raise up" those adjacent to it. In the 1960s, an outfit that both Saramaka and Ndyuka women favored for festive occasions consisted of a yellow skirt with blue or green stripes topped by a bright red kerchief or sash at the waist; in an identical spirit, Saramakas sometimes appliquéd a red border onto a yellow-and-green cloth to create the much-admired *bè-a-*

4.55. Detail of the Paramaka cloth in figure 4.45.

búka ("red-at-the-edge") style skirt. And women crocheting calfbands made an effort to choose colors for the center stripes that would "shine" or "burn" against the surrounding white. Cicatrizations were discussed in the same terms, and although people generally viewed the light skin color of albinos as distinctly unattractive, they praised their cicatrizations for the way the "green" of the scar tissue contrasted with the "white" of the skin around it. Likewise, shiny white teeth against deep black skin has always been a central ideal of physical beauty. Finally, coastal imports, whether plastic clothespins, boxes of detergent, or enamel cooking pots, have long been selected and displayed with an eye to color contrasts (see fig. 4.56), and even the arrangement of rice types within women's gardens constitutes an intentional patchwork of "red" and "white" varieties. The explosion of colors that distinguishes eastern Maroon men's art from that of the Saramaka merely confirms the centrality of this pervasive aesthetic ideal.

We have seen how the replacement of bits-and-pieces textiles by narrow-strip patchwork meant that the tricolor focus on red, white, and black/navy was complemented, and in some contexts upstaged, by a more fully multi-

4.56. Interior of a Ndyuka woman's house, Diitabiki, 1962. The spoons are aluminum; the decorative painting is predominantly red, white, blue, and black; the clothespins are red, white, yellow, and blue; the enamel ware is red, blue, yellow, and green; and the plastic tablecloth is green and white (see S. and R. Price 1980:29).

chrome aesthetic.[29] Among eastern Maroons, a parallel development occurred at the same time in men's painting, which had started out with a relatively cautious use of red, white, and black, but later evolved into a brilliant decorative art that drew, for example, on yellow, pink, light blue, and green (fig. 5.1; see also S. and R. Price 1980:plate V). In both media, the shift reflected external market conditions, which dictated the range of available materials, as well as internal aesthetic preferences that encouraged the introduction of new materials into the system. The earlier privileging of red, white, and black/navy has survived in a number of ways, however, and can still be counted as a fundamental feature of Maroon culture. The knitted ties that adorn some hammock covers have always been made with red, white, and black cotton, and many ritual objects continue to be decorated with designs of red annatto juice, white clay, and black soot. Linguistic terminology is more developed for these three colors than for any others, in that they are the only ones that can be intensified by a special modifier, and most other colors can be subsumed into the tripartite classification—okra sauce is "black," people are either "red" (light-skinned Maroons and Amerindians), "white" (albinos and Europeans), or "black," and varieties of wood and clay are distinguished in the same terms.

The interest in color contrast is complemented by an attention to positional contrasts within a two-dimensional grid (the juxtaposition and interplay of horizontally and vertically oriented shapes) and a tendency to crosscut linear patterns (to interrupt the main "grain" of a design). In narrow-strip capes, for example, the stripes woven into the trade cotton interrupt and offset the dominant vertical pattern created by the strips, and a decision to extend the vertical strips into the space normally occupied by horizontal strips both reflects a conscious aesthetic decision on the part of the seamstress and attracts notice for its artistic effect. In most capes embellished with appliquéd strips of cloth, eyelet, and ribbon, the design is formed by a horizontal band intersecting two verticals, and this "H-shaped" pattern is repeated in other items of Maroon material culture, providing one of the most widely utilized "frames" for textile arts, objects carved in wood, and even village entrance gates. Saramakas view the secondary incisions that crosscut the main elements of some calabash carvings as a way of "dressing up" the design, and the important "wood-within-wood" technique in woodcarving (see Chapter 5) can be interpreted as a way of crosscutting linear designs without denying their continuity. Extending our gaze beyond the realm of plastic arts, we notice that everyday speech, formal oratory, prayer, tale telling, song, and dance all require frequent "cuts" (interruptions) in the form of responses, digressions, or sudden shifts in style (see Chapter 7).

Symmetry constitutes another focus of aesthetic attention. From notions of proper posture (see fig. 4.21) to the placement of cicatrization designs (fig. 4.13), the symmetry of the human body stands as a firm ideal. Women are meticulous about adjusting their skirts so that left and right hems are even in front, and their waist ties so that the point (of Saramaka kerchiefs) or tassel (of Ndyuka cords) is not off center. We will see below the importance of building patchwork compositions symmetrically around a vertical center axis. Woodcarving designs almost universally observe at least one axis of symmetry, and even calabash carvings and embroidery designs are conceptualized in terms of (imperfectly executed) one- or two-axis symmetry. This is a particularly interesting principle to explore in its full cultural setting, since it has varied in importance over time (becoming more and more rigorously observed in the course of the twentieth century) and has a distinct gender dimension (being strongly associated with male artistic proclivities). The Maroons' "rhythmic" approach to color contrast, horizontal/vertical alternations, and interruptive patterns of speech, song, and dance has led many observers to comment on what they see as the "syncopated" quality of Maroon aesthetics. In terms of the artistic ideals that have dominated plastic/graphic media in the twentieth century, however, it is worth stressing that Maroons make a consistent and conscious effort to avoid details that would offset or compromise the central symmetry of their designs. While symmetry and variations on it seem in some ways to have been kept in a dynamic balance during much of Maroon history, the visual arts have been affected, for the last fifty years at least, by a gradual but undeniable trend toward a privileging of symmetry.

We conclude this chapter with a brief description of the setting in which Saramaka narrow-strip textiles were composed, as a way of underscoring the importance of supplementing formal visual analysis with detailed ethnographic contextualization. Although the following paragraphs focus on a single form as it was made at a particular time in a particular region, they point more generally to the relevance of production steps and techniques, the social dimension, aesthetic commentary, technical vocabulary, market changes, generational differences, and other local details for an understanding of the place of all art in the wider society and, ultimately, its connectedness to more global cultural narratives.

In planning a man's narrow-strip cape, a woman would work with a collection of perhaps a hundred cloth strips, each of which had been trimmed from the side or end of a two-ell length of trade cotton (figs. 4.57, 4.58). Women rarely composed capes alone, since they considered others' reactions useful as they made choices and decisions regarding color, pattern, and overall size. The first piece to be laid out on the ground was always the

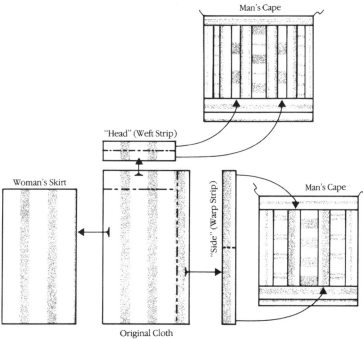

4.57, 4.58. A two-ell length of cloth is trimmed (dotted lines) along the warp and weft, creating a woman's skirt and several strips to be used, along with others, in a man's narrow-strip patchwork cape.

vertical center strip or "spine." Pikilio women preferred to use a "head" (a strip trimmed from the weft), but "sides" (strips trimmed from the warp) might be selected on the basis of other considerations, such as color or width. Most women agreed that the spine should be the widest strip in the composition. A pair of matching strips, chosen for their contrast with the spine, would then be placed at the sides, and the composition would continue to develop from the center out, with "heads" and "sides" alternating. Women gave careful attention to color contrast between adjacent strips and attempted to avoid excessive repetition of any one color. One to three "sides" (depending on the height of the man who would wear the cape) would be chosen for the lower edge (the *sepú búka*—"next to the calf-bands"). Another "side," preferably dominated by white, yellow, or some other unobtrusive color, would be placed along the top, with the selvage to the upper edge. Once a pleasing composition of the right size was achieved, the upper corners of the vertical strips were tacked loosely together with thread to mark their positions, and the sewing began. The seams were made either by hand or by hand-cranked sewing machine, but their raw edges were always tucked under with the point of a needle and sewn down by tiny hand-done stitches. The top would be left as selvage, and the other three edges would be given half-inch hems. After ties were sewn on at the upper corners, the cape would be washed in the river, dried, and folded, wrong side out, into a neat, small packet that could be handled easily for storage or traveling.

Several aspects of this production process merit our particular attention.

(1) Comments made by the women participating in these sessions (to each other as well as to us) made it clear that for them the general alternation of lengthwise and crosswise stripes that outside observers found so striking did not reflect an aesthetic preference, but rather resulted from a technically motivated attention to warp and weft. The proof that they were operating on the basis of warp and weft (as they claimed) rather than the more immediately visible variable of stripe direction, is seen in capes of the type illustrated in figures 4.59 and 4.60. Here, in contrast to the majority of capes, the alternation of warp and weft does not produce a consistent alternation of lengthwise and crosswise stripes. Instead, because some of the strips happen to "miss" the dominant stripe (which runs along the warp) but still catch the secondary stripe (running perpendicular to the warp), the patchwork is an alternation of warp and weft without being an alternation of lengthwise and crosswise stripes. In such cases, the seamstresses were unanimous that the composition was "correct," because, in their terms, it alternated "heads" and "sides."

(2) Similarly, occasional deviations from perfect mirror symmetry

MAROON ARTS

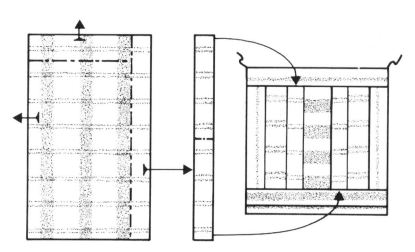

4.59, 4.60. Selvage trimmings sometimes miss the warp stripes, but catch those along the weft. This can produce a narrow-strip cape in which warp and weft alternate consistently but stripe direction does not.

(through staggered placement of crosswise stripes or modifications in the left-right matching of strips around the "spine") in no way reflected an aesthetic ideal of "syncopation," at least at the height of the narrow-strip art. What might once have been (and what might seem, from an outside perspective, still to be) the use of aesthetically sophisticated syncopated rhythms was in fact the result of inadequate resources. A woman who found herself without sufficient cloth of one pattern might reluctantly resort to misaligned stripes or even nonmatching strips by the time she reached the outer sides, but this was simply a matter of making do. By the 1960s, older women who had been active textile artists in the early twentieth century, when staggered or off-center compositions were more common, had adopted the new, more rigorous standards for matching the right and left sides, and were critical of their early, imperfectly symmetrical compositions, often remarking that their daughters and granddaughters had been more successful than they at working out the "proper" principles for the arrangement of strips.

(3) Technical considerations influenced the artistic possibilities of narrow-strip cloths in other ways as well. Around 1970, the introduction of a heavier grade of trade cotton, which shrank noticeably when it was washed, effectively segregated cloth strips into two categories that could not be combined. Women learned to keep this factor in mind as they planned their layouts, carefully avoiding the juxtaposition of these *dégi miñ* ("thickies") with strips of the thinner cotton, regardless of the attractiveness of the color combinations.

(4) Cultural ideas about beauty gave certain parts of the capes more aesthetic importance than others, and this too influenced the artist's decisions in creating the compositions. The bottom strips, which would fall next to the wearer's calves, were ideally brightly colored in order to call attention to this important part of the body (just as crocheted legbands do), while the top border was more appropriately an unobtrusive strip.

(5) Listening carefully to Maroons' technical and aesthetic commentary in the setting of their own artistic production helps us to understand other formal variables as well—why, for example, men's and women's garments receive different treatments in terms of symmetry and color combinations. In the late 1970s, women explained that the narrow-strip skirts they had begun to make (which were often machine sewn) exhibited uncentered patterns and apparently random color juxtapositions not because of an aesthetic of syncopation or some other artistic goal, but because they considered it inappropriate to lavish on their own clothing the same degree of care that they gave to men's garments, which constituted gifts of love. In effect, women saw themselves as preserving the social value of the labor

and artistic finesse represented in men's narrow-strip clothing by avoiding both hand-sewing and preplanning in narrow-strip clothes designed for their own use.

FOLLOWING A PHOTOGRAPHIC GALLERY of Maroon textiles, we will pass on to the medium of woodcarving, in which many of the same aesthetic principles come into play.

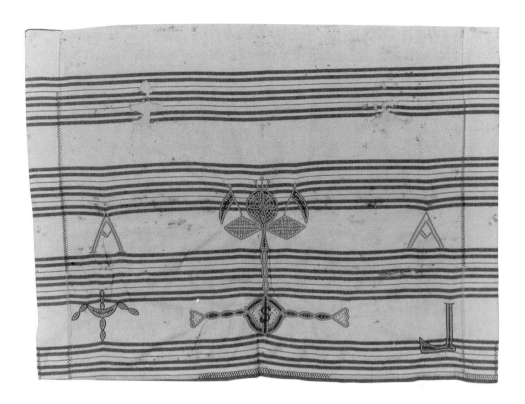

Maroon textile art has always included some kind of embroidery. The earliest style, especially popular at a time when men only rarely wore capes (about 1880–1920), was most often executed on skirts and breechcloths of white cloth with blue or gray stripes.

Opposite page: Breechcloth flaps
4.61. A breechcloth with edge strips in red appliqué and embroidery in red and black—collected 1960s, probably Saramaka.
4.62. A breechcloth embroidered in red, gray, and yellow—collected between 1932 and 1938.
4.63. A breechcloth embroidered in red, black, gray, and yellow with two openwork strips—made about 1910–15 by Ma Diala, from the Ndyuka village of Fandaaki.

Above:
4.64. A skirt embroidered in red, black, and yellow—made between 1890 and 1920 by an Aluku, probably from the village of Loka.

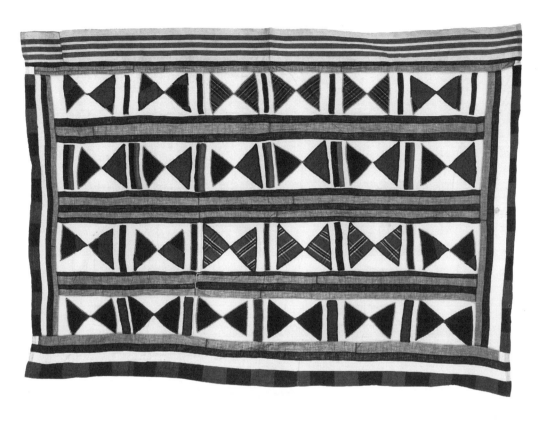

Patchwork was developed as an artistic medium at the end of the nineteenth century, with strips constructed from squares, rectangles, and triangles joined in symmetrical arrangements, mainly for men's shoulder capes. The dominant colors were red, white, and black or navy, though multicolor strips were often integrated in the composition as well.

4.65. Patchwork cape with unusual circular elements, probably Ndyuka.
4.66. Patchwork cape sewn about 1920 by a Saramaka woman from a village on the upper Gaanlio.
4.67. Patchwork cape collected 1924–25 in Saramaka.

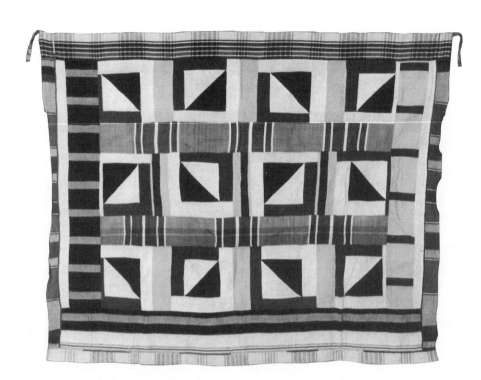

MAROON ARTS

4.68, 4.69, 4.70. Three capes sewn between 1920 and 1940
by Peepina, from the village of Totikampu (on the lower
Saramacca River), for her husband Agbago (Aboikoni), Saramaka paramount chief from 1951 until his death in 1989.
Panels composed of monochrome patches in red, white,
black, yellow, and pink are framed by multicolor striped
strips. (See also fig. 4.2.)

MAROON ARTS

Maroon seamstresses experimented in various ways with embroidery and patchwork.

4.71. A textile composed of small patches, narrow strips, and openwork embroidery. (For a similar Ndyuka textile made as an "overskirt for festive occasions," see fig. 4.44.)

4.72. A decorative cover for a hunting sack with red, black, and yellow embroidery on gray-and-white cloth, framed with strips in red, yellow, and blue that have been joined by openwork embroidery—sewn about 1910–15 by Ma Losa, from the Ndyuka village of Fandaaki.

4.73. A patchwork cape in monochrome patches of red, white, and black, striped patches in black, white, yellow, and a little red, and decorative embroidery along the "calfband" edge—collected 1928–29 (by Melville and Frances Herskovits) in the Saramaka village of Munyenyenkiiki. (For a color plate of this textile, see R. and S. Price 1992c:160.)

MAROON ARTS

As Maroon women shifted the focus of their patchwork textiles from "bits and pieces" of monochrome cloth to narrow strips of multicolor cloth, they sometimes made capes that straddled the line.

4.74, 4.75. Shoulder capes from the Suriname Museum collection.
4.76. A shoulder cape in which half of the narrow strips are composed of patchwork—sewn in the 1950s or 1960s.

MAROON ARTS

After about the 1940s, multicolor strips came to dominate Maroon patchwork, and monochrome cloth was used only rarely.

4.77, 4.78. Saramaka shoulder capes sewn about 1960.
4.79. A Saramaka hammock sheet, sewn by Chief Agbago's wife Apumba, from the village of Pempe, for her sister-in-law Naai, who gave it to us in 1968 when we left Dangogo after two years as her closest neighbors.

Over the course of the twentieth century, embroidery became more linear.

4.80. Man's dance apron collected 1968 in the Saramaka village of Dangogo. Threads extracted from scraps of imported trade cotton have been braided to form the ties.
4.81. Yellow-and-white skirt with red, green, and purple embroidery and red yarn border (detail)—sewn 1990s by Djam (Elefina), from the Saramaka village of Dangogo. Djam, who even as a child showed gifts that defied gender expectations (see S. Price 1993 [1984]:fig. 3), marks her own symmetrical designs and has even become a wood-carver (see figs. 1.1, 5.65).

Cross-stitch embroidery is still a popular form of decorative sewing in the 1990s, but reverse appliqué is gaining ground.

4.82. A Saramaka shoulder cape with red and blue embroidery on a bright yellow cloth—collected in the 1970s (detail).
4.83. Cut-outs in a white cloth expose an orange and green cloth underneath, in shapes edged with yellow and black embroidery. Sewn 1991 in the Saramaka village of Botopasi (unfinished).

4.84. Chief Agbago's textile-draped coffin is lowered into the canoe that will bear it to the cemetery.

4.85. Chief Agbago's coffin rests in the house of mourning during the three-month-long pre-burial rituals.

5.1. Eastern Maroon paddles.

Carving Histories 5

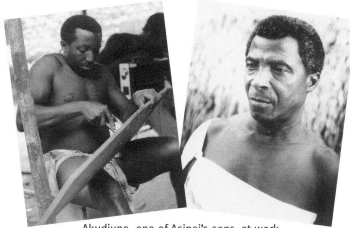

Akudjuno, one of Asipei's sons, at work
on a paddle, and Asipei, 1978.

JULY 1967. Asipei, an articulate and patient teacher, was trying to steer the discussion with R. P. away from its initial focus on "tradition," potential "Africanisms," and stylistic continuities and to get across a point about the way Saramaka woodcarving had changed since his youth in the 1920s. He wasn't finding it easy. "Look," he finally proposed, "think of it this way."

> When I went to the city as a kid, we were really impressed by the automobiles. But when we look back at them now they seem like a joke—so simple, so little power. Every few years, when I'd go back to the coast, I'd see that whitefolks had built better cars. And that kept happening until today. Now the cars they make do all sorts of fancy things. Well, friend, it's exactly the same with our woodcarving! My uncle's generation only knew how to make those big, crude designs—the ones we call "owl's eyes" and "jaguar's eyes"—but since then men have never stopped making improvements. Almost every year there's something new, something better. Right up to today.

His analogy scored a decisive point in the competition between our initial concerns, built up from our reading of the literature on African-American culture history and the rather different vision of art history held by Saramakas. It was just one of a number of settings in which Maroons forced us to understand that the discourse of progress, so central to late nineteenth-

5.2. Saramaka round-top stool, carved about 1915–20 by Seketima, village of Godo (see also fig. 5.21).

century modernism, was a fundamental aspect of their perspective too. And their own view of their art history, we began to realize in conversations with Asipei and other men and women, was based on a radical evolutionism, leading to a frequent denigration of the old in favor of the new.

Before our arrival in Suriname, art *history* had been virtually ignored in the two dozen books and articles that focused on "Bush Negro" art. Authors either treated art synchronically and typologically (e.g., Crowley 1956) or they dealt with history only in the conjectural sense of relating isolated traits to alleged "African" prototypes on the basis of formal similarities (e.g., Herskovits 1930, Kahn 1931, Lindblom 1924), often concluding that Maroon woodcarving was nothing less than "an original African art form" (Volders 1966); indeed, the subtitle of the most widely read book on the subject, Philip Dark's *Bush Negro Art* (1954), was *An African Art in the Americas*. The viewpoint that Asipei and others took about the development of Maroon woodcarving went in the same direction as their wives' insistence on technical and aesthetic progress in textile arts. Together, these perspectives opened the door for the historical investigations we conducted over subsequent decades, in the field and in archives and museums throughout the world.

DURING ASIPEI'S LIFETIME, every Maroon man was expected to produce a whole range of wooden objects for himself, his wives, and, to a lesser extent, his unmarried kinswomen. Men made canoes, paddles, stools, combs, food stirrers, winnowing trays, mortars, pestles, peanut-grinding boards, laundry beaters, houses, and architectural decorations. We begin our exploration of Maroon woodcarving with a brief overview of the forms and uses of these objects.

STOOLS. Along with hammocks, stools constitute the most essential furniture of Maroon houses. People bring their own stools to council meetings, oracle sessions, and ancestral rites, and sometimes take them along in the canoe when they make visits to other villages. Older stools are closely associated with the ancestors who originally owned them, and some come to symbolize the political or religious offices these elders held. In terms of form, the simplest is a squat, one-piece, usually undecorated stool which Saramakas claim was copied by the original runaways from a common Amerindian form (fig. 5.98).[1] One-piece stools have long been carved in a crescential form as well (fig. 8.6; see also S. and R. Price 1980:figs 119, 120). Composite stools with thick, round, concave seats are a third major stool form (fig. 5.2). Composite stools with rectangular tops are carved with both flat and curved seats (figs. 5.97, 5.103). And folding stools made from interlocked pieces have developed from simpler two-plank models to elaborations of Western reclining chairs made for sale to outsiders (fig. 5.101).

COMBS. Because combs are carved frequently (as gifts for wives and lovers) and sold with relative ease to outsiders (*pace* Crowley 1956:147), they are among the best-known forms of Maroon woodcarving. Some of them—especially those made for a girl by her first husband—are embellished with multicolor yarn woven through the upper portion of the tines and ending in a fluffy tassel. A more subdued precursor to this decorative touch can be seen on an old comb that still has the brittle remnants of a raffia-like fiber from the Mauritius palm carefully woven through the upper tines (figs. 5.27, 5.92; see also S. and R. Price 1980:fig 192b).

FOOD STIRRERS. These spatula-like utensils are used to stir rice and certain foods that are prepared for ritual occasions, and most women own several of them. They vary in both the shape of the blade and the size of the handle, and those made by Saramakas tend to be narrower than those made by eastern Maroons (figs. 5.3, 5.4, 5.5, 5.6). Food stirrers have also been a popular form for virtuoso carving (figs. 5.80, 5.81, 5.84).

5.3, 5.4, 5.5, 5.6. Food stirrers. *Left to right:* Aluku, Saramaka, and two from Ndyuka.

MAROON ARTS

TRAYS. Women use round trays mainly for winnowing rice, but also for carrying meals to the house where several men gather to eat together. Trays have served as a popular form for some of the most elaborate artistry produced by Maroon men for their wives. Highly prized by the women who own them, they constitute crucial ritual props when food offerings are presented to the ancestors (figs. 5.33, 5.37, 5.60, 5.61, 5.62, and 5.64). Many modern examples are only minimally incised, with arcs and circles made by a pair of compasses. Rectangular trays, less common than round ones, are used to carry food and dishes to men's meals (figs. 5.58, 5.59).

CANOES. Canoes, made from logs that are painstakingly dug out and then "opened" by fire, represent one of the most striking triumphs of Maroon art and technology (see figs. 2.9, 2.10, 2.11, 2.12; see also S. and R. Price 1980:fig. 5). Ranging from less than ten to more than fifty feet in length, canoes are decoratively carved on both ends and often on the plank seats as well. Eastern Maroons embellish their canoes with colorful painted designs, and in the 1970s, Saramakas sometimes painted the gunwales with a single color.[2]

PADDLES. Paddle size, shape, and decoration have varied greatly according to ownership, function, and region. In the late nineteenth and early twentieth centuries, the paddles used for large cargo canoes were very broad, but these became rare once men began installing outboard motors on large canoes. The paddles that women use (in a short, brisk rhythm that contrasts with the men's long, slow strokes) are often half the length of those used by men, and are more elaborately decorated. Eastern Maroons often embellish their paddles with carving and colorfully painted designs on both blade and handle (figs. 5.1, 5.7, 5.8, and 5.42).

5.7, 5.8. Saramaka woman's paddle collected 1928–29 near Ganiakonde, and Saramaka man's paddle collected 1966 in Godo.

LAUNDRY BEATERS. These clublike implements, used to beat hammocks and other bulky laundry on stones in the river, are especially popular among eastern Maroons. The form of the beating end varies from circular to long and narrow, and the shaft is often gently curved (figs. 5.82, 5.83).

PESTLES. The double-headed pestles used with a mortar to pound unwinnowed rice are large, heavy, and undecorated. Smaller, single-headed pestles are used to mash bananas, maize, and other ingredients for festive dishes, and may have elaborately carved handles (fig. 5.79).

PEANUT-GRINDING BOARDS. Peanuts are ground on these boards with a gourd or (rarely) a wooden roller, to produce the smooth paste that figures importantly in many festive dishes—peanut rice, peanut sauce for meat and fish, and many recipes involving bananas, rice flour, and coconut (figs. 3.12, 5.9, 5.55, 5.56, and 5.57). Many are elaborately carved at both ends.

DRUMS. Of the several distinctive drum forms made by Maroons, *apinti* "talking" drums are the only ones that are consistently—and often elaborately—treated with surface decoration (figs. 5.10, 7.8).

5.9. Saramaka peanut-grinding board, collected 1966 in Ganiakonde.

5.10. Saramaka *apínti* drum, collected 1928–29.

ARCHITECTURAL DECORATION. The decoration of Maroon houses seems to have been initiated by Saramakas during the second half of the nineteenth century. Contemporary observers sometimes commented explicitly on the lack of architectural decoration in Maroon villages (e.g., Cateau van Rosevelt and van Lansberge 1873:321), and one points out that the only decorated houses in an eastern Maroon village in the 1890s were three that had been made by visiting Saramaka men (van Panhuys 1928:232). Since then, Maroons have experimented with a wide variety of decorative techniques, including carving, painting, and wood inlays. Many different architectural elements have been embellished, from the ends of protruding beams to the crossed slats atop palm-leaf roofs. Furthermore, whole facades have been turned into massive works of art. Twentieth-century eastern Maroon carvers painted colorful designs on doors and house facades (until the practice began to decline in the 1960s), and central Maroons exploited openwork or bas-relief carving on house facades and doors on a similarly impressive scale during the same period (figs. 2.20, 2.21, 5.11, 5.12, 5.13, 5.54, and 5.106; see also S. and R. Price 1980:plateV, figs. 28, 142, 143). During the late nineteenth and early twentieth centuries, door locks provided an especially popular and aesthetic challenge to Maroon woodcarvers (figs. 5.74, 5.75, 5.76).[3] The carving of three-piece door frames continues as a lively art in Saramaka villages, reflecting both the creativity of individual carvers and the stylistic trends of particular villages and time periods.

5.11. A house with openwork carving, photographed early twentieth century in the Aluku village of Apatu.

5.12. A Saramaka house with openwork carving and painted decoration, probably made before 1950.

MAROON ARTS

5.13. Saramaka interior door, carved about 1930 by Heintje Schmidt, Ganzee.

OTHER OBJECTS. Maroons sometimes decide to add decorative carving to other kinds of objects, to carve wooden substitutes for things normally made from a different material, or to make a nonfunctional object just for the aesthetic pleasure that it brings. Pierced trays, openwork food stirrers, and virtuoso carvings with links or moveable parts are common, and we have seen carved wooden washboards, ceremonial swords, soap containers, hammock-threading tools, storage cabinets, carpenter's planes, model airplanes and helicopters, umbrellas, calabash-like ladles, and wooden substitutes for basketry fire fans, for the bottles used to make legbands, and for the corncobs used to clean them. In the same spirit, Maroon carvers have produced in wood everything from an armchair to a pith helmet to a sewing machine, and even the simple umbrella spokes that are used to crochet calfbands are sometimes set into decoratively carved wooden handles (figs. 5.14, 5.15, 5.16, 5.17, 5.47, 5.53, 5.66, 5.68, 5.69, 5.70, 5.85; see also S. and R. Price 1980:114–20).

5.14. Carved storage cabinet made from an imported wooden crate and local woods — collected 1960s (apparently in Saramaka).

5.15, 5.16, 5.17. A wooden pith helmet, a wooden sewing machine, and a soap box.

Though Maroon men carved a range of wooden objects in the nineteenth century, we now know that it was only in the second half of that century that decorative embellishment became widespread. Until the general emancipation of Suriname slaves in 1863, Maroons—who had been officially free since the 1760s—visited the coast with some trepidation, since they always risked being taken for slaves. Axes, machetes, knives, and other tools—items that had been liberated from plantations with great difficulty during the wars, then received by Maroons as periodic tribute after the treaties of the mid-eighteenth century—remained scarce and highly prized. The tools used in house and canoe construction and in basic woodcarving were shared among a group of kinsmen rather than owned individually. But after Emancipation, particularly beginning in the 1870s, when gold fever swept French Guiana, Maroon men flocked to the coast, often staying for years at a time and establishing a migratory labor pattern that has lasted for over a century. By the 1880s, when the first waves of men returned from French Guiana, almost all the tools of the modern woodcarver were present in Maroon villages—machetes and axes (for each of which several kinds are distinguished), four types of adzes, three gouges, two chisels, two augers of different sizes, a wooden-handled plane, compasses, compass saws, jack-knives, and hammers.[4] By the turn of the century, commercial paints had also been brought back home by eastern Maroon men, which allowed them to add a whole new dimension to their woodcarving. The stage was set for a series of remarkable artistic developments. Drawing on our fieldwork and museum research of the 1960s, we proposed a framework for studying and understanding these art historical developments based on a series of four decorative styles which affected all types of objects carved by Saramaka men, beginning a hundred years earlier.[5]

What we called Style I (which Saramakas usually refer to as "owl's eyes") was practiced during the second half of the nineteenth century. The oldest men we spoke with in the 1960s remembered the men of their grandparents' generation making crudely pierced holes—often large circles ("owl's eyes") or semicircles ("jaguar's eyes"). Their designs were simple—incised crescents, circles, or scrolls on smaller surfaces, and bas-relief free-forms (of which there were only a few types) on doors, drums, and trays. When they added "teeth" and cross-hatching, it was usually large and crude, and they tended to leave considerable portions of carvings empty. We illustrate typical examples of Style I in figures 5.10, 5.20, and 5.104.

Carving in Style II (which Saramakas usually call "monkey's tail") showed considerable technical refinement. Men began executing more delicate piercing (now with an auger instead of a knife) and "toothwork," and more frequent designs in bas-relief, often transforming a whole surface into

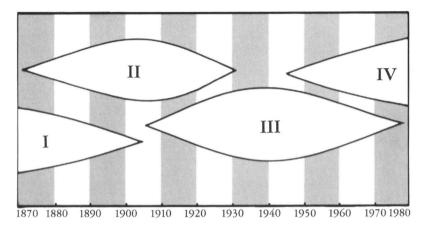

5.18. Schematic chronology of the major Saramaka woodcarving styles.

a stencil-like pattern. These carvings were relatively complex and busy, and free spaces were rare. Fancy scrolls or spirals (the "monkey's tails") became common and the use of decorative tacks bought on the coast, which had been quite limited in Style I, reached its apogee in the later carvings done in Style II. We illustrate Style II in figures 5.2, 5.7, 5.97, and 5.105.

Style III centered on the development of a completely new technique that dominated Saramaka carving for much of the twentieth century— interwoven bas-relief ribbons, known as "wood-within-wood." Its invention depended in part on the new use of an old tool, as compasses, which had been used for decades in plank making and calabash carving, were applied to the surface design of wooden objects.[6] These bas-relief ribbons formed sinuous, curvilinear designs, completely filling surfaces, as in the most complex designs in Style II. Decorative tacks, which were used liberally on early pieces in this style, gradually diminished in importance, but there continued to be technical development in toothwork and cross-hatching. Figures 5.102 and 5.103 illustrate characteristic Style III carving.

In Style IV the wood-within-wood technique continued to appear on most pieces but dominated design much less than in Style III, tended to be cast in angular rather than sinuous forms, and was almost always accentuated by an incised line through the center of each ribbon (in contrast to Style III, in which ribbons were more usually left blank or studded down the center with tacks). Bas-relief became less pervasive and many designs were executed exclusively with incised lines, characteristically reinforcing one another to compose concentric or nestled forms. There was widespread use of intricate toothwork, but piercing (especially on stools and paddles) and decoration with tacks became less frequent than before. For a comparison of Styles III and IV, see figure 5.19.

5.19. The handles of two Saramaka paddles: *left,* carved about 1920 by Seketima, Godo; *right,* carved about 1965 by Kondemasa, Dangogo.

Although all four styles were executed on the full range of objects that carvers made, each type of object posed distinctive challenges—woods have different characteristics, some forms (such as drums and winnowing trays) cannot be pierced, some objects have longer lifetimes than others (e.g., combs need to be replaced more quickly than doorposts), and so forth. Partly because of these considerations, the dates of the transitions between styles differed slightly from one type of object to another. For example, Style III replaced Style II on combs about fifteen years before the transition occurred on doorposts. In order to illustrate the four decorative styles in more detail, we now take a closer look at three types of carved objects: round stools, door frames, and combs.

ROUND STOOLS. Round-seated models are one of the five main forms of Saramaka stools. Though commonly used by men as well as women until the early twentieth century, they later came to be considered primarily women's stools.

MAROON ARTS

The Style I stool we illustrate in figure 5.20 belonged to Naai, older sister of Chief Agbago, who was our neighbor in Dangogo during the 1960s. Naai had been engaged to marry Akoosu, from the village of Godo, at the time he made the stool for her, sometime between 1900 and 1905. (There was also a second, larger stool, very similar in its form and carving, which he had made for his own use when he visited her village. During our years in Dangogo, Chief Agbago always sat on this stool when he visited

Naai in 1968.

his natal village.) The sides of Naai's stool show the characteristic "owl's eyes" and "jaguar's eyes" (from which the horizontal base has broken off), as well as the typically sparse decoration (very slightly exaggerated by wear in 1968, when we took the photo). Akoosu carved the seat with a simple single-line design and two sets of teeth—crude triangles around the center and a circle of dots along the edge. The presence of tacks (of which there were three types, only partially visible in the photo) mark this stool as a late example of Style I carving.

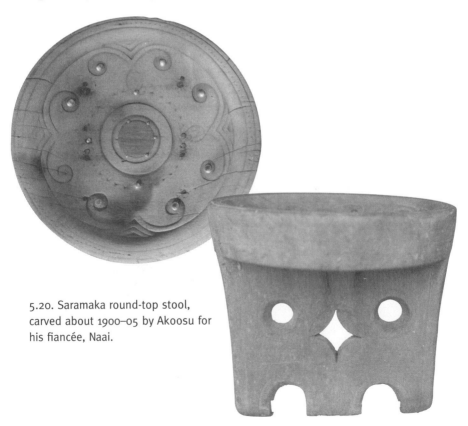

5.20. Saramaka round-top stool, carved about 1900–05 by Akoosu for his fiancée, Naai.

The Style II stool depicted in figures 5.2 and 5.21 was made about 1915–20 by Seketima—also from Godo and widely considered one of the greatest carvers of the century—for a wife from Dangogo named Ansebuka. Graceful bas-relief scrolls fill the broader side panels. The crown of the stool is rimmed with unusually fine cross-hatching. And the deep, concave seat forms a delicate, perfectly controlled composition, studded (like the rest of the stool) with the brass tacks so characteristic of later Style II work. The forms on the subtly carved narrow side panels recall those on the seat but are executed in piercing rather than bas-relief.

5.21. Saramaka round-top stool, carved about 1915–20 by Seke-tima, Godo (see also fig. 5.2).

Style III is illustrated by another stool made by Seketima for Ansebuka, probably in the late 1930s (fig. 5.22). Very similar in conception to the Style II example, it differs by having the wood-within-wood technique on the seat and the narrow side panels. This stool attests to the gifts of a master carver who participated in the style changes that occurred during his lifetime by successfully shifting his own techniques and artistic conceptions. Seketima's adaptability is evident on yet another stool that he carved for Ansebuka, about 1920, which combines characteristic Style II carving on the side panels with a flowing, delicately pierced Style III design on the seat (see fig. 5.39). Not all men achieved this level of mastery of changing fashions. Indeed, many spent their whole lives carving in the style they had learned as youths, and others enlisted the help of younger kinsmen to embellish their stools, made according to earlier conventions, with designs in the currently popular style.

5.22. Saramaka round-top stool, carved about 1930–35 by Seketima, Godo.

The Style IV stool in figure 5.23 was carved about 1963 by Akudjuno, a young man from Asindoopo, as a gift for his fiancée, Misakiya. The design is executed in intricate toothwork and linear incisions rather than in the bas-relief ribbons of Styles II and III, and the lines of teeth reinforce one another, creating a characteristic nestled design on the side of the stool. As in most Style IV pieces, tacks are used only sparingly.

COMBS. Because combs break and are discarded after several years' use, those we saw in the field were almost all carved in Style IV, and the large Suriname River collections made by Kahn and the Herskovitses in the late 1920s (filled with Style II and III examples) include only one Style I comb from this region. Several older Saramakas remembered Style I combs and told us they were very large, relatively broad, and decorated with crude piercing. On being shown photos of museum objects they suggested that

5.23. The seat and one side of the base of a Saramaka round-top stool, carved about 1963 by Akudjuno, Asindoopo.

the comb in figure 5.24 as well as the Aluku comb in Dark 1954:plate 2A would have been typical examples. The carving on Style II combs, which was characterized by scrolls, delicate piercing, and some studding, can be seen in figures 5.25, 5.86, and 5.92 (see also Dark 1954:plate 6G), and a typical Style III comb, with complex bas-relief ribbons, is illustrated in figure 5.26 (see also S. and R. Price 1980:fig. 190). Style IV combs, which were made in both wood and aluminum, are illustrated in figures 5.27, 5.87, and 5.88, and S. and R. Price 1980:fig. 192a, b. Note particularly the angularity of the wooden combs and the virtuoso appendages of the aluminum examples.[7] During the 1970s, men continued to carve most combs in the manner of the 1960s but made others by a new technique—using bicycle spokes for the teeth, and varnishing the wooden handle, which they incised with very simple designs (S. and R. Price 1980:fig. 192c, d).

5.24, 5.25, 5.26, 5.27. *Left to right:* A Ndyuka comb in Style I and Saramaka combs in Styles II–IV. The comb on the right was stolen from the Walters Art Gallery, Baltimore, during the 1981 exhibit "Afro-American Arts from the Suriname Rain Forest."

5.28. One of a pair of non-identical Saramaka door-posts, collected 1928–29 in Bendekonde. (The second was unavailable for illustration.)

Door frames. In Saramaka, the doors of all men's houses and many women's houses were framed by doorpost and lintel, almost always fashioned from cedar, until the late 1980s. Because older Saramakas could not recall ever having seen door frames in Style I and we have never seen one illustrated, we suspect they were not yet part of the standard house front. The earliest doorframes Saramakas remembered were made in the 1880s in Style II and, according to their descriptions, consisted simply of a single monkey's-tail spiral. Although to our knowledge no such pieces are extant, an 1894 sketch of a Saramaka door frame exactly matches their description (fig. 5.29). During the first fifteen years of this century, doorpost designs were rather standardized elaborations of the monkey's-tail spiral. Older Saramakas from Dangogo claimed that men simply stenciled whatever design was currently popular, and that about 1915 all doorposts in the village (perhaps fifty) were nearly identical. The vertical portions of the door frame in figure 5.30, carved by a young man in Dangogo about 1910, constitute the only example we saw of this particular Style II pattern.[8]

Soon after 1915, the practice of copying standard models faded out and men began creating original designs on door frames just as they had long been doing on other kinds of objects. The door frame in figure 5.31, made about 1920 by a twenty-year-old from Dangogo, was, according to the carver, a conscious attempt to transform the standard Style II pattern (illustrated in fig. 5.30) into Style III. Later door frame carvers further developed this style, using wider interwoven ribbons and, in many cases, brass tacks, much like two examples photographed by the Herskovitses in the late 1920s (1934:facing p. 284). Figure 5.32 shows a door frame made about 1966 by Gaduansu, a young man from Dangogo. The complex, intricate, and relatively angular design, the daringly thin connections between pieces, the delicate piercing, and (on the lower crosspiece) the nestled forms make this a characteristic example of Style IV work.

5.29. 5.30, 5.31, 5.32. *Top to bottom:* Saramaka door frames carved about 1890, 1910, 1920, and 1966, respectively.

Our stress on the distinctiveness of each of these four styles should not obscure the constant development through time from early to late work within each one. Just as women can distinguish early and late examples of particular sewing styles, men can distinguish early and late examples of each woodcarving style by taking into account the level of technical refinement and the particular artistic conventions that structure the design. They showed us, for example, how in Style III, early pieces are identifiable by such features as the relative breadth of their bas-relief ribbons (taking into account the kind of surface involved) or the way in which a ribbon may pass under several others before passing over one. Indeed, attention to the alternation of underpasses and overpasses was gradually modified until, by the time Style IV emerged, it was already considered a sign of technical ineptitude not to alternate them nearly perfectly (compare, for example, figures 5.56 and 5.9).

The style progression we discerned in Saramaka woodcarving is closely paralleled by that reported by Jean Hurault for the Aluku, suggesting the existence of broadly similar art histories among all Suriname Maroons. Hurault's museum-based study (1970) concludes that this art form is a New World creation and that it did not come into being until well into the nineteenth century. "Apparently created around 1830–1840," he writes, "it evolved rapidly, reaching what we might call the classic style by 1870–1880" (1970:84). Hurault divides the evolution of Aluku art into three style periods. In the first, or "archaic" style, which dominated Aluku woodcarving between 1830 and 1870, the exterior form of objects was relatively crude, their ornamentation was monotonous and poorly executed, designs consisted mainly of nonfigurative incisions, and an abstract sexual symbolism was, Hurault claims, already apparent (figs. 5.77, 5.78). In the "classic style" (1860s–1920s), which he describes as marking the apex of Aluku art, powerful yet simple compositions were conceptualized holistically, central motif and ornamentation were one, often executed in interwoven bas-relief ribbons, and there were frequent semi-figurative representations of humans and animals that were, he says, closely tied to sexual symbolism (figs. 5.33, 5.80, 5.81). Hurault does little to hide his distaste for the third style, "an impoverished art" that emerged in the 1920s and marked "a rupture with the principles of simplicity and sincerity that dominated the early art" (1970:119, 90; see the three rightmost paddles in fig. 5.73 as well as Hurault 1970:plates XVI-XIX). This "modern" style included a proliferation of geometric figures and nonsignificant decoration; symmetry came to dominate design; and there was a preoccupation with complexity and detail that attests to what Hurault calls an *horreur du vide*. In this mid-twentieth-century style, he claims, symbolic motifs developed to the point of forming a rudimentary language of conventional signs.[9]

MAROON ARTS

5.33. An Aluku winnowing tray carved in the early twentieth century.

If we look beyond the striking style progressions and technical evolution that characterize Maroon woodcarving of the past century and a half, we can discern a number of features that have appeared (whether by invention or introduction from the outside) at specific points in time, enjoyed a widespread popularity, and then gradually disappeared. Because of their temporal specificity, these features often provide important clues for the dating of individual pieces.

New shapes have appeared at one time or another during the history of almost every type of object carved by Maroons. We cite just two examples. The kind of comb that Saramakas refer to as a *sindó muyêè pénti* ("comb for a faithful woman") had a distinctive cylindrical handle, which sometimes formed a connecting piece with a flat decorated handle (see fig. 5.34, and Dark 1954:plates 5B and 7E). Developed about 1890, it was extremely popular for about twenty-five years and then gradually disappeared. Although almost all men who learned to carve before 1915 made such combs during their youth, those who began in the 1920s already considered the shape old-fashioned. Or again, around 1890 the blades of Saramaka food stirrers changed from shapes like those on canoe paddles (fig. 5.77, 5.78) to ones with straighter sides (fig. 5.4), and by 1910 only a few older men were still making the "paddle" forms.[10] Analogous examples could be cited from the history of stools, peanut-grinding boards, and other kinds of wooden objects.

Perhaps the most important change in Saramaka ideals of form came about 1900, when men began giving curvature to a variety of objects traditionally carved in the flat. Inspired by the "cocked" ends of canoes and one-piece crescential stools, they began for the first time to curve their composite plank-top stools and combs (compare, for example, figs. 5.104 and 5.103) as well as laundry beaters and even some food stirrers. One older Saramaka told us that aside from canoes and crescential stools, plank-top stools were the earliest items to be treated to this curved form, in conscious imitation of crescential stools. One unusual, apparently intermediate, stool now in the Tropenmuseum, which was collected in the 1890s, tends to support this claim (fig. 5.99). Though made from a single piece of wood (like a crescential stool), its seats and legs are uniformly thin (as in a plank-top stool) and the seat is gracefully curved.[11] Over the course of this century, curves have, when present at all, become increasingly pronounced. Each decade, for example, men have tilted the ends of canoes more sharply and executed the curve of their combs more daringly—even though this decreases the durability of all but the aluminum examples, in which (significantly) the concept is most fully realized (see S. and R. Price 1980:fig. 192a, b). One clear reflection of such changes in fashion is that forty-nine of the fifty-three combs collected by the Herskovitses in the 1920s were flat (Crowley 1956:152), while the very great majority of combs we saw in the field in the 1960s were curved. During the 1970s, flat combs again came into fashion and today they represent at least half of those being made.

5.34. A Saramaka "comb for a faithful woman," collected late 1920s.

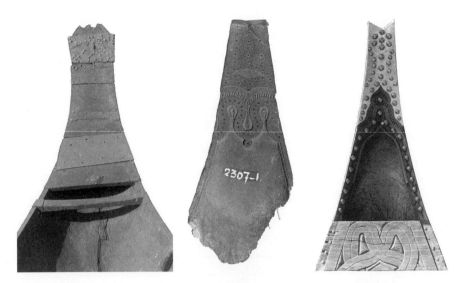

5.35. Saramaka canoe prows. *Left to right:* owned by Paramount Chief Akoosu (1888–97); probably carved in the 1920s; carved about 1965 by Adelmo, village of Heeikuun.

The decoration of the inside ends of canoes represents another change in woodcarving that is independent of the Style I–IV progression. During the past hundred years, these have received four distinct and quite standardized treatments in upper river Saramaka, the first lasting from sometime before the 1880s until about 1910, the second from about 1890 to the 1940s, the third from roughly 1910 to the 1950s, and the fourth from the 1930s into the present. Older Saramakas describe the earliest of these styles (which they'd been told about but had never seen) as a complete planking-over of the dugout portion at the ends of the canoe, with decoration on the planking. After hearing about this style in the field, we came upon a handsome example in the Tropenmuseum that had belonged to Saramaka Chief Akoosu (1888–97); its planked-over stern, which even includes a sheet of scrap iron, was decorated with a characteristic monkey's-tail design (fig. 5.35*left*). In the second of these styles (for which we have only Saramakas' descriptions and sketches), the planking stopped much farther from the two ends of the canoe and the dugout portion was considerably extended with a small gouge to form a crescent, giving this style its name, "new moon." In this and subsequent styles, the extreme tips of the canoe were covered with tin, cut to accentuate the carved design, and embellished with tacks.[12] In the third style (which Saramakas described and sketched for us), this gouge-work was extended still farther up the neck of the canoe, at both ends, in a complex form with delicate embellishment called "tapir's hoof."

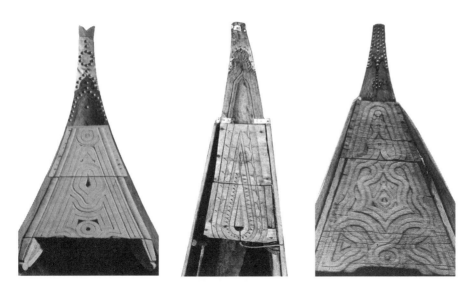

5.36. Saramaka canoe prows carved in the 1970s. *Left to right:* carved 1978 by Foto-bakaa, village of Asindoopo; carved in Pikiseei; carved in Kambaloa. (For a full view of Fotobakaa's canoe, see S. and R. Price 1980:fig. 5.)

Figure 5.35*middle* illustrates an example of this style in the Tropenmuseum. Finally, in the current style, the carved-out portion ends an inch or two lower, and is surmounted by a distinctive design (fig. 5.35*right*). The origin of this final style illustrates the role individual creativity can play even in such a standardized type of carving. In the late 1930s, a man named Alinzo from Asindoopo made a canoe which opened unevenly and, as was usual in such cases, did not bother to embellish it by fully carving out the ends in the "tapir's hoof" pattern. Instead, he cut a simpler variation, which was admired and copied by others, and which became by the 1960s the only style still seen on the upper river.[13]

Innovations in even minor details may suddenly become the rage and spread to distant villages. We cite three examples from Saramaka. About 1920 one distinctive curve that was cut into a comb handle in the village of Semoisi and another that was invented in Akisiamau became so fashionable in woodcarving that women throughout the region began cutting them as cicatrizations on their bodies. Around the same time, a man from Pempe created a comb handle in the shape of a gunstock which, by means of a boss, could be partially freed from the body of the comb. And another carver from Pempe figured out a way of cutting around the edge of a piece of wood in the center of a design in such a way that it rattled but did not fall out, a technique that was quickly imitated by other carvers (S. and R. Price 1980:fig. 203).

A number of minor decorative techniques used on all kinds of objects have undergone significant changes during the past century. Again, three examples will illustrate. First, branding. In the late nineteenth century, men often embellished their carvings by branding them with the heated sawed-off tip of an umbrella, an umbrella rib, or the point or head of a nail (see figs. 5.90, 5.96, and 5.98). A decade or two later these techniques had been replaced by incising lines with a hot machete or knife (fig. 7.11), and by the 1960s, branding was completely out of fashion, at least in upper river Saramaka. Second, decorative "teeth." In a certainly partial inventory, Saramakas showed or described to us eleven technically distinct, named types of toothwork, some long since abandoned and others introduced or invented during their own lifetimes. Finally, decorative tacks. The original popularity of large brass tacks or studs bought in Paramaribo, the later introduction of first one and then another type of small copper tacks from French Guiana, and the more recent decoration of house fronts with broad-headed galvanized nails from Paramaribo are all closely linked to the history

5.37. A Saramaka winnowing tray collected 1928–29 in Ganiakonde.

of coastal wage labor and to the role such nails have played as signs of success in the outside world.

Out of these sorts of creative innovation, and the varying responses to them in different villages, grows significant regional diversity. Maroons can usually identify the precise region in which a canoe was made by the type of carving at its prow (see fig. 5.36 for the designs associated with three Saramaka villages in the 1970s), and there are recognizable differences between the two tributaries of the Suriname River in the curvature of stools. Between one Maroon group and another the stylistic differences are yet more striking. Most Maroon men are confident that they can distinguish Ndyuka and Saramaka carving at a glance, and although (as with connoisseurs anywhere in the world) their confidence is not always borne out, it nevertheless reflects a generally valid stylistic divergence, both between the arts of these two largest Maroon groups and between the arts of the eastern and central groups collectively. We mention a few of the more notable differences.[14]

5.38. A Ndyuka winnowing tray collected in the 1960s on the Tapanahoni River.

The varying width of eastern Maroon ribbons, which often bulge and taper, contrasts with the more even-edged Saramaka style (figs. 5.93, 5.94, 5.95). Eastern Maroon carvers make less frequent use of compasses, producing freer undulations in the ribbons and a less strictly geometric effect than is seen in Saramaka patterns (fig. 5.40). The practice of dividing ribbons lengthwise into two or even three planes is common among eastern Maroons but extremely rare in Saramaka (fig. 6.26).[15] The ends of these ribbons are often pointed in eastern Maroon carvings, but almost always rounded in Saramaka ones (compare, for example, figs. 5.38, 5.91, and 5.95 with figs. 5.37 and 5.86). Interwoven ribbons are less important in eastern Maroon carvings, which have a great deal of piercing and bas-relief of other kinds, overlapping but not intertwining ribbons, and small, sloping planes (fig. 5.38).

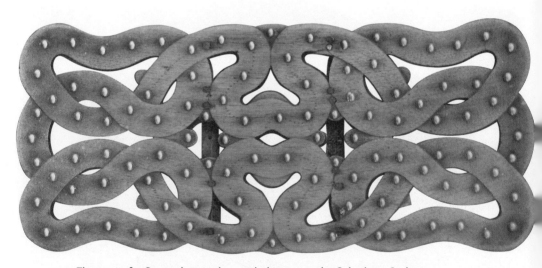

5.39. The seat of a Saramaka stool carved about 1920 by Seketima, Godo.

Brightly colored paints, which Saramakas do not use, contribute importantly to modern eastern Maroon decorative work, particularly on paddles, house fronts, and canoe tips (figs. 2.20, 2.21, 5.1, 5.42, and 5.109; see also S. and R. Price 1980:plate V, fig. 28).[16] Eastern Maroons continued to decorate by branding much longer than Saramakas did, sometimes using instruments unknown in Saramaka, such as lead pipes (figs. 5.90, 5.96, and 5.98). The shapes of many eastern Maroon objects are distinct from those made in Saramaka—for example, paddles and food stirrers have shorter, broader blades and larger, more ornate handles than those in Saramaka (fig. 5.6); canoes are narrower than in Saramaka; and combs were made in the gigantic, broad form decades after they had disappeared in Saramaka. Finally, naturalistic designs and aesthetically unintegrated clusters of "signs" have been carved by eastern Maroons more frequently than by Saramakas (figs. 5.89, 5.90, 5.96, S. and R. Price 1980:fig. 258).[17]

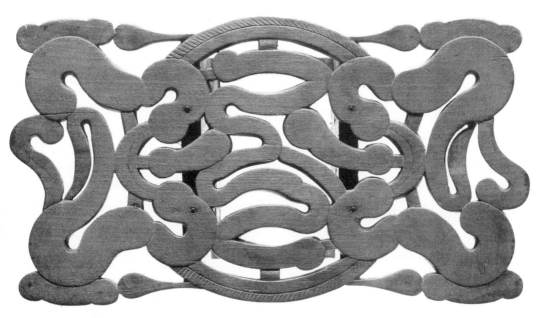

5.40. The seat of a plank-top stool with carving typical of eastern Maroons.

Although the very great bulk of woodcarvings have always been characterized by nonrepresentational, non-iconographic designs executed with purely decorative principles in mind, occasional Maroon carvings, especially in the early twentieth century, have incorporated stylized depictions of human figures, often in conventionalized sexual positions. Because at the time of our 1960s fieldwork the previous literature on this art had devoted such intense attention to its alleged symbolic content, we made it our business to engage in frequent discussions with Maroons about the "meaning" of their woodcarvings and, more importantly, to listen carefully when they addressed the subject among themselves. Again and again we were struck by their tendency to talk about art in terms of form and color, in terms of technical mastery, in terms of social uses and sentimental attachments, in terms of raw materials and the condition of objects, in terms of the innovations and stylistic imprints of particular individuals, and in terms of generational change and long-term developments—but not in terms of symbolic meanings or messages. And exhaustive inventories of wooden objects in a number of Saramaka houses revealed that the very great majority of woodcarving designs are neither named nor conceptualized as conveying a "meaning."

In contrast to woodcarving designs, many texturing patterns in woodcarving are indeed named, usually after natural or manufactured objects ("lizard's teeth," "beach-chair frame"), but these names are used descriptively, much as a European might talk about a "herringbone tweed" without evoking fishbones or proverbial wisdom about the sea. Likewise, the names that are attached to motifs or designs are after-the-fact descriptive labels ("monkey's tail," "tapir's hoof") and carry no symbolic charge. There are, however, a few conventionalized signs that men sometimes add to an object after the carving is finished, of which six transmit a message of love (like X's and O's at the bottom of a letter), two thank people for complimenting the piece, and six address a curse to anyone who insults it.

Among the eastern Maroons, iconography plays a similarly limited role, though representational motifs and conventionalized signs have at times been somewhat more common there than in Saramaka. Designs representing lizards, snakes, birds, and human forms have long played a role in the woodcarving of Ndyukas, Alukus, and Paramakas, and have sometimes appeared in their calabash and textile arts as well (see fig. 6.30F; S. and R. Price 1980:fig. 256). The depiction of such forms does not, however, constitute an iconographic system. Nor does it justify the widespread belief among outsiders that carvers are intending to convey abstract ideas in their art.

The literature on Maroons has been plagued by insistent assertions that their woodcarving centers on an iconographic system and carries specific symbolic messages. In this view, particular visual forms are directly translatable into such concepts as love, fertility, wealth, or death, and the determined outsider who manages to break through the Maroons' code of secrecy can, making some allowance for the artist's subjectivity, learn to "read" the carvings' deep meanings. The challenge of securing this inside knowledge has driven many investigators to interrogate Maroons with methods that cannot help but produce the desired results.[18] It quickly becomes clear what these visitors want and how much they are willing to pay for it, and Maroons have often cooperated, both out of indifference to what the outsider thinks and because there is a profit to be had.

The Herskovitses describe with candor how during their first trip to the interior of Suriname they were "completely balked by the unwillingness of the Bush Negroes to discuss their carvings." But refusing to take no for an answer, they persevered, and with the help of a teenager who was eager to sell them a crudely carved stool, finally created a critical vocabulary of their own, which they then offered to other informants as a prod for further stories of the sort they had in mind. "There are two snakes," they explained to a Saramaka artist, pointing to one of his own carvings. The artist apparently said nothing, but an onlooker murmured supportively, "Anacondas." Encouraged by this implicit confirmation, Melville Herskovits continued his elaboration of the kind of story he was looking for. "These," he said, "are the teeth of the great lizard—*bamba tande*—and this part . . . is a carved chain, and you call it *moni mo' muye*—money is more than woman." The Herskovitses report that the men laughed and said yes, "So it is. The man knows about Saramacca carving" (M. and F. Herskovits 1934:33–34, 276).

Other investigators have been equally resourceful in extracting exegeses from recalcitrant informants. The prolific writings of L. C. van Panhuys are replete with scenes in which denials give way to acquiescence, uncomprehending silences are filled in by the investigator, and carvings are turned upside down to produce forms that can be "read" as meaningful representations (for further examples, see S. and R. Price 1980:188–93).

Maroons react in variable ways to this sort of pressure. Occasionally we have heard a carver pronounce a defiant monologue about how other men may flatter the fantasies of tourists in order to make money, but how he has never compromised his integrity by such a demeaning practice and is not about to start now. More often carvers go along with the game.[19] In the late 1960s, one woodcarver set up a stall on the road to the Suriname airport, bought a copy of a popular book offering a dictionary of Maroon motifs and their "meanings" (Muntslag 1966), copied its illustrations onto his carvings, and referred his customers to the authoritative printed page (which he could not read) for the exegeses that, for them, lent enhanced value to their purchases.

WOODCARVING, LIKE MUCH ELSE in the life of the Maroons, has changed significantly since the late 1970s, when we wrote *Afro-American Arts of the Suriname Rain Forest*. Visiting Aluku villages in 1990, we found that the process of *francisation* had left no aspect of life in this remote corner of France untouched. The old village of Papaisiton had been abandoned, and some of its painted houses were being restored as tourist attractions through the efforts of French-sponsored associations charged with valorizing "traditional" ways of life. Meanwhile the village's former inhabitants had moved into modern cement or wooden houses, many built on a coastal model, in the new *chef-lieu*, officially called Pompidouville. Aluku woodcarving, which two decades before had still been a vibrant and dynamic art combining painting and sculpture, was now restricted to a handful of specialist practitioners. Those few Aluku men who continue to produce artworks, however, attest to a continuing mastery of the medium; see, for example, figures 5.41, 5.42, 5.67, and 5.109, and, for an illustration of the recently developed art of painting on canvas, figure 5.72.

5.41. An Aluku door carved 1990 in St. Laurent by Dakan Edouard Amaikon, from the village of Papaisiton, for the Musée Régional de Guyane.

The great bulk of carved objects that were in Aluku homes and villages two decades ago have by now been sold off to outsiders—tourists, gendarmes, soldiers, and the occasional collector. In our 1990 expedition to collect for the future Musée Regional de Guyane, we were able with some difficulty to find examples of all the objects once routinely carved by Aluku men (paddles, laundry beaters, food stirrers, combs, hammock threaders, mortars and pestles, stools, and winnowing trays) and a few of these objects were still in use, but most had been set aside and were being held as keepsakes (see R. and S. Price 1992a for sketches).

On our visits to Ndyuka villages along the Tapanahoni in 1991 we found greater poverty and slower change than we had seen in Aluku territory. But Western influences on housing and furniture were contributing to changes in artistic production, or at least providing alternatives in the form of imported manufactured goods. We saw numerous carved and painted house fronts whose earlier beauty had been faded by time, weather, and lack of maintenance, but an even greater number of houses were unembellished

5.42. Aluku carved and painted paddles: *left two,* made about 1987 and 1982 by Feno Obentié, Loka; *right,* made in 1990 by Toma Peeyon, Asisi.

and influenced by coastal models, with windows, three to four rooms, and greatly enlarged living spaces. Wooden objects with sculptural detail and decorative painting were more in evidence than in contemporary Aluku or Paramaka villages, but even on the Tapanahoni, the involvement of all adults in artistic production, which had been such an essential aspect of life in Maroon groups of every region a couple of decades earlier, was clearly beginning to give way to a commoditized and monetized Western-oriented material culture within which actively practicing artists were on their way to becoming the exception rather than the rule.

Carving is also becoming increasingly specialized in Saramaka, but remains more widely practiced there than among other Maroons. A round-seated stool, a winnowing tray, and a peanut-grinding board, carved in 1990 by men from different regions, bear witness to continued mastery (figs. 5.43, 5.63, 5.108). In 1997, outside Cayenne, we happened upon a thirty-year-old Saramaka finishing a stool for his wife that demonstrates ongoing technical prowess and aesthetic innovation (fig. 5.107). Saramakas have also nearly monopolized the art of woodcarving for the tourist trade. From the early beginnings of a Maroon airport art in the 1960s, which developed as a distinctive variant of the carving style then being produced in Kambaloa and neighboring villages (in the middle river region of Saramaka), the market has expanded dramatically, both in Paramaribo and—more profitably—in French Guiana. Carvings, usually in soft cedarwood, are characterized by relatively large toothwork and other devices that permit rapid production. Two types of folding stools form the bread and butter of most commercial carvers (fig. 5.101 and R. and S. Price 1992a:256), but they are comple-

5.43. Saramaka peanut-grinding board carved in 1990 in Cayenne by Mando Amimba, from the village of Kambaloa, for the Musée Régional de Guyane.

mented by a variety of new forms, and innovations are constantly extending the repertoire—owls, turtles, toads, caymans, fish, and armadillos, Ariane rockets set on maps of French Guiana, small boxes with sliding covers, lacquered attaché cases, ingeniously constructed carafes that incorporate a Heineken bottle inside, helicopters and other toys for children, coffee tables, and other forms (figs. 5.44, 5.45, 5.46, 5.47, 5.66, 5.69; see also R. and S. Price 1992a:284). We have seen an elaborate baby's crib, toy Cessnas have

5.44, 5.45, 5.46, 5.47. Carvings made in Mando's atelier—an Ariane rocket by Apinda-goon, armadillos (*above*) by Miseli and (*below*) by Elion (all for the tourist trade), and a helicopter that Mando made for his six-year-old son.

given way to Boeing 747s, and even the anti-AIDS campaign of the 1990s has been creatively exploited. After some Saramaka carvers were asked by health workers in French Guiana to provide a wooden form for demonstrating the use of condoms (to replace the bananas and vibrators they had started out with), the artists began producing giant "articulating" penises for sale to tourists, thus launching one of their most lucrative commercial items. In the early 1990s, carvers along the road between St. Laurent and Mana began carving in highly polished letterwood and were soon producing almost every tourist item in that more-difficult-to-carve and higher-priced medium (fig. 5.65).[20]

Our 1980 book on Maroon art alluded in passing to the practice of direct copying—whether a late nineteenth-century carver replicating another man's doorpost, a Christian Saramaka woman embroidering a cross-stitch diagram from a needlework magazine, or the innovative "motor boat" form for calabash bowls being imitated by neighbors of the Saramaka woman who invented it. Since then, both the practice of copying and our own awareness of it have expanded in new directions. In particular, the use of books, which was a curiosity in the 1970s, has become standard among professional carvers. In French Guiana, where Hurault's lavishly illustrated book on Aluku carving is easily available, and where many Saramaka carvers still have the copies of *Afro-American Arts of the Suriname Rain Forest* that we have distributed as gifts over the years, objects modeled on images in these books have become especially common—see, for example, figure 5.50.[21]

5.48. Konfa in 1968.

5.49. Two combs illustrated in S. and R. Price 1980 (figs. 191a, 190c).

This trend was confirmed twenty-five years after our first trip up the Suriname River, when we stopped at a woodcarving shed by the side of the road near St. Laurent and had a serendipitous reunion with Konfa Vola, whose father was our close neighbor in Dangogo. A child when we'd last seen him, Konfa had become a professional woodcarver and moved to French Guiana. After we caught up on news, he showed off his wares, many of which were copied directly from illustrations of Maroon woodcarvings in the same book that shows him, at the age of five or six, with his mother and baby sister (fig. 5.48). We learned that he and his coworkers in French Guiana had already sold numerous copies of the Style I and Style II stools pictured in figures 5.20 and 5.21 and the snake motif stool in figure 5.97, as well as many of the trays and combs in the book, literally retracing the artistry of their fathers, grandfathers, and great-grandfathers. Their current best sellers were high-polish letterwood versions of the book's illustrations of Style III carvings. Designs that had been popular in the interior of Suriname before they were born were thus being married to a precious wood that sold well to late twentieth-century European tourists on the coast of French Guiana.

5.50. Three combs made for the tourist market by Saramakas living near St. Laurent, modeled on illustrations in *Afro-American Arts of the Suriname Rain Forest* (see fig. 5.49). *Left to right:* carved 1990 by Soni Bodji from the village of Semoisi; carved 1995 by George or Simeon Paulus from Botopasi; carved 1995 by George or Simeon Paulus from Botopasi.

5.51. Distinguished art historian Robert Farris Thompson,
Master of Timothy Dwight College, Yale University.

5.52 "Saramaka tray for festive occasions," Cayenne.

But this was far from the most startling of our discoveries about the recycling potential of woodcarving designs. That same year we encountered, on the living room wall of a bourgeois French household in Cayenne, an object of recent Saramaka manufacture modeled on an Akan throne whose image holds pride of place in a Yale College master's quarters. We choose to leave the intriguing story behind these look-alike carvings untold here, but invite our readers to turn back to the vignette with which this book opens and, time permitting, to pick up a slim novel called *Enigma Variations*, in which the dilemmas raised by this and other copies are explored in greater depth.

5.53. An umbrella, carved by a Saramaka for the tourist trade, 1979.

5.54. A Saramaka door and frame collected before 1933.

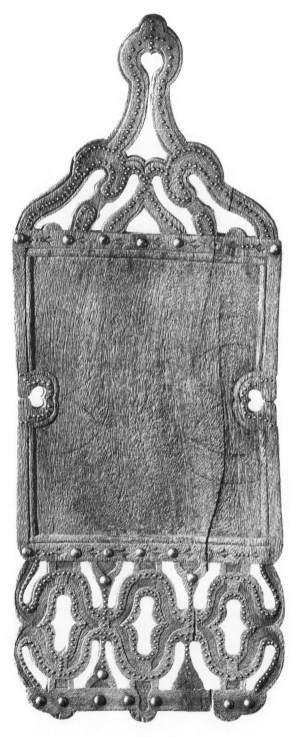

5.55. A Saramaka peanut-grinding board, collected 1928–29 in Asindoopo.

5.56. A Saramaka peanut-grinding board and gourd roller, carved about 1900 on the upper Gaanlio.

5.57. A Ndyuka peanut-grinding board, collected late 1920s in Moompusu (Tapanahoni River).

5.58. A Saramaka tray carved about 1960 in Kampu by Tebini, who inscribed on it the first letter of his own name and that of the wife for whom it was a gift.
5.59. A Ndyuka tray carved about 1970 by Yoping Kanape, Sanbendumi.

5.60. A winnowing tray carved with human figures, collected before 1933.
5.61. A Saramaka winnowing tray, collected 1928. (See M. and F. Herskovits 1934:282–83 for a discussion of the carving.)

5.62. An Aluku winnowing tray carved between 1905 and 1920. (For a sketch of the tray before its restoration by the Bureau du Patrimoine Ethnologique, Guyane, which patched cracks and filled holes, see R. and S. Price 1992a:218.)

5.63. A Saramaka winnowing tray carved in Cayenne by Ziveti Bento Gaagaa, village of Kambaloa(?). It was commissioned (as an example of the kind of tray he would carve for a wife) for the Musée Régional de Guyane in 1990.

5.64. Front (*left*) and back of a winnowing tray collected before 1932.

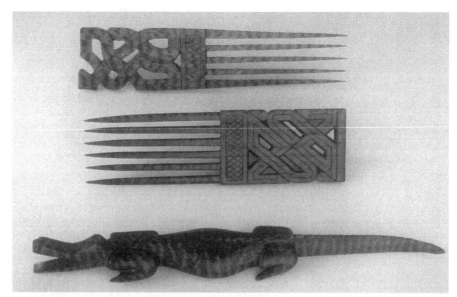

5.65. Tourist carvings in letterwood, made by Saramakas living on the Route de Mana, French Guiana: lower comb carved in 1995 by Konfa Vola, village of Bofokule; upper comb carved in 1997 by Meo Vola, village of Bofokule; cayman carved in 1997 by Djam (Elefina), village of Dangogo (see also fig. 1.1).

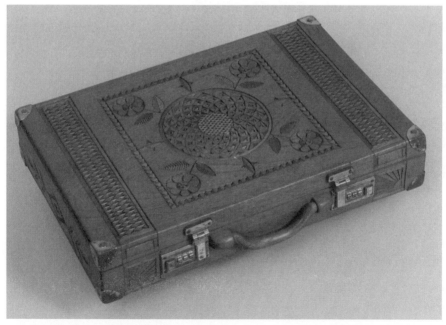

5.66. A Saramaka attaché case carved 1990 in Kourou for sale to tourists by Basia Kaneli, from the village of Dan. In 1993 we saw an identical case being carried by a Dutch businessman in the Caracas international airport.

MAROON ARTS

5.67. A stereo chest, sculpted and painted about 1985 by Feno Obentié, from the Aluku village of Loka. There are feet on three sides, permitting different surfaces of the chest to be displayed.

5.68. A carpenter's plane carved 1989 in St. Laurent by Marcel Doye, whose father was Saramaka and whose mother was from the Aluku village of Asisi.

Opposite page:
5.69. A Saramaka wooden carafe with a Heineken beer bottle mysteriously imbedded in it, carved near St. Laurent for the tourist trade in 1995 by Simeon Paulus, village of Botopasi.
5.70. A Saramaka wooden roller for grinding peanuts, collected late 1920s in Bedoti. This carved object represents an elegant substitute for the more usual gourd roller.
5.71. Wooden ladles carved in the shape of calabash ladles (see fig. 6.5 and S. and R. Price 1980:fig. 215): *left,* collected 1932–38; *right,* collected 1960s in the Saramaka village of Tutubuka.

5.72. An Aluku painting on canvas, for sale to outsiders, made 1990 by Antoine Din-
guiou, village of Papaisiton.
5.73. Aluku paddles. *Left to right:* carved late nineteenth century, carved 1920–30,
carved 1940–45, carved 1945, carved 1955.

5.74. A Maroon door lock collected before 1916.

Opposite page:
5.75. Front and back of a Ndyuka door lock collected before 1922 in Gaamanstaalkonde, said by the collector to have been carved sixty years earlier.
5.76. A Maroon door lock collected before 1883.

MAROON ARTS

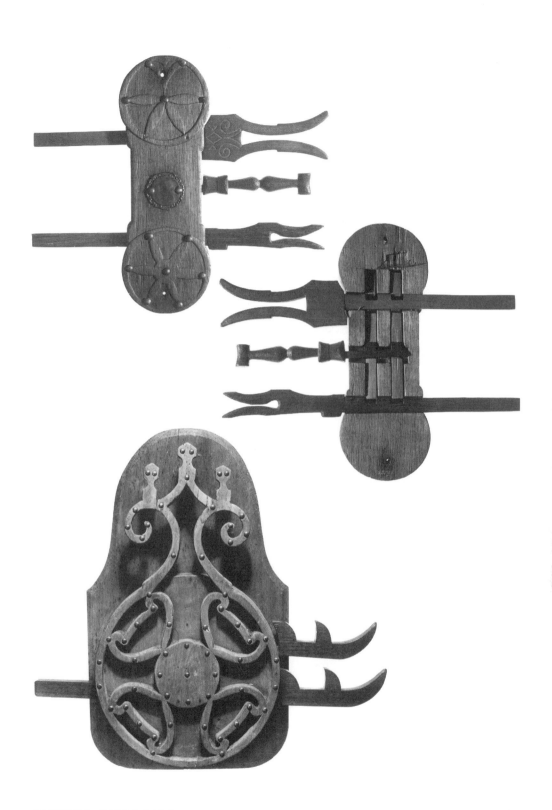

5.77, 5.78, 5.79, 5.80, 5.81. *Left to right:* A food stirrer collected before 1883 and another before 1897, a pestle collected 1966 in the Saramaka village of Tumaipa, and Aluku food stirrers collected before 1901 and 1939. The last two are decorative (non-functional) utensils.

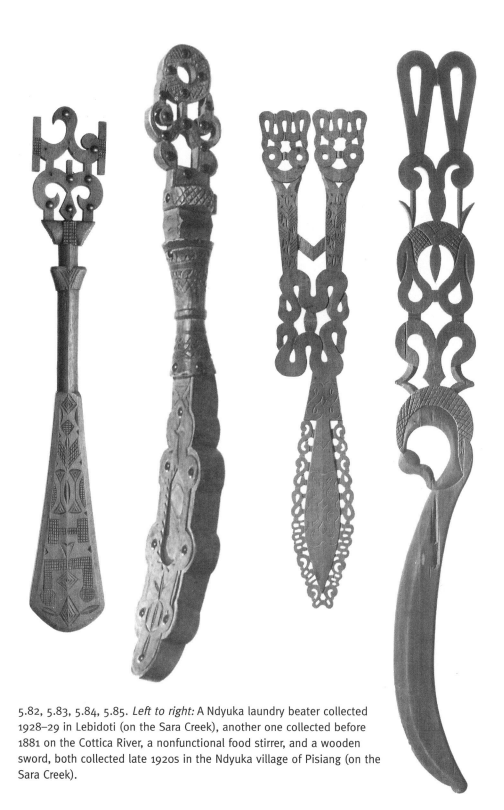

5.82, 5.83, 5.84, 5.85. *Left to right:* A Ndyuka laundry beater collected 1928–29 in Lebidoti (on the Sara Creek), another one collected before 1881 on the Cottica River, a nonfunctional food stirrer, and a wooden sword, both collected late 1920s in the Ndyuka village of Pisiang (on the Sara Creek).

5.86, 5.87, 5.88. Saramaka combs. *Left to right:* one collected before 1899 and two carved about 1963 on the Pikilio.

5.89, 5.90, 5.91. *Left to right:* two Ndyuka combs from villages on the Tapanahoni River (collected 1893–96 and late 1920s) and an Aluku comb collected before 1939.

5.92, 5.93, 5.94. *Left to right:* a comb collected 1928–29, probably in Saramaka, a Ndyuka comb collected in Diitabiki, and a comb with late nineteenth-century style carving (see Hurault 1970:116).

MAROON ARTS

5.95, 5.96. *Left,* A Ndyuka comb collected 1961 in the village of Mooitaki; *right,* an Aluku comb collected before 1901.

5.97. A stool with cowrie shell inset, collected late 1920s in Ganiakonde. This unusual example of representational carving by Saramakas was used in rituals.

5.98. An Aluku stool carved from a single piece of wood and decorated by branding, collected before 1939.

Opposite page:

5.99. A one-piece stool, collected about 1895.

5.100. A Saramaka folding stool carved from a single piece of wood, collected 1928–29.

5.101. A Saramaka folding chair carved in the early 1970s from a single piece of wood for sale to tourists. This form, like that illustrated in R. and S. Price 1992a:296, developed out of the early twentieth-century stool type illustrated in figure 5.100.

MAROON ARTS

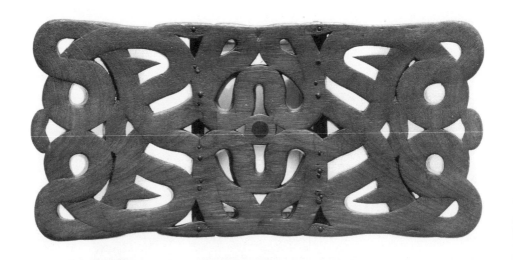

5.102. A Saramaka rectangular-top stool carved by Apenti (c. 1885–1970), Dangogo and Kayana.

5.103. A rectangular-top stool.

5.104. A plank-top stool collected before 1883.
5.105. A Saramaka round-top stool, collected late 1920s from a headman in Lombe
(see S. and R. Price 1980: note 43).

5.106. A Saramaka door collected 1960s in Semoisi.

5.107, 5.108. *Left,* a Saramaka round-top stool, carved 1997 in Cayenne by Menie Bet-
ian, village of Kambaloa, for a wife; *right,* a Saramaka round-top stool, carved 1990 in
St. Laurent by Alimoni Mayoko, village of Godo, commissioned (as example of the kind
of stool he would carve for a wife) for the Musée Régional de Guyane.

MAROON ARTS

5.109. An Aluku door painted in 1990 by Lamoraille, village of Apatou, commissioned for the Musée Régional de Guyane.

6.1 (*opposite page*). A Saramaka calabash bowl in
the American Museum of Natural History, New York.

Calabash Arts

New York City, 1950. Scratches. . . . Most likely incised with fingernails. . . . Documentation indicates that some were made by the women. . . . Perhaps their kind of doodling. . . .

WORKING IN A WINDOWLESS STOREROOM of the American Museum of Natural History, straining to understand unfamiliar objects that hadn't left their dust-covered shelves in twenty years, the young researcher formulates hypotheses as best he can. He has read the anthropological literature on the Bush Negroes, so he knows that it is the men, masters in the art of wood-carving known as *tembe*, who are the real creative artists in these societies. Melville Herskovits, after spending two summers among them, had written categorically, "'*Tembe no muje sundi*,' . . . 'Wood-carving is not a woman's affair.'" The researcher notes that some of the bowls on the shelves have external designs reminiscent of the men's woodcarvings, though quite possibly incised with a fingernail, and many others have been decorated on the insides in what he views as an "alien" style. From his background reading he suspects that the women are more susceptible to novelty. And it strikes him that while the men's carvings are all well considered, clearly marked, and conceived in relation to a definite surface, the women's sometimes overflow the design space and show none of the aesthetic considerations so evident in the men's work. *Make a note: the aesthetic field divides into active and passive participants—men produce the art and women play the role of connoisseurs. Thinking more broadly in terms of personality configurations, we might well conclude that the men are more conservative and the women more fickle.*[1]

If the first anthropological analysis of Maroon calabash art took off from these sorts of ruminations, the reasons may be traced at least partly to the setting. The contemplation of objects that have been removed from their habitual environment and transported to a distant museum can be instructive, but it also invites the observer to draw heavily on cultural preconceptions, since few competing sources of interpretation are readily available. Let's return to these same calabashes, this time in the hands of the people who carve them. The story begins with a tree.[2]

Calabash trees, which are planted in villages and garden camps, produce green fruits that are generally between baseball- and basketball-sized (fig. 6.2) and may be spherical, oblong, or pear-shaped. The best way to decide if they're ripe, Saramaka women say, is by the sound they make when they're knocked with the handle of a knife—a dull "*pòpòpò*" means that the fruit needs more time, but a sharp "*ká! ká! ká!*" says that it's ready to pick. Once severed from the tree, the heavy globes are sawed in half and the white, inedible pulp removed. The resulting shells are immersed in a vat of boiling water over a wood fire for something under half an hour, and the remaining

6.2. A calabash tree (*Crescentia cujete*) in the Saramaka village of Dangogo.

MAROON ARTS

mushy pulp is scraped out with a spoon at the river's edge (fig. 6.3). At this point, some of the calabashes may be given to a man for exterior decoration, but most are kept by the woman herself, who shapes the edge of each bowl or ladle by breaking off protrusions with her teeth or fingers and scraping it smooth with a knife. Next she prepares her carving tool, smashing a bottle to produce sharp pieces of glass and selecting one to use for incising the lines of her design. Often the first line she draws is a border along the inside edge of the bowl. She then marks out the central design, rotating the bowl thoughtfully and lightly indicating the lines but not yet executing them in full bas-relief. The piece of broken glass is then pressed deeper, going over each line firmly several times to make one edge sharp and clear and give the other a softer, shaded effect. A band may then be scraped along the exterior edge, and the carving is finished. The freshly carved bowls are soaked in water, rubbed smooth with a sandpaper-like leaf and then with fine sand, dried in the sun, rubbed with lime halves, rinsed, and dried again. They are now ready to use.

6.3. A Saramaka woman boils a vat of calabash shells.

Maroons distinguish at least seven varieties of the calabash tree, and use them selectively for different utensils. Most of the finished products fall into three main types—covered containers, open bowls, and various utensils used as spoons and ladles—each of which is further subdivided according to form and function.

Covered containers are made by cutting the fruit along the equator (fig. 6.4). Their decoration is entrusted to men, who work with their standard woodcarving tools, principally knives, chisels, and compasses, and produce densely textured geometric designs. Large containers may either be decorated and used to store rice or left plain and used to store salted meat and fish. Medium-sized containers are generally carved in intricate designs and used by women, for example to carry winnowed rice on their visits to a husband's village. Small containers, which are not decorated, may hold salt or ritual ingredients such as herbs and white clay. When men are away from home for the day they sometimes carry their lunch (food, calabash spoon, and drinking cup) in a calabash container, tied in a cloth to keep the top on.

Bowls are produced by cutting a calabash fruit through the stem end. Maroons distinguish five forms—baby cups (small, sparsely decorated, and used for water), two kinds of medium-sized bowls that are handsomely decorated and used at men's meals (round, hemispheric models used for drinking water and shallow, slightly elongated ones used to rinse hands after eating), rice-rinsing bowls (large and sparsely decorated), and bowls used for ritual purposes (very large and completely undecorated). These forms are illustrated in S. and R. Price 1980:fig. 213a.

6.4. Saramaka calabash containers.

Calabashes cut through the stem into more than two pieces are made into spoons, ladles, and rice mounding utensils (fig. 6.5). Maroon terminology distinguishes "small spoons" (for eating), "okra ladles" (for everyday cooking), "large ladles" (for communal cooking projects), and "rice mounders" (used to scoop rice out of the pot and shape it into a smoothly hemispheric shape in the serving bowl). Sometimes rice mounders are made by recycling a broken calabash bowl, trimming it to the correct proportions.

In addition to these items, rattles are fashioned out of small calabashes, and people used to make calabash rings, or "stools," on which they could set their bowls. Calabashes perform a variety of medicinal jobs as well; we once witnessed a birth, for example, at which the woman was smeared all over with the pulp of a freshly picked calabash to stimulate her contractions, and calabash discs may be affixed to a person's chest as a cure for certain physical ailments.

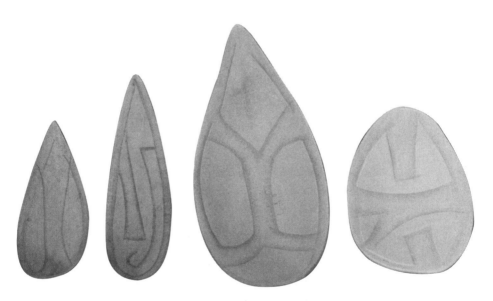

6.5. Spoons, a ladle, and a "rice mounding" utensil made from calabashes.

Examination of historical accounts, archival documents, and museum collections suggests that over the past three centuries, Maroons and other Surinamers have decorated calabashes with many different techniques and in many different styles. The shells have been painted, varnished, pierced with round holes, turned into elaborate mesh baskets, set on pedestals, carved in bas-relief, embellished with natural dyes, rubbed with kaolin, lacquered with urine, topped with elaborately carved wooden handles, and adorned with cloth and paper appliqués. The designs have ranged from angular to curvilinear, abstract to representational, geometric to free-form, and busily ornate to starkly minimalist.

The history of calabash art among the Maroons spills over into that of Amerindians and coastal Afro-Surinamers because of trading relations, cooperative production, and stylistic borrowing.[3] Although the written reports of early observers sometimes leave doubt about whether a particular calabash was the work of coastal Afro-Surinamers, Amerindians, or Maroons, we do know that Maroons have been fashioning calabash spoons, bowls, and covered containers since their very earliest years in the interior, and that these were being decoratively embellished by about 1800 (Schumann 1778: s.v. *gollu, kallabas, kuja, kujeri, tappadorro*; Staehelin 1913–19, III ii:198, 213; von Sack 1810:81).

Afro-Surinamers first learned how to prepare calabash shells from Suriname Indians, who employed them as their "everyday dishware and kitchen equipment" (Fermin 1769, I: 194), as well as for spindle whorls and rattles. We have reason to believe that the earliest extant calabash alleged to represent Maroon artistry (fig. 6.6) was in fact made by Amerindians. Part of a stylistically homogeneous set of calabashes in the Musée de l'Homme that was collected sometime before 1792 but carries museum documentation made in the late nineteenth century, this remarkable piece is the only one of that group attributed to Maroons. Its high gloss and intricately painted exterior and interior designs, in yellow, blue-gray, and white on a black ground, are not only stylistically unlike anything we know to have been made by Maroons, but also an excellent example of a style commonly made by tropical forest Indians. A nineteenth-century naturalist, writing of his travels on the lower Amazon, describes Amerindian-made *"cuyas"* as

> sometimes very tastefully painted. The rich black ground-colour
> is produced by a dye made from the bark of a tree called
> Comateü, the gummy nature of which imparts a fine polish. The
> yellow tints are made with the Tabatinga clay; the red with the
> seeds of the Urucú, or anatto plant; and the blue with indigo,
> which is planted round the huts. (Bates 1873:116)

Nearby, on the upper Rio Negro, Indians also produced highly polished calabash containers. There,

> the cups are polished brown on the outside and lacquered black on the inside; while the edge or the whole exterior is ornamented with incised patterns. The lacquering is done in a curious way. The calabash, after being well smoothed on the inner surface and washed with a decoction of carayuru (Bignonia) leaves is turned upside down over some cassava leaves sprinkled with human urine, where it remains until such time as the inside becomes black and shiny. (Koch-Grünberg 1910, II:232, translated in Roth 1924:302)

Because all the pieces in the set of eighteenth-century calabashes at the Musée de l'Homme conform quite precisely to the range of colors and the polished surfaces described in these passages, and because they are unlike anything known to have been produced by Maroons, we feel safe in concluding that they were all produced by Amerindians, most probably groups living to the south of the areas inhabited by Maroons. It is likely, however, that such calabashes were known, and perhaps owned, by Maroons, since calabashes figured importantly in the active trading networks that different Amerindian groups had with each other and with Maroons. In addition to this kind of painting, Amerindians have decorated calabashes with carving, but we have no evidence of their artistic influence on Maroon calabash carving. Although historical accounts refer to Amerindian calabashes

6.6. An eighteenth-century calabash bowl from Suriname.

decorated with incisions (see, for example, Roth 1924:302), those few documented examples available in museum collections are, compared to Afro-Suriname calabashes, very minimal in design and rather crude in execution (see S. and R. Price 1980:figs. 217, 218). The first calabashes we know to have been decorated by Afro-Surinamers were carved on their exterior surfaces with textured geometric (often circular) designs and rubbed with kaolin. As one observer reported,

> There are some Negroes who engrave on the convexity of this fruit compartments and grotesques in their own style, the hatchings of which they then fill in with chalk; which produces quite a pretty effect; and although they employ neither straight-edge nor compasses, these designs do not fail to be quite exact and quite agreeable. (Fermin 1769, I:194; see also Stedman 1988 [1790]:413)

This eighteenth-century style of calabash decoration is visually similar to certain decorative styles used on the exteriors of gourds in West Africa (see, for example, Chappel 1977, and Griaule and Dieterlen 1935). The earliest extant example of this style is a calabash rattle in the Rijksmuseum voor Volkenkunde in Leiden, which was collected in 1818 (fig. 6.7). This African-looking style, in which rosaces, other geometric shapes, border designs, and

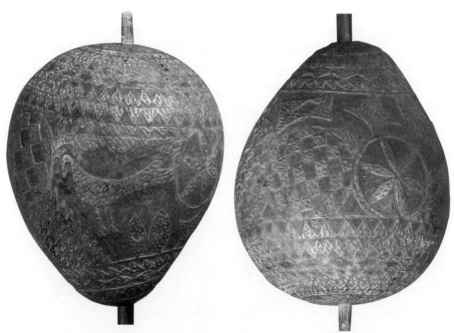

6.7. A calabash rattle used at dances by Afro-Surinamers, collected in 1818 (see S. and R. Price 1980:155 for further commentary).

sometimes animal figures are textured with incised flecks and rubbed with kaolin, continued to be found in Suriname—sometimes in Maroon villages—until the second half of the nineteenth century (fig. 6.8).[4]

During the second half of the nineteenth century, Maroon men began using compasses to incise the exteriors of some calabashes with sets of concentric arcs and circles in a style that lasted only a few decades (fig. 6.9). And Maroon women began experimenting with the interior surfaces of

6.8. Late nineteenth-century calabashes (with undecorated interiors).

6.9. A covered container collected before 1912 (with undecorated interior).

calabashes, often working on the same bowls whose exteriors were decorated by the men (fig. 6.10; see also S. and R. Price 1980:figs. 223, 224).[5] During the same period, calabashes provided a meeting ground for the artistry of Maroons and coastal Afro-Surinamers. Late nineteenth-century collections of Suriname artifacts abound in calabash bowls colorfully embellished inside and out with hearts, Dutch aphorisms, scenes of daily life, and garlands of flowers executed with glossy commercial paints. These are attributed to former plantation slaves in the coastal region and bear no technical or stylistic resemblance to contemporary Maroon calabash art (see S. and R. Price 1980:fig. 225a). There are also many calabashes, however, that have coastal-style paintings on one surface and incised Maroon circle-and-arc designs on the other (fig. 6.11). Museum catalogs list some of these mixed pieces as plantation artistry and others as the work of Maroons.

6.10. An Aluku calabash bowl carved on the outside (*left*) and inside (*right*), collected 1878–81.

But it seems clear that each one was in fact decorated first by a Maroon and later by a coastal Surinamer. Although such "bicultural" artifacts have become increasingly rare over the past several decades, they have not disappeared entirely. Suriname's independence in 1975 inspired some fine examples, with Maroon women's carvings on the inside and painted depictions of urban Surinamers in Afros and platform shoes on the outside (fig. 6.12). And while browsing around souvenir shops in Paramaribo, Cayenne, and St. Laurent, we have occasionally seen later examples of this same collaborative type.

6.11. A calabash bowl with carved exterior and painted interior, probably made between 1850 and 1870.
6.12. A calabash bowl with painted exterior and carved interior, bought in a Paramaribo souvenir shop in 1978.

6.13. A calabash container carved by an Aluku man and embellished with a wooden handle, collected before 1932, and a calabash bowl carved on the inside by a Sara-maka woman in the 1960s.

By the end of the nineteenth century, two styles of carving had come to dominate Maroon calabash art, and these have persisted with only minor change into the present (fig. 6.13). Men were using chisels and pocket knives to create the complex textured designs that became the universal mode for the exterior decoration of two-piece calabash containers (fig. 6.14; see also S. and R. Price 1980:figs. 228–30), and women were using pieces of broken glass to carve the roughly symmetrical designs that became standard on the interiors of open bowls (fig. 6.15).

6.14. A Saramaka calabash container collected late 1920s in the village of Bedoti.
6.15. The interior of a Maroon calabash bowl collected before 1894.

The development of women's calabash carving during the twentieth century has followed the regional division that we have already seen in other artistic media. With calabashes, the main distinguishing feature concerns the definition of figure and ground. Saramaka designs are dominated by bands that are even-sided or concave and "shaded" (darkened by scraping) to the inside. Eastern Maroon designs are formed by bulging shapes whose shaded effect is to the outside. The difference, which is readily perceptible on visual grounds, is reflected in the way women from the different regions talk about their carving. Almost all of the names that Saramakas use to designate calabash designs refer to the even or concave shapes with internal shading, and those utilized by eastern Maroons focus instead on the convex shapes formed by external shading.[6] Figure 6.16 illustrates the difference.

Calabash designs that can be viewed either in terms of their concave, internally shaded forms or their convex, externally shaded forms suggest that the two styles of carving may well have had a common origin. If further

6.16. Saramakas carve concave shapes that are shaded on the inside, while eastern Maroons carve convex shapes that are shaded on the outside. *Left,* a small Saramaka drinking bowl collected 1976 in Asindoopo; *right,* a larger Aluku one collected in 1990.

MAROON ARTS

research were to determine that "ambiguous" designs like the one in figure 6.17 predated the two dominant styles of the twentieth century, we would be in a position to propose that a shared style gradually came to be "read" with inversed definitions of figure and ground by eastern and central Maroon women respectively. Alternatively, it is possible that eastern Maroon women once conceptualized designs according to a "Saramaka" definition of figure and ground, that a few women began experimenting with the "background" shapes of their designs, that these became the focus of their artistic attention, and that their innovative approach was copied and eventually became universal in eastern Maroon villages. This latter hypothesis finds support in the fact that the earliest extant examples of designs formed by scraped bands, from both eastern and central groups, are carved in the "Saramaka" mode. In either case, a sensitivity to the contours of the "ground"—which is frequently evident in aesthetic commentary by Maroon women and which has come into play in Maroon textile arts (see Chapter 4)—seems to have contributed to the development of contrastive regional styles.[7]

6.17. A Ndyuka calabash from the village of Diitabiki. Ndyuka design names have been penciled (by the collector?) onto the convex, externally shaded shapes, but the concave, internally shaded shapes of the background are common Saramaka design elements.

Even within particular groups, calabash carvings reflect regional diversity. In Saramaka, for example, the point at which two scraped bands merge is frequently closed off in carvings from the downstream village of Santigoon but almost always left open in those made by women living elsewhere (compare, for example, the carvings illustrated as 4d and 4e in S. and R. Price 1980:fig. 232). Women from the northern half of Saramaka territory scrape no borders on their bowls, but a border is an absolute requirement for bowls made in the villages to the south. And particular bowl forms and decorative designs often have strong associations with the village where they were first created and where they are most frequently made. Pointed (rather than rounded) ends on rice mounders and variants of the "Indian arrow" motif in carvings, for example, are viewed as "Pempe style" (fig. 6.18; see also S. and R. Price 1980:figs. 214a, 232/4g). Notched hand-washing bowls and the "embroidery design" motif are thought of as belonging to the village of Asindoopo (fig. 6.18; see also S. and R. Price 1980:figs. 232/5b and 5d). And spade-shape motifs are considered "Godo-style" carving (see S. and R. Price 1980:fig. 234).

6.18. Two hand-washing bowls carved in the "embroidery design" motif (one with the notched "motor boat" shape), and a drinking bowl carved with the Indian arrow motif associated with the village of Pempe.

MAROON ARTS

Our visits to eastern Maroon villages in 1990 and 1991 reinforced the ideas about regional variation that we had originally formed on the basis of fieldwork in Saramaka and examination of museum collections. The calabashes that we saw in Aluku, Ndyuka, and Paramaka villages had no "Saramaka-style" borders scraped into their exterior edges, and generally followed the "eastern Maroon" design style centering on convex, externally scraped shapes. They also confirmed, once again, the dynamism of Maroon art. Even though imported kitchenware was clearly gaining ground on calabashes for both cooking and meal service, and even though fewer and fewer women were continuing to carve, the designs that *were* being produced reflected lively artistic creativity and innovation. One new idea that was being played with by a number of women was the segmentation of the surface into three parts, creating a "patchwork" effect, as if the lines separating the segments were seams joining different pieces of cloth (fig. 6.19).

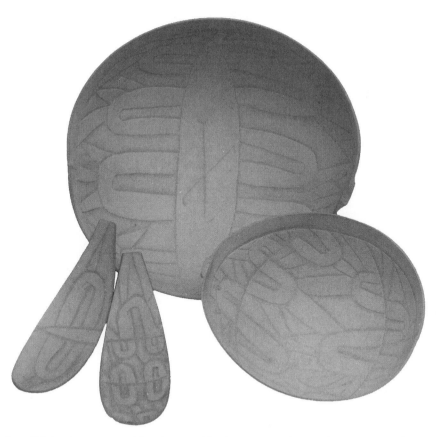

6.19. Calabash spoons and bowls carved in the 1970s and 1980s by Ma Legina, from the Aluku village of Komontibo.

Maroons have often experimented with the adaptation of designs and art styles from other media to calabash carving. The Asindoopo "embroidery design" motif was inspired directly by textile art (fig. 6.20; see also S. and R. Price 1980:fig. 261). The design on figure 6.21*left* may have been modeled on the bands with zig-zag "filler" stitches that were common in contemporaneous embroidery (fig. 6.21*right*). And it seems quite possible that the idea for the decoration shown in figure 6.22*left* came from bits-and-pieces patchwork (fig. 6.22*right*), which was being produced at the time this container was made.

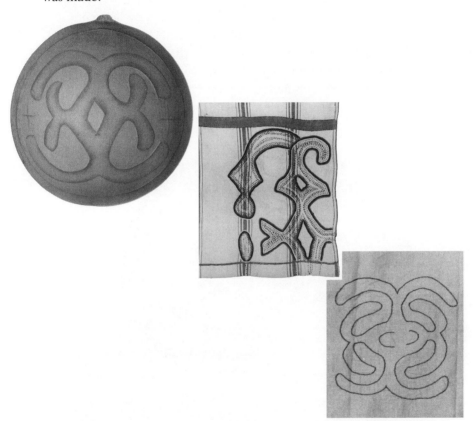

6.20. A calabash bowl carved in the 1960s by Yimbaa-muyee, village of Asindoopo; detail of the breechcloth in figure 4.61; and embroidery on a cape sewn in the 1950s or 1960s by Kaadi, Chief Agbago's wife from the village of Botopasi.

Opposite page:
6.21. The top of a calabash container, probably Aluku, collected before 1935 (see S. Price 1993 [1984]:96-99), and embroidery on a skirt collected 1960 in the Saramaka village of Lombe.
6.22. The bottom of a calabash container collected late 1920s in the Ndyuka village of Maipaondo, on the Sara Creek, and detail of the shoulder cape shown in figure 4.36.

Calabash carvings have also reflected the stylistic influence of woodcarvings (fig. 6.23). Some have imitated the even-sided "wood-within-wood" ribbons of Saramaka carvings (fig. 6.24), others have replicated the bulging shapes and layered bands of eastern men's carvings (figs. 6.25, 6.26), and in conversation women have often cited the men's art as the inspiration for calabash designs that to us were less obviously imitative. Finally, a hairstyle known as "around the head" gave one woman the idea for a calabash design of the same name (fig. 6.27).

The implications of these inter-media relationships for Maroon culture history will be addressed in Chapter 8.

6.23. The calabash bowl in figure 3.7 and the seat of the round-top stool in figure 5.23.

6.24. Wood-within-wood carving on a Saramaka calabash bowl (made 1931 in Ganzee) and the peanut-grinding board in figure 5.9.

6.25. Eastern Maroon carving on a Paramaka calabash bowl collected in the 1970s and the comb in figure 5.94.

6.26. Layered bands carved on a Ndyuka calabash bowl collected in 1991 and an Aluku comb collected before 1939.

6.27. A calabash bowl collected in 1968 on the Pikilio and the "around-the-head" hairdo that explicitly inspired it. See figure 3.1 for an illustration of a cassava cake with the same design.

6.28. Aluku calabashes (see key on p. 232).

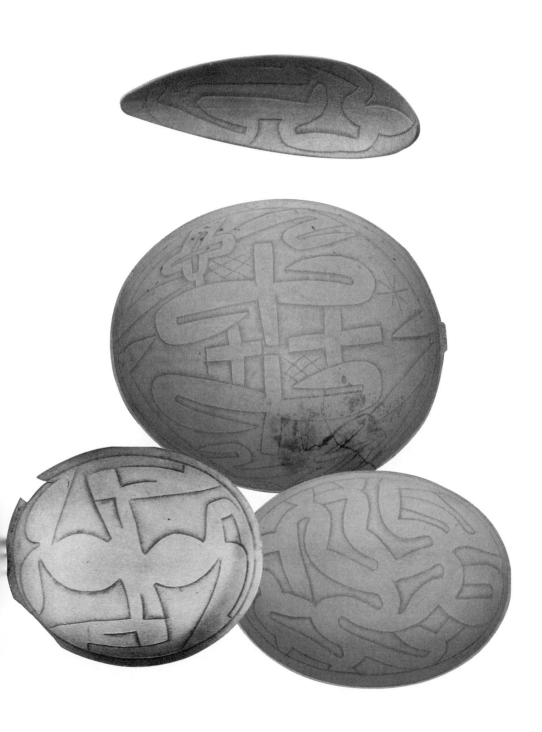

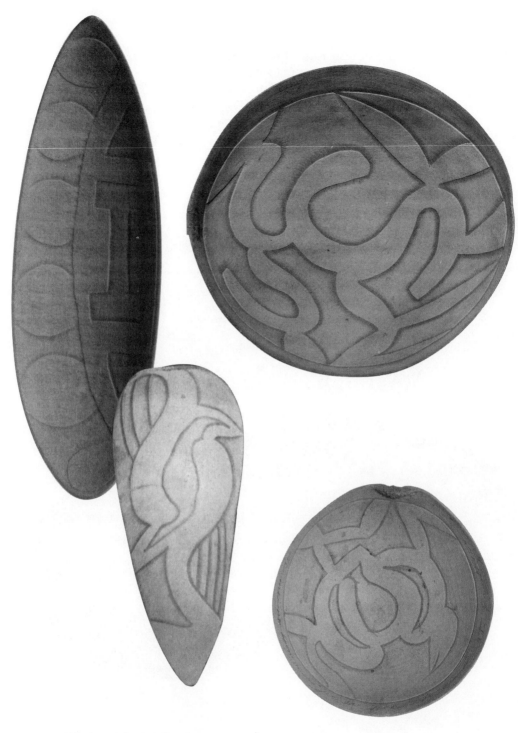

6.29. Ndyuka calabashes (see key on p. 233).

6.30. Paramaka calabashes
(see key on p. 234).

6.31. Saramaka calabashes
(see key on p. 235).

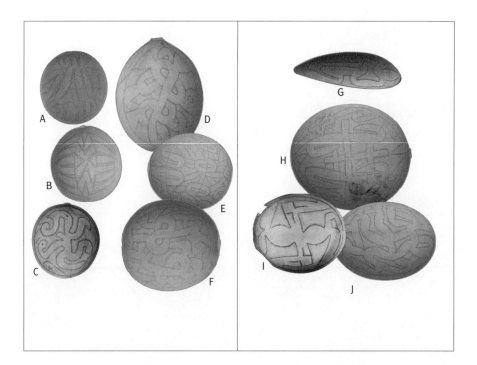

Key for fig. 6.28. Aluku calabashes:

    A. Carver undocumented (collected 1990).

    B. Carved by Ma Atubun, Komontibo, about 1989.

    C. Carved by Ma Anaaweli, Papaisiton, before 1978.

    D. Carved by Ma Bodomma, Asisi, before 1990.

    E. Probably carved by Ma Betsi, Maripasoula (collected 1990).

    F. No documentation.

    G. Carver undocumented (collected before 1935).

    H. Carved by Ma Alelia, Kotika, probably in the 1950s.

    I. Carver undocumented (collected before 1939).

    J. Carved by Ma Bodomma, Asisi (collected 1990).

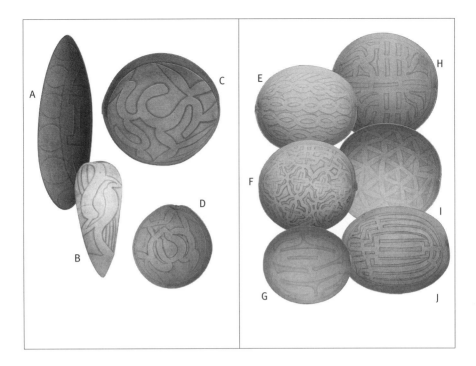

Key for fig. 6.29 Ndyuka calabashes:

    A. Carver undocumented (collected before 1881).

    B. Carver undocumented (collected late 1920s).

    C. Carver undocumented (collected before 1932).

    D. Carver undocumented.

    E. Collected 1991 in Tabiki.

    F. Carved by Amenta, Tabiki (collected 1991).

    G. Carved by Ma Abele, Tabiki (collected 1991).

    H. Carved by Telia, Tabiki (collected 1991).

    I. Collected 1991 in Fandaaki.

    J. Carved by Ma Deni, Fandaaki (collected 1991).

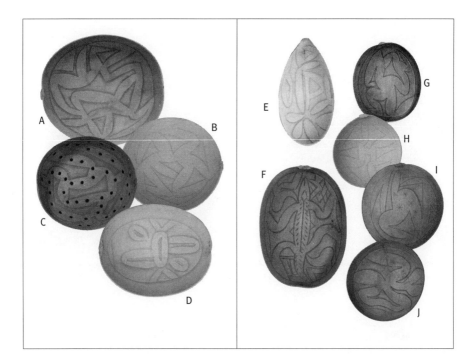

Key for fig. 6.30. Paramaka calabashes:

A. Collected 1991 in Nason.

B. Carved by Sa Koyon, Loka Loka, late 1980s.

C. Collected 1965 in Langatabiki.

D. Carved by Maktalena, Loka Loka, about 1985.

E. Collected 1991 in Nason.

F. Collected 1965 in Langatabiki.

G. Collected early 1970s.

H. Carved by Sama Mma, Langatabiki, about 1988.

I. Collected early 1970s.

J. Collected early 1970s.

Key for fig. 6.31. Saramaka calabashes:

     A. Collected 1978 in Pikiseei.

     B. Collected in the late 1920s.

     C. Collected 1991 by Mando Amimba in the region of Kambaloa.

     D. Carved 1970s in an upper-river village.

     E. Collected 1979.

     F. Carved about 1978 in Pempe.

     G. Collected 1991 by Mando Amimba in the region of Kambaloa.

     H. Collected in the late 1920s.

     I. Carved 1970s in Pempe.

     J. Carved by Keekete, Asindoopo, 1950s–60s.

7.1. 1707 painting by Dirk Valkenburg of a slave "play" on the Suriname River plantations of Palmeneribo-Surimombo, from which the ancestors of the Saramaka Dombi
clan escaped soon thereafter.

Playing

7

After a few hours, the relatives of the deceased, and other negro men and women who wished to participate in this scene of bereavement, began arriving from neighboring villages. There was a constant stream of canoes coming downstream, each with three or four people, and by nightfall there were some five hundred visitors. With the setting of the sun, the formal death music—with fife, drums, and musket salutes—began. More than a hundred human voices accompanied the music, and this incredible noise lasted the entire night till dawn. . . . Negro men and women streamed in from distant places, until the village began to resemble a populous European market town. . . . At nine in the morning the funeral commenced. First the corpse was laid in a coffin built of cedar wood, in front of the deceased woman's hut so people could pay their respects. Then all the female sorcerers arrived in pairs, led by the person who was to fill the position that had been held by the Grang-Mama. She had in her hand a scepter made from tree-shoots, with which she consecrated the deceased, amidst grimaces and rites, and then danced three times around the coffin with amazing skill, considering her age, accompanied by fife and drums. The most remarkable aspect of her death-dance was that she could move about without her feet ever leaving the ground, while every part of her body moved in perfect time to the music. As she danced, she also consecrated several of her companions with the scepter. Before she finished, her next companion began to dance, and this continued until all were dancing, and then they all danced together. After a solid hour, this painful dance of death was over. This is such a strenuous dance that one can see every muscle of the naked negro bodies moving.

—*Moravian Brother Johann Riemer,*
missionary to the Saramaka, 1780

The large-scale communal events that Maroons call "plays" (Sar. *pêè,* Ndy. *pee*) bring together their most complex, most intense, and most stylized performances.[1] Often lasting till dawn and bringing together festively dressed people from a number of villages to participate in multimedia performances of song, dance, and drumming, plays are organized on a variety of occasions and serve also as the primary public opportunity to meet potential lovers and spouses. They form the high point of each of the several stages of funeral rites. They accompany the installation of chiefs, headmen, and other officials. And they are used to honor particular gods and ancestors. Whether a gathering in honor of a forest spirit or the climactic rite of a funeral, each play calls for a specialized set of dances, drum rhythms, and kinds of singing.

The 1707 painting of a "play" on the Dombi plantation (fig. 7.1) provides striking visual evidence of continuities in performance principles, depicting dancing, drumming, and meetings between lovers in a scene uncannily like a modern Maroon play. In addition to the features discussed in Chapter 4 (n. 2), there are numerous postures and gestural attitudes which could as easily have been taken from a twentieth-century photograph—the standard stance with shoulders and hips thrust back, the "getting-down" position in solo dancing, the way two men dance at each other in the background on the right, the way infants are tied on women's backs, the posture of the person carrying water, and the way one of the dancers wipes the sweat from a drummer's face.[2]

THE EMPHASIS ON INDIVIDUALITY, expressiveness, and personal style— which we described in Chapter 4 in regard to clothing and adornment—is a pervasive aspect of the culture of Maroons, influencing music, artful speech, and all sorts of verbal play as well as the more formal genres of performance. Even in the broader comparative context of African-American societies (where performative and expressive events play such a central role), Maroons exhibit an unusually keen appreciation of nuance in voice, phrasing, accent, gesture, and posture. Playfulness, creativity, and improvisation permeate conversation, and spontaneously invented elliptical phrases frequently substitute for standard words—a watch may become a "back-of-the-wrist motor," food "under-the-nose-material," a stool "the rump's rejoicing," swimming "underwater work." Speech play assumes other forms as well: verbal dueling by young men (involving the improvisation and recital of run-on strings of wittily phrased insults); the casual insertion of foreign-language expressions (from French Guiana Creole, from coastal Suriname Creole, from Dutch, or from English); and elaborate secret play languages (usually developed by groups of young men).

Maroons' interest in individual mannerisms inspires frequent verbal and gestural mimicry. We once saw two friends silently greeting each other across a roaring rapids—one beginning with a humorous imitation of a fellow villager's idiosyncratic dance style, and the second countering with his own rendition of another man's equally recognizable performance of the same dance. Maroon women are especially adept at comic impersonations of their husband's other wives. The expressive, dramatic quality of Maroon life also comes through in the spontaneous songs and dances that are sparked by mundane but happy events. An elderly woman who had been fishing without success for over an hour and finally caught one tiny fish, dropped into a sitting position in the shallow water and broke into a sinuous dance of celebration with her upper torso. Another time, a woman noticed S. P. passing by her door with a new enamel bucket on her head, and invented a little song: "The red bucket suits my 'sister-in-law'—look how the red bucket suits my 'sister-in-law.'"

This kind of spontaneous expressiveness shades directly into more formally delineated styles of music, dance, and verbal art. The melodic phrase a woman uses to break the monotony of a morning of rice cutting may later be expanded by a repeated response and sung by a soloist and chorus at the next community-wide celebration in her village. A hunter's humorous description of an agouti he happened upon, washing itself in the forest, is stylized into a dance that is performed to the accompaniment of drums and handclapping. And another man's rendition of the rhythms of a Coca-Cola bottling machine he saw in Paramaribo becomes a popular piece for local drummers. Just as Maroons incorporate into their visual aesthetic framework such features of everyday life as tin lanterns, outboard motors, or different-colored varieties of rice, they enjoy building the sounds, gestures, and language of daily living into their more formal performing arts.

Maroon expressive events at all levels of formality are characterized by total participation and by the highly structured (though at the same time fluid) nature of the interplay among participants, rendering inappropriate the analytical use of Western distinctions between "audience" and "performer." There are, for example, certain stylized contrapuntal patterns that recur in everyday speech and gossip, in the formal rhetoric of ritual and judicial sessions, in public song/dance/drum performances, and in the telling of tales. Normal conversations are punctuated by supportive comments such as "That's right," "Yes indeed," or "Not at all." Even when men living on the coast send tape-recorded messages back to their villages, they leave pauses after each phrase, so that the "conversation" may assume its proper two-party form once the tape is played. In formal settings, stylized responses become more frequent, and responsibility for providing them is assumed by a particular individual. Discussions involving the paramount chief, for example, are always conducted with the rhetorical aid of a third party, who explicitly represents "the public." Prayers also assume an antiphonal structure, as participants support the speaker's words at intervals with slow handclapping and specially intoned declarations of "Great thanks." Solo work songs are interrupted by the comments of others present, and popular songs involve the alternation of a soloist and a responsive chorus. Whatever the specific context, this fundamental dialogic pattern—which characterizes folktales as well—privileges the ongoing, active engagement of those who are not the principal speaker or "performer" of the moment.

A closely related feature of Maroon performance is role-switching between the (temporary) soloist and other participants. For example, song/dance/drum plays are characterized by the emergence of a succession of individual soloists, each of whom briefly enjoys center stage and then yields to another. In other words, Maroon "performances" more closely resemble a jam session than the playing of a piano concerto, balancing the complementary values of individual virtuosity and full communal participation.

Many kinds of Maroon cultural events exhibit a common diachronic structure characterized by repeated interruptions. An initial exposition is interrupted by another, which in turn may be interrupted by a third, with subsequent portions of each unfolding—often with further interruptions—throughout the performance. For example, a formal court session or a divinatory seance with an oracle might proceed from A (the first case) to B, to a continuation of A, to the end of B, to a continuation of A, to the beginning of C, to the whole of D, to another continuation of A, to the end of C, and finally to the end of A. The description of tale-telling at the end of this chapter offers a concrete example: the telling of a tale about the origin of drums is interrupted by one about a wrestling match, then continued briefly, then interrupted again by a tale about an extraordinary dance performance, and followed by a tale about the Devil, before continuing on, with three more interruptive tales, to its conclusion. And this practice of interrupting and overlaying segments strung out through time is closely related to central features of Maroon musical performance, such as drummers' or singers' staggered points of entry and the pervasiveness of polyrhythms.

Another widespread feature of Maroon performance is the creative use of indirection and ellipsis—the art of allusion through proverbs or other condensed verbal and gestural forms, and other spontaneous and conventional means of avoiding direct reference. Although the use of such devices intensifies in formal contexts (prayer, council meetings, and so forth), even everyday ways of addressing or referring to people are treated as a complex and subtle art. We have heard people managing to avoid uttering a person's name, for example, by substituting kin terms, official titles, references to kinship ("So-and-so's mother"), residence ("the man up the hill"), physical characteristics ("the dark one"), temporary states ("the woman who was sick"), and recent actions ("the man who killed the tapir"). Reference sometimes becomes a kind of sophisticated word play in which the speaker uses progressively less ambiguous terms seriatim until the listener finally understands. This same kind of ellipsis appears in many Maroon folktales, where, for example, Anaconda may be referred to as "the Long One," Elephant as "the Big Guy," and Jaguar as "the Old Man."

From a Maroon perspective, the ability to use proverbs—or, more frequently, cryptic proverbial allusions—represents the ultimate achievement in the verbal arts. Proverbs form a central repository of moral wisdom and values, and they play an important role in almost any formal conversation. As people grow older they tend to use proverbs with greater frequency and skill—which means more elliptically and more often in esoteric ritual languages. Proverbs are also "spoken" on the *apinti* (talking) drum, for example as a running commentary on the debates in a tribal council meeting. They are often preceded by a reference to the person, animal, or other being conventionally credited with the observation ("The elders say, 'Spider monkeys don't beget howler monkeys'" [like father, like son]; "Lizard says, 'Speed is good, but so is caution'"). Although proverbs are occasionally spoken as full sentences ("If you don't poke around in a hole, you won't know what's in it"), they are more frequently left half-finished ("If you don't poke around in a hole . . ."), in the expectation that listeners will complete it mentally themselves. In many cases, one or two key words from a proverb are cited in isolation, or an allusion is simply made to its characters or to the being credited with its invention. To mention "the one about River Grass" communicates the moral of a proverb expressed, in its full version, in terms of a conversation between a certain fish and the vegetation in a rapids, and "the talk of Chicken" represents the wisdom of a proverb introduced as having originally been spoken by that fowl.

Such condensed allusions in everyday speech are not always to proverbs; they may be made to folktales, to so-called "dilemma tales," to well-known proclamations or favorite aphorisms of living elders, or to any philosophical fragment that a speaker can expect a listener to have heard. The mere mention of "*nóuna*," for example, can serve as an effective warning from one Saramaka to another to be on guard about revealing information to an outsider, since in a well-known folktale that nonsense word is used to protect secret knowledge from discovery (R. and S. Price 1991:16–19). In Saramaka tale-telling, the art of allusion reaches a high point in the "tale-nuggets" that interrupt longer narratives. Here, as in proverbial allusions, a part is artfully offered for the whole, and the communicative process takes on a fully dialogic form, as listeners are called on to fill in, silently, a whole folktale on the basis of a few cryptic phrases of narrative or, often, of song.

Finally, as we have already implied, playfulness and the appreciation of novelty are as important in Maroon performance as in the graphic and plastic arts. Just as Maroons have admired the innovative carving of a folded umbrella in the medium of wood, participants in village plays have delighted in such novelties as one dancer's use of a Chinese paper fan, which he gradually and deliberately unfolded as he danced. We have seen how everyday speech is peppered with creative indirection and how speech play takes other forms as well—verbal dueling, the frequent borrowing of words from other languages, and the creation and use of secret play languages.[3] As we will see, creativity and play are an equally important aspect of formal song, dance, drumming, and tale-telling performances, and contribute both to the enormous vitality of these arts and to the ongoing processes of stylistic change through time.

These very general features of the Maroon arts of performance are part of the historical synthesis that the original Maroons and their immediate descendants forged during the late seventeenth and early eighteenth centuries. Historical evidence makes it clear that many of them—antiphonal speech and song, "interruption" as a syntagmatic principle, interactive participation in performative events, and verbal indirection, ellipsis, and play—were already firmly established by the time of the treaties, in the middle of the eighteenth century. On the plantations of coastal Suriname, call-and-response slave songs were described from a European viewpoint as "melodious but without Time; in Other respects not unlike that of some Clarks reading to the Congregation, One Person Pronouncing a Sentence Extemporary, which he next hums or Whistles, when all the others Repeat the Same in Chorus, another sentence is then Spoke and the Chorus is Renew'd a Second time & So ad perpetuum" (Stedman 1988 [1790]:516). Eighteenth-century German missionaries—who commented frequently in their diaries about Saramakas' attention to performance in daily life, the value they placed on eloquence, their "frivolous" love of novelty, and their consuming interest in singing, dancing, drumming, and other music—also complained that their own speech was repeatedly disrupted. "My sermon," wrote one missionary, "was frequently interrupted. One [Saramaka] said, 'Teacher, today we understand your words.' Another, 'What you say is the truth.' A third, 'I see that our Obia men (sorcerers) have deceived us.' A fourth, 'I believe that the Great God is the only one'" (translated in R. Price 1990:254). Even central Maroon evaluative terms such as (Sar./Ndy.) *súti/switi*—today a term of strong approbation used for speaking, singing, dancing, drumming, tale-telling, and sexual performance—appear in the eighteenth-century materials.

Such historical continuities in fundamental features of performance and the general structure of plays have been complemented by considerable dynamism. Songs, dances, and figures of speech are constantly being created, play languages are frequently invented, and whole new styles of song, dance, and drumming are periodically added to the repertoire. While the overall form of Saramaka funeral plays, for example, has remained relatively constant since the eighteenth century, this did not preclude the introduction of a musical novelty in the 1960s (*kawina*, a calypso-type song/drum/dance performance at a designated point in the festivities) or its replacement, after the introduction of gasoline-powered generators in the 1970s, by soul music combos using Japanese-made electric instruments. Or again, at the climax of these same rites, masked dancers have always appeared in order to expel the departing ghost definitively from the village, but while the young men who make and wear these masks have always striven for novel ways to increase the scariness of their own creations (fig. 7.2), they welcomed the appearance of commercial rubber Halloween masks in the coastal stores of the 1960s as an additional resource (fig. 7.3). As with clothing styles, woodcarving, or cicatrization, the long-term history of the Maroon arts of performance has been characterized by continuities of aesthetic ideas combined with ongoing change on the level of form.

IN THE REMAINDER of this chapter, we present an overview of some of the Maroon arts of performance—dance, song, drumming and other instrumental music, and selected verbal arts. Although we address each one in turn, we ask readers to keep in mind that they are not generally performed in isolation but are embedded and combined in immensely rich public events. Funerals, for example, involve a complex interworking of cooking, dress, grooming, song, dance, drumming, riddles and tales, prayer, oratory, divination, and purificatory rites in prescribed combinations and sequential orders over a series of many months.

7.2. Saramaka mask used in funeral rites, made about 1965 in Dangogo.

7.3. Saramaka masked dancers at a funeral. One wears a rubber Richard Nixon mask bought in Paramaribo.

DANCE

Kenneth Bilby, writing about the Aluku, has described a scene that is equally common in Saramaka villages: "One of the first experiences of an infant is to be 'danced' by its mother, who 'stands' the child on her lap, holding it under the arms and singing playfully, tapping rhythms with her fingers on its back. And as the child is being danced, the mother—all the while singing—bestows its *pikin nen*, the intimate nickname it will thenceforth be known by" (1989:53). Maroon children are encouraged to dance—hands on their hips, torsos rotating rhythmically, and feet planted firmly in one spot— as soon as they can stand, and they become adept at a whole range of dance styles by the time they are five or six years old (fig. 3.11).

Eighteenth-century missionaries treated the subject of dance, like that of ritual, through disparaging remarks more than ethnographic description, yet their dismay at the competence of even very young children in performing the dances of various possession gods and at the importance of dance to even the very oldest women indicates that this was as central an activity then as it is today (R. Price 1990). At the end of the nineteenth century, a missionary to the Aluku offered a description that could almost have been written today:

> The women . . . stand in a semi-circle. One sings a recitatif which the others answer by a chorus. . . . All hold their arms straight out and raised toward the sky. Without the slightest movement of their feet, they move left and right to the sounds of the drums and repeat the chorus. This can go on for hours or even the whole night.
>
> Into the semicircle formed by the women, a man advances, with knees bent as if he were sitting, wearing a fringed breechcloth and cloth over his shoulders, and holding a handkerchief in his hand, arms outstretched and slightly raised. . . .
>
> The supreme accomplishment is to follow exactly the sounds of the two drums, one rapid and the other slower. With his right foot, he stomps the ground in time with the small drum, and with his left, he follows the rhythm of the larger, slower drum.
>
> This gymnastic effort, as one might suppose, is very tiring. And the applause of the crowd is unreserved for those who are skilled and able to keep it up for several minutes at a time. (Brunetti 1890:195–96, cited in Bilby 1989:52)

Maroon dance styles exhibit the same regional diversity and tendency toward evolution through time as other kinds of Maroon performance. During the 1960s, 1970s, and early 1980s, the most popular dance styles at funerals and other large public events were Saramaka *tjêke* and Ndyuka and Aluku *awasa*. *Tjêke*, which is danced by both men and women against an accompaniment of *sêkêti* singing and handclapping, alternates between a low-key "holding pattern" and intense periods of light, rapid footwork that almost seems to lift the dancer off the ground. Dancers delicately manipulate arms, wrists, and fingers, and periodically descend to a crouching position while balanced on the balls of the feet, a position considered the ultimate demonstration of agility and grace (fig. 7.4; S. and R. Price 1980:plate XVIII). *Awasa*, performed to the accompaniment of a drum choir, is danced with thick anklets of seed pods on each leg, which rhythmically accentuate the dancer's hard-stomping footwork (see figs. 4.17, 7.5).

7.4. Saramakas dancing *tjêke* to the accompaniment of singing and handclapping.

Many other dance styles are known—passing from one region to another, dropping in and out of fashion, and undergoing changes in the settings in which they are considered appropriate. *Susa* and *agankoi*, for example, are considered Ndyuka or Aluku dances, but both enjoyed a brief period of popularity several decades ago in Saramaka villages.[4] Likewise, *lama*—originally a dance from the coastal area—moved from the missionized villages of the lower Suriname River to the upper river region in the 1930s, enjoyed a period of intense popularity, and was dropped. *Alesingô*, in which a male dancer balances on long horizontal poles manipulated by two men, was imported to the Pikilio in the 1950s but was upstaged in the late 1970s by a new form of dancing on vertical stilts. *Adunké*, which preceded *tjêke* as the most popular secular dance in Saramaka, has now taken on historical associations (as has its associated song and drumming style) and is performed only at rites honoring those ancestors who were accustomed to it during their lifetimes (it was danced/sung/drummed, for example, in honor of the First-Time ancestors at the climactic moment of Paramount Chief Agbago's funeral in 1989). Because of the ephemeral nature of dance, even compared with the other performing arts, our information on the variety of dance styles through time is fragmentary, but we have collected enough names and descriptions of now-obsolete styles to know that stylistic evolution and love of novelty are as central an aspect of Maroon dance as they are of other Maroon arts.

During much of the twentieth century, the most prestigious, highly stylized form of Saramaka dance has been *djómbo* (jumping) *sêkêti*, performed by a male soloist accompanied by a *sêkêti* drum choir. Unlike most dance styles, *djómbo sêkêti* is performed by only a few masters in any region during a given period. A great *sêkêti* dancer must frequently create new dances, each of which is named and mimetic, and the general repertoire is in constant flux.

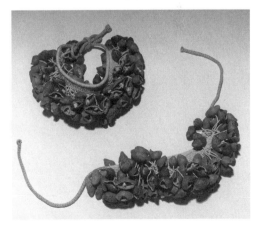

7.5. Dance anklets (Sar. *kawái*/ Ndy. *kawai*) worn by eastern Maroons and Saramakas for *awasa* and by Matawais for *bandja* dancing.

On the evening of the performance, typically as part of funeral celebrations involving visitors from a number of villages, the dancer carefully prepares himself for this most virtuoso of all Saramaka performances. Before entering the dance area, he carefully dresses in a specially faded short cape, a broad embroidered dance apron over his breechcloth, and a home-sewn cotton cap or a fashionable store-bought hat. He smears white bands of kaolin around his calves and puts on black cotton anklets filled with specially prepared ingredients that insure lightness of step and provide protection from jealousy and sorcery that could make him lose his balance. As women flap lengths of cloth up and down before him to create a breeze and others hoot constantly with cupped hands over their mouths, the dancer positions himself regally on a stool, legs relaxed, head high, face expressionless, waiting for the right moment to begin. As the drums take up the rhythm, he stands and deliberately adjusts his cape and apron, then suddenly bursts into motion—his face an unmoving mask, his every movement bespeaking absolute muscular control. Various stylized gestures, lasting some twenty seconds each, alternate with less spectacular holding patterns. The intense bursts of brilliance are varied—stylized imitations of a

7.6. Ndyuka "play" honoring snake gods.

MAROON ARTS

rodent digging up sweet potatoes in a garden, a hummingbird drinking nectar, a man sawing planks from a log, a jaguar killing a turtle, or a steamship leaving the Paramaribo pier. At certain times his feet are stamped down flatly, at other times they move with lightning speed to give a striking "off the ground" effect. Dance/drumming sequences of two or three minutes alternate with rest periods when he returns to his stool for a minute or so and is fanned by some of the women while others hoot continuously. Then the drums begin again and the dancer strikes a pose, holds it, executes a few quick steps, and strikes it again, emphasizing the perfect balance and symmetry that are such an important part of this tense, highly controlled style of dance.

At plays for the various gods, people perform the dances associated with them whether or not they have ever been possessed, both to celebrate these spirits and—they say—in order to be prepared in case such a god should decide to enter their head (figs. 7.6, 7.7). Such dances differ dramatically. In Saramaka, forest spirits characteristically hop on one foot at a time, warrior gods swoop with arms outstretched like a buzzard or pad stealthily like a jaguar, and snake gods dance with arms whipping gracefully from side to

7.7. Ndyuka "play" honoring snake gods.

side, index fingers pointing to the ground. Other types of dancing are integrated into various rites. In a major ceremony aimed at cleansing the village after a funeral, masked dancers who have concealed every part of their bodies (with cloth, leaves, gloves, and other coverings) dance obscenely with long wooden penises, simulating copulation with drums and making suggestive advances toward other participants in the event. The masks worn by these dancers may be large wooden or gourd faces embellished with peccary or other animal hair, jaguar skin, and locally made dyes or, today, commercial rubber masks imported from the coast (figs. 7.2, 7.3). Furthermore, the great powers credited with supporting particular clans during the original wars of liberation are each honored with a special type of dancing (as well as distinctive drumming and song). Finally, there are other dances appropriate to a broad range of settings. Saramaka *bandámmba*, for example, is a sexually suggestive women's dance, accompanied by its own style of drumming. It is closely associated with fertility and the cult of twins, but it is also used in rites dedicated to the First-Time Maroon ancestors (who are said to have enjoyed it) as well as in less formal celebrations such as the return of a long-absent man from a coastal trip. When Maroons visited Washington, D.C., as part of the 1992 Festival of American Folklife, Saramaka women's exuberant *bandámmba* provoked a large audience to nearly get out of hand (R. and S. Price 1994:59–60).

SONG

The missionaries who lived in Saramaka villages in the eighteenth century made frequent reference to singing, even mentioning one type that has since disappeared—songs sung by groups of men paddling large canoes, characterized by "a sprightly melody and countless repeats" and addressed to various spirits for protection on the river or for success in hunting and fishing (R. Price 1990:384). Today, in special contexts, Maroons continue to perform certain songs they say were sung by their eighteenth-century ancestors. These are normally reserved for rituals honoring the First-Time ancestors but they also form important interludes in men's narrations of early history (for numerous examples, see R. Price 1983a). When the great Saramaka historian Tebini recounted the celebration that followed the conclusion of the 1762 peace treaty, he performed several songs that had been sung on that day and then described the *aléle*, a play that is still remembered as the climax of the festivities. He then explained the origin of an *adunké* song, dating from the same moment, that commemorates the frustration of a woman whose jealous husband, named Kwasi, locked her in her house to prevent her from attending the *aléle* play.[5]

By the time they had finished praying, it was the dead of night. The women said it was time to dance—until morning! The men said, "Let's dance. Let's celebrate. Peace has come!" Then they sang out:

Fíí kó,—— kó dén-de fíí—— o.—— Kó dén-de,

"Peace has come, *kó dénde*, Freedom. *Kó dénde*, Peace."

Peace had come. . . . Then they said, "Well, women, it's time to strut your stuff, to dance *aléle*." And they sang out:

Ka- lí- ka- tí tu- lé- le, ka- lí- ka- tí tu- lé- le, ka- lí- ka- tí tu- lé- le, ka-

lí- ka- tí tu- lé- le, ka- lí- ka- tí tu- lé- le, ka- lí- ka- tí tu- lé- le.

Then the women danced *gílin gílin gílin*. The men danced, moving their hips. . . . The house . . . the whole village was going *zzzz* [with excitement]. . . . Well, that night they played *aléle* . . . all night long, *gbele, gbele, gbele*. Everyone was dancing it! . . .

When they finished this celebration . . . one woman said to another, "Child [term of affection], with the size of our celebration at Baakawata, with that fantastic *aléle*, how come *you* didn't show up?" The other said, "Oh! My husband locked me up and left me in the house [because he was jealous]. That [untranslatable pejorative expletive] Kwasi didn't want me to come." Then the first woman sang out [composing a new *adunké* song, still sung today]:

Dií- ta- wén-djè-má- nu, An- dí-mbéi-ián kó na a- lé- le? Hóó-kóó.——

Bê- le- kí- si- gba-da- Kwa-sí- án kê mi kó!——— Hóó- kóó.

"Diítawêndjèmánu [the woman's play name], why didn't you come to the *aléle? Hóókóó* [expression of joy]. [Expletive] Kwasi didn't want me to come. *Hóókóó.*"

The use of songs as social commentary has continued into the present, though their style has been modified over time. Saramakas draw a sharp distinction, for example, between the *adunké* style of popular song, which lasted into the twentieth century, and the *sêkêti* style that displaced it, though the two share certain central features, from the recursive structure of their lyrics to the kinds of incidents and personal idiosyncrasies they depict. A late-nineteenth-century *adunké* song that we heard in Saramaka recounts how a brash young married woman from the Pikilio called out audaciously to her lover during a large play, defiantly publicizing her affair to the entire community and, with the aid of her sister, summoning him to her (see R. and S. Price 1977 for a recording and transcription). The performance that we heard of this song was followed by a description of how the woman's husband, who was also present, angrily tried to grab his wife but caught only her skirt, and how she escaped by running naked through the large crowd.

Today among the Saramaka, popular *sêkêti* songs (like *awawa* songs among the Aluku) treat much the same subject matter, concentrating on local scandals, interpersonal disputes, and the joys and sorrows of lovers. People sing these songs as an accompaniment to the daily round—while harvesting rice, paddling a canoe, carving a comb, composing a textile design, or engaging in any other quiet activity. During the course of a community play, these same songs become a central public activity. Individual men and women take turns performing them as soloists, often while executing a dance, and are supported by a chorus of women who provide the responsive segments and accompany the entire performance with a strong beat of steady handclapping. We illustrate this type of song with the lyrics of a few representative examples, giving the response of the chorus in parentheses. (For additional examples and discussion, see S. Price 1993 [1984]:167–94).

Do you see that walk she's walking?
Woman, I want/love you.
Wilhelmina, the queen.
Mademoiselle, Mademoiselle *sisiyééni* [Sicilian?],
What about it?
Do you see that walk she's walking?
Woman, I want/love you.
(Wilhelmina the Queen)
> [A man expresses his desire for a woman whose way of walk-
> ing attracts his eye. He extends the compliment through refer-
> ence to the former Dutch queen—meaning, in this case,
> someone very special—and adds a further romantic touch by
> calling to her in a foreign language.]

She's jilted me.
Sister-in-law became a co-wife of mine.
(Sister-in-law became a co-wife of mine.)
> [A woman accused her sister-in-law of being unfriendly by compar-
> ing her behavior to that expected of a co-wife.]

Seliso, your mother telephoned.
Yes, yes, your mother.
Seliso, Seliso,
Your mother telephoned.
(Seliso, your mother telephoned.)
> [Because "to telephone" is a euphemism for lying, this simple song
> was an effective way for one man to insult a fellow villager with
> whom he was having problems.]

The rapidity with which these songs pass in and out of the repertoire of
any region is closely related to the focus of their lyrics. As the incident that
inspired each song becomes a part of social history, so does the song itself,
and Maroon popular songs are as short-lived as their counterparts in Europe
and the United States. During 1975, in going over a list of 156 *sêkêti* songs
we had heard in Saramaka in 1967–68, we found not a single one that was
still being sung. Although residents of the region remembered the melody
and lyrics of each one (as well, in most cases, as the incidents that had
inspired them), they had replaced them with a new and equally extensive
pool of songs that commented on more current social events.

The songs sung by Saramaka men engaged in hard physical labor—felling trees with axes or hauling timber through the forest to the river—are very different from these popular songs both musically and linguistically. Small bits of their lyrics are in the language of everyday speech, but most lyrics are expressed in phrases used to communicate with forest spirits or in other esoteric languages, and many of the words are used exclusively for these two types of singing. These long, linguistically complex songs summon a variety of ancestors and gods (especially the forest spirits who have jurisdiction over the part of the forest where the work is taking place), and ask them to give the men strength, to lighten the work, and to provide protection against injury. In a boastful and arrogant tone, the singers describe their strength, courage, and skill, recite their praise names, quote appropriate proverbs, and command the women to fetch water and food. (See R. and S. Price 1972b and, for a recording of a tree-felling song, R. and S. Price 1977.)

In Saramaka, men call on their knowledge of yet other esoteric languages in the songs that culminate certain night-long ceremonies held after a death. *Papá* designates a complex of language, songs, and drum rhythms that are closely associated with the concept of death and surrounded by ritual prohibitions which provide protection from their strong and potentially dangerous powers. Men's *komantí* songs constitute another immensely rich and varied set of musical forms. Other songs, drum rhythms, and dances are performed by male and female adepts in the cults of forest spirits, snake gods, river gods, and sea gods, and in each of the localized "great *óbia*" cults owned by particular clans and villages. And each of the other Maroon groups has its own complex musical repertoire, which overlaps only partly with that of the Saramaka. Indeed, it would appear that the degree of variation present in the visual arts of the various Maroon groups is fully matched or even surpassed by the variation in styles of dance, drumming, and song—although systematic comparative studies are still lacking.

There are indications that stylistic change in song parallels that in other arts but we are unable to describe it in any detail. Saramakas perceive gradual, ongoing change in all kinds of song, and have pointed out to us changes in both *sêkêti* and *papá* singing since the early twentieth century as examples. But until musicologists find ways of analyzing what changes have taken place, for example, since *sêkêti* was first described by travelers in the mid-nineteenth century (Cateau van Rosevelt and van Lansberge 1873: 323–24), we can only echo Saramakas' own assertions of significant change in their vocal music.

DRUMS AND DRUMMING

Among the Maroon performing arts, drumming holds pride of place. Even the folktale that recounts the original discovery of drums in the land of the devils presupposes (anachronistically) that the main characters understand the centrality of drums in Maroon life. Said a son to his dying father:

> Well, the thing known as Drum—I keep hearing its name, but, well, I don't know it firsthand. But wherever Drum may be, I'm going to go get it and bring it back to play at your funeral, play the *apínti* drum at the head of your coffin, even if it's not till the day they bury you, even if it's the seventh day of your funeral, I will absolutely play it at the head of your grave. Because, well, the thing that's called *apínti*, I hear people saying that it's, well, that it's a really important thing in Bush Negro land.

In other words, it is almost as if it were impossible for Maroons to imagine a time when drumming did not exist.[6]

Maroons classify drums not only by their form but also by the role they play in particular types of performance. For example, Saramakas call the kind of drum shown in figures 5.10 and 7.8 an *apínti* when it is played alone as a talking drum but a *tumáu* when it takes on a specialized rhythmic role in the drum choirs that accompany women's *bandámmba* dancing and rites

7.8. Paramaka *apinti* drum, collected late 1920s, on the French Guiana side of the Marowijne River.

for warrior gods or forest spirits. Likewise, the Aluku drum normally called a *tun* is called *atompai*, *sebikede*, or *pudja* in specialized musical contexts (Bilby 1989:57). The major Maroon forms are illustrated in figure 7.9. Different drum choirs and particular styles of drumming mark each of a large number of specialized performance contexts—rites for forest spirits, snake gods, warrior gods or early ancestors; various stages of funeral rites (fig. 7.10); and a variety of secular settings. Each such style of drumming is specialized, sometimes involving formal apprenticeship, and the repertoire of pieces within each style is large and ever-changing. Even in the styles considered, for ideological reasons, least subject to change, such as the Saramaka *papá* drumming that is played during the climactic night of a funeral, there has been significant change and development over time. The *papá* style of today's fifty-year-old masters is recognizably different from that of the oldest living generation of players, and Saramakas make it clear that this has always been the case.

Most Maroon men acquire a basic proficiency in the common drum rhythms, but drumming—in contrast to most artistic talents—is often spoken of as a natural gift, and there is clear recognition of the "masters" in any village or region. Skill in drumming, as in other performing arts, brings prestige. A gifted drummer easily persuades the waiting gods and spirits to

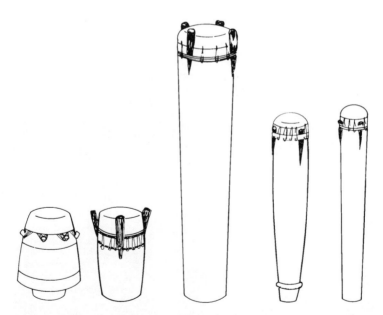

7.9. Five Saramaka drum types (*left to right*): *apínti; deindein* (beaten with sticks), *agidá* (the principal drum at snake-god rites, played horizontally with one stick and one hand); *apúku doón* (the principal drum at rites for forest spirits); and *lánga doón* (the principal drum at *papá* funerary performances).

join villagers through possession, and is rewarded with frequent congratulatory embraces from participants, as well as by food, liquor, cloth, and other gifts. While many drum styles are used throughout a region, others are restricted to particular villages or clans. Regional differences in drumming parallel those in the visual arts. Although a Ndyuka drumming style occasionally becomes fashionable for a brief period in Saramaka, for example, differences in "tribal" drumming styles are as marked as the linguistic differences between the groups.

The *apinti* is a "talking drum" used at major council meetings and at certain important rituals. (It is not unique in its "speech" function—the Saramaka *agidá*, for example, communicates in similar paralinguistic forms with the various kinds of snake spirits.) The *apinti* acts as town crier at certain community events. At Saramaka council meetings, for example, its rhythms officially open the proceedings; summon and greet particular gods, ancestors, and public officials; comment on current events; help set the tone for the meeting through the imaginative use of proverbs; and formally dismiss people at the end. (At the 1992 pan-Maroon Peoples' Meeting held under Smithsonian auspices in Washington, D.C., Saramaka, Ndyuka, and Aluku

7.10. Aluku drummers at a funeral rite (Jean Hurault, *Africains de Guyane*).

apinti players took turns doing similar honors—see R. and S. Price 1994:69–76.) Saramaka oral traditions describe the use of *apínti* drums during the eighteenth century, and the "drum names" used at that time to summon important people to council meetings are still used to summon the spirits of those ancestors today.[7] Each drum phrase can be transposed into a rhythmically similar verbal form (either in one of several esoteric languages or in special *apínti* language), which is translatable into the language of ordinary speech. For example, the Saramaka *apínti* rendering of the proverb "Smoke has no feet, but it makes its way to heaven" is based on the rhythm of the proverb as expressed in the language of their *komantí* warrior gods (*Dabikuku misí améusu*) rather than its form in ordinary Saramaccan (*Simóko án a fútu ma a nángo a gádu*). On the drum, "Good morning," which is simply "*wéki*" in everyday Saramaccan, becomes an elaborate rhythmic phrase which Saramakas verbalize in "*apínti* language" as "*Keí keí dí día, kêtekeí dí día, kilinkilíng kidíng tjêkeledíng ding ding ding . . .*"

We offer here a transcription of an actual *apínti* performance from the beginning of a Saramaka tribal council meeting in 1968. Spaces indicate pauses between phrases, during which one of two simple "holding" rhythms is played; square brackets indicate Saramaccan translations for which we have no verbalized *apínti* equivalents. We do not indicate consecutive repetition of phrases. (For a recording of this performance, see R. and S. Price 1977.)

Ting; tjêkele gín din gín din . . . gilíng.	"Listen"; opening call.
Asantí kotoko bu a dú okáng, kobuá, o sá si watera dján de, djantanási, dum de dum; kediamá kédiampon ódu a sáisi ódu a kêèmponu sasi naná bêtiè.	Recital of the drum's "praise name," including words for its parts (wooden body, pegs, ties, head); call to supreme god and the earth.
Opête nyán opête; sêmbè sindó gêde gêde gêde, sêmbè sindó gêde hía.	Call to junior assistant headmen; remark that "many people have sat down."
Gídi gídi kúndu bi a kúndu; opête nyán opête; kokóti bái batí.	Call to senior assistant headmen; call to junior assistant headmen; call to headmen.
Kásikási têgètêgèdé. Keí keí dí día, kêtekeí dí día, kilinkilíng, kidíng tjêkele ding,	Call to senior women. Good morning; call to the paramount chief; proverb ("However

tjêkeledíng, ding ding . . .; kilíbe tente, odú akásambile fu wán pandási; sekúinya ti sekúinya kata kái na tí sekúinya; [begi].

great the problem, the paramount chief can take care of it"); prayer.

Kediamá kédiampon ódu a sáisi ódu a kêèmponu sasi naná bêtiè.

Call to supreme god and the earth.

Kilíbe tente, odú akásambile fu wán pandási; alíbête benté, bébetiêbenté a falí; otíbilíbití tja ko bêèdjô; kilíng king diá keng dia kéng eti; kásikási têgètêgèdé; fébe tutú máfiakata bánta nási betê; [piimísi]; atupeteezú atuá petee zú ahuun wásikan djáni bobo; [piimísi].

Call to the paramount chief; proverb ("The water hyacinth floats downstream with the ebb tide, but the tide will bring it back up as well"); call for liquor; apologies to the elders; call to senior women; proverb ("When the mouth starts moving, hunger is afraid"); apologies (for anything bad that might have inadvertently been drummed); call to "headmen of the river" (gods); apologies.

Kokóti bai batí; asákpa a pênde, makáiya pênde; gídi gídi bú a fô.

Call to headmen; call (by name) to two important ancestors.

Ahála ba tatá gánda volabutan; Dabikúku misí améusu; [begi]; [piimísi]; kokóti bai batí; kilíbe tente, odú akásambile fu wán pandási; ma in tênè, ma in tênè búa.

Call to city officials; proverb ("Smoke has no feet, but it makes its way to heaven"); prayer; apologies; call to headmen; call to the paramount chief; proverb ("When a leaf falls in the water, it's not the same day that it starts to rot").

Tjaketeke [. . .]; [piimísi]; [gaamá ku mása gaán gádu]; ding ding ding . . ., kokóti bai batí; ding ding ding . . ., gídi gídi kúndu bi a kúndu; gidi gidi bêeyo; ding ding ding . . . .

Proverb ("You can't measure your foot against the paramount chief's"); apologies; call to the paramount chief and supreme god; "The paramount chief is walking"; call to headmen; "The paramount chief is walking"; call to senior assistant headmen; call for food to be brought; "The paramount chief is walking."

OTHER MUSICAL INSTRUMENTS

In spite of the cultural preeminence of drums, Maroons have always played a variety of other musical instruments. Some are combined with drums in prescribed ritual contexts, some are important solo instruments in specific settings, and others are played informally, purely for entertainment. Calabash rattles (fig. 6.7) and iron "gongs" have always been the most widely used accompaniments to drum choirs in specified rituals. For example, rattles play a central role in snake god, forest spirit, and warrior god rites (sometimes in accompaniment to singing without drumming), and gongs—usually composed of a metal hoe blade struck with an old machete blade—are an essential part of plays for warrior gods and *papá* performances.[8] Other, more specialized instruments are associated with particular localized cults—for example, the members of the Nasí clan are said to use a serrated wooden cylinder called a *gombí* or *kumbí* scraped with a second piece of hardwood in certain rites.[9]

Wooden signal horns or trumpets (*tutú*), found today only in a few villages in Saramaka, were until recent times a ubiquitous feature of council meetings, funerals, and certain other public gatherings (fig. 7.11). During the wars of liberation, they were used "to Command Advancing, Retreating, &c" (Stedman 1988 [1790]:540; see fig. 7.12), and the European commander arriving in Saramaka to seal the peace in 1762 was greeted with "horns blaring" (R. Price 1983a:178). During the eighteenth century, wooden trumpets were used for general celebration: "They are blowing *tutù*, some men have returned from the city" (Schumann 1778, s.v. *tutù*). Well into the twentieth century, each important man (and some women) had a "horn name," which was blown on the horn to summon him to council meetings and important rites, particularly funerals. (A separate system of drum names has always been used, as we have seen, in many of the same contexts.) As with the *apínti*, horns not only called names but also spoke in proverbs, and older Saramakas are still able to give the verbal "translations" of certain horn phrases.[10]

7.11. Saramaka wooden signal horn, collected 1928–29 in Dangogo.

Among the Aluku, the use of flutes (which might be related to the fifes reported for eighteenth-century Saramaka) persists in altered form. While in the past Alukus apparently used flutes to communicate between canoes traveling the river, today they use them solely for entertainment. And though they no longer make their own flutes from wood but buy Western models instead (most often recorders), the melodies they play are profoundly their own (Bilby 1989:65).

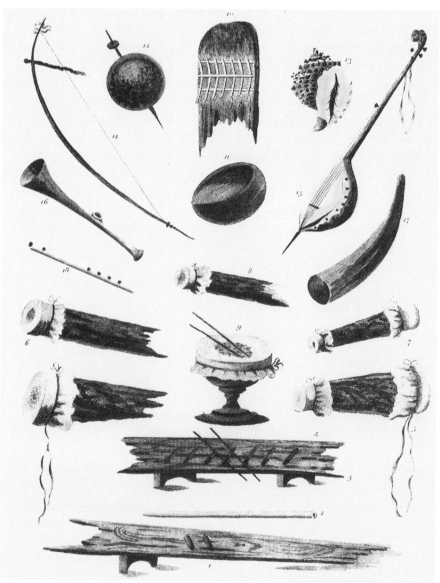

7.12. "Musical Instruments of the African Negroes [Suriname slaves, 1770s]" (Stedman 1988 [1790]:539).

Two other instruments, both of which are played solo and familiarly called *bèntá*, have been important for entertainment throughout Maroon history: the *agwado* or *gólu-bèntá*, consisting of three "musical bows" inserted through a gourd, and the *papái-bèntá* (split-reed *bèntá* or "finger piano"), made from four or five split reeds fastened tightly over two wooden bridges to a flat board (figs. 7.13 and 3.14). Though the *agwado* appears to have disappeared among the Saramaka, it is still played by the Aluku: "The musician holds the instrument between his legs and taps rhythms with his fingers on the gourd as he plucks melodies on the three strings and sings his song" (Bilby 1989:65). In Saramaka, the *papái-bèntá* is a young man's instrument, played for individual pleasure or to entertain others. The gift of *bèntá* virtuosity is held to demonstrate an affinity with forest spirits, and it is said that some legendary players were able to walk on water across the river while playing. Like the rhythms played on the *apínti* and some other Saramaka drums, the *bèntá* plays rhythms that are "transformable" or "translatable" into verbal sounds. Some pieces imitate bird or animal calls, some comment on personalities or current events (much in the manner of *adunké* or *sêkêti* songs), some imitate rhythms played on drums, and others are used in children's games (to indicate, for example, whether the person looking for a hidden object is "hot" or "cold"). We cite as an example the verbal version of a *bèntá* composition that comments satirically on an event in the Saramaka village of Bofokule:

Djebikese kulé butá dí kándu	Djebikese runs to place the "protective charm."
Adombokui kulé butá dí kándu	Adombokui runs to place the "protective charm."
Djebikese kulé tí kangóti	Djebikese runs *tí kangóti* [sound of his running].
Djebikese tungi mi túngi	Djebikese runs *tungi mi túngi*.
Djebikese tá séti bô	Djebikese sets up the bow [a particular type of "protective charm" in the form of a bow].

Both the *agwado* and the split-reed *bèntá* represent important continu-ities with the African past, in terms of their form, their association with forest (and other) spirits, and their imitations of other cultural sounds. Yet the materials used to make them, the particular spirits with which they are associated, and the drum rhythms they imitate are distinctly Maroon—Aluku *agwados* were in the past used in warrior spirit rites (Bilby 1989:65). These instruments represent, then, a good example of the ways in which Maroons adapted widespread African forms (along with some of their asso-ciated meanings) and transformed them into something very much their own.[11]

We know of still other instruments used at one time or another by Maroons, and there are undoubtedly others that have disappeared without a trace. A Maroon "xylophone" was described in the early nineteenth century (von Sack 1810:82–83), but does not seem to have survived. Likewise, Stedman's eighteenth-century drawing depicts other instruments made by Suriname slaves—a musical mouth bow called *benta*, a nose flute, and others (fig. 7.12)—but we have no specific indications regarding their use by Maroons. The most interesting of all eighteenth-century musical instru-

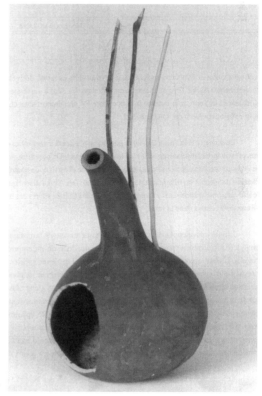

7.13. An Aluku *agwado.*

ments from Suriname is a calabash banjo, made by a slave and collected by Stedman in the 1770s (fig. 7.14). It represents, to our knowledge, the oldest extant banjo from anywhere in the Americas, and is a fine example of the four-stringed instruments made and used at least since the seventeenth century by Afro-Americans in many parts of the hemisphere (see, for example, Epstein 1977:1–46; see also R. and S. Price 1979:131, 138).

Finally, Maroons have always enjoyed novelty in music making, as well as in the other arts. One of the rare eighteenth-century Saramaka converts to Christianity apparently became adept at playing a kind of French (or hunting) horn (R. Price 1990:193–95); late-nineteenth- and early-twentieth-century Maroon visitors to French Guiana occasionally returned with concertinas that they had learned to play; and a set of Yamaha electric instruments imported to Saramaka in the 1970s encouraged young boys to make and master wooden guitars that were excellent copies of the imported plastic-and-chrome models.

RECENT MUSICAL TRENDS

Summing up Maroon music as of the late 1970s, Bilby wrote that it "combined elements from several different parts of the African continent, had remained almost entirely free of European influence . . . [and] constituted what was probably the most thoroughly African musical corpus in the entire Western Hemisphere" (1995:225). But in recent years it has been evolving in new directions and has even been making its mark on the world music scene. Let us listen to the rest of the story as recounted by Bilby, who has been following these trends for nearly twenty years.

7.14. A four-stringed calabash banjo made by a Suriname slave, collected in the 1770s by John Gabriel Stedman.

In the last few decades, a host of vibrant new musics has sprung up from the Afro-Surinamese roots. The three most popular current styles [are] *kawina*, *kaseko*, and *aleke*. . . . The origins of *kaseko*, Suriname's homegrown counterpart to calypso, are not entirely clear. . . . But . . . after World War II . . . it gradually emerged as the all-embracing national popular music of Suriname. . . . Toward the end of the 1970s, a particularly interesting new phase commenced as Maroon musicians entered the *kaseko* scene in full force . . . [with] unprecedented numbers of young people from the interior, especially Saramaka and Ndyuka Maroons, migrating to the coastal towns. They became attracted to the new urban sounds, and within a few years, their contributions came to dominate developments in *kaseko*, which was now often sung in the Maroon languages Saramaccan and Ndyuka as well as Creole Sranan. . . . One could hear the Maroon influence, for instance, in the Saramaka and Ndyuka texts of many songs, in the constant references to Maroon culture and to traditional life in the interior, in vocal and guitar stylings, in the occasional *kaseko* recordings containing sections based on rhythms of one or another kind of [Maroon] *obia pee*, in the transfer of specific Maroon rhythmic patterns to *kaseko* instruments like the *skratji* [bass drum], and in the occasional appearance of actual Maroon drums. Even Creole and Holland-based bands began to incorporate these influences. (1995:222–25)

Bilby goes on to describe yet more recent developments, as eastern Maroon *aleke* music came more fully into its own. Originating in a Ndyuka drumming style called *lonsei*, especially popular in the 1960s when it was played on traditional drums, Aluku *aleke* was, by the late 1970s, "played on an ensemble of three [Maroon-made] conga-like '*aleke*-drums,' a bass drum and high-hat set called *djas* (jazz), and other percussion instruments" (1995:227–28). Bilby's description of what happened next is worth quoting at length, as it follows the migration of Maroon music beyond its longtime rainforest home.

In the shared spaces of coastal Suriname and French Guiana, *aleke* brought together young Maroons from different clans and ethnic groups. By the early 1980s, it had come to reflect the wide range of influences around them, both in lyrics and in sound. Singers experimented with Pentecostal church melodies and French Antillean Carnival tunes; they stripped down reggae rhythms, transferring them to drums and percussion to come up with something like a Rastafarian *nyabinghi* beat. New songs were constantly composed, reflecting contemporary life on the margins of the coastal towns. Many songs were concerned with relations between the sexes, but political commentary became common, especially after the outbreak of civil war in 1986. Many *aleke* songs obliquely denounced the atrocities perpetrated against Maroon civilians by the military government, while other songs called for a healing of wounds and the restoration of democracy, peace, and harmony—a goal that, as of 1995, has yet to be fully accomplished, although fighting has stopped for the time being.

It was not until the late 1980s that Disco Amigo and other [Paramaribo] record stores began bringing out studio recordings of *aleke* on cassette. While the drumming style of *aleke* remains firmly anchored in [Maroon] tradition, many modern *aleke* songs sold on cassette today deal with decidedly modern themes, from AIDS and poverty to the pros and cons of condoms. Yet traditional Maroon concerns remain as much in the foreground as ever, and it is this mixture of new and old that makes *aleke* special: it speaks to the experience of both those living in the traditional Maroon villages and those who have settled in coastal towns. Indeed, on some occasions, *aleke* is still played in the old

7.15. The Aleke band Sapatia, 1987, made up of Ndyukas and Alukus.

way, on traditional Ndyuka drums, and is danced in ring formation; at other times, the same musical style appears in its newer
incarnation, featuring the long drums and *djas*, electrically
amplified vocals, and dance floors filled with couples in close
embrace. One of the latest developments is the emergence of a
new blend called *aleke-kaseko*, played by electric dance bands on
modern instruments. This new type of *kaseko* is among the most
popular Surinamese styles today, both in Paramaribo and the
Netherlands. (1995:228–30; see also Bilby 1990:458–70)

Bilby has elsewhere summed up the recent internationalization of Suriname
musics, including those played by Maroons. "In any random selection of
kaseko, *kawina*, and *aleke* recordings made during the past five years, one is
liable to detect strains of Jamaican reggae and dancehall, Central African
soukous, French Antillean *zouk*, Haitian *kompa*, Dominican *merengue*,
South African *mbube*, Trinidadian soca, North American funk, hip-hop, and
'house,' Brazilian *samba*, or any number of other foreign styles" (Bilby 1999).

But such trends—with "most recent kaseko hits in Suriname having been
by bands made up primarily or entirely of Saramaka and Ndyuka Maroons"
(Bilby 1999)—are not unidirectional. During the past two decades, young
Maroon musicians have been bringing other musics back home. As Bilby
describes it,

> While carrying out anthropological fieldwork among the Aluku
> Maroons in their traditional territory during the 1980s, I was
> repeatedly struck by the extent to which foreign styles of popular
> music with international distribution had begun to penetrate
> their society. One night in 1984, for instance, I was present when
> a Ndyuka *aleke* band, the Alcoa Boys, visited a funeral ceremony
> in the Aluku village of Kotika. . . . Among the songs they per-
> formed that night was a modified version of "Shine Eye Girl,"
> by the Grammy Award–winning Jamaican reggae band Black
> Uhuru; using nothing but *aleke* drums and percussion, they
> accompanied the song with a newly invented reggae-based
> rhythm. (1999; see also Bilby 1990:225–26)

Or again,

> As for the neo-African *aleke* recordings produced primarily for
> Ndyuka Maroon consumption, recent releases, though still
> firmly anchored in older Ndyuka drumming and vocal traditions,
> show evidence of the same cosmopolitan openness displayed by
> *kaseko* and *kawina* bands. A good example is "Mani Mani," by

Bigi Ting. Prefaced by a bit of Brazilian *samba*-style drumming, the piece then kicks off in typical *aleke* style with a section in the Ndyuka language; eventually the melody changes, and the lyrics (quoting a number of hit songs by other Surinamese bands) begin to shift back and forth between Sarnami Hindi [the language of Suriname's East Indian population], English, Ndyuka, and Sranan [the Creole language of coastal Suriname]; this part of the song alternates with yet another section consisting of an *aleke* version of James Brown's "Sex Machine," rendered in an approximation of African-American Vernacular English (over typical Ndyuka *aleke* drumming). (Bilby 1999)

In today's Maroon villages of the interior, then, "traditional" musics such as secular *sêkêti* or ritual *komantí* are sharing the scene with new forms that mix in elements from every corner of the African diaspora—and beyond.

RIDDLES AND FOLKTALES

Saramaka folktales (*kóntu*) are closely associated with funeral celebrations.[12] The immediate goal of every Saramaka funeral (which serves ultimately to usher a recently deceased member of the community into the world of the ancestors) is "to bury the deceased with celebration." Amidst the hectic weeks of drumming, dancing, singing, feasting, and complex rituals that contribute to these festivities, the telling of folktales—which takes place during the night after the actual burial (and for some deaths, on subsequent nights as well)—constitutes a special moment for people of all ages. The setting is more intimate than other funeral-related gatherings, typically involving some thirty to forty kinsfolk and neighbors, who sit on stools before the deceased's doorstep. Together, they in effect agree to transport themselves into a separate reality that they collectively create and maintain: *kóntu-kôndè* ("folktale-land," an earlier time as well as a distant place), where animals speak, where the social order is often inverted, where Saramaka customs have been only partially worked out, and where the weak and clever tend to triumph over the strong and arrogant. For Saramakas, folktales are sharply distinguished from history; *kóntu* are fictions with deep moral lessons for the present, not accounts of "what really happened."[13] Sitting by torchlight or the light of the moon, the participants at a tale-telling wake come face to face with age-old metaphysical problems and conundrums; by turns frightened by the antics of a villainous monster, doubled over with laughter at a lascivious song, or touched by a character's sentimental farewell, they experience an intellectually and emotionally rich evening of multimedia entertainment.

An evening of *kóntu* begins with riddling, a long string of witty prompts and responses performed by two people at rapid-fire pace, ideally without pause, prefaced by the conventional exchange— *"Híliti"* / *"Dáiti."* People memorize the answers they hear others giving to these riddles (*kísi kóntu*) rather than figuring them out on the spot when they take part in the verbal performance, and it is not uncommon for a person to know the answer to a riddle without being able to explain the rationale behind it. Riddles tend to be told in clusters that share a common form—those based on imitation of particular sounds, those that refer to the speaker's father, and so forth. A riddling session we recorded in Dangogo in 1968 gives something of the flavor:

—*Híliti.*

—*Dáiti.*

—A creek splits into twelve tributaries.

—Silk-cotton tree [which has a long trunk topped with a complex branch formation].

—*Híliti.*

—*Dáiti.*

—A single man at the prow of a ship headed out to sea.

—Needle.

—*Híliti.*

—*Dáiti.*

—I make a house for myself. I paint the outside with green paint. I paint the inside with red paint. All the people who are inside wear black jackets.

—Watermelon.

—*Híliti.*

—*Dáiti.*

—Indian up high.

—Awara [a tall palm tree with bright orange fruit]. . . .

—*Híliti.*

—*Dáiti.*

—Two brothers go hunting. They see a tapir behind a stone. One takes a gun and shoots the stone, pierces it, and kills the tapir. The younger one walks through the hole and takes the tapir away. The sister is back in the village boiling its liver and has it ready for them to eat when they return. Who is the cleverest one?

—The sister. . . .

—*Híliti.*

—*Dáiti.*

—*"Kolólo kolólo."*

—Okra's gone from the plate [i.e., the sound of the spoon scraping an empty plate].

—*Hílíti.*

   —*Dáíti.*

—*"Tjobó tjobó."*

   —Dog swimming.

—*Hílíti.*

   —*Dáíti.*

—*"Kalala kom."*

   —Poling stick [of a canoe] hits a rock. . . .

—*Hílíti.*

   —*Dáíti.*

—My father has a dog that barks from morning to night. It's never silent.

   —Rapids.

—*Hílíti.*

   —*Dáíti.*

—My father has a jug. He loads it with water again and again. It never gets full.

   —Ants' nest.

After a few minutes of riddling, someone calls out *"Mató!,"* the opening formula for tales, another responds vigorously, *"Tòngôni!"*[14] At this signal, everyone present steps over the invisible barrier into folktale-land.

By calling out *"Mató!"* a person appropriates center stage as the narrator of the first tale. By answering *" Tòngôni!"* another person assumes the role of *píkima* ("responder" or "what-sayer"), thereby agreeing to punctuate the narration at frequent intervals, usually with the conventional *"íya,"* but occasionally varying with "That's true," "Really!," or "Right," and shifting to the negative ("Certainly not!," "Not at all," or simply "No") at appropriate points in the story. All present informally monitor the conscientiousness of this responder, whose performance is essential to the proper telling of the tale, complaining when the responses are too widely spaced or weakly delivered, and collectively insisting that the telling maintain a clear call-and-response pattern. The teller and responder are often close friends or relatives, and play out their interaction with joking, teasing, and collegial criticism that heightens the pleasure of the session.

Another way in which a teller can frame a narrative involves the explicit suspension of everyday etiquette. For example, before launching into a ribald nugget, one man pleaded for understanding, arguing with mock seriousness that "When you're doing tale-telling like this, there are certain things you say, so everybody please excuse me. If fathers-in-law are present . . . If mothers-in-law are present, we're not doing that kind of [polite] talking. Today is for Anasi-stories, not for father-in-law or mother-in-law matters! We mustn't take offense."

Once underway, a tale should be interrupted periodically by tale-nuggets; Saramakas use the word *kóti* ("to cut [into, across, off]") in talking about this interruptive pattern. Each nugget briefly evokes a longer tale, often simply through a song that plays a pivotal role when fuller versions of that folktale are told. There is a presumption that most people present will be able to grasp the allusion, and this lends further force to the complicitous character of the tale-telling event. The announcement of such a nugget comes without warning, in many cases interrupting the narrator in mid-phrase: "Just as such-and-such was happening [referring to the action currently underway in the main story], I was there." "Really?" the narrator may ask, "And what did you see?" The nugget unfolds in a combination of speech and song (often enhanced by dance and mime), with the narrator of the main tale temporarily taking on the role of responder (and usually providing more varied responses than those punctuating the main tale); the end is signaled with a remark to "go on with your story." The person offering a tale-nugget stitches it into the fabric of the tale it is interrupting in some more or less imaginative fashion—by selecting a nugget that has some intrinsic parallel with the plot or characters of the main tale, by singing a song associated with a character or musical instrument from the main tale, by altering the usual plot of the nugget in order to blend it into the current action in the main tale, or by inserting characters from the main tale into the plot of the nugget.

The aesthetic success of an evening of tale-telling depends explicitly on listeners cutting into longer narratives. When a tale goes on too long without interruption, people chide one another until someone cuts in and restores the evening's rhythmic momentum. As we wrote in *Two Evenings in Saramaka*,

> One late-night contribution by Kandámma was accompanied by frequent criticisms and excuses about the lack of interruptions, as listeners began to feel sleepy and think about dispersing. "Won't somebody cut this tale, my god?!" pleads Asabôsi. Akóbo seconds her concern: "You men should cut it. Those machetes you carry around with you, what about using them?" Kasólu pleads a lack of options: "All I could do would be to make something up," and Akóbo quickly pins him: "Well, make it up then and let's hear it!" But Kasólu (a prolific narrator but a reluctant

singer in tale-telling) still begs out: "I always forget the songs when I sing and it ends up being a half-assed thing." There follows a prolonged silence, broken finally when Asabôsi calls out to Kandámma: "'Mmá, at that time, I was already there. . . .'" At other times, the synergistic effect of frequent interruptions by tale-nuggets builds dramatically, and people almost queue up to make their contribution. When Kasindó interrupted a tale by Aduêngi with a particularly sweet tale-nugget, Aduêngi jumped right back in with a tale-nugget of his own—in effect "interrupting" his own tale and stepping up the rhythmic pace of the session—loudly defending his unconventional move by saying, "If a man kicks you, you have to kick him back." (R. and S. Price 1991:4–5)

The narrator of a tale ends it by any one of several conventions. It might be a simple "That's where my story ends" or "That's as far as my story goes"; it might be a moral lesson, perhaps prefaced by a several-phrase synopsis of the plot; or, if the tale began by noting the once-upon-a-time absence of a particular feature of Saramaka life (polygyny, drumming, all night dancing, etc.), it might be an expression of gratitude to one of the tale's characters for having carved out this aspect of current custom. A tale's "moral" may bear only tangentially on its content or be ironic or humorous, and listeners sometimes volunteer humorous "morals" of their own invention. When the tale ends, there usually follows some mix of compliments on its telling, animated discussion of its content and style, and extraneous conversation—but more or less quickly someone in the gathering calls out "*Mató!*," a second person responds with "*Tòngôni!*," and the next tale is already underway.

Our book about Saramaka folktales makes a point of presenting tales in their full social and performative context. Here we briefly summarize one *kóntu*, in the hope of giving some idea, no matter how pale, of this vibrant oral genre.

> Long ago, there was an old man who had three daughters and three sons. Feeling that his time to die was drawing near, he summoned his children and asked them how they planned to honor him at his funeral. The oldest son said he would cry and cry for days. The oldest daughter said she would dance and sing until her voice gave out. The middle son planned to construct a magnificent coffin and supply great riches to distribute among the guests. The middle daughter would prepare a great feast. The youngest daughter said she would volunteer her sexual favors for every male guest, to assure that they would feel welcome. Finally,

the youngest son offered to discover Drum, and to bring it back to play at his father's graveside. He had heard that the (*apínti*) drum was "an important thing in Bush Negro land," and vowed to make whatever journey was necessary to find it. The old man was indeed pleased.

Three days later, the old man died, and the children did just as they had said. The oldest son's crying was so loud that no one could hear anything else. The oldest daughter sang until her voice gave out, and then she drank an herbal mixture and started right in again.

> (Here, someone briefly interrupted the speaker, relieving his narrative with a fanciful description of a wrestling match between Squirrel and Mouse and a little song in the language of warrior gods. When he was done, he told the speaker to go on with his story, and the tale of the funeral continued.)

The feast prepared by the middle daughter was so lavish that no one in the village could eat another bite.

> ("Well, the man they were burying there was old Anasi's father-in-law," broke in another man, and he went on to describe how well Anasi [the spider] honored him at the funeral:) Anasi captured a little bird and had someone hold it until he was ready to dance. Quietly, he slipped the bird under the front of his breechcloth and began his dance, while the bird sang:

> > *Tjéin tjéin tjééin kína-ee.*
> > *Tjéin tjéin tjééin kína-oo.*
> > *Tjéin tjéin tjééin kína.*
> > *Tjéin tjéin tjééin kína-ee.*
> > *Tjéin tjéin tjééin kína-oo.*
> > *Tjéin tjéin tjééin.*

Everyone rushed to Anasi to congratulate him for his magnificent performance. The bird had already flown off.

> ("And while that little thing was chirping inside Anasi's breechcloth," broke in an old woman, "the Devil was right there, thinking about eating the [old man's youngest] boy." Her song, also in the language of warrior gods, was the Devil's rejoicing over the meal he was about to savor. The

woman signaled the end of her interruption with a conventional phrase, and the principal tale was resumed.)

The beauty of the coffin and the quantity of goods provided were beyond belief, and the youngest daughter's house was turned into a veritable one-woman brothel. Meanwhile, the youngest son prepared for his journey by finding three parrot feathers, three cowrie shells, and three balls of kaolin. He walked along until he came to a river, but there was no way to cross.

(Here, another woman interrupted, describing how Spider Monkey was watching the boy at the river's edge and sang a little song [in conventional "folk-tale language"] about him. Then she passed the narrative back to the main speaker.)

Finally, a large cayman appeared and the boy arranged—in exchange for a payment of one feather, one cowrie shell, and one ball of kaolin—to be transported across on its back. The cayman also promised to be available for the boy's return trip.

(The woman who had last interrupted broke in again: "I was standing right there when the cayman took the boy across," she said, and sang the boy's song to the cayman—in the esoteric language known as *Púmbu*—before turning attention back to the first speaker.)

The boy continued his journey, and was transported across two more bodies of water by two more caymans, providing the same payment to each. The last one offered detailed advice, describing the land of the devils which the boy was about to enter, and specifying exactly which drum would be safe to take. The boy did just as he was told and started back with the correct drum. But he was so struck by its beauty that he couldn't resist trying it out, and sat down to play a little song: *tim! tim! tim! tim!*

> *Kaadím, kaadím, mitóóliaa.*
> *Kaadím, kaadím, mitóóliaa.*
> *Sibámalé, sibámalé.*
> *Kaadím, kaadím, mitóóliaa.*

This song was heard by the devils, who had been away at work, and they rushed back in a fury to punish the trespasser.

(In the final interruption of the tale, a man declared that he had been present at the river's edge as the devils were imploring the cayman to drown the boy, and that he had witnessed another event there as well. He told, in kernel form, the story of a fish that dragged a canoe carrying a woman and her child down into a deep in the river, ending with a song in "folk-tale language" and a conventional phrase that returned attention to the tale of the drum.)

The boy's return journey was filled with suspense. The devils were in desperate, violent pursuit and each cayman insisted on hearing the drum's song before taking the boy on its back. Just as final preparations for burial were being completed, the boy arrived back in the village. He played the drum at the head of his father's coffin, before it was finally carried off for burial.

The tale ended with an acknowledgment of the importance of the boy's journey for Maroon life and a conventional concluding remark: "That's as far as my story goes."

The Changing Same

IN PREVIOUS CHAPTERS, we have explored the richness and variety of art forms produced by Maroon men and women. We have traced their development over the past hundred and fifty years, as materials, techniques, motifs, and styles have evolved from one generation to the next. We have explored the ideological background of these arts—gender associations, ideas about tradition and innovation, attitudes toward copying and ownership, understandings about meaning. And we have followed the arts as they move from context to context—in peoples' homes in the villages of the rainforest, at funeral rites and other community celebrations, in woodcarvers' workshops and souvenir stores on the coast, in the diaries, reports, and photographs of Western observers, in the museums of Europe and North America, and on the stages of Berlin, Washington, and other world capitals. We are now finally ready to confront what is undoubtedly the most difficult, politically charged, and hotly debated aspect of the study of these arts: their deep culture-historical roots.

We will begin by focusing on the formative moment when women and men from a wide variety of West and Central African societies arrived in chains to labor on the plantations of the Guianas, and we will attempt to characterize the challenges they faced and the resources they brought to the task. Following the Maroons into their early years in the rainforest, we will consider their adaptation to an unfamiliar and hostile environment, the ways they drew on their diverse cultural backgrounds to build a new communal life, and the unique cultural synthesis that emerged in the Suriname rainforest in the eighteenth century. We will next review the history of Maroon arts since that initial synthesis, summarizing materials presented in detail in previous chapters. All this will prepare us to address the question of Africa, looking at interpretations of the African legacy put forward in the literature, testing them against the full set of understandings that we have now assembled regarding the culture history of the Maroons and proposing new perspectives on the processes by which once-enslaved Africans joined forces in the Suriname interior to create a life at once indebted to their Old World heritages and responsive to the creative energies of each new generation. By addressing the whole broad sweep of Maroon art history, we make explicit our conclusion that the arts of the Maroons represent a unique balance of continuity and change that makes them, in the fullest sense, Afro-American.

The Formative Years

Building on our initial fieldwork of the 1960s in Suriname, conceptual insights developed in the early 1970s (Mintz and Price 1992 [1976]),[1] and subsequent historical, ethnographic, and museum research that we conducted primarily in Suriname and the Netherlands, the picture of early Maroon culture history that we presented in *Afro-American Arts of the Suriname Rain Forest* suggested that the heterogeneity of the initial groups of escaped slaves was of absolutely central importance in the formation of the cultures and societies they subsequently created in the New World. More recent research (R. Price 1983a, 1983b, 1990) has provided further evidence that each early band of Maroons was composed of Africans who had for the most part been slaves (for varying periods of time) on the same or neighboring plantation(s) in coastal Suriname, but who came from a number of different ethnic ("tribal") and linguistic backgrounds in Africa.

Some idea of the ethnic diversity of the Africans transported to Suriname can be gleaned from the lists of "nations" of origin used by Suriname planters to classify their slaves. At least fifty are mentioned in colonial sources—and labels commonly used by planters, such as "Kongo" or "Koromantee" (the first encompassing a vast and ethnically diverse kingdom, the second the name of a port through which people of varied ethnic origins were shipped), often lumped together slaves who had very different cultural backgrounds. Table 1 illustrates the geographical spread of African ports of shipment for Suriname slaves through time.[2]

TABLE 1. *The African origins of Suriname slaves*

	1650s–1700	1701–1725	1726–1735	1736–1795
Windward Coast ("Mandingos")	—	—	—	43%
Gold Coast ("Koromantees")	2%	12%	61%	23%
Slave Coast ("Papas")	46%	72%	31%	2%
Loango/Angola ("Loangos" or "Kongos")	52%	16%	8%	32%

NOTE: For present purposes, our "Windward Coast" corresponds to the coastal regions of modern Guinea-Bissau, Guinea, Sierra Leone, and especially Liberia and Ivory Coast; our Gold Coast is roughly coterminous with modern Ghana; our Slave Coast corresponds to the coastal regions of present day Togo and Benin; our Loango/Angola stretches from Cape Lopez south to the Orange River.

In Suriname, the cultural heterogeneity of the African labor force was further maintained as a matter of policy. For reasons of security, planters—using a divide-and-rule strategy—routinely separated out newly arrived shipments of slaves, "not putting any two in one Lot, because they would separate 'em far from each other; nor daring to trust 'em together, lest Rage and Courage should put 'em upon contriving some great Action, to the Ruin of the Colony" (Behn 1688:166). And during the first hundred years of the colony's existence, other local management practices further encouraged Suriname slaves to orient their allegiances in New World rather than African directions. Planters routinely refused to break up slave families by selling members to different masters, and made it a practice (for business rather than humanitarian reasons) to avoid separating mothers from children, or husbands from wives. Suriname plantation slaves were, in effect, considered to belong to the soil, and were not to be sold as individuals or even family groups. Ownership changed only when the estate itself changed hands, and even then efforts were made to keep the whole group together on the old plantation. As a result, extended kinship groups and strong attachments to particular localities developed rapidly among the slaves. Not only did the slave force of each plantation soon develop a distinctive character and identity (many, for example, possessing their own recognizable style of drumming), but they also called one another by a special term, *sibi*, originally a form of address for Africans who had shared passage on the same slave ship.

Early Suriname plantations (which were quite large compared to those in many parts of the Americas) were the matrix for a rapidly developing Afro-American culture, including a new (creole) language, a new religious synthesis, and new principles of social organization. Because of high mortality among slaves and severely repressive practices by local planters, the colony could keep up its labor force only by maintaining unusually high levels of imports from Africa. This meant that at any time during roughly the first hundred years of the colony's existence, more than seventy-five percent of plantation slaves were African-born, over half had been brought from Africa within the previous decade, and about a third had arrived only within the previous five years. Those slaves who "marooned" ran off individually or in small groups more often than in large bands, but they usually regrouped in the forest with others from the same or neighboring plantations. Their new communities were constituted, then, of people who were almost all African-born (from a wide variety of societies), with varying degrees of exposure to plantation society and culture, depending on the amount of time they had spent in the New World.

The early bands of Maroons confronted challenges of remarkable complexity. Seeking refuge in a harsh and hostile environment, they were faced with the task of creating a whole new society and culture even as they were being relentlessly pursued by armed troops bent on the destruction of their communities. Let us consider briefly the cultural resources they brought to bear.

First, the members of a Maroon band cannot be said to have shared any particular African culture. Although most of them had spent their formative years somewhere in Africa, they came from a variety of ethnic groups, spread across the whole of West and Central Africa. Except in very limited realms, such people were in no position to try to carry on the cultural traditions of their individual home societies, which would have differed substantially from those of others in the group.[3] Immense quantities of knowledge, information, and belief must have been brought to Suriname in the minds of the enslaved Africans, but they were not able to bring with them the human complement of their traditional institutions. Members of tribal groups of differing status, yes; but different status systems, no. Priests and priestesses, yes; but priesthoods and temples, no. Princes and princesses, yes; but courts and monarchies, no. In short, the personnel responsible for the orderly perpetuation of the specific institutions of African societies were not transferred intact to Suriname. Thus, the organizational task facing the newly escaped slaves was that of creating institutions—institutions that would prove responsive to the needs of everyday life in a largely unfamiliar forest environment.

Second, the members of each band did share at least some familiarity (depending upon the length of their stay on the coast) with the newly developed culture of Suriname slaves. This cultural core—which had been developed on plantations by Africans interacting with one another as well as with Amerindian fellow sufferers and with Europeans—formed an important common base on which Maroons would later elaborate their own way of life.[4]

Finally, although early Maroons could not be said to have shared any particular African culture, they did share certain general cultural orientations that, from a broad comparative perspective, characterized West and Central African societies as a whole. In spite of the striking variety of socio-cultural forms from one African society to the next, there existed, we believe, certain underlying principles and assumptions that were widespread: ideas about social relations (what values motivate individuals, how one deals with others in social situations, the complementarity and relative independence of males and females, matters of interpersonal style); ideas about the way the world functions phenomenologically (ideas about causality, how particular causes are revealed, the active role of the dead in the lives of the living, and the intimate relationship between social conflict and illness or misfortune); ideas about reciprocity and exchange (compensation for social offenses, the use of cloth as currency);[5] and broad aesthetic ideas (which we discuss below). We would suggest that these common orientations to reality would have focused the attention of individuals from different West and Central African societies upon similar *kinds* of events, even though the culturally prescribed ways of handling these events may have been quite diverse in terms of their specific form. For example, the Yoruba "deify" their twins, enveloping their lives and deaths in complex rituals, while the neighboring Igbo summarily destroy twins at birth—but both peoples may be seen to be responding to the same set of underlying principles having to do with the supernatural significance of unusual births. In other words, the sharply divergent practices of deifying twins or killing them may be considered, at a deeper level, variations on a common cultural theme.[6]

For the ethnically diverse Africans who made up any early Maroon group, such deep-level common cultural principles would have represented a crucial resource, providing mutually acceptable frameworks and catalysts in the complex process by which new practices, institutions, and beliefs were developed. As we have seen, the process of culture-building by Maroons involved contributions by individual Africans with unique cultural knowledge, who shared a general openness to new cultural ideas and a firm commitment to forging a way of life together, as well as a familiarity with plantation culture, and certain more abstract, often unconscious, understandings that were part of a generalized African heritage. A hypothetical example may help illustrate how this process unfolded (Mintz and Price 1992 [1976]:46).

Let us imagine that one of the women in an early Maroon band gives birth to twins (or becomes insane or commits suicide or experiences any one of a number of events that would have required *some* kind of highly specialized ritual attention in almost any society in West or Central Africa). It is clear to all that something must be done, but neither the young mother herself nor any of the others from her particular ethnic background possess the special expertise needed. However, another woman, one of whose relatives may have been priestess of a twin cult in another part of Africa, takes charge of the situation and performs the rites as best she can remember them. By dint of this experience, then, this woman becomes *the* local specialist in twin births. Performing the special rites that would be necessary should the twins fall sick or die, and caring ritually for their parents, she may eventually transmit her special ritual knowledge (which represents a fairly radical selection and elaboration of what her relative's cult had been) to others, who themselves carry on (and further elaborate) the new knowledge, as well as the statuses and roles associated with it.

The result of such processes and events, multiplied a thousandfold, was the creation of societies and cultures that were at once new and immensely dynamic. African in overall tone and feeling, they were nonetheless wholly unlike any particular African society. The governing process had been a rapid and pervasive inter-African syncretism.[7]

Twentieth-century Maroon historians show their awareness of the role of such processes in the formation of their societies, though they narrate them in more human, less abstract terms and embed them in their own culture's understandings about interactions between the worlds of humans, nature, and spiritual forces. Modern Saramaka historians recount, for example, the experiences of their earliest remembered ancestors at the end of the seventeenth century, soon after their successful rebellion and escape from the Suriname plantation of Imanuël Machado, which documentary sources allow us to date to 1690 (R. Price 1983a:43–52). These stories evoke individual names and personalities in describing how, during the group's stay at Matjau Creek (while fomenting new rebellions among slaves they had known in whitefolks' captivity, and conducting periodic raids on vulnerable plantations), Lanu, Ayako, Seei, and the other Matjau people were engaged in the everyday process of building new lives in the unfamiliar forests—forging anew everything from horticultural techniques to religious practices, drawing on their diverse African memories as well as their New World experiences with both transplanted Europeans and local Amerindians. They tell how, as these early Maroons prepared their fields for planting, they encountered for the first time local forest and snake spirits and had to learn, by trial and error, to befriend and pacify them. They tell how a mother of twins from the Watambii clan inadvertently discovered, through the intervention of a monkey, the complex rituals that would forever thereafter be a necessary accompaniment to the birth of Saramaka twins. And they tell how newly found gods of war joined those remembered from across the waters in protecting and spurring on Saramaka raiders when they attacked plantations to obtain guns, pots, and axes, and to liberate their brothers and, particularly, sisters still in bondage (see R. Price 1990:18, *passim*).

We would note that the trial and error by which early Maroons learned to identify, befriend, and pacify local forest and snake spirits involved a tightly interwoven complex of pan sub-Saharan African ideas and practices regarding illness, divination, and causality. A misfortune (an illness or other affliction) automatically signaled the need for divination, which in turn revealed a cause—often a previously unknown local deity (previously unknown since these people had never before lived in this particular environment). The idea that local deities could cause illness when they were not respected (for example, by having a field cut too close to their abode in a large tree or boulder) was widespread in rural West and Central Africa, but the identity of the deities, their specific definitions, varied widely.

Here the process of communal divination, with people from a diversity of African origins asking questions together (through a spirit medium or other divinatory agent) of a god or ancestor in order to evoke a detailed picture of the personality, whims, and foibles of a new type of local deity, permitted the codification by the nascent community of new, African-American religious institutions—classes of gods such as *apúku*s (forest spirits) or *vodú*s (boa constrictor deities) or *wínti*s (saltwater gods), each of which had (and has) a complex and distinctive cult, including shrines, drum/dance/song plays, languages, and priests and priestesses. And the establishment of a new kind of ancestor shrine generations later, during the 1840s, by a similar kind of communal divination, shows how ongoing religious change in these communities is similarly produced and sanctioned (R. Price 1983a:5–6). Indeed, such public divination, a kind of communal creation of new cultural forms, works as effectively as it does in part because of the widespread African assumption that additivity rather than exclusivity is desirable in most religious contexts.

While twentieth-century Maroons recounting their early years in the forest envision a repeated process of discovery—an unfolding series of divine revelations that occurred in the course of solving the practical problems of daily life—we might describe the process, rather, as one in which these particular spirits were being created or invented to fit into a generalized religious model that would have been familiar to most members of the various African ethnic groups present.

The Watambii mother of twins provides a somewhat different kind of example of Maroon conceptualizations of this culture-building process. Here the metaphor is not divination but a kind of direct divine intervention. Nevertheless, it represents a precise Maroon way of speaking about the process of legitimizing a newly created institution nearly two centuries earlier. The story, as told to us in 1978 by our Saramaka friend Peleki, runs as follows:

> Ma Zoé was an early Watambíi-clan runaway. Once in the forest, she gave birth to twins. One day she went to her garden, leaving the infants in a nearby open shed. But when she returned for them, she saw a large monkey sitting right next to them. So she

hid to watch what would happen. She was afraid that if she star-
tled the animal, it might grab the children and carry them into
the trees. She was beside herself and didn't know what to do. So
she just kept watch. She saw that the monkey had amassed a
large pile of selected leaves. It was breaking them into pieces.
Then it put them into an earthenware pot and placed it on the
fire. When the leaves had boiled a while, it removed them and
poured the leaves into a calabash. With this it washed the child.
Exactly the way a mother washes a child! Then it shook the water
off the child and put it down. Then it did the same with the other
child. Finally, it took the calabash of leaf water and gave some to
each child to drink. The woman saw all this. Then, when it was
finished, the monkey set out on the path. It didn't take the twins
with it! And the mother came running to her children. She examined the leaves—which ones it had given them to drink, which
had been used for washing. And those are the very leaves that
remain with us today for the great Watambíi twin óbia. (R. Price
1983a:60–61)

Today, this Watambii cult services all twins born in Saramaka, involving
their parents and siblings in a complex set of rituals that draws on ideas and
practices from a variety of West and Central African societies (including the
widespread African association of twins with monkeys). In our view, Peleki,
who was himself a twin and therefore a frequent witness to the Watambíi
rites, is describing—through this metaphorical historical fragment—a particularly pure example of the process of inter-African syncretism. Indeed, it is
almost uncanny that Mintz and Price—several years before we heard
Peleki's story, and thinking as much of early Haiti (Saint-Domingue), where
an elaborated African-American twin cult had been much written about, as
of Suriname—imagined the more general culture-building process in terms
of a hypothetical twin birth.

As for the newly found gods of war who joined those remembered from
across the waters in protecting and spurring on Saramaka raiders, inter-
African syncretism again dominated the culture-building process. Each of
the great war óbias known to us (many of which are discussed somewhere in
R. Price 1983a or 1990), including those with names that point to a particular African people or place, such as Komantí, are in fact radical blends of
several African traditions, forged by processes very similar to the one that
produced the Watambii twin cult.

In early Maroon societies, rapid intermarriage among Africans of different origins, with no efforts we know of to preserve African ethnic lines

through endogamy, quickly created highly creolized societies—but creolized in the inter-African, not Europeanized sense.[8] By the time the Ndyukas and Saramakas signed peace treaties with the Dutch crown in 1760 and 1762, after nearly a century of guerrilla warfare, there were few African-born Ndyukas or Saramakas still alive and their cultures already represented an integrated, highly developed African-American synthesis whose driving force had been inter-African syncretism.[9]

When we go on to consider the subsequent two centuries of Maroon culture history, we are struck by a strong sense of continuity on the level of fundamental cultural principles, in spite of the existence of considerable surface change. From this earliest period of Maroon cultural formation, continuity-in-change—what Amiri Baraka called "the changing same" (Jones [Baraka] 1967)—seems the key theme. Let us now turn back to the arts to examine the way these general cultural processes influenced their development.

In spite of marked differences of form between the arts of one West or Central African society and the next, a large number of fundamental aesthetic ideas were widespread in the region—ideas about the human body as an aesthetic form, notions about rhythm (in music, in speech, in the visual arts), expectations about dynamism and change in the arts, understandings about the relationship between performers and audiences, and the concept of multimedia "plays." Indeed, aesthetics is probably one of the areas of life for which the hypothesis of a widely shared set of fundamental assumptions can be most persuasively argued (see, for example, Armstrong 1971, Lomax 1970, Szwed and Abrahams 1977, Thompson 1966, 1974, 1983). And, as we have seen, certain aspects of the horrendous experience of enslavement and transport tended to further reinforce selected features of this broadly African aesthetic—the stress on individual style and dramatic self-presentation, the openness to new ideas, and the value placed on innovation and creativity.

Out of these shared African aesthetic orientations and common New World experiences emerged a new cultural synthesis that was unique to the Suriname Maroons. Already perceptible in the earliest accounts of these societies, it continued as a dominant thread in the succeeding centuries. In earlier chapters we have laid out its components, including a special appreciation of individuality and personal style; a love of novelty, innovation, and creative playfulness; an expectation of constant change and development in artistic forms; a keen attention to rhythmic interruption in everything from music and speech to woodcarving and patchwork; specific notions concerning color contrast; concepts of formal balance and symmetry; ideas about the relationship of names to the people and things they label; aesthetic principles concerning the human body; and understandings about the nature of meaning in the arts. This complex of features has constituted a central continuous force throughout Maroon art history.

A Recap of Maroon Art History

While the synthesis of aesthetic principles we have just described had already become established in Maroon life by the eighteenth century, the visual arts themselves developed considerably later. Having presented the history of the principal art forms in some detail in previous chapters, we run through them again very briefly here, first medium by medium and then in terms of general kinds of change, in order to lay the groundwork for a consideration of the light that Maroon art history may shed on debates about African-American culture history more generally.

From their very first years in the forest, Maroon men worked in wood. Using axes, machetes, knives, and other tools imported from the coast, they built houses and canoes and made objects such as stools and cooking utensils, but all the available evidence points to an initial absence or extreme poverty of decorative embellishment. The silence about carving by eighteenth-century commentators, who provided extensive documentation on Maroon artistic life in many other realms, combined with the internal evidence of stylistic and technical development seen in museum collections, strongly suggests that woodcarving did not develop as an art form until the first half of the nineteenth century. Over the past hundred and fifty years it has undergone a striking efflorescence and stylistic evolution.

Textile arts followed a parallel course. Some sewing was done from the first, and needles, cloth, and red, white, and blue thread were among the items that Maroons insisted on receiving as a condition of the treaties. Yet neither written descriptions, visual depictions, or museum collections from the eighteenth century suggest that women engaged in decorative sewing as opposed to practical hemming and seaming. Artistically motivated sewing and embellishment seems to have emerged, largely as an art produced by women for men, toward the middle of the nineteenth century, when migratory wage labor altered sex ratios and increased the supply of trade cotton in the villages of the interior. Embroidery was technically developed by the end of that century, and has continued to evolve stylistically right up to the present moment. Toward the end of the nineteenth century, women also developed a new textile art, one in which small pieces of cloth were juxtaposed to create an aesthetically pleasing composition, and this too has moved through a series of distinctive styles.[10]

Calabash carving presents a somewhat more complex picture, and must be considered in terms of both the external and the internal decoration of the shell. Until well into the nineteenth century, calabash decoration, like almost all "calabash" art in Africa, was limited exclusively to the fruit's exterior surface. The earliest examples combine geometric shapes and representational figures in a style reminiscent of several African models. Although in many cases we cannot be certain whether these early examples were carved by Maroons or by plantation slaves (or whether the carvers were African- or Suriname-born), it is clear that this style was at least known to Maroons. By the mid-nineteenth century, when the arts of Maroon woodcarving, embroidery, and cicatrization were in their infancy, this style of calabash carving seems to have been abandoned in favor of two totally new modes of decoration then taking shape. The first was the rigidly geometric, nonrepresentational style with which men embellished the exteriors of two-piece containers. The second was a revolutionary use of the fruit's interior surface; a new technique which utilized broken glass (rather than knives or chisels) was joined with a design style based on roughly symmetrical arrangements of curved bands and soon became a central medium for Maroon women's artistic expression. By the late nineteenth century, the main lines of men's and women's calabash arts were firmly established and aside from regional differences in the definition of figure and ground, the subsequent development of each has been characterized by minor changes within a relatively stable stylistic mode.

Finally, the history of cicatrization closely parallels that of women's interior calabash carving. Absent as a developed art until the mid-nineteenth century, its technique and overall style emerged in a basic form that has remained relatively stable, except at the level of specific designs, for the full course of its history.[11]

It has now been nearly thirty years since we first contested the prevailing image of Saramaka woodcarving as simply "an African art in the Americas" and proposed tentatively that it had its formal beginnings in the Suriname rainforest during the early nineteenth century (R. Price 1970b; see also Hurault 1970). Soon thereafter, we came to similar conclusions regarding cicatrization and textile arts (R. and S. Price 1972a, S. and R. Price 1980). During the past thirty years we have spent countless hours in museum storerooms around the world, made many additional trips to Suriname and French Guiana to conduct further fieldwork with Saramakas, Paramakas, Ndyukas, and Alukus, and engaged in comprehensive research with archival documents bearing on Maroon life in the eighteenth century—none of which has brought to light any evidence that would alter our earlier assessments. Nor has the subsequent research conducted by other scholars in any way modified that picture (see S. Price n.d.).

SINCE THE MAIN ARTISTIC GENRES and techniques first took shape in the nineteenth century, they have evolved in the context of changing materials, demographic shifts, the dynamic creativity of individuals, and the appreciation of novelty that has always contributed to the cultural life of these societies. Several different kinds of processes have been at work.

First, a kind of continuous, almost organic development can be seen in the history of many artistic media and performance genres. Examples include the progression of distinctive styles in woodcarving, changes in the colors and contours of embroidery designs, and the stylistic evolution of *sêkêti* singing and *papá* funerary performances. Such developments, which are long-term and unidirectional, involve shifts in generally accepted concepts of form that gradually become institutionalized ideologically.

Secondly, the introduction of new materials and new ways of using old materials has periodically been exploited creatively by Maroon artists. We have seen, for example, how the arrival of multichrome trade cotton in the stores of coastal Suriname led to the development of narrow-strip patchwork, allowing women to realize their love of bright color contrast more fully than had been possible with the limited color spectrum of the earlier bits-and-pieces textiles. In men's arts, the availability of commercial paints after World War I led to an explosion in the use of color in eastern Maroon woodworking. And when Maroons who had jobs as industrial metalworkers learned to work with sheet aluminum after World War II, they transferred their woodcarving skills to this new medium, which allowed them to overcome certain structural limitations of wood and produce, for example, combs with more pronounced curvature. Such examples suggest that the introduction of unfamiliar materials, rather than fostering radically new arts, has tended to permit or encourage the development of familiar aesthetic ideas in directions not previously possible.

The transfer of ideas and forms from one medium to another has also contributed to the development of Maroon arts. On a general stylistic level, the fact that each person works in more than a single medium means that artistic ideas can flow easily from one to another. This feature of Maroon artistic life has contributed importantly to the distinctiveness of "male" and "female" design styles. We have also seen the importance of conscious copying that crosses boundaries between media. In addition to the examples illustrated in Chapter 6, we might cite a woman's hairdo and a cicatrization design that imitate the radial spokes of a half-finished basket or the parallel between certain woodcarving "teeth" and embroidery stitches of the same names. And virtuoso pieces are occasionally created that reproduce objects from one medium in the materials of another, such as carved wooden versions of "calabash" ladles or "basketry" fire fans.

Virtuoso inventions of this sort, like other new artistic ideas, are highly appreciated, are sometimes named after their originators, and may even be celebrated in song, all of which has favored our efforts to learn how, where, and when they were introduced for the first time. We know from both popular songs and people's commentaries, for example, that the notched version of calabash hand-washing bowls was invented in the late 1950s or early 1960s by Keekete, of Asindoopo, who drew her inspiration from the way men were beginning to carve out the rear portion of their canoes in order to accommodate outboard motors. And we have seen how the ingenuity of a woman from the Saramaka village of Abena-sitoonu, who first sewed the current appliqué style on a breechcloth for her husband, is honored through the term *abena kamísa* ("*abena* breechcloth"), a designation that people often use even when the sewing is executed on garments other than a breechcloth.

Artistic ideas have also been extremely mobile in terms of localities. Throughout Maroon history, contact between people from different villages and regions, as well as members of different groups such as Saramakas and Ndyukas, has led to intermarriage, ritual exchange, political cooperation, and artistic borrowing. A man who marries a woman from a group other than his own is, in effect, importing a set of "foreign" artistic skills and conventions that may be selectively adopted by his fellow villagers. His kinswomen, who supervise the ceremonial unloading of the marriage basket that the new wife brings when she arrives in his village for the first time, are careful to note the artistic features of her calabash containers, the flavor of each specially prepared delicacy, and even the selection of items included in the basket. Over the course of the marriage, some of her cultural imports may be imitated and partially incorporated into local artistry. Or again, when Saramaka men went to work in the gold mining villages along the Marowijne River in the late nineteenth century and when Ndyukas worked at the hydroelectric project on the Suriname River in the 1960s, the scene was set for frequent cultural exchanges. And throughout their history Maroons have engaged in travel explicitly aimed at making use of the special bodies of ritual knowledge and expertise associated with particular groups. Through such contacts, a Ndyuka dance style was taken over and developed by Saramakas in the early twentieth century, the bits-and-pieces patchwork style sewn by Saramakas during that same period resurfaced in the 1970s as the height of fashion among the Matawai, and so on. The recycling process represented by our own introduction in the 1960s of a calfband style from the 1920s must have occurred countless times as styles and techniques traveled, disappeared, and reemerged in new settings, leading in yet another sense to an art world characterized by the changing same.

And then there are the short-lived fads and fashions, artistic ideas that move rapidly in and out of the universe of any Maroon group. In contrast to unidirectional trends, these fads and fashions do not reflect fundamental changes in aesthetic ideas. Always innovative and surprising on the micro-level, they nevertheless represent "more of the same" when viewed from a distance. As Jean Hurault has pointed out for the Aluku, the introduction of new fads is particularly lively among the young, producing a rapid turnover in everything from woodcarving motifs and play languages to children's games and popular songs (1970:91). In earlier chapters we have cited examples from every Maroon group—dramatic changes in the length and width of men's necklaces and breechcloths, subtler variations in the size and placement of stripes on legbands, the endless succession of decorative "teeth" in woodcarving, the fleeting popularity of particular secular dances. In short, the rate of change in contemporary Western culture (often attributed largely to market forces)—whether in the fashions of Paris women's clothing, the fads of North American teenage footwear, or the turnover of songs on the industrial world's hit parade—is fully matched by the pace of innovation and obsolescence in Maroon sartorial and musical domains.

Finally, moving to the opposite extreme from fads and fashions, we come to a consideration of the kinds of change that cut across the whole range of artistic media, where we note several very gradual, unidirectional developments. Generalizing broadly, we have seen that larger patterns have tended to give way to smaller ones, that intricacy and busyness have increased, that a relatively simple tripartite color scheme has been largely replaced by fuller exploitation of the color spectrum, and that irregularity and asymmetry have yielded to greater uniformity and symmetry.

The long-term reduction in the overall size of designs is perhaps most easily seen in the arts of woodcarving and cicatrization. Increased intricacy is especially evident in the development of embroidery (compare, for example, late nineteenth-century designs with cross-stitch patterns from the 1970s) and woodcarving (where the simple circles and crescents of Style I gradually evolved into the complexly textured designs of Style IV). The gradual trend toward regularity and symmetry is particularly striking in the textile arts and in woodcarving—in the near-total disappearance of free-form embroidery, for example, and its replacement by highly geometrical compositions, in the gradual regularization over time of bilateral symmetry in narrow-strip capes and woodcarving designs, and in the parallel development of an insistence on the regular alternation of over-and-under bas-relief ribbons in woodcarving and warp and weft strips of cloth in patchwork. Long-term trends in the uses of color can most readily be seen in textile arts and eastern Maroon painting: by the 1930s the red, white, and navy combinations that had dominated turn-of-the-century embroidery and patchwork had given way to the use of a strikingly varied set of colors, and the red, white, and black color scheme that early-twentieth-century Aluku, Ndyuka, and Paramaka men used to embellish their woodcarvings blossomed into the almost electric multichromatism of the post–World War II era.

We would suggest that these long-term unidirectional trends in the arts may be related to broader developments in Suriname Maroon societies— their changing relationship to the world outside and the resulting changes in their self-perception and ideology. We might tentatively relate the shift toward greater regularity (fewer free-form designs, more insistent symmetry) and more concern with technical exactitude to increased exposure to Western technology, in particular to the products of literacy (magazines, newspapers, books). This trend has been accompanied by a gradual shift in the balance of gendered aesthetic principles, with the more mechanically oriented, Western-influenced men's styles gaining precedence; for example, embroidery designs marked out by men with a carpenter's compass and straight-edge largely won out over female-marked free-form designs, and some women taught themselves how to "mark" designs in the "men's" mode. Women's cross-stitch embroidery—often copied from (or based freely upon) examples in needlework books—represents another extreme along this continuum, as does the arrival of Maroon men on the pop music scene of Paramaribo and Cayenne. We are thinking less, however, of a simple process of direct "Westernization" (as the last two examples might imply) than of the subtle and gradual influence of Western notions of technical regularity, straight lines, and male technical dominance, which we believe have strongly influenced the course of Maroon arts since the mid-nineteenth century as a consequence of increased contact between Maroons and the society of the coast. If some outside critics have denounced the effect of these changes as the triumph of technique over aesthetic integrity and declared nostalgic longing for the good old days (see, for example, Hurault 1970:90), it should be remembered that it was this same trend toward regularity and symmetry that produced the woodcarving style of the 1920s, considered by these same critics as the very height of Maroon artistic accomplishment.

More generally, we would suggest that the initial blossoming of aesthetic sensibilities into technically and stylistically definable art forms during the second half of the nineteenth century was triggered in complex ways by economic developments in the Dutch colony and its neighbors, which opened up wage-labor opportunities for Maroon men, increased the consumer offerings that they could buy with their earnings, altered the sex ratios in Maroon villages by giving men an incentive to spend years at a stretch away from home, and in this way fundamentally altered the tone of marriage and the relationship between men and women in the villages of the interior. These developments not only made large amounts of imported trade cotton available, but also encouraged women to explore ways of turning it into artistic offerings that could play into their efforts to attract husbands from a diminishing pool of available men. And it was in this same setting that women began devoting considerable artistic attention to the development of calabash carving, mainly on bowls that they used to enhance the visual attractiveness of their husbands' meals.

THE SEARCH FOR AFRICAN CONTINUITIES

Most attempts to understand the contribution of Africa to the cultural history of Maroons have reflected one of two conceptual visions. In the first, Maroon societies are viewed as some *particular* African society simply transplanted to South American soil—such a view might argue, for example, that a substantial cohort of Ashanti slaves, joined by a smattering of slaves from other African groups, recreated in the interior of Suriname a more or less faithful copy of the society and culture they had left behind. In the second view, Maroon cultures are seen as mosaics, as the product of contributions from a number of ethnic groups in Africa whose juxtaposition was fixed some three hundred years ago in the rainforest, and whose discrete individual origins are still identifiable. Divergent in certain respects, these two approaches nevertheless share a fundamental assumption about African-American culture history—the notion of cultural stability over time. Each assumes that if not for external pressures for change and assimilation to another way of life, Maroon societies (whether "transplants" or "mosaics") would retain their original shape and remain suspended in time.

Behind such views, and perhaps motivating them, is the myth that so-called primitive societies exist outside of history, that they are strongly resistant to change, and that if they are seen to evolve in new directions it is only because of the impingement of other (typically, "Western") societies (see S. Price 1989). In the case of the Maroons, this myth has a specific corollary, which is that resistance to change reflects a conscious fidelity to Africa.

In fact, we now know that societies differ enormously in their attitudes toward change and in their degree of internal cultural dynamism. And, as we hope to have shown in earlier chapters, Suriname Maroon societies, like the vast majority of societies in pre-twentieth-century West and Central Africa, have always been particularly dynamic. For Maroons, change has never been equated with assimilation into the world of whitefolks or urban Creoles, and it has never been considered in any way an infidelity to a collective African past or their allegiance to that generalized land of origin. On the contrary, Maroons have always found it possible to be fiercely anti-European in their outlook yet enthusiastically supportive of creative new cultural ideas developed on their own terms. Indeed, the fact that the original groups of ethnically diverse escaped slaves shared no one set of African beliefs, institutions, or cultural forms made them particularly inclined to understand cultural change not as loss and attrition, but rather as a creative way of making things truly their own. It will be useful to examine more closely the discrepancy between the views of change held by Maroons and those held by outside observers in order to propose fruitful avenues for the interpretation of their culture history, and more specifically of their arts.

Maroon societies have often been portrayed as a direct offshoot of Africa. Scholarly articles bear such titles as "Little Africa in the Americas" (Kahn 1954), "We Find an African Tribe in the South American Jungle" (Vandercook 1926), "African Customs and Beliefs Preserved for Two Centuries in the Interior of Dutch Guiana" (van Panhuys 1934), and "Africa's Lost Tribes in South America: An On-the-Spot Account of Blood-Chilling African Rites of 200 Years Ago Preserved Intact in the Jungles of South America by a Tribe of Runaway Slaves" (Kahn 1939). In a book describing their experiences among Maroons in the 1970s, two African-American visitors declared that "we had never expected the people to be this classical, . . . this purely African and isolated from the outside world. . . . It seemed that for every mile we had traveled into the rain forest we had traveled back about a year in time, until we had gone back more than two centuries," thus elaborating on their earlier assessment that twentieth-century Maroon communities were "more African than much of Africa" (Counter and Evans 1981:32–33; n.d.:2). As an earlier visitor had put it, "The flush tides of imperialism have passed over these people, leaving them practically unaltered and unknown, unique among the Negro peoples of the world. They still maintain the life of jungle dwellers of the immemorial past" (Kahn 1931:3).

The arts have figured importantly in this image. Philip Dark subtitled his book *Bush Negro Art* (1954) *An African Art in the Americas*, a Dutch observer declared that Maroon woodcarving was "an original African art form" (Volders 1966:141), and in an article entitled "Bush Negro Art," Melville Herskovits characterized Maroons as having "remained faithful to their African traditions [thus presenting] the unique phenomenon of an autonomous civilization of one continent—Africa—transplanted to another—South America" (1930:160).

Such general claims that the Maroon arts are, as Kahn put it, "African survivals" (1931) are often supported by visual comparisons of Maroon objects and carefully selected look-alikes from particular African cultures, aimed at pinpointing the specific source of inspiration. One scholar presents side-by-side images of an Akan throne from Ghana and a Saramaka peanut-grinding board from Suriname (see fig. 8.1), commenting that "the Akan preference for arabesques in openwork, for even-sided flat bands, and for brass studs to enhance curvilinearity . . . [is] also present, rearranged and reconsidered" in the Maroon carving (Thompson 1970:18).

A second example of this "matching" strategy is provided by William Fagg, who suggests that there exists a "marked affinity" between the carving styles on stools made by the Duala of Cameroon and those made by the Suriname Maroons, and backs up his position by illustrating a Duala stool (see fig. 8.2) and pointing to its "resemblance of form and feeling to the generally sinuous character of Bush Negro carving" (Fagg 1952:121–22).

And a third example can be seen in the juxtaposition of textiles from both sides of the Atlantic (fig. 8.3) to support an argument that the "vibrant visual attack and timing" of African-American patchwork, especially that of the Maroons, is "unthinkable except in terms of partial descent from Mande cloth" (Thompson 1983:208).

We have argued that this research procedure, an ideologically driven enterprise in which similar looking pieces are juxtaposed as evidence of specific historical connection, relies on methodological practices and

8.1. An Akan throne made about 1700 and a Saramaka peanut-grinding board collected in 1929. (See also figs. 5.51, 3.12.)

8.2. "Carved stool from Duala, French Cameroons" (Fagg 1952).

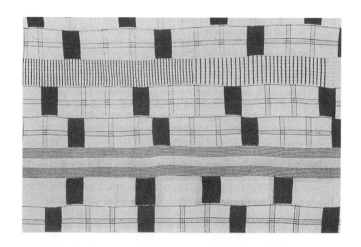

8.3. Narrow-strip textiles: *top,* "early Asante cloth of the nineteenth century, when weavers were working under Mande influences"; *bottom,* a "splendid multistrip cape" from twentieth-century Saramaka (Thompson 1983:215–17).

conceptual premises that are flawed. It is based on a biased selection of examples; it infers specific historical continuities on the basis of visual similarity; it underestimates Maroon agency and creativity; and in focusing on form rather than process, it misconstrues the nature of cultural change.[12]

Clearly, a determined researcher who is intent on proving a chosen historical scenario can almost always locate some objects or design styles in one tradition that closely resemble some objects or design styles in another, even when dealing with peoples that have had virtually no contact with each other. Compare, for example, the two carvings illustrated in figure 8.4—an Alsatian chair carved with an interlaced motif from the High Middle Ages and a Saramaka peanut-grinding board carved in the 1960s. Or again, note the similarity between the designs on a bone betel-chewing implement from Indonesia and a calabash drinking bowl from Saramaka, illustrated in figure 8.5.

8.4. Interwoven ribbons in woodcarving: *left,* a mid-nineteenth-century Alsatian chair known as *"Brettstellstuehl,"* carved in a motif from the High Middle Ages; *right,* a twentieth-century Saramaka peanut-grinding board (see fig. 5.9).

8.5. Designs carved (*left*) on a bone lime tube from Timor (Indonesia) and (*right*) a Saramaka calabash drinking bowl from Asindoopo.

The task of finding visual matches within pools of Maroon and African materials is, of course, much easier than that of pairing Maroon art with objects from Alsace or Indonesia, since the historical connection between the Maroons and West and Central Africans has in fact lent greater visual resemblance to their arts. But this does not mean that one simply emerged from the other. As we have already seen, much happened between the arrival of Africans in Suriname, in the late seventeenth and early eighteenth centuries, and the development of the Maroon arts being held up as African survivals—arts which emerged only in the mid- to late nineteenth century. It is both obvious and undeniable that, as we have already argued, common threads of different sorts run through the artistic life of the Maroons and those of any number of West and Central African societies. At the same time, because the cultural fabric of each of the many groups in this transat-lantic complex is so richly textured, because influences from so many other sources have been woven into each of them over the centuries, and because art is such a fundamentally creative undertaking, it is essential not to assume that this relationship takes the form of (uninterrupted) visual con-tinuities. We need, in other words, to go well beyond a look-alike logic and to trace the evolution of Maroon arts in the context of their full social, eco-nomic, and cultural settings as they unfolded over time in the New World. We return briefly to our three examples of African/African-American matches in order to clarify the argument.

First, the carving on the Akan throne and the Maroon peanut-grinding board. Regarding the "arabesques in openwork," we have seen in Chapter 5 that Maroon openwork developed only during the second half of the nine-teenth century. Likewise, the Saramaka use of brass studs—which Hers-kovits, too, interpreted as "the survival of the African ornamentation of woodwork with iron" (1930:162–63)—represents no simple historical conti-nuity. Brass studs came into use on Saramaka woodcarvings only in the mid-nineteenth century, when trading contact with the coast was regular-ized. And the fact that in the 1920s carvers from upstream villages made more frequent use of studs than men living in villages closer to the coast was not due to a survival of the use of metal in, as Herskovits put it, "the deep interior . . . where the African elements have been most faithfully retained," but rather by the very different patterns of wage labor and atti-tudes toward coastal goods that existed in the two regions at that time (with upper river men migrating to the coast more often and for longer periods of time).

Secondly, the stools. Although both Herskovits (1952:158) and Fagg (1952) saw Maroon stools as an African survival, and others have claimed that they were derived directly from Ashanti models (Volders 1966:141), historical research reveals that the curved, sometimes crescential stools whose origins these scholars were attempting to pinpoint were first made by Maroon woodcarvers only in the late nineteenth century. It has also become clear that these stools were at first simple and relatively unembellished, and that they were only gradually developed, with the popularization of piercing and brass studs, into the sometimes elaborate compositions that have been seen as reminiscent of African models. Indeed, the strongest Maroon parallel for Fagg's Duala stool known to us dates only from the first quarter of the twentieth century and the stool with the next most striking resemblance was carved in the 1960s (figs. 8.6, 8.7). Furthermore, we now know that the Amerindians with whom Maroons were in direct contact from their earliest years in the forest carved stools with curved seats that could also have provided models (fig. 8.8; see also Ahlbrinck 1931:fig. 79).

Finally, in the realm of textiles, our caution regarding the interpretation of Maroon arts as holdovers from specific African traditions follows a similar logic. The Maroon form that bears the closest visual similarity to an African textile form is clearly that of narrow-strip patchwork cloths, and yet, as we have seen, these represent an art that did not develop until the twentieth century, when changing consumer offerings in the stores of coastal Suriname and changing economic opportunities for Maroon wage laborers provided fertile soil for the implementation of aesthetic preferences that had previously found expression in completely different realms of life. We elaborate this example at the end of this chapter.

We wish to emphasize that our rejection of these proposed continuities of form, and the methodology used to discover and document them, is in no way intended to cast doubt on the monumentality of Africa's cultural contribution to Maroon life. Rather we are making a plea for greater recognition of the importance of the initial process of inter-African syncretism and the pervasive changes that occurred during the subsequent centuries of Maroon history. Two brief examples will illustrate this distinction. Finger pianos, which can be traced to African origins as firmly as any object in the Maroon repertoire, are used to imitate the latest Maroon drum rhythms and songs, not to repeat those of seventeenth- or eighteenth-century African ones, and they put the player in a special relationship with specifically Maroon (not African) forest spirits. And fighting rings and bracelets, which have specific historical parallels in many parts of Africa and were described by missionaries living with Maroons during the period immediately after their peace treaties in the mid-eighteenth century, were made of filed-down pieces of sugar-mill machinery from coastal plantations and used as part of a distinctly Maroon process for the settlement of disputes, a process developed in the New World.

8.6. A Saramaka crescential stool, collected 1928–29 in Botopasi. (The stool was destroyed during the allied bombing of Hamburg in World War II.)

8.7. A Saramaka stool carved 1966 in Lombe for John C. Walsh in dual celebration of his birthday and the rescue of the 5000th animal (a giant armadillo) from the rising waters behind the Afobaka dam (Walsh and Gannon 1967).

8.8. Three Amerindian stool forms from Suriname.

Without in any way questioning the poignancy of those formal continuities that have been maintained by Maroons, we wish merely to call attention to the limitations posed by an exclusive focus on form, by a search for African cultural "traits," and by an essentializing vision of African societies as discrete, stable cultural units that contribute identifiable bits and pieces to the fabric of Maroon life. How, then, can we redefine our undertaking to reflect an awareness of the full environment in which Maroon cultures, and more specifically Maroon arts, developed and continue to flourish?

PROCESS OVER FORM

In this final section, we wish to propose the usefulness of turning one's attention away from comparisons of particular African and African-American forms and focusing instead on the creative processes that have generated them. Our research in the Guianas, combined with our reading of the literature on African-American culture history more generally, has persuaded us that if the Maroons of Suriname and French Guiana may be said to be the "most African" of all African Americans, it is not because they have "retained" more African cultural traits than their brothers and sisters elsewhere in the Americas. In fact, in many domains they have not. Rather, it is often the case that a tenacious fidelity to African forms by a given African-American society reflects the stagnation of once-vital cultural principles from the African past. And that a readiness to extrapolate new forms from old reflects a maintenance of the internal dynamism, the ability to grow and change, that constitutes one of the most striking features of West and Central African cultural systems.

For example, in a study of African-American personal naming systems (R. and S. Price 1972b), we were able to demonstrate that the strength of African influence on the actual pool of names in use within a given society is often inversely related to the strength of African influence on ways names are created, used, and attached to their bearers. That is, we found that societies with a relatively high proportion of (lexically) African names (such as Cudjo, Kwasi, or Chitunda) could diverge sharply from African models in terms of the ways that names are created, conceptualized, and used, while other African-American groups with very few lexically "African" names remained extremely similar to African systems in terms of broader principles and practices of naming.

The difference can be seen by comparing naming practices of the Gullah, in coastal South Carolina and Georgia, with those of the Saramaka Maroons. Among the Gullah, a locally used name is "nearly always a word of African origin" (Turner 1949:40), while in Saramaka, African words represent only about one-sixth of the names in use. We would suggest, however, that the Saramaka, whose cultural traditions were developed with minimal Western influence, have enjoyed the freedom to be mildly prodigal with their gradually declining pool of lexically African names at the same time that they have remained more faithful to West African naming principles at a deeper level. We have in mind such principles as the naming of newborns after events that occurred during the mother's pregnancy or particular circumstances of the birth itself; the subsequent accumulation of additional names in recognition of the person's appearance, personality, or life experiences; the danger of pronouncing certain "heavy" names assigned to a person early in life; the practice of intoning strings of "praise names" as a kind of ritual boasting; an etiquette of name avoidance in favor of elliptical equivalents; and verbal play in which, for example, a woman named *Sakuima* is also called *Atasakwe* (translatable as "Thresher" and "She Is Threshing," respectively), or a man whose name is *Asipei* becomes known also as *Luku-fesi* ("Mirror" and "Face-Looker").

Roger Bastide, considering the general question of "Africanisms" in the New World, drew a distinction between African-American religions that are *en conserve* ("canned" or "preserved")—such as, he claimed, Brazilian *candomblé* or Cuban *santería*—and those that are *vivantes* ("living"), like Haitian *vodoun*. The former, he argued, represent a kind of "defense mechanism" or "cultural fossilization," reflecting a fear that any small change might bring about the end, while the latter are more secure of their future and freer to adapt to the changing needs of their adherents (1967:133–55).[13] As he argued, African-American adaptation to changing conditions "does not imply breaking with the past. It is in point of fact the most touching evidence for fidelity. Survival does not imply rigidification, separation from the ever-changing flow of life. . . . On the contrary, survival presupposes plasticity" (1967:45).

It can legitimately be argued that of all African-American peoples, the Maroons of the Guianas have had the greatest freedom to combine and extrapolate African ideas and to adapt them creatively to changing circumstances. This perspective, which focuses attention on process rather than form, helps us to understand why observers of Maroon life find it so "African" in feeling even though it is virtually devoid of directly transplanted African systems.

THE CULTURAL HETEROGENEITY of the original Maroons gives the immediate lie to the notion of a whole African civilization having been transplanted to the New World. And our examination of the initial processes of culture-building, as well as our review of the extraordinary panorama of change and development since those beginnings, should shake the credibility of the view that an African mosaic was, early on, cemented together once and for all deep in the forests of the Guianas. What we might imagine instead (recognizing that it has all the weaknesses of a partial metaphor) is a kind of kaleidoscope, in which the principles of combination are broadly African (and shared by most Maroons), the initial multicolored chips come from a diversity of African societies, and new chips (Amerindian, African, European) are added from time to time.

Let us pursue this image further. There are, on the one hand, the central, fairly stable principles at the heart of the system—broad aesthetic ideas, including attitudes about dynamism and change. And on the other hand there is an original vocabulary of forms from a variety of African sources, with further forms from African, Amerindian, and other sources added as time goes on. Such a general device, because of its very nature, would assure that invention or creation would often mean reinvention or recreation. And such processes are frequently attested to in Maroon history—both within and across the boundaries of particular areas of culture. In fact, the whole culture history of the Maroons has been characterized by such continuity in change, by creative and dynamic processes operating within a general framework of broadly African aesthetic ideas.

Earlier we suggested how this system worked through time in the realm of personal naming patterns. Three more examples—calfbands, cloth names, and patchwork—which pick up on specifics introduced in previous chapters, may further clarify the ways in which continuities with a broad-ranging African heritage, the influence of Amerindian and European contacts, and the input of innovative individuals have come together to produce cultures that are African-American in the fullest sense of the term.

CALFBANDS. Many seventeenth-century Africans wore fiber ties, sometimes strung with beads, just below the knees, and these were among the few material items that survived the Middle Passage to arrive intact in Suriname (fig. 8.9). As we saw in Chapter 4, Maroons have, at every point in their history, had the option of wearing some kind of ornamentation on their calves—simple strings, white "crocheted" bands, colorfully striped bands (often embellished with braided ties or tassels), or strings hung with feathers, tassels, shells, or animal teeth. One might therefore be tempted to view Maroon calfbands as a direct continuation in the Americas of a specific item of African dress. But the origin of Maroon calfbands becomes more complex as soon as we take into consideration the full range of models available to slaves and early Maroons. Stedman's account of Suriname Indian dress in the eighteenth century, for example, describes how the young girls wore "a kind of *Cotton Garters* round their ankles, and the same under their knees, which being very tight, and remaining for ever, occasions their Calves to Swell to an enormous degree, by the time they are grown Women" (Stedman 1988 [1790]:308). In fact, the specific parallels include much more than the garment itself. Among both Maroons and Amerindians, the bands are intended to fit as tightly as possible, even to the point of serious discomfort; ideals of physical beauty favor large calves, which the constricting bands are thought to enhance; the bands may be fashioned either on a wooden cylinder or directly on the wearer's legs; the single-element, interlooped stitch (executed from left to right with an eyeless needle in a continuous circle) is identical in the calfbands of Maroons and Amerindians; and, to cap it all off, the Maroon term for calfbands (*sepu*) is of Amerindian origin. (On Suriname Amerindian calfbands, see Roth 1924:105.) This, then, is an example of a form that was both familiar to the early Maroons from African precedents and shaped by contact with local aboriginal cultures, most notably through new construction techniques.

But the Maroons also developed the idea of calf ornamentation in ways that were uniquely their own and that responded to general trends in their art and material culture. The decline in the popularity of men's ritual jewelry during the early twentieth century coincided with the abandonment of protective hangings on calfbands, and the dramatic efflorescence of color in Maroon woodcarving and textile arts was paralleled in contemporaneous calfband fashions, as pure white gave way to models with conservative monochrome stripes and later to bold combinations of multicolor stripes,

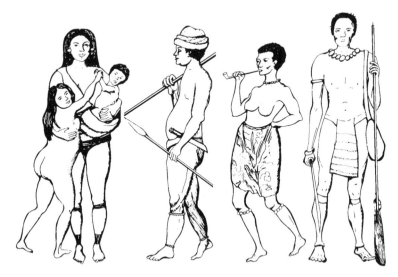

8.9. Calfbands worn by (*left to right:*) an eighteenth-century Carib Indian in Suriname, an eighteenth-century African in West Africa, an eighteenth-century African arrivant in Suriname, and a nineteenth-century Maroon.

THE CHANGING SAME

edging decoration, and large yarn tassels. Maroons also made calfbands their own in other ways: the cylinders and needles used to construct them and the "corncob" utensils used to clean them were all embellished with distinctively Maroon styles of woodcarving; they created special forms for infants just learning to walk; they turned calfbands into an explicit emblem of a wife's faithfulness and affection; they institutionalized them as an important part of burial rites; and they assigned to different styles the kinds of specific regional associations that characterize every kind of Maroon artistry.

CLOTH NAMES. The names that Maroons attach to particular cloth patterns also reflect the process by which African cultural principles were creatively implemented in the New World. In Chapter 4 we saw how the introduction of particular clothing styles, jewelry, cloth patterns, and hair-dos is celebrated by the bestowal of special names. As fashions come and go, as particular fads rise and fall in popularity, so do the names and terms that are coined to refer to them. Praise gives way to derision, and linguistic connotations shift along with the fashions themselves. (For more on the role of terminology in Maroon fashion history, see S. Price 1993 [1984]:162–64.)

Among the hundreds of cloth-pattern names that we have heard, none is recognizably "African" in origin (in contrast to the words used in many areas of life—see, for example, R. Price 1975a). Yet the principles of the system— the ways in which special labels are assigned, used, manipulated, and eventually discarded—display striking parallels with those that have been reported in West and Central Africa (see, for example, Lamb 1975, Mack 1980, Posnansky 1992, Rattray 1927, Warren and Andrews 1977). The similarities begin with the importance accorded to "the language of fashion," and especially the creative assignment of names to individual patterns, whether on locally woven cloth (in Africa) or imported trade cotton (in Suriname).

The kinds of names that are invented, though not the names themselves, are generally similar. Some commemorate events—compare, for example, *gaamá baasá gaamá,* "chief embraces chief" (in honor of a meeting between Saramaka Chief Aboikoni and Ndyuka Chief Akoontu Velanti) and *kyere 'twie,* "catch the leopard" (after Ashanti King Kwaku Dua I gave orders to have a leopard caught alive). Some pick up on visual similarities with plants or animals—*kankan fátu,* "blackbird fat" (for a cloth as orange as the fat of a blackbird) and *asambo,* "breast of the guinea fowl." Others refer to wealth or prices—*ôndo kólu,* "a hundred guilders" (for a particularly expensive grade of trade cotton) and *nyawoho,* "he has become rich" (for a cloth that, it was said, only a person worth £1000 in gold dust was allowed to wear) or *silaliko ópo lágima,* "Suralco raised up the poor man" and *biribi ne hia nse,* "there is nothing so bad as poverty" (a poor man's cloth). Others express respect for political leaders and royalty—*wemína bánti*, "[Queen] Wilhelmina's belt" and *mamponhema*, "the Queen Mother of Mampon." Others honor professional entertainers—*makeba* (after Miriam Makeba performed in Paramaribo) and *suom gye wo adowa* (the name of a popular song by the African Brothers Band of Ghana). And still others reflect sexual jealousies—*siló a bédi*, "sloth in bed" (after a Saramaka woman's caustic remark when her husband replaced his other wife's hammock with an imported bed) and an Ewe pattern named *atsusikpɔdzedzome*, "the second wife saw it on her rival and jumped into the fire" (after an Ashanti man bought this particularly beautiful cloth for the wife he loved the most). Many more examples could be cited—all lexically divergent, but closely related by the principles of their formation.[14]

Furthermore, the "floating" of several potential names before one becomes accepted, the expectation that people will have familiarity with a vast number of cloth names, and the acceptance of flexibility in name/pattern correspondences are common to African and Suriname Maroon cloth naming traditions. Maroons often cited names in a qualified form ("sort of like X," "the red version of Y"), and accounts of naming systems in Africa make reference to disagreements, regional differences, and qualifying prefixes. Parallels can also be seen in the way that the daily use of names for cloth patterns and clothing styles involves playful manipulation, abbreviation, and disguise. A cloth named "Agbago traveled in an airplane" (after the Saramaka chief took his first plane ride) is often referred to as "the chief went to heaven," one called "Aviee caused havoc at Djumu" (after a man stole from Peleki's store at the Djumu mission post) can also be called "Aviee ruined Peleki," and a third named "Agbago threw Venipai out of his office because of bad living" is sometimes spoken of as "Venipai cried." A similarly playful attitude apparently characterizes the Akan use of names for clothing fads. Warren and Andrews describe the situation when flared trousers were in fashion.

> "Perhaps you feel shy" ("*Gyama wo fere*") refers to a type of Afro trousers with [only] moderately flared bases. . . . "Gun and bullet" ("*Tunabo*") is a teasing title for a pair of trousers without a flared base. The trouser leg represents the gun and the [person's] leg, the bullet. "*Po*," the sound made by a gun shot, is the same as "*Tunabo*." "*Po*" was introduced after people were beaten up for shouting "*Tunabo*." At times the "critics" don't say anything, but rather run past and fall down in front of the person indicating that he has shot the "critic" dead with the "*tunabo*." (1977:15, 14)

Or again, they tell how young Akan women disparaged a style of head kerchief worn mainly by old women by calling it *wo daa ho bɔ* ("Do you still use it?"), but contritely rebaptized the same style as *medwanetoa* ("I apologize") when it came back into fashion (1977:15). Maroons rename clothing styles in a similar spirit to reflect changing fashions. As we saw in Chapter 4, the bits-and-pieces textiles that had been so prized in the early decades of this century were given a name that made fun of their pretentiousness and garishness as soon as narrow-strip patchwork came into favor. And the narrow-strip patchwork was, in its turn, denigrated by new terms such as "[outboard] motor cover" when cross-stitch embroidery took over the fashion scene.

We would argue that while the actual clothing styles of the Maroons have undergone continual change, with fashions coming in and going out at a particularly rapid rate, certain very basic attitudes toward dress have remained constant. And while Maroons' talk about cloth and clothing has also been characterized by a particularly rapid turnover of terms, the ways in which those terms are created, played with, used, and discarded continue to reflect a heritage that is shared by their African contemporaries.

PATCHWORK. Finally, we return to the dilemma of visual similarities between Maroon narrow-strip patchwork and parallels from weaving traditions in West Africa. As we argued in Chapter 4, interpreting this Maroon art form as a straight-line historical continuity with African precedents raises more questions than it answers, given the fact that it only began to be made in the twentieth century.[15] But this does not necessarily diminish the strength of cultural connection, or the usefulness of understanding how it came about. At earlier points in this book, we have presented all the ingredients of our explanation, which hinges on continuities in fundamental cultural ideas despite discontinuities in the forms through which they are realized. Here we merely recall them in the context of our more general argument about the dynamics of Maroon culture.

First, the technique of patching for practical (rather than aesthetic) ends—whether cutting and realigning a single piece of cloth to change its proportions or sewing several pieces of cloth together to form a larger whole—has been practiced throughout Maroon textile history.

Second, an aesthetic appreciation of sharp color contrast has run through the full culture history of the Maroons, and has permeated countless aspects of their lives, from the choice of garments to wear together or imported cookware to hang on a wall to the arrangement of "red" and "white" rice varieties in a garden, the paints to use on a house front, or the wood inlays to set into a carved stool.

The material means for combining the practice of patching and the aesthetics of color contrast became available only during the twentieth century. At that time, male wage-labor opportunities provided money, coastal stores began importing multichrome trade cotton, and the reduced presence of men in the villages gave women a special incentive to create artistic offerings as a way of attracting husbands. It was in this setting that Maroon women brought together the longstanding aesthetics of color and the equally longstanding technique of cloth-patching, creating a distinctly innovative art out of distinctly non-innovative components of the culture.[16]

In short, basic notions about clothing construction and the aesthetics of color combination, which grew out of the Maroons' African cultural heritage, have remained remarkably constant over the course of Maroon history. The variable element has been availability of materials—cloth scarcity during the early years, chromatically limited fabrics during the late nineteenth century, and an abundance of colorfully striped trade cotton in the twentieth century. Thus the maintenance of a basic technique and of certain broad aesthetic values allowed for the creative, prototypically African-American reinvention, once favorable material and social conditions were in place, of a distinctively African mode of artistic expression.

THESE THREE EXAMPLES (calfbands, cloth names, and patchwork) are intended to stand for a general aspect of the culture history of the Maroons that we have attempted to lay out more comprehensively in the body of this book and which we reiterate in nutshell form here. On the one hand, there are the relatively unchanging features of Maroon artistry (regarding color contrast, symmetry, and so forth), which are based on a broadly African set of aesthetic principles. On the other, there is the celebration of artistic innovation and individual creativity, which guarantees that Maroon artists are ever modifying, inventing, and playing with new forms and techniques. The result is a set of arts which are at once African and American, reflections of cultural processes that are uniquely African-American.

We have seen how the initial synthesis of aesthetic ideas, drawn from a variety of African cultures, was forged during slavery and the earliest years of Maroon existence. This set of ideas has always pervaded Maroon life, even outside the realm of "artistic" production. Aesthetic considerations are important, for example, in posture, the layout of rice fields, the serving of meals. Discussions of imported manufactures, from pots to cloth to soap, are also permeated by aesthetic concerns. All of this is crucial in helping us comprehend how ideas that in the twentieth century have been realized in woodcarving, strip-sewing, or calabash carving could have been maintained and passed down, first during slavery and then during a long period of relatively reduced formal artistic production. Even under the maximally repressive conditions of slavery in Suriname and during the century-long period of guerrilla warfare against the colonists, people still made use of opportunities for story-telling, dancing, drumming, and singing; they made choices about the way they walked, carried their babies, and wore their hair; they expressed aesthetic preferences in the arrangement of their house furnishings, the mending of their clothes, the serving of their meals, the layout of their gardens, and countless other aspects of life that did not require the specific resources of elaborately developed art forms. Throughout a long period of material hardship—first during slavery and then in the rainforest—artistic production was to a great degree curtailed, but ideas capable of influencing the character of formal arts were kept alive through the ongoing activities of everyday life and, most important of all, through daily talk about aesthetics. Even in the absence of any particular artistic activity, then, a panoply of aesthetic ideas, from the general to the extremely specific, would have been passed on from one generation to the next.

We have also seen that Maroons enjoy artistic innovation, play, and creativity in every domain of life. Whether in their woodcarving or textiles, hairdos or songs, Maroons display a recurrent inventiveness and an irrepressible dynamism that provide a telling contrast to the popular image of "traditional" artists in non-industrial societies.

Viewed in a broad comparative context, the history of Maroon arts is characterized by continuity-in-change, by Amiri Baraka's "changing same." In building creatively upon their collective past, the early Maroons synthesized African aesthetic principles and adapted, played with, and reshaped artistic forms into arts that were new, yet still organically related to that past. The arts of the Maroons, forged in an inhospitable rainforest by people under constant threat of annihilation, stand as enduring testimony to African-American resilience and creativity and to the exuberance of the Maroon artistic imagination working itself out within the rich, broad framework of African cultural ideas.

Notes

Chapter 1: Souvenirs

1. http://www.findinfo.com/adiante

2. Not that we failed to notice the kinds of things that have, since that time, taken on a privileged status, both in our own work and that of the discipline more generally. During our second week in Saramaka territory, more than thirty years ago, R. P. penned into his notebook,

> One of the most striking things about Saramakas is their use of gadgets, machines, and manufactured items in general. They draw on the whole world: lots of stuff from West Germany (hunting equipment, fishing line, lanterns), England (cutlasses), USA (tools, guns, outboards), France (gunpowder, food), Holland (food, tape recorders, radios, magazines), Spain (gunpowder), Red China (cloth, flashlights, batteries), etc. etc. From their attitude toward such things, I can almost imagine that Saramakas have always bought, traded, stolen such goods—in no way do I feel that super-duper tape recorders are "spoiling" Saramaka. . . . One guy, Abateli, showed me an electric lightbulb he'd bought. He said now he just needed a car battery and he'd have electric light. Guys here don't just have ordinary flashlights—they have ones that blink on and off with flashing red lights.

Yet when we sat down to write a book about Maroon art in the late 1970s, we were still not very far removed from academic concerns of the 1960s, formed through graduate courses centered on Raymond Firth and A. R. Radcliffe-Brown, summer fieldwork designed to put Malinowski's theory of magic to the empirical test, structuralist seminars run by Claude Lévi-Strauss at the École Pratique des Hautes Études, and classes on ethnoscience in Harvard's Department of Social Relations. And we were only a few years past our first book-length description of Suriname Maroon society (R. Price 1975b, actually finished in 1969), with its kinship charts, bar graphs, and use of capital letters to represent individuals and kin groups. Abateli's lightbulb, which in a later era would have made a fitting rhetorical companion to the New Guinea flashbulbs that were deconstructed first by Jim Clifford (1985:173) and then by Marianna Torgovnick (1990:79), was left as an aside in our notebook, along with other untapped first impressions.

3. See, for example, Dening 1980 and Rosaldo 1980.
4. See, for example, R. Price 1983a and 1990, S. Price 1993 [1984].
5. The best books are Aboikoni 1997 and Scholtens et al. 1992. The latter work, written in Dutch with an extended summary in English, contains over a hundred and twenty illustrations, many in color. The senior author, anthropologist Ben Scholtens, was murdered in Paramaribo on the eve of his flight to the Netherlands to defend his Ph.D. dissertation.
6. On the whole, these shifts in the academic landscape have been salutary. At the same time, as Donna Haraway has cautioned, some of the most "persuasive and enabling" ideological stances carry serious risks of introducing "false harmonies" into the stories we tell, precisely because they are so compelling. See Haraway 1989:6 and, for an application of this line of reasoning to interpretations of Maroon life, S. Price 1994.
7. Contributions to these changes are too myriad to enumerate here, but a few markers from the past decade and a half may serve to evoke the general trend. In 1984, prestigious New York City art museums hosted simultaneous celebrations of "tribal and modern affinities" in art, Maori art (organized by Maori curators and inaugurated with ceremonies that included nose-rubbing greetings between the city's mayor and Maori elders flown in from New Zealand), Ashanti artifacts crafted from gold (for which the mayor returned as ceremonial host, this time participating in a massive parade through Central Park), American Indian art from the Pacific Northwest, and African arts of adornment. The Center for African Art opened its doors for the first time; Sotheby's and Christie's both held large, widely publicized auctions of "primitive" art; and the College Art Association decided to add sessions on anthropological themes to its annual meeting. In 1988 and 1989, the Smithsonian sponsored major symposia exploring the role of museums in a rapidly evolving social and cultural environment, and National Public Radio formed the carefully multicultural "Working Group on a New American Sensibility" to discuss the same range of issues for radio. Paris mounted "Magiciens de la Terre," a global art extravaganza so ambitious that it took both the Pompidou Center and the vast La Villette complex to hold it. With vigorous local participation, community museums sprang up in unprecedented numbers, providing active loci for grassroots cultural creativity. And a wave of publications, seconding the collective message of numerous traveling exhibitions, pulled into the mainstream a whole range of political, economic, and ethical issues that had previously sat at the margins of art historical concerns (see, for example, Clifford 1988, Cole 1985, Coombes 1994, Greenfield 1989, Hall and Metcalf 1994, Henderson and Kaeppler 1996, Hiller 1991, Krech 1989, Lippard 1990, Mar-

cus and Myers 1995, Messenger 1989, Michaels 1993, Myers n.d., O'Hanlon 1995, Pearce 1993 and 1995, Phillips and Steiner 1999, Plattner 1996, Rhodes 1994, Root 1996, Schildkrout and Keim 1990, Steiner 1994, Thomas 1991, Vogel 1988, Ziff and Rao 1997).

Chapter 2: Maroons of the Guianas

The quote from Captain Kala of Dangogo, teaching R. P. in 1978, is adapted from R. Price 1983a:47–48.

1. The early history of the Maroons—the powerful and sacred period of "First-Time" from which each group derives its distinct identity—has been studied by several scholars during the past twenty-five years. For early Saramaka (and Matawai) history, see R. Price 1983a, 1983b, and 1990; for the Ndyuka, see Thoden van Velzen and van Wetering 1988; for the Aluku, see Bilby 1990, Hoogbergen 1990, and R. and S. Price 1992b.

2. Maroon languages divide similarly into two groups—variants of Saramaccan, which are spoken by Saramakas, Matawais, and Kwintis, and variants of Ndyuka, which are spoken by Ndyukas, Alukus, and Paramakas. In citing Maroon terms in this book, we employ a modified version of the orthography developed by Jan Voorhoeve: vowels have "Italian" values except that è is pronounced like the e in English "met," and ò is pronounced like the a in "all"; vowel extension in speech is indicated by vowel repetition in writing; and in Saramaccan, an acute accent (´) indicates high tone, while low tones are unmarked. In the spelling of Saramaka proper names of both people and places, we follow the Suriname convention of omitting diacritical marks. As a rough pronunciation guide for English speakers to some of the personal names, place names, and other terms used in the text, we list a few examples: Agbago = Ah-gbah-GO, aseésènte = ah-SAY-sen-tay, Boo = Baw, Faansisonu = Fahn-see-SO-nu; Kaadi = Kaah-dee, Keekete = Keh-keh-tay, Peepina = Pay-PEE-na, Pete = Peh-teh, Seketima = Seh-KEH-tee-ma, Takite = Ta-kee-TAY.

3. For a photo from the 1980s of a Ndyuka woman's house in which aluminum and enamelware are displayed along with woodcarvings, family snapshots, and a calendar, see van Binnendijk and Faber 1992:27.

Shiva Naipaul's impressionistic view of Maroon women's life is illustrated by a photo of a well-supplied house interior and the explanation that "the lives of Bush Negro women seem to revolve around this interminable cleaning and burnishing of kitchenware. There is something obsessive about it. . . . Every hut is arrayed with glittering displays of these pots and bowls and enamel basins. . . . The number of pots is a sign of wealth, and the shinier they are, the better they protect their owners from evil spirits" (1981:86). In this journalist's "Tableau of Savage Innocence," cleanliness among "savages" can be understood only by recourse to the spirit world and pagan superstition.

4. Eighteenth-century documents clearly show that men's ownership and display of selected imported items dates from the earliest years of Maroon history (R. Price 1983b, 1990). During periods of relative Maroon prosperity, such as the French Guiana gold rush years at the turn of the twentieth century, outside observers expressed wonderment at Maroons buying "tea sets, clocks, and boxes," and dragging pieces of fancy European furniture over the rapids back to their villages (van Panhuys 1908:38; Franssen Herderschee 1905:53–54; see also de Beet and Thoden van Velzen 1977).

5. In the past, calabash bowls were sometimes set on decorative rings made of pottery, wood, or calabash. Although we have seen a number of these in museum collections, they have not, to our knowledge, been used by Maroons for several decades.

6. Hurault has presented detailed descriptions of the construction and layout of mid-century eastern Maroon house types (1970:40–54), as well as photographs and line drawings which give an excellent sense of the range of aesthetic treatments applied to individual dwellings.

Chapter 3: Art and Aesthetics

1. For further discussion of art and gender in Maroon societies, see S. Price 1993 [1984].

2. Maroons' view of their culture as a sharply diversified whole is even more frequently expressed in terms of language. People often explained to us, in an admittedly overstated rhetoric, why Saramaka ways are more difficult to learn (they claimed) than those of other societies. As one young man put it, "It's because every village has its own language. Akisiamau and [its stone's-throw neighbor] Asindoopo don't speak the same language, though we do understand each other. When you get to Langu [the Gaanlio], differences get really fierce—there you might as well be in Matawai!"

3. Although we have been present many times when men returned from the coast and were showered with gifts of celebration, our ethnographic notes are less successful in capturing the flavor and cultural significance of the event than this idealized description by a Saramaka woman, which we have translated from a 1976 recording. In addition to the sequence of exchanges she mentions, our own notes describe spontaneous singing and dancing and the participation of a somewhat wider

range of relatives.

4. For Maroon men living on the coast, commercial woodcarving was already a well established money-making option in the 1970s. Carvers' stands along the highway between Paramaribo and the Suriname airport offered souvenirs for departing visitors; there were a number of souvenir shops in Paramaribo stocked largely with Maroon-made combs, food stirrers, paddles, and even coffee-table tops; and some carvers were peddling their wares through the city on foot.

Chapter 4: Cloths and Colors

1. See figures 4.84 and 4.85, as well as the illustrations in van Binnendijk and Faber 1992:35 and in Scholtens et al. 1992:71, 80–86.

2. A 1707 painting by Dirk Valkenburg of a slave "play" on the Suriname River plantations of Palmeneribo-Surimombo, from which the ancestors of the Saramaka Dombi clan escaped during the second or third decade of the eighteenth century, provides an invaluable view of the clothing, postures, and musical instruments used by the very slaves who rebelled and became Maroons just a few years later (fig. 7.1, R. Price 1983a: 108–111). The men are wearing breechcloths but no covering on the upper torso; one appears to be wearing a fancy soft hat at a rakish angle, another sports small protruding braids, and others seem to be wearing earrings. Aside from two long, gathered (apparently European) skirts, the women are wearing knee-length wrap-skirts much like those in use by Maroons today. Infants are tied onto the backs of women just as they are among present-day Maroons, and one is wearing a cap identical to those we often saw in Saramaka. The woman standing at the painting's right edge sports decorative cicatrizations on her belly and chest. Finally, the white kerchiefs on the heads of several dancers are identical to those used in countless ritual and performative settings by twentieth-century Maroons of all regions.

3. The stitch in infants' calfbands looks just like the stitch in Western knitting, but is made with two short reeds, split to hold the thread, rather than two skewer-like needles. For a description and diagram of this stitch, which is used also by some groups of Carib Indians in the Guianas, see Roth 1924:104 and Ahlbrinck 1931:119, 444–45.

4. In 1997, Saramakas told us that adolescent girls had generally stopped wearing the aprons, but that they were always given one just before being passed ritually into adulthood so that they could "replace" their apron with a woman's wrap-skirt.

5. When men gather of an evening and swap stories of women they have known and loved, an important rhetorical role is played by vivid descrip-

tions of cicatrizations—how those of a certain woman glistened in the sunlight, and so forth. Women sometimes heighten their tactile effect during love-making by donning a multi-stranded "wrestling belt" given to them at the time of their first marriage and treated as an intimate, personal, and private possession (see S. and R. Price 1980:fig. 110). Men other than the woman's husband or lover must not see it, and in upper river Saramaka, a woman traditionally gave it to her husband when he left for an extended trip to the coast, as a token of her intended faithfulness. Similar beaded belts, with similar functions and associations, have been made in West Africa (see, for example, Sieber 1972:142–43), and beads possess more general erotic associations in some African societies (Warren and Andrews 1977:15–16).

6. During the same period, young men in a Cottica Ndyuka village were reported to have attended a feast for the dead wearing garments "with a yard-long train which is carried by children" (Köbben 1968:86). The contemporaneous rage in Saramaka was a shoulder cape, often made from a terrycloth beach towel, that reached all the way to the ground and was worn only by men in their late teens and early twenties.

7. As our discussion of textile art history later in this chapter shows, this "new" style represented, from a non-Matawai perspective, an interesting recycling of an important earlier Maroon fashion.

8. In the 1970s we heard Saramakas proclaim that "funeral rites are not [should never be] conducted without calfbands," reflecting the fact that although calfbands are optional for everyday dress, they were considered *de rigueur* for public celebrations. When men were away on the coast, each wife was careful to make at least one pair of them, in order to "give thanks" properly for the goods he would present to her upon his return, people wearing a new pair of calfbands were often congratulated on them (either verbally or by a spontaneous song and dance), and when a corpse was laid out for burial it was dressed in new calfbands, with several other pairs laid ceremoniously on top. One man told us that he never wore calfbands because he didn't like the way they got stained and unsightly whenever he underwent ritual washings for a chronic illness, but that his trunks were filled with those that his wives had nevertheless presented to him at various times. When, during a 1997 trip to French Guiana, we interviewed Saramakas about changes in the way people were dressing in the villages of the interior, they all said that men were wearing Western clothes more and more, but that the custom of donning calfbands was still very much alive. (For an idea of the frequency of their use in 1989, see Scholtens et al. 1992.)

9. For an illustration of Aluku anklebands, see Crevaux 1879:361.

10. Morton Kahn reported that in the 1930s not all Maroon men owned a pair of pants. "If a Bush Negro is not fortunate enough to own a pair of trousers, he may rent one for ten Dutch cents a day . . . from small shopkeepers who have their stores near the bank of the river" (1931:47).

11. Ken Bilby reports that Aluku officials have traditionally worn uniforms provided by the French government and modeled on French military attire, but that they prefer the look of the Suriname uniforms and have been lobbying for change (e-mail, 28 May 1997). For other illustrations of Maroon officials' uniforms, see Kahn 1931, Scholtens et al. 1992, Thoden van Velzen and van Wetering 1988, and de Beet and Sterman 1981.

12. See Bonaparte 1884, Cateau van Rosevelt and van Lansberge 1873, Crevaux 1879, Joest 1893, and Spalburg 1899.

13. In 1887, a group of one hundred Saramaka men were reported to have been working for the past ten years out of Mana, French Guiana, canoeing supplies upriver to gold miners. By 1936, it was estimated that sixty percent of all Saramaka men were temporarily working in French Guiana. And during 1967–68, when we were living in a village on the Pikilio, about half the local men were in Kourou, helping to build the European Space Center (see R. and S. Price 1989).

14. For a detailed study of the effects of male emigration on Saramaka marriage, see R. Price 1970a. Eastern Maroon men also participated in the new wage-labor opportunities, but because they left their villages for shorter periods of time (months rather than years), the social and cultural consequences of their migration were less dramatic than in Saramaka.

15. A small amount of weaving has been done by Maroons since the formation of their societies in the eighteenth century (see, for example, Schumann 1778: s.v. *fumm krossu*). In the 1960s, many older Saramakas remembered, from their childhood, seeing people weaving hammocks; Chris de Beet and Miriam Sterman told us in 1980 that some Matawais still wove hammocks in the 1970s; and in 1990, Ken Bilby and R. P. collected a hammock woven from Aluku-grown cotton some eighty years earlier, from a man who said the last Aluku who knew the craft had died around 1970. Throughout Maroon history, however, cloth supplies have been heavily dominated by imported commercial cotton.

16. The sewing on these cloths was remarkably fine, often surpassing thirty-five stitches per inch. This might be compared to Amish patchwork quilts, on which the most highly skilled seamstresses "often 'put in' twenty stitches per inch" (Bishop and Safanda 1976:6). The Singer sewing machine in our house gives options ranging from six to twenty stitches per inch, plus one last setting designated only as "fine."

17. See M. and F. Herskovits 1934:facing p. 332, for an illustration from 1928.

18. Expectations concerning the quantity of cloth brought back from a coastal trip have varied dramatically, depending on wages and the price of cloth, as well as the length of time spent away. Saramakas claimed that around the turn of the century men sometimes brought as many as 300 skirt-length cloths for each wife. During the 1920s and 1930s, 12–20 cloths was a more usual amount, and in the 1960s most men brought between 50 and 100, though some provided as many as 150 for each wife.

19. Saramakas told us about five named models of women's tin lanterns, each of which was popular at a particular time. Those that we saw in use did not, as far as we know, have distinctive names, though subtle differences in their shapes and surface textures were a common topic of aesthetic discussion. Four modern examples are illustrated in S. and R. Price 1980:fig. 100.

20. In 1967–68, we elicited 65 cloth names in the villages of the Pikilio and in Pokigoon, partly on the basis of 89 sample swatches kindly provided by Ahmad El-Wanni, owner of the largest Paramaribo cloth store catering to Maroons. Anthropologist Leslie Haviland then showed the swatches to Saramakas living in the village of Brownsweg, who concurred on just over fifty percent of the names. In 1976 and 1978, women on the Pikilio helped us expand the sample to 121 names, including many for cloth patterns that had been introduced after 1968. For further discussion of cloth names, and many more examples, see S. and R. Price 1980:ch. 3 and S. Price 1993 [1984]:chs. 6 and 7. Although all the names and etymologies that appear in these publications were given by at least two people, no one person knew them all and disagreement on the name of a particular cloth was not rare. (A cloth pattern named during Chief Agbago's funeral rites in 1989—"the chief is sleeping"—attests to the continuing practice; see Scholtens et al. 1992:155.)

21. The longer version of this name is *bómbo de a saáfu dá pipí* ("cunt is in slavery to penis"). Like cloth names, many Saramaka proverbs can be cited in longer or shorter versions. We once, for example, heard a man commenting on a conjugal feud whose origin he did not know by declaring, "The person who sleeps in the house . . ." The person he was talking to supplied the rest mentally (". . . knows where the roof leaks") and nodded in agreement.

22. Upon reading a final draft of these pages, Ken Bilby wrote, "I can attest to an almost identical pattern of cloth naming in Aluku (at least back when narrow strip patchwork was in vogue there)" and told us about a 1991 visit with an elderly Aluku couple. Together they examined dozens

of old pieces of clothing and reminisced about cloth patterns.

Among the names for different types of cloth that were present as strips within larger compositions were: *apodo* (because of the color as well as the pattern, said to resemble clusters of *apodo* palm nuts); *sapakaa* (in reference to the *sapakaa* lizard, because the stripe pattern resembled the lizard's skin); *Yobo sonali* (Yobo's newspaper—referring to some gossip associated with a woman named Ma Yobo); *palulu kama* ("wild-banana leaf bed"—after an embarrassing incident in which an Aluku woman was discovered *in flagrante* with a visiting city Creole on a wild-banana leaf "bed" the man had hastily made in the bush). (Ken Bilby, e-mail, 3 July 1998)

23. This paragraph refers most specifically to Saramaka, though the main lines of the fashion history it describes apply also to the eastern Maroons.

24. Needlework books and magazines have come from a variety of sources. Those we saw in Saramaka ranged from North American publications showing Santa Clauses and angels to a French booklet illustrating seventeenth- and eighteenth-century Turkish saddlebag trimmings. For an example from the late 1980s that features a knight on horseback, see Scholtens et al. 1992:77.

25. Hurault documents "clothing" in two line drawings and a page of text which extols its hygienic advantages over Western clothing, asserting four separate times that it involves "no sewing aside from hemming the edges," and making no mention of the embroidery that appears in one of these sketches (1970:57–58). In fact, at the time of his visits to their villages, Alukus were engaged in decorative sewing as elaborate as that of Saramakas.

26. The visual comparison of narrow-strip textiles from Africa and Suriname also obscures fundamental technical differences. In West Africa, looms are used to weave long strips, which are then generally joined by edge stitching (which forms no seam). Among the Maroons, commercial trade cotton is cut or ripped to produce raw-edged strips, which are then joined by seams. Maroon women take pains to make the raw edges of these seams as inconspicuous as possible, turning them under and fixing them in place with meticulous stitching, but their patchwork, unlike the West African equivalent, always carries narrow lines of extra thickness on the "wrong" side of the garment.

27. For further commentary on the ethnography of art and the art of ethnography, see S. Price n.d. Although in this book we are primarily concerned with New World materials, it is clear that research on African/American cultural connections depends equally on comprehen-

sive historical ethnography in the relevant societies of Africa. Recent reflections on the historically conditioned and ever-changing nature of ethnic identities on that continent provide essential cautions for scholars attempting to trace the roots of cultural phenomena in the Americas (see especially Appiah 1992).

28. As one late nineteenth-century observer remarked, their clothing "is always of a jumping-at-the-eye color" (van Coll 1903:538). However, Maroons view color contrast, like other aesthetic ideals, as a principle that can be overdone, and they are critical of what they consider excesses. An unusually colorful hammock, for example, may be criticized by Saramakas as "too patterned" (*pèndê pói*) and one of their terms for color contrast (*apísi ku wána*) is frequently used in a derogatory sense.

29. Eighteenth-century Moravian diaries make clear that the use of red, white, and "black" goes back to the earliest years of Maroon history (see, for example, Staehelin 1913–19, III iii:131).

Chapter 5: Carving Histories

1. Such stools, among both Amerindians and Maroons, may or may not have carrying handles, sometimes elaborated into animal heads or tails (Roth 1924:275). There are possible African models for this stool type as well (see, for example, Sieber 1979:30). It may well have been this type of simple stool that the European commander described during the final peacemaking ceremonies with the Saramakas in 1763. While wooden trumpets blared forth their messages and muskets fired celebratory salutes, the most important dignitaries were seated on "low blocks of wood" (R. Price 1983a:178).

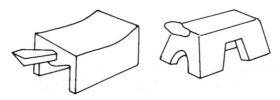

A Saramaka *bógolo* stool and the Amerindian form on which it was modeled.

2. For an excellent discussion of Maroon canoe construction, see Hurault 1970:62–79.

3. Wooden door locks with a mechanism similar to that found on Maroon examples are known from ancient Egypt (Oudschans-Dentz 1935/36). They had a broad distribution in pre-colonial Africa, apparently spread-

ing from the Sudanic region to the Gold Coast and Slave Coast, and by
1000 C.E. they were found in parts of Europe as well (Joest 1893, Lindblom 1924, van Panhuys 1925). Apparently present among plantation
slaves in eighteenth-century Suriname (Hartsinck 1770:17), they continued to be made by non-Maroon Afro-Surinamers well into the twentieth
century (van Panhuys 1925:273). Whether knowledge of wooden door
locks arrived in Suriname via Portuguese-Brazilian slave masters or with
African slaves themselves, the style of decoration on Maroon examples
has always been closely related to contemporaneous Maroon woodcarving fashions.

4. Each of these tools serves specialized functions. For example, the three
   kinds of gouges are used, respectively, to decorate the extreme ends of
   canoes, to shape drums, trays, and round stools, and as a "drill" for
   piercing, and they are in no sense interchangeable.

5. This discussion of Saramaka woodcarving is adapted from R. Price
   1970b, which provides more detailed information on such things as early
   tools, native terms, and types of wood. The chronology is based on a
   combination of oral history, Saramakas' age rankings of living and dead
   villagers, museum documentation, and archival records on such events
   as the installations and deaths of village officials. While it should be
   apparent that we employ the idea of "style" as a classificatory conve-
   nience (cf. Thompson 1969:158), we want to emphasize that both the
   categories and the elements or traits which define these styles were
   identified in the process of examining objects in the field with Saramakas, and that the classification depends substantially on their own
   critical distinctions.

6. Saramakas assert that wood-within-wood carving was invented not long
   after Djankuso became paramount chief (1898), and that knowledge of
   the technique (and the use of compasses with which it was always executed) soon spread from the upper river region to the rest of Saramaka
   and to Ndyuka. Their date and location for this invention—probably the
   most revolutionary in Maroon carving—are supported by the independent dating of objects in the field, examination of the numerous
   museum pieces collected in the late nineteenth and early twentieth centuries, and perusal of the literature, which illustrates a number of
   pieces from the 1890s.

7. Carving in aluminum, using hacksaws, special files, drills, and so forth,
   was a new craft in the 1960s, and was learned only by a few young Saramakas. The aluminum was appropriated by men working for Suralco (an
   Alcoa subsidiary). Decorative yarn tassels, as on the wooden comb in
   figure 5.27 or the aluminum example in S. and R. Price 1980:fig 192b,

were becoming popular on such things as lanterns, umbrellas, and even the protective rings worn by men on their biceps. (See Chapter 3 on the somewhat older art of decorative carving on imported aluminum eating spoons.)

8. We suspect that the lintel, carved with the wood-within-wood technique, was not made at the same time as the vertical pieces but was substituted some years later for the Style II lintel which normally accompanied this standard design.

9. Aluku men, who have always lived in close proximity to Ndyukas and Paramakas, carved in styles that were closely related to the styles of these two groups. In addition, for the past hundred years there had been a significant presence of Saramaka men in Aluku villages. Plying the Marowijne as canoemen since the gold rush, Saramakas often settled down for a while with Aluku wives. (Indeed, the presence of non-Aluku husbands in Aluku villages means that a certain number of the older pieces collected from women there, and therefore assumed by the collector to be Aluku-made, could easily have been sculpted by Saramakas or Ndyukas.) Aluku woodcarving developed in a particularly rich context of intercultural encounter and it is clear that it ranks aesthetically with the work of the finest carvers from any of the Maroon groups.

10. This particular change—which took place in the upper river region of Saramaka—is, to our knowledge, the most purely local of those described in this chapter. During the 1960s, the "paddle" form continued to be made at least occasionally lower down the Suriname River and remained common among the Ndyuka.

11. A similar one-piece stool, with a thin, curved seat, was carved in the second half of the nineteenth century by Gwentimati, founder of the Aluku village of Asisi. For a sketch, see R. and S. Price 1992a:172.

12. Formerly this metal came from old cans (as on the canoe pictured in S. and R. Price 1980:fig. 201b). More recently it has been salvaged from the tin liners of empty import crates, bought in the city (as on the canoe in S. and R. Price 1980:fig. 201c). Two variants adopted in the 1960s involved heating corrugated galvanized roofing metal to fit the canoe tips or using thin sheet aluminum appropriated by men working for Suralco.

13. There is at least one rival story claiming that the current design was originated by a Dangogo man working in French Guiana and was carried back to Saramaka by men from the village of Pempe—which could in fact account for its name, *Pempe bêtè* ("Pempe chisel-work"). There is no disagreement, however, about the date or suddenness of this innovation.

14. By the early 1970s, woodcarving was apparently no longer practiced among the Kwinti, the smallest and westernmost group of Maroons. What little we know of the history and characteristics of Kwinti carving is summarized in S. and R. Price 1980:note 52.

15. See figure 6.25 for a Paramaka adaptation of this practice to calabash carving.

16. Early twentieth-century paintwork by eastern Maroons was largely limited to red and black designs on canoe paddles (Kahn 1931:197). During the mid-1970s, Saramakas for the first time adopted a (highly selective) use of paints—on the gunwales of canoes, as accents on plank house fronts—but they have not attempted the complex compositions that characterize Aluku, Ndyuka, and Paramaka work.

17. During the early twentieth century, a Ndyuka man invented an indigenous writing system, known as the "Afaka script," which has received considerable attention from scholars (for references, see R. Price 1976:61 and Dubelaar and Pakosie 1988, 1993). The signs that make up this script, however, were never used decoratively.

18. Likewise, Venice Lamb has traced R. S. Rattray's "quest for clan symbolism in Asante cloth" to the power of the "desire to attach names and meanings to art forms," which could have led him "to read more into these patterns than was originally intended. The weavers, particularly when being subjected to questioning by an outsider, may well feel under some obligation to construct meaningful stories and legends to explain abstract patterns which in themselves are really just beautiful examples of textile design" (1975:136).

19. The larger set of games to which this one belongs, often referred to in the United States as "puttin' on ole massa," arises from the asymmetry of slave/master relations, and pervades the history of Africans throughout the Americas. Maroons have also enjoyed playing it in contexts other than artistic exegeses. For example, Saramakas serving as informants for government workers mapping their territory have provided Saramaccan obscenities as village names, and these have been dutifully entered onto official maps. They have taken similar pleasure in telling unsuspecting census takers, when asked, that their mother's or father's current address is the village of Paasitonu (a local cemetery).

20. In 1994, a small group of schoolteachers, researchers, and artists based in Mana formed the multicultural collective, "Chercheurs d'Art," which promotes work by a combination of Western, Amerindian, and Maroon artists.

21. One Saramaka entrepreneur in Suriname is apparently running a whole atelier of carvers who model their work on photocopies that he makes

from our 1980 book, and exports their wares as "authentic art from the rain forest" to Paramaribo, the Netherlands, Belgium, Martinique, and Germany (Bröer 1997:623–24). For an illustration of a particularly poor copy from our book—this one apparently made in Kourou—see Bruné 1995:113.

Chapter 6: Calabash Arts

1. As a Yale graduate student, Philip J. C. Dark undertook a museum-based study of the arts of the Maroons (then being called "Bush Negroes"). His attention to calabash carving was a significant departure from previous studies, which had focused more exclusively on wood-carving. If some of his conclusions seem dated today, it is important to acknowledge that the dominant understandings about gender were very different at the time he wrote. Our italicized passages are paraphrased from Dark 1951, 1954; the Herskovits quote is from 1930:159. See also Herskovits's crispy comment on Dark's "pseudo-psychological conjecture" about gender relations (1951) and Dark's reply (1952).

2. The similar-looking "calabashes" (more properly called "gourds") that contribute to the art and material culture of many societies in Africa are grown on vines (most commonly *Lagenaria siceraria* [Molina] Standley) and are botanically unrelated to the fruit of the calabash tree (*Crescentia cujete* L.). Maroons grow gourds as well, fashioning them into water containers, rolling pins for processing peanuts, bowls for ritual uses, musical instruments, masks, children's dolls, and tiny disks strung onto the ankles of small children when they are beginning to walk, as a medicine to aid their progress. But these items are virtually never decorated artistically. For more on the uses of gourds by Maroons, see S. Price 1993 [1984] and S. and R. Price 1980:164–65; the difference between "calabashes" in Africa and the Americas, and the implications of this difference for African-American culture history, are explored in S. Price 1982.

3. Traces of the complex history of Maroon calabashes are still evident in the Maroon languages. Saramakas call calabash bowls *kúya*—a word that is likely to have come, like its Brazilian homophone, from the Tupi word *kuia*, which their ancestors could have heard either in the forest (directly from Amerindians) or on the coast (from the slave masters who had come to Suriname from Brazil, or perhaps from their slaves). Saramakas call calabash spoons *kuyêè* (apparently from the Portuguese word *colher*) and eastern Maroons call them *supun* (from the English word *spoon*, presumably introduced by the English settlers who owned the plantations of coastal Suriname between 1651 and 1667). The word

apaki, which is used by both Saramakas and eastern Maroons (to refer to covered calabash containers and to covered gourd containers, respectively), seems to derive, like the Jamaican word *packy* (which can designate a calabash tree, a calabash fruit, a calabash container, or a calabash bowl), from the Twi word *apákyi*. (Eastern Maroons use the word *pakiba* for the covered calabash containers that Saramakas call *apakí*.) See Schumann 1778:s.v. *kuya, kujeri*, and Cassidy and Le Page 1967:s.v. *packy*. We are grateful to Ken Bilby for information on Jamaican and Aluku terminology.

4. See also Hurault 1970: plates III–V and, for an unusual example collected in the early 1800s, Neumann 1961.

5. Elsewhere we have suggested that in calabash decoration as in textile arts (see Chapter 4), women have often worked out new styles and techniques in "marginal" spaces, and that as their experimentation enters the mainstream of artistic production the designs themselves also move to a central position on the object being made or embellished. S. Price 1993 [1984] and 1999 present this argument in more detail and offer illustrations of the early experimental carvings.

6. The creation, naming, and meaning of calabash motifs is discussed in S. Price 1993 [1984]:117–21, which illustrates fifteen named design elements.

7. Similarly, Bill Holm has demonstrated the sensitivity of Northwest Coast Indian artists to the contours of ground areas ("negative space") and has traced the origin of certain of their figures to the gradual standardization of these (back)ground areas. That is, particular shapes (in painted wood, weaving, appliqué, and silverwork) that began as carefully controlled backdrops to the design have evolved, over time, into elements of the design itself (1965:57, 80–82).

Chapter 7: Playing

The passage from the writings of Moravian Brother Johann Riemer is taken from R. Price 1990:215–16.

1. Multimedia "plays" are a widespread historical feature of African-American life throughout the hemisphere. The term "play," generally used by Euro-Americans with an implied contrast to "work" or seriousness, is widely used by African Americans to refer to "*the* activity by which Afro-American individuality is asserted and maintained" (Szwed and Abrahams 1977:78, their italics).

2. The most striking departure from the painting's general style of ethnographic realism is its depiction of a public kiss. Stedman's eighteenth-century observation about Suriname slaves—"Such is the Delicacy of

these People, that I dont Remember ever /Amongst the many thousands that I did live With/ to have Seen one offer a Kiss in public to a Woman" (1988 [1790]:526)—corresponds to our own observations among modern Maroons. For a recent detailed analysis of this painting, see Kolfin 1997:23–29.

3. These play languages are structured by rules for the distortion of words from Maroon and other languages and are intensely enjoyed as a vehicle for the expression of peer group exclusivity (R. and S. Price 1976, Hurault 1970:19).

4. Bilby describes Aluku *susa* as "a competitive dance-game for men, who must execute the precise step at the right moment. The rivals dance in an open space before the drums, encircled by spectators and a group of women singers. When one of the dancers succeeds in 'killing' his adversary, the latter steps away and is replaced by another." And he describes *agankoi*, also called *songe*, as imitating the graceful movements of the fish of that name and danced by men and women wearing *kawai* anklets (1989:59).

5. For a recording, see R. and S. Price 1977, and for more details, R. Price 1983a:175–81.

6. Eighteenth-century European documents frequently mention the importance of drumming in various aspects of Maroon life, but little is said of style. And while Maroon oral history also makes frequent reference to drums in the eighteenth century (in rituals of diverse kinds, in signaling, and in "speaking" proverbs at council meetings), documentary evidence about early drum history is slim. The plantation drums in figures 7.1 and 7.12 represent the only relevant eighteenth-century depictions known to us.

7. The origins of the form of the *apinti*, once simply presumed to be Akan, now appear to be more complex. Recent work on the subject suggests that in the seventeenth and eighteenth centuries peoples of both the Slave Coast and the Gold Coast had drums of this general type—Ewe *kagan*, Yoruba *apinti*, and Akan *apentemma*. The Saramaka drum's "praise name" for itself, played at the beginning of each *apínti* performance, refers specifically to Asante.

8. The separate origins of the gongs used in *komantí* and *papá* performances are reflected in their Saramaka names. In the former rites, which in Saramaka ideology are related to Asante, the instrument is known as *dáulo* (apparently from Twi *adawuru*), while in the latter— which preserves in the name *papá* the seventeenth/eighteenth-century Yoruba name for coastal Ewe, "Popo"—the instrument is called *gan* (apparently from the identical Ewe word).

9. Closely related Afro-Caribbean rasp instruments include the recently obsolete coastal Suriname *grumi* (Wooding 1972:530) and the eighteenth-century Jamaican *goombah* (Long 1774, II:423–24).

10. Wooden horns were always closely associated with Maroon funerals. In the 1970s in Saramaka, store-bought bugles were used extensively by the gravediggers' association, as they traveled the river from village to cemetery and back. African wooden signal trumpets, played like Maroon ones through a hole in the side, have a wide historical distribution on that continent (Lindblom 1924:68–70). Lindblom's attempt to pin down the African origins of the Maroon trumpet, however, pays too little attention to the variation evident among extant Maroon examples. The *abeng* of the Jamaica Maroons, though usually fashioned from cow-horn, is also blown through a hole in the side and used in similar ways to the Suriname Maroon signal trumpet (see, for example, Cassidy and Le Page 1967:2).

11. For a study of the very widespread African instruments called *mbira* or *sanzhi*, see Berliner 1978. The term *bèntá* derives from West African words for "musical bow," e.g., Twi ɔ-*bentá* and Ewe *béta*. Afro-Caribbean musical bows are also reported for Jamaica (*benta* or *bender*) and Curaçao (*benta*) (Cassidy and Le Page 1967:38; van Meeteren 1947:39–40).

12. The following paragraphs follow closely R. and S. Price 1991:1–9. We feel insufficiently acquainted with riddling and folktales among other Maroon groups to write about them here. But it is clear that eastern Maroon tale-telling, which is also associated with funerals, unfolds in a style very unlike that of Saramaka. In 1990, we witnessed part of a funeral in the Aluku village of Loka. As we wrote,

> The evening music began with a couple of hours of *aleke* singing and drums, a recent Aluku style for which we have not yet acquired a taste. Around midnight, fifty or so people (largely young, largely female) crammed into the funeral hangar—an open shed draped with embroidered cloths, with drums at one end—and began to "play *mato*." This distant cousin of the narrative folktales that Saramakas [tell] . . . rang unfamiliar to our ears. Brief shouted vignettes, brief songs, lots of hooting, backed by drums. Many of the stories recounted recent local gossip, scandal stories that Saramakas would have fed into popular songs or cloth names. Much more raucous than Saramaka tale-telling, much less attentive listening. (R. and S. Price 1992a:195)

In other words, from our brief experience, and from what little others have written on the subject, eastern Maroon tale-telling sessions seem far more "activated" and contestational, and less narrative-centered, than the generally "sweet" and intimate tale-telling sessions we witnessed in Saramaka. (For a recent collection of Aluku tales with French translations, see Anelli 1991.)

13. For Saramakas, both *kóntu* and First-Time (historical) knowledge are central cultural resources, important components of their collective identity, but they occupy separate spheres. Though the morals, as well as certain rhetorical devices, of folktales may overlap with those of particular First-Time stories, Saramakas maintain a clear distinction between the two—both in the contexts in which they are communicated and the kinds of characters and incidents they depict.

14. Rarely, Saramaka tales are told outside of the context of wakes—most commonly by children or during a relaxed evening in a horticultural camp; *Mató* and *Tòngôni* are prohibited for such occasions, and the opening for riddles (*Hílíti/Dáíti*) is substituted.

Chapter 8: The Changing Same

1. This section on "The Formative Years," first drafted in 1979, drew on ideas and prose in two earlier publications which contain fuller expositions of the central argument as well as supporting evidence (R. Price 1976; Mintz and Price 1992 [1976]). In adapting these earlier statements to the needs of this section, we found it more graceful, stylistically, not to separate quotations or paraphrases from the surrounding prose. We are grateful to Sidney W. Mintz for permission to use materials from the Mintz and Price study in this way.

   The generalizations in this section have since been reexamined in some detail. See, for example, R. Price 1983a, 1983b, and 1990, which contain considerable oral and archival testimony regarding the origins, migrations, and social and cultural history of each of the original groups of maroons who became Saramakas.

2. Earlier versions of table 1 were presented in R. Price 1976:13–16 and S. and R. Price 1980:195. Considerable further research by Johannes Postma (1990), Alex van Stipriaan (1993a, b) and Jacques Arends (1995) has improved our understandings, "although the general picture presented by Price 1976 is by and large confirmed" (Arends 1995:251). We draw on this more recent research, particularly Arends 1995:251 and van Stipriaan 1993a, in constructing table 1.

3. In response to those claiming the existence of an overarching African culture, Kwame Anthony Appiah has retorted that "whatever Africans share, we do not have a common traditional culture, common lan-

guages, a common religious or conceptual vocabulary," adding that "Africans share too many problems and projects to be distracted by a bogus basis for solidarity" (1992:26). More recently, he has stated that "the central fact of African life, in my judgment, remains not the sameness of Africa's cultures, but their enormous diversity. . . . Religious diversity, political diversity, diversity in clothing and cuisine: Africa has enough cultural diversity to satisfy the wildest multiculturalist" (1997:47).

Appiah has also written eloquently on the historically contingent nature of African ethnic identities—part of the reason why the idea of establishing an African "baseline" for New World studies has been so fraught with problems. Appiah cites Chinua Achebe's remarks about the relative recency of the "Igbo" identity in Nigeria: "For instance, take the Igbo people. In my area, historically, they did not see themselves as Igbo. They saw themselves as people from this village or that village. . . . And yet, after the experience of the Biafran War, during a period of two years, it became a very powerful consciousness." And then he cautions that

> recognizing Igbo identity as a new thing is not a way of privi-
> leging other Nigerian identities: each of the three central eth-
> nic identities of modern political life—Hausa-Fulani, Yoruba,
> Igbo—is a product of the rough-and-tumble of the transition
> through colonial to postcolonial status. David Laitin has
> pointed out that "the idea that there was a single Hausa-
> Fulani tribe . . . was largely a political claim of the NPC
> [Northern Peoples' Congress] in their battle against the
> South," while "many elders intimately involved in rural Yoruba
> society today recall that, as late as the 1930s, 'Yoruba' was not
> a common form of political identification." . . . Modern Ghana
> witnesses the development of an Akan identity, as speakers of
> the three major regional dialects of Twi—Asante, Fante,
> Akuapem—organize themselves into a corporation against an
> (equally novel) Ewe unity. . . . Identities are complex and mul-
> tiple and grow out of a history of changing responses to eco-
> nomic, political, and cultural forces, almost always in opposi-
> tion to other identities. (1992:177–78)

Thus when we briefly contrast Igbo and Yoruba in terms of their "traditional" treatment of twins, we are using an anthropological shorthand that in other contexts would require considerable historicizing.

4. In general, Amerindian influence has been far greater on technical than on conceptual aspects of Maroon life. Fish drugs, bows and arrows, and

traps, as well as a large variety of hunting techniques, were learned from the Indians. A wide range of basketry forms—including the cassava press and sieve, various containers, and several kinds of fire fans—have always been an important part of Maroon subsistence (figs. 4.56, 2.14; see also S. and R. Price 1980:fig. 257, Wilbert 1975:56–57, 76–77, and Yde 1965:55). As we have already mentioned, the techniques for constructing calfbands and for split-reed "knitting" were taken over from Amerindians (see Roth 1924:104–5), and adolescent girls wear "aprons" which closely resemble those of Amerindian women, and are called by an Amerindian term (figs. 4.7, 4.21, S. and R. Price 1980:fig. 109).

5. The widespread use of cloth as a medium of exchange has been well documented for pre-colonial West and Central Africa (see, for example, Johnson 1980, Hodder 1980, Edwards 1992). In Maroon societies, transactions involving payments (e.g., for ritual services), social obligations (e.g., between spouses and affines), religious offerings (e.g., to honor an ancestor or appease a god), or reparations (e.g., for adultery or theft) are routinely expressed, in large part, as quantities of cloth. In the late 1960s, when a skirt-length piece of cloth cost one Suriname guilder, Saramaka women used it conceptually as the basic monetary unit. Those selling rice or peanuts to the local mission, for example, would express their prices as a certain number of *koósu* ("cloths" or "skirts"), though they were paid in the equivalent number of guilders.

6. In a nuanced discussion of Ogun in Africa and the New World, Sandra Barnes has made an analogous argument, proposing that throughout the continent African ironworkers "are exceptional members of society with particularly high *or low* status (since their work makes them either feared *or revered*)" (1989:4, our italics). Once again, what matters most is not the form but the underlying principle. Or, as Lawrence Levine has put it more generally, African slaves "though they varied widely in language, institutions, gods and familial patterns . . . shared a fundamental outlook toward the past, present and future and a common means of cultural expression" (1977:4).

7. A study of the *malungu*—"shipmate"—complex in southern Brazil (Slenes 1991–92) helps nuance the notion of inter-African syncretism by pointing to some of its micro-processes. (The broader distribution and significance of similar "shipmate" institutions in Jamaica, Suriname, Haiti, and Trinidad is discussed in Mintz and Price 1992 [1976]:43–44.) Here, an eighteenth-century word that existed in variant forms across the large southern part of Africa where people spoke one or another of the languages in the Bantu family is shown to have merged its several related meanings—"big canoe," "companion of suffering," "shipmate,"

and "companion on the journey from life to death across the sea"—soon after the arrival of slaves from this broad region to Brazil. Slenes argues that during the late eighteenth and early nineteenth centuries, when tremendous numbers of new Bantu-speaking slaves were introduced into the state of Rio de Janeiro, an ideal situation existed for the creation of inter-Bantu syncretisms. "Slaves who spoke a Bantu language found themselves not only in the same semantic ship but in the same ontological sea" (ibid.:52). As with the creation of creole languages in the Americas, a necessary condition for the process to develop seems to have been the interaction of speakers of several different African languages who were in a relationship of relatively equal power and who shared certain deep-structure linguistic principles but whose languages were not mutually intelligible.

8. On the large slave plantations of late eighteenth-century Suriname, where some seventy percent of slaves were still African-born (and half of whom had arrived in the New World only during the previous decade), lively rituals and "plays" associated with Loango, Papa, Nago, and other African "nations" were commonly performed (see, for example, Stedman 1988 [1790]:292, 646–47). But similarly named rites among mid-eighteenth-century Saramakas, hardly any of whom were African-born, had already become fully creolized—with a good deal of inter-African exchange and New World elaboration (see R. Price 1990).

There is a longstanding, complex debate about the role of African ethnicity as an ongoing functional principle on New World plantations. For example, Monica Schuler has taken R. P. to task for (over)emphasizing the rapidity of creolization and has, in contrast, stressed what she sees as the continuing importance of African ethnic solidarity (Schuler 1970, 1979, 1980; see also Karasch 1979). Some scholars have claimed that planters in some colonies at some moments encouraged the maintenance of African ethnic solidarity as a means of control, while others have pointed to widely documented planters' practices of separating slaves of a particular ethnic origin for the same purpose (see, for references, R. Price 1979:142). R. P. has cautioned that "such statements, which originate in data from particular societies at particular historical moments, can be converted into generalizations only at the risk of obscuring the very variation that is crucial to understanding the nature of New World slavery" (ibid.:143). Nevertheless, our reading of the broad historical record suggests that the great bulk of cases of strong ethnic solidarity among New World slaves occurred relatively late (during the nineteenth century), and that the initial cultural processes on New World plantations involved a shift in commitment from exclusivistic African to open-ended creole realities. In most cases of ethnic-based organization, late-coming slaves (or liberated Africans or indentured Africans) arrived into already creolized, fairly ancient (former) slave cultures where at first they simply banded together as "foreigners." Roger Bastide, working with Brazilian materials, gave an overview that dissolves many of these difficulties.

> We know little about Afro-Brazilian religions in those distant times, but we should certainly give up the notion of [African] cult centers surviving through centuries down to the present day . . . and think rather of a chaotic proliferation of cults or cult fragments arising only to die out and give way to others with every new wave of [African] arrivals. The *candomblés*, *xangôs* and *batuques* of today are not survivals of ancient sects reaching back into the Brazilian past but relatively recent organizations. . . . We should therefore think of the religious life of Africans that were broken and resumed but that nevertheless retained from one century to the next . . . the same fidelity to the African mystique or mystiques. (1978 [1960]:47–48)

And J. Lorand Matory's recent research on Bahian *candomblé* and on Yoruba religion lends considerable muscle to Bastide's assertions (1999).

We are in sympathy with Edward Kamau Brathwaite's poetic and imaginative critique of Monica Schuler's attempt to specify Jamaican *myal* as a solar, "Kongo" retention. "It may," writes Brathwaite, "have been so in Central Africa, but in Jamaica it was (and is) a fragment or aspect of a larger creolised form which includes *obiah*, *jonkonnu*, and *kumina/pukumina*, 'convince,' *congo* and *ettu*" (1979:152 *et passim*).

In any case, for the Maroons of Suriname the situation is relatively clear. All evidence shows that there was early and quite thorough creolization, consisting largely of inter-African syncretism. New World, local realities quickly became the focus of people's attention, and the core of personal and group identity. (See van Stipriaan 1993 for an analogous argument regarding the culture of slaves in Suriname.)

9. It may be useful to comment here on a common misreading of the model of creolization that was proposed programmatically in Mintz and Price 1992 [1976] and has been developed in more concrete terms in S. and R. Price 1980 and in the present book. Some scholars have gone so far as to (mis)interpret our position as a denial of the existence of an African cultural heritage in the Americas. As the 1992 preface to Mintz and Price 1992 [1976] noted,

> It seemed that many such reactions originated in a desire to

polarize Afro-Americanist scholarship into a flatly "for" or "against" position in regard to African cultural retentions. For instance, Mervyn Alleyne dubbed us "creation theorists," charging us with exaggerated attention to the cultural creativity of enslaved Africans in the New World; yet his own book reaches conclusions close to our own (1988). Daniel Crowley castigated Sally and Richard Price's *Afro-American Arts of the Suriname Rain Forest*, which develops the conceptual approach in a particular historical context, as "badly overstat[ing] a good case" (1981). Joey Dillard found the authors "not completely on the side of the angels," their arguments "controversial if not positively heretical" (1976).

In a similar, more recent misreading, John Thornton claims that we depict "the resulting mixture" as "distinctly European and European-oriented, with the African elements giving it flavor rather than substance" (1992:184–85). On the question of the heterogeneity of Africans imported into the New World, Thornton writes that "on the whole, modern research has tended to side with Mintz and Price, who argue that there were major differences among the cultures of the Atlantic coast of Africa" (1992:184), but he then tries to show that this represents an exaggeration and that Africans were "not nearly so diverse as to create the kind of cultural confusion posited by those who see African diversity as a barrier to the development of an African-based American culture" (1992:187). Needless to say, we have never imagined that there was "cultural confusion," nor have we seen diversity as a "barrier." Rather, we have consistently presented cultural diversity as an encouragement to inter-African syncretism and creolization. Thornton takes great pains to demonstrate that on large plantations in the Americas, "slaves would typically have no trouble finding members of their own nation with whom to communicate" (1992:199) and that "the slave trade and subsequent transfer to New World plantations was not, therefore, quite as randomizing a process as posited by those who argue that Africans had to start from scratch culturally upon their arrival in the New World" (1992:204). We would note that the idea of Afro-Americans "starting from scratch" is not a position anyone has endorsed for decades, perhaps since the days of E. Franklin Frazier (1939).

For all his contestational rhetoric, Thornton in the end (like Alleyne) comes back to a position very close to our own. After asserting that "African slaves arriving in Atlantic colonies did not face as many barriers to cultural transmission as scholars such as Mintz and Price have maintained" (1992:206), he writes, "However, they probably did not simply recommence an African culture in the New World. . . . They were, after all, in a new environment. . . . Even if they were able to transmit their culture to a new generation, the culture passed on was not the original African culture. . . . Afro-Atlantic culture became more homogenous than the diverse African cultures that composed it, merging these cultures together and including European culture as well. The evidence suggests that the slaves were not militant cultural nationalists who sought to preserve everything African but rather showed great flexibility in adapting and changing their culture" (1992:206).

Ideology and rhetoric aside, there is certainly a continuing need for careful studies of the processes by which Africans in the New World, in diverse circumstances and at different times, became Afro-Americans. For an excellent recent overview of these issues, see Morgan 1997.

10. Our announcement, in a 1980 recap of textile art history, that patchwork arts were "finally abandoned in the 1970s," was, we now understand, premature.

11. The various illustrations of cicatrized slaves in Suriname all depict people born in Africa, not the New World. For discussion of the history of cicatrization in Suriname, see R. and S. Price 1972a, and S. and R. Price 1980:88–92.

12. It was to explain such independent invention of similar cultural forms by widely separated peoples that early twentieth-century anthropologists coined the "Principle of Limited Possibilities" (see, for example, Goldenweiser 1913). More recently, William Sturtevant has presented an excellent methodological critique of the reconstruction of culture history from the spatial distribution of cultural traits, and has gone on to argue that certain formal similarities between the aboriginal cultures of southeastern North America and the Antilles cannot be construed as proof of historical contact (1960). Alfonso Caso, in reevaluating the case for cultural diffusion between the Old and New Worlds, has argued on the basis of a large number of fascinating examples that "resemblances of form have very little value as evidence [of historical connection] even when they are obvious" (1964:55). Long ago, Robert Lowie stated the general case more boldly: "The sensible traits of an ethnographic object may determine its character from the standpoint of a curiosity dealer, but never from that of a scientific ethnologist" (1912:331).

13. The fact that in some ways time has proven Bastide's classification of *candomblé* and *santería* inexact does not weaken the ideological distinction he was drawing. That we now know, for example, how dynamic and ever changing *candomblé* has been through time in no way cancels out its adherents' continuing commitment to the idea of an African authen-

ticity (see Matory 1999).

14. The African examples in this paragraph are taken from Lamb 1975:
    134–36, Posnansky 1992:126, Rattray 1927:240–46, and Warren and
    Andrews 1977:14. For more on Maroon cloth names, including addi-
    tional examples, see Chapter 4.

15. Robert Farris Thompson has made a valiant effort to document histori-
    cally intermediate textiles that would maintain a medium-specific conti-
    nuity. But none of his examples, which are based on such practices as
    "correcting" original collection data, hold up under close examination—
    see S. Price n.d.

16. Nearly twenty years ago, we raised the possibility that similar processes
    had contributed to the development of U.S. African-American quilts,
    but noted that "the historical research necessary to reconstruct this art
    in the United States is still in a very early stage (S. and R. Price 1980:
    223). Since then, these quilts have inspired considerable attention
    among collectors, art historians, and folklorists, and been the focus of
    numerous exhibitions and art catalogues. Excellent work has begun to
    appear on the biographies and aesthetic perspectives of individual
    artists (see, for example, Ferris 1982, Grudin 1990, Leon 1992, and
    Wahlman 1993), but almost nothing has yet been uncovered regarding
    the early developmental history of the art.

References

Aboikoni, Laurens

    1997   *Di duumi u Gaama Aboikoni (The funeral of Granman Aboikoni)*. Paramaribo, Suriname: Summer Institute of Linguistics.

Ahlbrinck, W.

    1931   "Encyclopaedie der Karaïben." *Verhandelingen der Koninklijke Akademie van Wetenschappen te Amsterdam (Afdeeling Letterkunde, Nieuwe Reeks)* 27:1–555.

Alleyne, Mervyn

    1988   *Roots of Jamaican Culture*. London: Pluto Press.

Anelli, Serge

    1991   *Mato: Contes aloukous*. Cayenne, French Guiana: Mi Wani Sabi et Apelguy-Les Deux Fleuves.

Appiah, Kwame Anthony

    1992   *In My Father's House: Africa in the Philosophy of Culture*. New York: Oxford University Press.

    1997   "The Arts of Africa." *The New York Review of Books* 44(7):46–51 (April 24).

Arends, Jacques

    1995   "Demographic Factors in the Formation of Sranan." In *The Early Stages of Creolization*, ed. Jacques Arends, 233–85. Amsterdam: John Benjamins.

Armstrong, Robert Plant

    1971   *The Affecting Presence*. Urbana: University of Illinois Press.

Barbot, John

    1732   "A Description of the Coasts of North and South Guinea." In *A Collection of Voyages and Travels*, ed. Awnsham Churchill, vol. 5. London.

Barnes, Sandra T.

    1989   *Africa's Ogun: Old World and New*. Bloomington: Indiana University Press.

Bastide, Roger

    1967   *Les amériques noires*. Paris: Payot.

    1978 [1960]   *The African Religions of Brazil: Toward a Sociology of the Interpenetration of Civilizations*. Baltimore: Johns Hopkins University Press.

Bates, Henry Walter

  1873   *The Naturalist on the River Amazons*. 3rd ed. London: John
          Murray.

de Beet, Chris, and Miriam Sterman

  1981   *People in Between: The Matawai Maroons of Suriname*. Utrecht:
          Krips Repro Meppel.

de Beet, Chris, and H. U. E. Thoden van Velzen

  1977   "Bush Negro Prophetic Movements: Religions of Despair?"
          Bijdragen tot de Taal-, Land- en Volkenkunde 133:100–35.

Behn, Aphra

  1688   *Oroonoko, or The Royal Slave: A True History*. London: W. Can-
          ning.

Benoit, P. J.

  1839   *Voyage à Surinam: Description des possessions néerlandaises dans
          la Guyane*. Bruxelles: Société des Beaux-Arts.

Berliner, Paul F.

  1978   *The Soul of Mbira: Music and Traditions of the Shona People of
          Zimbabwe*. Berkeley: University of California Press.

Bilby, Kenneth M.

  1989   "La musique aluku." In *Musiques en Guyane*, ed. Marie-Paule
          Jean-Louis et Gérard Collomb, 49–72. Cayenne, French Guiana:
          Bureau du Patrimoine Ethnologique.

  1990   *The Remaking of the Aluku: Culture, Politics, and Maroon Eth-
          nicity in French South America*. Unpublished Ph.D. dissertation,
          Johns Hopkins University.

  1995   "Introducing the Popular Music of Suriname." In *Caribbean
          Currents: Caribbean Music from Rumba to Reggae*, by Peter
          Manuel, with Kenneth Bilby and Michael Largey, 221–31.
          Philadelphia: Temple University Press.

  1999   "'Roots Explosion': Indigenization and Cosmopolitanism in Con-
          temporary Surinamese Popular Music." *Ethnomusicology* 43.

van Binnendijk, Chandra, and Paul Faber

  1992   *Sranan: Cultuur in Suriname*. Amsterdam: Koninklijk Instituut
          voor de Tropen.

Bishop, Robert, and Elizabeth Safanda

  1976   *A Gallery of Amish Quilts: Design Diversity from a Plain People*.
          New York: Dutton.

Bonaparte, Prince Roland

  1884   *Les habitants de Suriname, notes recueillies à l'exposition colo-
          niale d'Amsterdam en 1883*. Paris: A. Quantin.

Brathwaite, Edward Kamau
   1979   "Commentary Three." *Historical Reflections* 6:150–55.
Bröer, Christian
   1997   "Leven met twee landen: De veranderende sociale positie van Surinaamse remigranten." *Amsterdams Sociologisch Tijdschrift* 23(4):608–39.
Bruné, Paulin
   1995   *Sièges & Sculptures chez les Noirs-Marrons des Guyanes.* Cayenne, French Guiana: Editions Equinoxe Communication.
Brunetti, Jules
   1890   *La Guyane Française: Souvenirs et impressions de voyage.* Tours, France: Alfred Mame et Fils.
Bruyning, C. F. A. and Lou Lichtveld
   1959   *Suriname: A New Nation in South America.* Paramaribo, Suriname: Radhakishun.
Caso, Alfonso
   1964   "Relations between the Old and New Worlds: A Note on Methodology." *Proceedings of the 35th International Congress of Americanists*, vol. 1 (Mexico 1962):55–71.
Cassidy, F. G., and R. B. Le Page
   1967   *Dictionary of Jamaican English.* Cambridge, England: Cambridge University Press.
Cateau van Rosevelt, J. F. A., and J. F. A. E. van Lansberge
   1873   "Verslag van de reis ter opname van de Rivier Suriname." In "Uit de geschiedenis der opening van het Surinaamsche binnenland," by W. R. Menkman. *De West-Indische Gids* 27 (1946):182–92, 289–99, 321–43.
Chappel, T. J. H.
   1977   *Decorated Gourds in North-Eastern Nigeria.* Lagos, Nigeria: Federal Department of Antiquities.
Clifford, James
   1985   "Histories of the Tribal and the Modern." *Art in America* 73(4):164–77.
   1986   "Partial Truths." In *Writing Culture: The Poetics and Politics of Ethnography*, ed. James Clifford and George E. Marcus, 1–16. Berkeley: University of California Press.
   1988   *The Predicament of Culture: Twentieth Century Ethnography, Literature, and Art.* Cambridge, Massachusetts: Harvard University Press.
   1997   *Routes: Travel and Translation in the Late Twentieth Century.* Cambridge, Massachusetts: Harvard University Press.

Colchester, Marcus

    1995   *Forest Politics in Suriname*. Utrecht: International Books (in collaboration with the World Rainforest Movement).

Cole, Douglas

    1985   *Captured Heritage: The Scramble for Northwest Coast Artifacts*. Seattle: University of Washington Press.

van Coll, C.

    1903   "Gegevens over land en volk van Suriname." *Bijdragen tot de Taal-, Land- en Volkenkunde* 55:451–635.

Coombes, Annie E.

    1994   *Reinventing Africa: Museums, Material Culture, and Popular Imagination*. New Haven: Yale University Press.

Coster, A. M.

    1866   De Boschnegers in de kolonie Suriname, hun leven, zeden, en gewoonten. *Bijdragen tot de Taal-, Land- en Volkenkunde* 13:1–36.

Counter, S. Allen, Jr., and David L. Evans

    n.d.   *The Bush Afro-Americans of Surinam and French Guiana: The Connecting Link*. Pamphlet.

    1981   *I Sought My Brother: An Afro-American Reunion*. Cambridge, Massachusetts: MIT Press.

Crevaux, Jules

    1879   "Voyage d'exploration dans l'intérieur des Guyanes, 1876–77." *Le Tour du Monde* 20:337–416.

Crowley, Daniel J.

    1956   "Bush Negro Combs: A Structural Analysis." *Vox Guyanae* 2:145–61.

    1981   "Review of S. and R. Price, *Afro-American Arts of the Suriname Rain Forest*." *African Arts* 16:27, 80–81.

Dark, Philip J. C.

    1951   "Some Notes on the Carving of Calabashes by the Bush Negroes of Surinam." *Man* 51:57–61.

    1952   "Bush Negro Calabash Carving." *Man* 52:126.

    1954   *Bush Negro Art: An African Art in the Americas*. London: Tiranti.

Dening, Greg

    1980   *Islands and Beaches. Discourse on a Silent Land: Marquesas 1774–1880*. Honolulu: University Press of Hawaii.

Dillard, J. L.

    1976   *Black Names*. The Hague: Mouton.

Dubelaar, C. N., and André Pakosie

    1988   "Seven Notes in Afaka Script." *New West Indian Guide* 62:146–64.

1993 "Kago Buku: Notes by Captain Kago from Tabiki, Tapanahoni River, Suriname, Written in Afaka Script." *New West Indian Guide* 67:239–79.

Edwards, Joanna P.

1992 "The Sociological Significance and Uses of Mɛnde Country Cloth." In *History, Design, and Craft in West African Strip-Woven Cloth*, ed. Sylvia H. Williams et al., 133–68. Washington, D.C.: National Museum of African Art.

Eilerts de Haan, J. G. W. J.

1910 "Verslag van de expeditie naar de Suriname-Rivier." *Tijdschrift van het Koninklijk Nederlandisch Aardrijkskundig Genootschap* 27:403–68, 641–701.

Epstein, Dena J.

1977 *Sinful Tunes and Spirituals: Black Folk Music to the Civil War.* Urbana: University of Illinois Press.

van Eyck, J. W. S.

1830 "Beschouwing van den tegenwoordigen staat, zeden en gewoonten van de Saramaccaner bevredigde Boschnegers, in deze kolonie." In *Surinaamsche almanak voor het jaar 1830*, 260–77. Amsterdam: C. G. Sulpke.

Fagg, William

1952 "Notes on Some West African Americana." *Man* 52:119–22.

Fermin, Phillippe

1769 *Déscription générale, historique, géographique et physique de la colonie de Surinam.* Amsterdam: E. van Harrevelt.

Ferris, William

1982 *Local Color: A Sense of Place in Folk Art.* New York: McGraw-Hill.

Forest Peoples Programme

1998a "Suriname Information Update," 20 April. Internet.

1998b "Suriname Information Update," 7 May. Internet.

Fotografie

1990 *Fotografie in Suriname 1839–1939 / Photography in Suriname 1839–1939.* Amsterdam: Fragment Uitgeverij.

Franssen Herderschee, A.

1905 "Verslag van de Gonini-expeditie." *Tijdschrift van het Koninklijk Nederlandisch Aardrijkskundig Genootschap* 22:1–174.

Frazier, E. Franklin

1939 *The Negro Family in the United States.* Chicago: University of Chicago Press.

de Goeje, C. H.

    1908   "Verslag der Toemoekhoemoek-expeditie." *Tijdschrift van het Koninklijk Nederlandisch Aardrijkskundig Genootschap* 25:943–1169.

Goldenweiser, A. A.

    1913   "The Principle of Limited Possibilities in the Development of Culture." *Journal of American Folklore* 26:259–90.

Greenfield, Jeanette

    1989   *The Return of Cultural Treasures*. Cambridge, England: Cambridge University Press.

Griaule, Marcel, and Germaine Dieterlen

    1935   "Calebasses Dahoméennes." *Journal de la Société des Africanistes* 5:203–7.

Grudin, Eva Ungar

    1990   *Stitching Memories: African-American Story Quilts*. Williamstown, Massachusetts: Williams College Museum of Art.

Hall, Michael D., and Eugene W. Metcalf, Jr. (eds.), with Roger Cardinal

    1994   *The Artist Outsider: Creativity and the Boundaries of Culture*. Washington, D.C.: Smithsonian Institution Press.

Haraway, Donna

    1989   *Primate Visions: Gender, Race, and Nature in the World of Modern Science*. New York: Routledge.

Hartsinck, Jan Jacob

    1770   *Beschrijving van Guyana of de Wilde Kust in Zuid-Amerika*. Amsterdam: Gerrit Tielenburg.

Henderson, Amy, and Adrienne Kaeppler (eds.)

    1996   *Exhibiting Dilemmas: Issues of Representation at the Smithsonian*. Washington, D.C.: Smithsonian Institution Press.

Herlein, J. D.

    1718   *Beschryvinge van de Volk-plantinge Zuriname*. Leeuwarden: Meindert Injema.

Herskovits, Melville J.

    1930   "Bush Negro Art." *The Arts* 17, no. 51:25–37. (Reprinted in *The New World Negro*, ed. Frances Herskovits, 157–67. Bloomington, Indiana: Indiana University Press, 1966.)

    1951   "Bush Negro Calabash Carving." *Man* 51:163–64.

    1952   "Note sur la divination judiciaire par le cadavre en Guyane Hollandaise." In *Les afro-américains. Mémoires de l'Institut Français d'Afrique Noire* 27:187–92.

Herskovits, Melville J., and Frances S. Herskovits

    1934   *Rebel Destiny: Among the Bush Negroes of Dutch Guiana*. New York: McGraw-Hill.

Hiller, Susan (ed.)

 1991   *The Myth of Primitivism: Perspectives on Art*. London: Routledge.

Hodder, B. W.

 1980   "Indigenous Cloth Trade and Marketing in Africa." In *Textiles of Africa*, ed. Dale Idiens and K. G. Ponting, 203–10. Bath, U.K., Pasold Research Fund.

Holm, Bill

 1965   *Northwest Coast Indian Art: An Analysis of Form*. Seattle: University of Washington Press.

Hoogbergen, Wim

 1990   *The Boni Maroon Wars in Suriname*. Leiden: E. J. Brill.

Hurault, Jean

 1961   *Les Noirs Réfugiés Boni de la Guyane Française*. Dakar: Institut Français d'Afrique Noire.

 1970   *Africains de Guyane: La vie matérielle et l'art des Noirs Réfugiés de Guyane*. Paris-The Hague: Mouton.

Joest, Wilhelm

 1893   "Ethnographisches und Verwandtes aus Guyana." *International Archives of Ethnography* 5, supplement.

Johnson, Marion

 1980   "Cloth as Money: The Cloth Strip Currencies of Africa." In *Textiles of Africa*, ed. Dale Idiens and K. G. Ponting, 193–202. Bath, U.K.: Pasold Research Fund.

Johnston, Harry H.

 1910   *The Negro in the New World*. London: Methuen.

Jones, LeRoi [Amiri Baraka]

 1967   *Black Music*. New York: William Morrow.

Kahn, Morton C.

 1931   *Djuka: The Bush Negroes of Dutch Guiana*. New York: The Viking Press.

 1939   "Africa's Lost Tribes in South America: An On-the-Spot Account of Blood-Chilling African Rites of 200 Years Ago Preserved Intact in the Jungles of South America by a Tribe of Runaway Slaves." *Natural History* 43:209–15, 232.

 1954   "Little Africa in America: The Bush Negroes." *Américas* 6(10):6–8,41–43.

Kappler, August

 1854   *Zes jaren in Suriname*. Utrecht: W. F. Dannenfelser.

Karasch, Mary

 1979   "Commentary One." *Historical Reflections* 6:138–41.

Köbben, A. J. F.

    1968   "Continuity in Change: Cottica Djuka Society as a Changing System." *Bijdragen tot de Taal-, Land- en Volkenkunde* 124:56–90.

Koch-Grünberg, Theodor

    1910   *Zwei Jahre unter den Indianern: Reisen in Nordwest Brasilien, 1903–05.* Berlin.

Kolfin, Elmer

    1997   *Van de Slavenzweep en de Muze: Twee Eeuwen Verbeelding van Slavernij in Suriname.* Leiden: KITLV.

Krech, Shepard, III

    1989   *A Victorian Earl in the Arctic: The Travels and Collections of the Fifth Earl of Lonsdale, 1888–89.* Seattle: University of Washington Press.

Lamb, Venice

    1975   *West African Weaving.* London: Duckworth.

Leon, Eli

    1992   *Models in the Mind: African Prototypes in American Patchwork.* Winston-Salem North Carolina: Winston-Salem State University.

Levine, Lawrence W.

    1977   *Black Culture and Black Consciousness: Afro-American Folk Thought from Slavery to Freedom.* New York: Oxford University Press.

Lindblom, Gerhard

    1924   *Afrikanische Relikte und Indiansche Entlehnungen in der Kultur der Busch-Neger Surinams.* Gothenburg: Elanders Boktryckeri Aktiebolag.

Lippard, Lucy R.

    1990   *Mixed Blessings: New Art in a Multicultural America.* New York: Pantheon.

Lomax, Alan

    1970   "The Homogeneity of African-Afro-American Musical Style." In *Afro-American Anthropology: Contemporary Perspectives,* ed. Norman E. Whitten, Jr., and John F. Szwed, 181–201. New York, Free Press.

Long, Edward

    1774   *The History of Jamaica.* London: T. Lowndes.

Lowie, Robert H.

    1912   "On the Principle of Convergence in Ethnology." Reprinted in *Lowie's Selected Papers in Anthropology,* ed. Cora Du Bois, 312–35. Berkeley: University of California Press, 1960.

Mack, John

    1980   "Bakuba Embroidery Patterns: A Commentary on their Social
           and Political Implications." In *Textiles of Africa*, ed. Dale Idiens
           and K. G. Ponting, 163–74. Bath, U.K.: Pasold Research Fund.

Marcus, George E., and Fred R. Myers (eds.)

    1995   *The Traffic in Culture: Refiguring Art and Anthropology*. Berkeley:
           University of California Press.

Matory, J. Lorand

    1999   *The Trans-Atlantic Nation: Tradition, Transnationalism, and
           Matriarchy in the Afro-Brazilian Candomblé*. Princeton, New
           Jersey: Princeton University Press.

van Meeteren, Nicolaas

    1947   *Volkskunde van Curaçao*. Willemstad, Curaçao.

Messenger, Phyllis Mauch (ed.)

    1989   *The Ethics of Collecting Cultural Property: Whose Culture?
           Whose Property?* Albuquerque: University of New Mexico Press.

Michaels, Eric

    1993   *Bad Aboriginal Art: Tradition, Media, and Technological Horizons*.
           Minneapolis: University of Minnesota Press.

Mintz, Sidney W., and Richard Price

    1992 [1976]   *The Birth of African-American Culture: An Anthropological
           Approach*. Boston: Beacon Press.

Morgan, Philip D.

    1997   "The Cultural Implications of the Atlantic Slave Trade: African
           Regional Origins, American Destinations, and New World Devel-
           opments." *Slavery & Abolition* 18:122–45.

Muntslag, F. H. J.

    1966   *Tembe: Surinaamse houtsnijkunst*. Amsterdam: Prins Bernard
           Fonds.

    1979   *Paw a paw dindoe: Surinaamse houtsnijkunst*. Paramaribo, Suri-
           name: Vaco.

Myers, Fred R.

    n.d.   *The Practice of Pintupi Painting: Nation, State, and Aboriginal
           Fine Art*. Berkeley: University of California Press.

Naipaul, Shiva

    1981   "Suriname: A Tableau of Savage Innocence." *Geo* 3(3):74–94.

Neumann, Peter

    1961   "Eine verzierte Kalebassenschüssel aus Suriname."
           *Veröffentlichungen des Städtischens Museums für Völkerkunde zu
           Leipzig* 11:481–98.

O'Hanlon, Michael

 1995   *Paradise: Portraying the New Guinea Highlands*. London: British
          Museum Press.

Oudschans-Dentz, Fred.

 1935/36 "Het boschnegerdeurslot: Zijn oorsprong en toepassing." *De
          West-Indische Gids* 17:228–30.

Oudschans-Dentz, Fred., and Herm. J. Jacobs

 1917   *Onze West in beeld en woord*. Amsterdam: J. H. de Bussy.

van Panhuys, L. C.

 1899   "Toelichting betreffende de voorwerpen verzameld bij de Aucaner
          Boschnegers." In *Catalogus der Nederlandsche West-Indische
          tentoonstelling te Haarlem*, 74–82.

 1908   "Iets over de Marowijne rivier en hare geschiedenis." *Bulletin
          van het Koloniaal Museum te Haarlem* 12:15–66.

 1925   "Contribution à l'étude de la distribution de la serrure à
          chevilles." *Journal de la Société des Américanistes, Paris* 17:271–74.

 1928   "Quelques ornements des nègres des bois de la Guyane Néer-
          landaise." *Proceedings of the International Congress of American-
          ists* 22:231–74.

 1934   "African Customs and Beliefs Preserved for Two Centuries in the
          Interior of Dutch Guiana." *Proceedings of the International Con-
          gress of Anthropological and Ethnological Sciences* 1:247–48.

Pearce, Susan M.

 1993   *Museums, Objects, and Collections: A Cultural Study*. Washing-
          ton, D.C.: Smithsonian Institution Press.

 1995   *On Collecting*. London: Routledge.

Phillips, Ruth B., and Christopher B. Steiner (eds.)

 1999   *Unpacking Culture: Art and Commodity in Colonial and Postcolo-
          nial Worlds*. Berkeley, California: University of California Press.

Plattner, Stuart

 1996   *High Art Down Home: An Economic Ethnography of a Local Art
          Market*. Chicago: University of Chicago Press.

Polimé, T. S., and H. U. E. Thoden van Velzen

 1988   *Vluchtelingen, opstandelingen en andere Bosnegers van Oost-
          Suriname, 1986–1988*. Utrecht: Instituut voor Culturele
          Antropologie.

van de Poll, Willem

 1951   *Suriname: Een fotoreportage van land en volk*. The Hague: W.
          van Hoeve.

Posnansky, Merrick

 1992   "Traditional Cloth from the Ewe Heartland." In *History, Design,* and Craft in West African Strip-Woven Cloth, Sylvia H. Williams et al., 113–32. Washington, D.C.: National Museum of African Art.

Postma, Johannes Menne

1990   The Dutch in the Atlantic Slave Trade 1600–1815. Cambridge, England: Cambridge University Press.

Price, Richard

1970a   "Saramaka Emigration and Marriage: A Case Study of Social Change." Southwestern Journal of Anthropology 26:157–89.

1970b   "Saramaka Woodcarving: The Development of an Afroamerican Art." Man 5:363–78.

1975a   "KiKoongo and Saramaccan: A Reappraisal." Bijdragen tot de Taal-, Land- en Volkenkunde 131:461–78.

1975b   Saramaka Social Structure: Analysis of a Maroon Society in Surinam. Río Piedras, Puerto Rico: Institute of Caribbean Studies of the University of Puerto Rico.

1976   The Guiana Maroons: A Historical and Bibliographical Introduction. Baltimore, Maryland: Johns Hopkins University Press.

1979   "Commentary Two." Historical Reflections 6:141–49.

1983a   First-Time: The Historical Vision of an Afro-American People. Baltimore, Maryland: Johns Hopkins University Press.

1983b   To Slay the Hydra: Dutch Colonial Perspectives on the Saramaka Wars. Ann Arbor, Michigan: Karoma.

1990   Alabi's World. Baltimore, Maryland: Johns Hopkins University Press.

1995   "Executing Ethnicity: The Killings in Suriname." Cultural Anthropology 10:437–71.

1996 [1973]   Maroon Societies: Rebel Slave Communities in the Americas, ed. R. Price, 3rd edition. Baltimore, Maryland: Johns Hopkins University Press.

1998   "Scrapping Maroon History: Brazil's Promise, Suriname's Shame." New West Indian Guide 72:233–55.

Price, Richard, and Sally Price

1972a   "Kammbá: The Ethnohistory of an Afro-American Art." Antropológica 32:3–27.

1972b   "Saramaka Onomastics: An Afro-American Naming System." Ethnology 11:341–67.

1976   "Secret Play Languages in Saramaka: Linguistic Disguise in a Caribbean Creole." In Speech Play, ed. Barbara Kirshenblatt-Gimblett, 37–50. Philadelphia: University of Pennsylvania Press.

1977   Music from Saramaka: A Dynamic Afro-American Tradition.

Phonograph record/cassette, with ethnographic notes. New York: Folkways FE 4225. Available from Smithsonian Folkways, Washington, D.C.

1979   "John Gabriel Stedman's Collection of 18th-Century Artifacts from Suriname." *Nieuwe West-Indische Gids* 53:121–40.

1988   "Introduction." In *Narrative of a Five Years Expedition against the Revolted Negroes of Surinam,* by John Gabriel Stedman [1790], ed. Richard Price and Sally Price, xiii–xcvii. Baltimore, Maryland: Johns Hopkins University Press.

1989   "Working for the Man: A Saramaka Outlook on Kourou." *New West Indian Guide* 63:199–207.

1991   *Two Evenings in Saramaka.* Chicago: University of Chicago Press.

1992a   *Equatoria.* New York: Routledge.

1992b   *Stedman's Surinam: Life in an Eighteenth-Century Slave Society.* An abridged, modernized edition of *Narrative of a Five Years Expedition against the Revolted Negroes of Surinam,* by John Gabriel Stedman, ed. Richard Price and Sally Price. Baltimore, Maryland: Johns Hopkins University Press.

1992c   "Widerstand, Rebellion und Freiheit: Maroon Societies in Amerika und ihre Kunst." In *Afrika in Amerika,* ed. Corinna Raddatz, 157–73. Hamburg: Hamburgisches Museum für Völkerkunde.

1994   *On the Mall.* Bloomington: Indiana University Press.

1995   *Enigma Variations.* Cambridge, Massachusetts: Harvard University Press.

Price, Sally

1978   "Reciprocity and Social Distance: A Reconsideration." *Ethnology* 17:339–50.

1982   "When Is a Calabash Not a Calabash?" *New West Indian Guide* 56:69–82.

1983   "Sexism and the Construction of Reality: An Afro-American Example." *American Ethnologist* 10:460–76.

1989   *Primitive Art in Civilized Places.* Chicago: University of Chicago Press.

1993[1984]   *Co-Wives and Calabashes.* Ann Arbor, Michigan: University of Michigan Press.

1994   "The Curse's Blessing." *Frontiers: A Journal of Women's Studies* 14(2):126–45.

1999   "The Centrality of Margins in African-American Art." In *The African Diaspora: African Origins and New World Self-Fashion-*

ing, ed. Carole Boyce Davies, Isidore Okpewho, and Ali Mazrui. Bloomington, Indiana: Indiana University Press.

n.d. "At the Cutting Edge: Patchwork and the Process of Artistic Innovation." In the forthcoming *Essays in Honor of William C. Sturtevant,* ed. Ives Goddard and William Merrill. Washington, D.C.: Smithsonian Institution.

Price, Sally, and Richard Price

1980 *Afro-American Arts of the Suriname Rain Forest.* Berkeley: University of California Press.

Rattray, R. S.

1927 *Religion and Art in Ashanti.* Oxford, England: Oxford University Press.

Rhodes, Colin

1994 *Primitivism and Modern Art.* London: Thames and Hudson.

Riemer, Johann Andreus

1801 *Missions-Reise nach Suriname und Barbice zu einer am Surinamflusse im dritten Grad van Linie wohnenden Freinegernation.* Zittau und Leipzig.

Root, Deborah

1996 *Cannibal Culture: Art, Appropriation, and the Commodification of Difference.* Boulder, Colorado: Westview Press.

Rosaldo, Renato

1980 *Ilongot Headhunting 1883–1974: A Study in Society and History.* Stanford, California: Stanford University Press.

Roth, Walter Edmund

1924 "An Introductory Study of the Arts, Crafts, and Customs of the Guiana Indians." *Thirty-Eighth Annual Report of the Bureau of American Ethnology,* Washington, D.C.:25–745.

von Sack, Baron Albert

1810 *A Narrative of a Voyage to Surinam.* London: W. Bulmer.

Schildkrout, Enid, and Curtis A. Keim

1990 *African Reflections: Art from Northeastern Zaire.* Seattle: University of Washington Press.

Scholtens, Ben, Gloria Wekker, Laddy van Putten, and Stanley Dieko

1992 *Gaama Duumi, Buta Gaama: Overlijden en Opvolging van Aboikoni, Grootopperhoofd van de Saramaka Bosnegers.* Paramaribo, Suriname: Cultuurstudies/Vaco.

Schuler, Monica

1970 "Akan Slave Revolts in the British Caribbean." *Savacou* 1:8–31.

1979 "Afro-American Slave Culture." *Historical Reflections* 6:121–37.

1980 *"Alas, Alas, Kongo": A Social History of Indentured African Immi-*

gration into Jamaica, 1841–1865. Baltimore, Maryland: Johns
Hopkins University Press.

Schumann, C. L.

1778   "Saramaccanisch Deutsches Wörter-Buch." In "Die Sprache der
Saramakkaneger in Surinam," Hugo Schuchardt (*Verhandelingen
der Koninklijke Akademie van Wetenschappen te Amsterdam*
14[6], 1914, pp. 46–116). Amsterdam: Johannes Müller.

Sieber, Roy

1972   *African Textiles and Decorative Arts*. New York: The Museum of
Modern Art.

1979   "African Furniture and Household Goods." *African Arts*
12(4):24–31, 90.

Slenes, Robert W.

1991-92 "*Malungu, ngoma vem!*': África coberta e decoberta no Brasil."
Revista USP 12:48–67.

Spalburg, J. G.

1899   *Schets van de Marowijne en hare bewoners*. Paramaribo, Suriname: H. B. Heyde.

Staehelin, F.

1913–19 *Die Mission der Brüdergemeine in Suriname und Berbice im
achtzehnten Jahrhundert*. Herrnhut: Vereins für Brüder-
geschichte in Kommission der Unitätsbuchhandlung in Gnadau.

Stedman, John Gabriel

1988 [1790] *Narrative of a Five Years Expedition against the Revolted
Negroes of Surinam*, ed., with an introduction and notes, by
Richard Price and Sally Price. Baltimore, Maryland: Johns Hop-
kins University Press.

1796   *Narrative, of a Five Years' Expedition, against the Revolted Negroes
of Surinam*. London: J. Johnson and J. Edwards.

Steiner, Christopher B.

1994   *African Art in Transit*. Cambridge, England: Cambridge University Press.

van Stipriaan, Alex

1993a   "'Een verre verwijderd trommelen. . .' Ontwikkeling van Afro-
Surinaamse muziek en dans in de slavernij." In *De Kunstwereld:
Produktie, distributie en receptie in de wereld van kunst en cul-
tuur*, ed. Ton Bevers, Antoon Van den Braembussche, and
Berend Jan Langenberg, 143–73. Hilversum: Verloren.

1993b   *Surinaams contrast: Roofbouw en overleven in een Caraïbische
plantagekolonie, 1750–1863*. Leiden: KITLV Press.

Sturtevant, William C.

1960   *The Significance of Ethnological Similarities between Southeastern North America and the Antilles*. Yale University Publications in Anthropology 64. New Haven: Department of Anthropology, Yale University.

Szwed, John F., and Roger D. Abrahams

1977   "After the Myth: Studying Afro-American Cultural Patterns in the Plantation Literature." In *African Folklore in the New World*, ed. Daniel J. Crowley, 65–86. Austin, Texas: University of Texas Press.

Thoden van Velzen, H. U. E., and W. van Wetering

1988   *The Great Father and the Danger: Religious Cults, Material Forces, and Collective Fantasies in the World of the Surinamese Maroons*. Dordrecht: Foris.

Thomas, Nicholas

1991   *Entangled Objects: Exchange, Material Culture, and Colonialism in the Pacific*. Cambridge, Massachusetts: Harvard University Press.

Thompson, Robert Farris

1966   "An Aesthetic of the Cool: West African Dance." *African Forum* 2(2):85–102.

1969   "Abatan: A Master Potter of the Egbado Yoruba." In *Tradition and Creativity in Tribal Art*, ed. Daniel Biebuyck, 120–82. Los Angeles: University of California Press.

1970   "From Africa." *Yale Alumni Magazine* 34(2)16–21.

1973   "Yoruba Artistic Criticism." In *The Traditional Artist in African Societies*, ed. Warren L. D'Azevedo, 19–61. Bloomington, Indiana: Indiana University Press.

1974   *African Art in Motion*. Los Angeles: University of California Press.

1983   *Flash of the Spirit: African and Afro-American Art and Philosophy*. New York: Random House.

Thornton, John

1992   *Africa and Africans in the Making of the Atlantic World, 1400–1680*. Cambridge, England: Cambridge University Press.

Tripot, J.

1910   *La Guyane: Au pays de l'or, des forçats, et des peaux rouges*. Paris: Plon-Nourrit.

Torgovnick, Marianna

1990   *Gone Primitive: Savage Intellects, Modern Lives*. Chicago: University of Chicago Press.

Turner, Lorenzo Dow

    1949   *Africanisms in the Gullah Dialect*. Chicago: University of Chicago Press.

Vandercook, John Womack

    1926   "We Find an African Tribe in the South American Jungle." *The Mentor* 14(3):19–22.

Vogel, Susan Mullin (ed.)

    1988   *ART/artifact: African Art in Anthropology Collections*. New York: Center for African Art.

Volders, J. L.

    1966   *Bouwkunst in Suriname: Driehonderd jaren nationale architectuur*. Hilversum: G. van Saane.

Wahlman, Maude Southwell

    1993   *Signs and Symbols: African Images in African-American Quilts*. New York: Studio Books.

Walsh, John, and Robert Gannon

    1967   *Time Is Short and the Water Rises*. New York: E. P. Dutton.

Warren, D. M., and J. Kweku Andrews

    1977   *An Ethnoscientific Approach to Akan Arts and Aesthetics*. Philadelphia: I.S.H.I.

van Westerloo, Gerard, and Willem Diepraam

    1975   *Frimangron*. Amsterdam: de Arbeiderspers.

Wilbert, Johannes

    1975   *Warao Basketry: Form and Function*. Los Angeles: UCLA Museum of Cultural History.

Wolf, Eric R.

    1982   *Europe and the People Without History*. Berkeley: University of California Press.

Wooding, Charles J.

    1972   *Winti: Een Afroamerikaanse godsdienst in Suriname*. Meppel: Krips Repro.

Yde, Jens

    1965   *Material Culture of the Waiwái*. Copenhagen: Nationalmuseets, Ethnografisk Roekke X.

Ziff, Bruce, and Pratima V. Rao (eds.)

    1997   *Borrowed Power: Essays on Cultural Appropriation*. New Brunswick, New Jersey: Rutgers University Press.

Additional Information on Illustrations

1.1. Collection of Richard and Sally Price—W97.3 (16 cm.). Photo by Martha Cooper (1998).

1.2. The Prices in Dangogo. Photos by Sally Price and Richard Price.

1.3. Photos by Martha Cooper (Asindoopo).

2.1, 2.2, 2.3. William Blake's early 1790s engravings, made in London, were modeled on Stedman's 1770s drawings made in Suriname (see R. and S. Price 1988).

2.4. Map drafted by Heather Harvey.

2.5. Faanselia, on the upper Pikilio, 1968. Photo by Richard Price.

2.6. Brownsweg. From van Westerloo and Diepraam 1975:158. Photo by Willem Diepraam (1973–75).

2.7. Photo by Richard Price (1968).

2.8. Photo (1962) courtesy of Dr. J. B. Ch. Wekker, Centraal Bureau Luchtkartering, Paramaribo.

2.9. From Joest 1893:plate VI (4).

2.10. Photo by Richard Price.

2.11. Photo by Richard Price.

2.12. Photo by Richard Price.

2.13. Photo by Richard Price (Dangogo, 1968).

2.14. House of Kabuesi, Dangogo. Photo by Richard Price (1968). (For a portrait of Kabuesi, see R. and S. Price 1991:48.)

2.15. Photo by Richard Price (Dangogo, 1968).

2.16. From van de Poll 1951:plate 198.

2.17, 2.18. Photos by Richard Price (Dangogo, 1968).

2.19. The house of Doote, priest of the Gaan-Tata oracle. Photo by Richard Price (Niukonde, 1968). (For a portrait of Doote, see R. and S. Price 1991:196.)

2.20. From Hurault 1961:facing p. 76. Photo by Jean Hurault (Loabi).

2.21. From Hurault 1970:plate 9. Photo by Jean Hurault (Tapanahoni, 1957).

3.1. These cassava cake patterns were made with fine white sand during a 1968 interview in Dangogo. Photos by Sally Price.

3.2. Photo by Richard Price (Dangogo, 1968).

3.3. Collection of Richard and Sally Price—K78.12 (14 cm.). Photo by Antonia Graeber (1980).

3.4. Photo by Richard Price (Dangogo).

3.5. Collection of Richard and Sally Price—T68.10 (62 cm.). Photo by Antonia Graeber (1980).

3.6. Photo by Richard Price (Asindoopo, 1978).

3.7. Collection of Richard and Sally Price—K76.229 (18 cm.). Photo by Antonia Graeber (1980).

3.8. Collection of Richard and Sally Price—K76.109 (26 cm.). Photo by Antonia Graeber (1980).

3.9. Collection of Bonno Thoden van Velzen and Ineke van Wetering, Bosch en Duin. (16 cm.) Photos by Antonia Graeber (1980).

3.10. From Hurault 1970:plate 41. Photo by Jean Hurault.

3.11. Moina and Anaweli dance for Headman Kala as Faanselia and Yegi look on. Photo by Richard Price (Dangogo, 1968).

3.12. Melville J. and Frances S. Herskovits Collection—S 108, Schomburg Center for Research in Black Culture (65 cm.). Photo by Antonia Graeber (1980).

page 53: "Quinze!" Photo by Richard Price (Asindoopo, 1978).

4.1. Sewn early twentieth century—see further information in text. Photo by Richard Price (Asindoopo, 1978).

4.2. Sewn by Peepina, village of Totikampu, about 1920–40. Collection of Richard and Sally Price—T78.2 (115 cm.). Photo by Richard Price (Asindoopo, 1978).

4.3. Musée des Cultures Guyanaises—90.8.144 ("cushion" = 13 cm.). Photo by Pierre Buirette (1997).

4.4. Ad for American Museum of Natural History installation of "Afro-American Arts from the Suriname Rain Forest," *New York Times*, 6 November 1981, p. C30.

4.5. Dominant colors are red, white, navy, and yellow. Collection of Richard and Sally Price—T92.1 (126 cm.). Photo by Hans Lorenz (1997).

4.6. Photo courtesy of the Photothèque, Musée de l'Homme, Paris (negative no. D.32.2022.53).

4.7. Photo courtesy of the Surinaams Museum, Paramaribo.

4.8. From Kahn 1931:facing p. 162. Photo by Klein.

4.9. Photo by Ineke van Wetering (Diitabiki, 1961).

4.10. Photo by Richard Price (Dangogo, 1968).

4.11. Photo by Richard Price (Dangogo, 1968).

4.12. Photo by Richard Price (Dangogo, 1968).

4.13. Drawings by Margaret Falk, after field sketches by Sally Price (Dangogo, 1968).

4.14. From Bruyning and Lichtveld 1959:59. Photo by C. F. A. Bruyning (Saje, 1952).

4.15. Photo by Richard Price (Niukonde, 1968).

4.16. Photo by Ineke van Wetering (Diitabiki, 1962).

4.17. Photo by Chris de Beet.

4.18. Pete, Dangogo, 1968. Photo by Sally Price.

4.19. *Top to bottom*: collected 1932–38, Rijksmuseum voor Volkenkunde, Leiden—2452-449 (6 cm. wide); collected late 1920s, American Museum of Natural History, New York—26.72 (6 cm. wide); the next four are from the Fowler Museum of Cultural History, Los Angeles—X72-111, X71-629, X72-112, X72-113, X71-630, all collected in the 1960s (8–11 cm. wide); collected before 1906, Museum voor Land- en Volkenkunde, Rotterdam—9808 (2 cm. wide). Photos by Antonia Graeber (1980).

4.20a. *Left to right*: Surinaams Museum T79 (30 cm.); Rijksmuseum voor Volkenkunde, Leiden—2452-466 (20 cm.). Photo by Antonia Graeber (1980).

4.20b. *Left to right*: Collection of Richard and Sally Price—M78.1 (24 cm.); Surinaams Museum, Paramaribo—H726 (30 cm.). Photo by Antonia Graeber (1980).

4.21. Photo by Richard Price (Dangogo, 1968).

4.22. From Tripot 1910:facing p. 136.

4.23. Photo courtesy of the Koninklijk Instituut voor de Tropen, Amsterdam.

4.24. From M. and F. Herskovits 1934:facing p. 24.

4.25. Photo courtesy of the Surinaams Museum, Paramaribo.

4.26. From Johnston 1910:plate 103. Photo by H. van Cappelle.

4.27. From Johnston 1910:plate 102. Photo by H. van Cappelle.

4.28. From *Fotografie* 1990:79. Photo by Augusta Curiel.

4.29. From Kahn 1931:facing p. 16.

4.30. Tropenmuseum, Amsterdam—H2475 (116 cm.). Photo by Antonia Graeber (1980).

4.31. From Eilerts de Haan 1910:fig. 24.

4.32. Collection of R. and S. Price—T78.10 (97 cm.). Photo by Antonia Graeber (1980).

4.33. Rijksmuseum voor Volkenkunde, Leiden—2452-431 (28 cm.). Photo by Antonia Graeber (1980).

4.34. Drafted by Margaret Falk, after a sketch by Sally Price.

4.35. Drafted by the Photographic and Illustrations Department of Johns Hopkins University, after a sketch by Sally Price.

4.36. Tropenmuseum, Amsterdam—3290-237 (108 cm.). Photo by Antonia Graeber (1980).

4.37 *left*. Sewn by Buka, village of Soola, for her husband Faansisonu, about

1940. Collection of Richard and Sally Price—T78.43 (130 cm.). Photo by Antonia Graeber (1980).

4.37 *right.* Surinaams Museum, Paramaribo—T63 (113 cm.). Photo by Antonia Graeber (1980).

4.38. Photo by Richard Price (Asindoopo, 1978).

4.39 *left.* Collected 1932–38. Rijksmuseum voor Volkenkunde, Leiden—2452–456 (99 cm.). Photo by Antonia Graeber (1980).

4.39 *right.* Collected 1978 in the Saramaka village of Pikiseei. Collection of Richard and Sally Price—T78.46 (99 cm.). Photo by Antonia Graeber (1980).

4.40. In 1980 we wrote, "About 400,000 yards of such cloth are imported to Suriname each year, now mainly from the Peoples Republic of China and from Japan, for sale to Maroons" (S. and R. Price 1980:85). We do not have comparable information for the 1990s. Photo by Sally Price (Paramaribo, 1979).

4.41. Photo by Richard Price (1968).

4.42. Adelmo of Heeikuun visiting Kulia in Dangogo. Photo by Richard Price (1968).

4.43. Elema and Suyeti on the doorstep of our house. Photo by Richard Price (Dangogo, 1968).

4.44. Musée des Cultures Guyanaises—91.8.220 (130 cm.). Photo by Pierre Buirette (1997).

4.45. Musée de l'Homme, Paris—38.21.1. Photo by the Photothèque, Musée de l'Homme (negative no. D.80.673–493).

4.46. Musée des Cultures Guyanaises—90.8.41 (166 cm.). Photo by Pierre Buirette (1997).

4.47. White cloth with pink and blue edging strips and multicolor embroidery. Collection of Richard and Sally Price—T68.11 (79 cm.). Photo by Antonia Graeber (1980).

4.48. Musée des Cultures Guyanaises—91.8.95 (54 cm.). Photo by Pierre Buirette (1997).

4.49. Black and yellow embroidery on orange cloth. Collection of Richard and Sally Price—T68.2 (77 cm.). Photo by David Porter (1978).

4.50. Black embroidery on yellow cloth. Collection of Richard and Sally Price—T78.34 (88 cm.). Photo by Antonia Graeber (1980).

4.51. Red and blue embroidery on bright yellow cloth. See also uncaptioned photo on p. 113. Photos of Lamei by Richard Price (Asindoopo, 1976).

4.52. Collected by Mando Amimba for the Musée Régional de Guyane. Musée des Cultures Guyanaises—91.9.259. Photo by Pierre Buirette (1997).

4.53. Collected near St Laurent. Collection of Richard and Sally Price—

T97.1 (97 cm.). Photo by Hans Lorenz (1997).

4.54. Collected near St. Laurent. Collection of Richard and Sally Price—T97.3 (106 cm.). Photo by Karen McCluney (1997).

4.55. See figure 4.45.

4.56. Photo by Ineke van Wetering.

4.57. Collection of Richard and Sally Price—T78.32 (94 cm.). Collected 1978 in Dangogo. Photo by the Photo and Illustrations Department of Johns Hopkins University.

4.58. Drafted by Margaret Falk, after a sketch by Sally Price.

4.59. Sewn in upper river Saramaka in the 1960s. Collection of Richard and Sally Price—T78.23 (81 cm.). Photo by A. Vonk.

4.60. Drafted by Margaret Falk, after a sketch by Sally Price.

page 113. See information on figure 4.51, above.

4.61. Fowler Museum of Cultural History, Los Angeles—X72-118 (111 cm.). Photo by Antonia Graeber (1980).

4.62. Rijksmuseum voor Volkenkunde, Leiden—2452-441 (112 cm.). Photo by Antonia Graeber (1980).

4.63. Musée des Cultures Guyanaises—91.8.204 (104 cm.). Photo by Pierre Buirette (1997).

4.64. Musée des Cultures Guyanaises—90.8.101 (100 cm.). Photo by Pierre Buirette (1997).

4.65. Surinaams Museum, Paramaribo—T27 (105 cm.). Photo by Antonia Graeber (1980).

4.66. Collection of Richard and Sally Price—T78.38 (97 cm.). Photo by Antonia Graeber (1980).

4.67. Indiana University Museum, Bloomington—1732b1/26 (131 cm.). Photo by Antonia Graeber (1980).

4.68. Chief Agbago attributed this cape to Peepina but was not certain. Collection of Richard and Sally Price—T78.3 (112 cm.). Photo by Antonia Graeber (1980).

4.69. Collection of Richard and Sally Price—T78.4 (107 cm.). Photo by Antonia Graeber (1980).

4.70. Collection of Richard and Sally Price—T78.1 (103 cm.). Photo by Antonia Graeber (1980).

4.71. Surinaams Museum, Paramaribo—94 (131 cm). Photo by Antonia Graeber (1980).

4.72. Musée des Cultures Guyanaises—91.8.219 (63 cm.). Photo by Pierre Buirette (1997).

4.73. Sammlung Herskovits 1930, Hamburgisches Museum für Völkerkunde—30.51.66 (96 cm.). From R. and S. Price 1992c:160.

4.74. Surinaams Museum, Paramaribo—T36 (90 cm). Photo by Antonia

Graeber (1980).

4.75. Surinaams Museum, Paramaribo—T35 (93 cm). Photo by Antonia Graeber (1980).

4.76. Collection of Richard and Sally Price—T78.15 (89 cm.). Photo by Antonia Graeber (1980).

4.77. Collection of Richard and Sally Price—T78.28 (99 cm.). Photo by Antonia Graeber (1980).

4.78. Collection of Richard and Sally Price—T78.29 (84 cm.). Photo by Antonia Graeber (1980).

4.79. Collection of Richard and Sally Price—T68.7 (185 cm.). Photo by Antonia Graeber (1980).

4.80. Collection of Richard and Sally Price—T68.3 (39 cm.). Photo by Antonia Graeber (1980).

4.81. Collection of Richard and Sally Price—T97.4 (130 cm.). Photo by Karen McCluney (1997).

4.82. Collection of the late Robin "Dobru" Ravales, Paramaribo (92 cm.). Photo by Antonia Graeber (1980).

4.83. Collected by Mando Amimba for the Bureau du Patrimoine Ethnologique, Guyane. Musée des Cultures Guyanaises—91.9.260 (93 cm.). Photo by Pierre Buirette (1997).

4.84. Photo by Martha Cooper (Asindoopo, 1989).

4.85. Photo by Martha Cooper (Asindoopo, 1989).

5.1. *Left to right*: Tapanahoni Ndyuka, collected 1971, Fowler Museum of Cultural History, Los Angeles—X73-444; Fowler Museum of Cultural History, Los Angeles—LX78-412; Tapanahoni Ndyuka, collected 1920s, American Museum of Natural History, New York—26.717; Paramaka child's paddle, Surinaams Museum, Paramaribo—H44; Tapanahoni Ndyuka, collected 1971, Fowler Museum of Cultural History, Los Angeles—X73-443. Photo by Antonia Graeber (1980). Lengths vary from 45 to 168 cm.

page 131. Photos by Richard Price, Asindoopo and Dangogo.

5.2. Collection of Richard and Sally Price—W76.1 (26 cm.). Photo by Antonia Graeber (1980).

5.3. Collected before 1932. Musée de l'Homme, Paris—32.96.6 (49 cm.). Photo by Antonia Graeber (1980).

5.4. Carved 1955–65, upper river Saramaka. Collection of Richard and Sally Price—W68.13 (46 cm.). Photo by Antonia Graeber (1980).

5.5. Collected before 1932. Musée de l'Homme, Paris—47.14.19 (59 cm.). Photo by Antonia Graeber (1980).

5.6. Collection of Silvia W. de Groot, Amsterdam (48 cm.). Photo by Antonia Graeber (1980).

5.7. Sammlung Herskovits 1930, Hamburgisches Museum für Völkerkunde—30.51.96 (131 cm.). Photo by Antonia Graeber (1980).

5.8. Surinaams Museum, Paramaribo—H916 (235 cm.). Photo by Antonia Graeber (1980).

5.9. Collection of John C. Walsh, Boston (61 cm.). Photo by Antonia Graeber (1980).

5.10. Melville J. and Frances S. Herskovits Collection—S 110, Schomburg Center for Research in Black Culture (43 cm.). Photo by Antonia Graeber (1980).

5.11. From Oudschans-Dentz and Jacobs 1917:fig. 120.

5.12. Photo by Silvia W. de Groot (Kambaloa, 1961).

5.13. Surinaams Museum, Paramaribo (137 cm.). Photo by Antonia Graeber (1980).

5.14. Fowler Museum of Cultural History, Los Angeles—X72-94 (85 cm.). Photo by Antonia Graeber (1980).

5.15. Collected before 1961. Museum voor Land- en Volkenkunde, Rotterdam—54444 (39 cm.). Photo by Antonia Graeber (1980).

5.16. Surinaams Museum, Paramaribo—H550 (39 cm.). Photo by Antonia Graeber (1980).

5.17. Collected 1928–29 in the Saramaka village of Ganzee. Sammlung Herskovits 1930, Hamburgisches Museum für Völkerkunde—30.51.59 (42 cm.). Photo by Antonia Graeber (1980).

5.18. Drawn by Margaret Falk, after a sketch by Richard Price (1969).

5.19. Photo by Richard Price (Dangogo, 1968).

page 145. Photo by Richard Price, Dangogo.

5.20. Photo by Richard Price (Dangogo, 1968).

5.21. Collection of Richard and Sally Price—W76.1 (26 cm.). Photo by Antonia Graeber (1980).

5.22. Collection of Richard and Sally Price—W68.8 (33 cm.). Photo by Richard Price (Dangogo, 1968).

5.23. Photo by Richard Price (Dangogo, 1968).

5.24. Collected late 1920s in the Sara Creek village of Pisiang. American Museum of Natural History, New York—26.360 (29 cm.). Photo by Antonia Graeber (1980).

5.25. Collected 1974 in Niukonde. Collection of Silvia W. de Groot, Amsterdam (26 cm.). Photo by Antonia Graeber (1980).

5.26. Melville J. and Frances S. Herskovits Collection—S 2, Schomburg Center for Research in Black Culture (22 cm.). Photo Museum of African Art, Washington, D.C. (1980).

5.27. Carved 1979 in Guyaba. Collected by Richard and Sally Price—labeled W79.7 (26 cm.)—now stolen. Photo by Antonia Graeber (1980).

5.28. Sammlung Herskovits 1930, Hamburgisches Museum für Völkerkunde—30.51.104 (191 cm.). Photo by Antonia Graeber (1980).

5.29. Carved by a Saramaka for his house on the Marowijne River near Albina. From van Panhuys 1928:fig. 1.

5.30. The lintel may represent a later addition. Photo by Richard Price (Dangogo, 1968).

5.31. Photo by Richard Price (Dangogo, 1968).

5.32. Carved by Gaduansu—for a full view of the house front, see S. and R. Price 1980:fig. 184. Photo by Richard Price (Dangogo, 1968).

5.33. Collection of Jean Hurault (50 cm.). From Hurault 1970:plate XIV.

5.34. American Museum of Natural History, New York—26.2 (43 cm.). Photo by Antonia Graeber (1980).

5.35. *From left to right:* Tropenmuseum, Amsterdam—H2780, photo by Tropenmuseum; Tropenmuseum, Amsterdam—H2307-1, photo by Tropenmuseum; photo by Richard Price (Dangogo, 1968).

5.36. *From left to right:* Fowler Museum of Cultural History, Los Angeles—X79-495, photo by Antonia Graeber (1980); two photos by Richard Price (1978).

5.37. Sammlung Herskovits 1930, Hamburgisches Museum für Völkerkunde—30.51.119 (64 cm.). Photo by Antonia Graeber (1980).

5.38. Collection of Silvia W. de Groot, Amsterdam (70 cm). Photo by Antonia Graeber (1980).

5.39. Photo by Richard Price (Dangogo, 1968).

5.40. Surinaams Museum, Paramaribo—H649 (46 cm.). Photo by Antonia Graeber (1980).

5.41. Musée des Cultures Guyanaises—90.8.3 (90 cm.). Photo by Pierre Buirette (1997).

5.42. The paddle on the left has birdshot embedded in the center of the handle, so that it makes a shaking sound when moved. Musée des Cultures Guyanaises—90.8.4, 90.8.89, 90.8.226 (132, 126, 120 cm.). Photo by Pierre Buirette (1997).

5.43. Musée des Cultures Guyanaises—90.9.21 (87 cm.). Photo by Pierre Buirette (1997).

5.44. Apindagoon is from the village of Kambaloa and was nineteen when he carved this piece. Musée des Cultures Guyanaises—90.9.22 (56 cm.). Photo by Pierre Buirette (1997).

5.45. Miseli is from the village of Dangogo and was twenty-three when he carved this piece. Musée des Cultures Guyanaises—90.9.17 (36 cm.). Photo by Pierre Buirette (1997).

5.46. Elion is from the village of Gaantatai and was fifteen when he carved this piece. Musée des Cultures Guyanaises—90.9.16 (25 cm.). Photo by

Pierre Buirette (1997).

5.47. Collection of Richard and Sally Price—W95.4 (16 cm.). Photo by Pierre Buirette (1997).

5.48. Detail of figure 4.10.

5.49. From S. and R. Price 1980:figs. 191a, 190c.

5.50. *From left to right*: Musée des Cultures Guyanaises—90.9.12 (34 cm.); collection of Richard and Sally Price—W95.6 (33 cm.); collection of Richard and Sally Price—W95.5 (36 cm.). Photos by Pierre Buirette (1997).

5.51. From *Yale Alumni Magazine* (November) 1995, p. 47. We are grateful to Sidney W. Mintz for providing this photo.

5.52. From R. and S. Price 1995:79.

5.53. Collection of Richard and Sally Price—W79.5 (65 cm.). Photo by Antonia Graeber (1980).

5.54. American Museum of Natural History, New York—26.847a,b (133 cm.). Photo by Antonia Graeber (1980).

5.55. Sammlung Herskovits 1930, Hamburgisches Museum für Völkerkunde—30.51.55 (65 cm.). Photo by Antonia Graeber (1980).

5.56. Collection of Richard and Sally Price—W68.3, M68.18 (53 cm., 17 cm.). Photo by Antonia Graeber (1980).

5.57. American Museum of Natural History, New York—26.588 (51 cm.). Photo by Antonia Graeber (1980).

5.58. Collection of Richard and Sally Price—W76.5 (51 cm.). Photo by David Porter (1978).

5.59. Collection of Richard and Sally Price—W79.3 (51 cm.). Photo by David Porter (1978).

5.60. American Museum of Natural History, New York—26.810. Photo by American Museum of Natural History.

5.61. Melville J. and Frances S. Herskovits Collection—S 106, Schomburg Center for Research in Black Culture (64 cm.). Photo by Antonia Graeber (1980).

5.62. Musée des Cultures Guyanaises—90.8.174 (65 cm.). Photo by Pierre Buirette (1997).

5.63. Musée des Cultures Guyanaises—90.9.20 (60 cm.). Photo by Pierre Buirette (1997).

5.64. Musée de l'Homme, Paris—47.14.49 (60 cm.). Photo by Antonia Graeber (1980).

5.65. *From top to bottom*: collection of Richard and Sally Price—W97.1 (24 cm.), the carver was born in 1974; collection of Richard and Sally Price—W95.1 (21 cm.); collection of Richard and Sally Price—W97.5 (30 cm.), the carver was born in 1958. Photo by Hans Lorenz (1997).

5.66. Musée des Cultures Guyanaises—90.9.23 (47 cm.). Photo by Pierre Buirette (1997).

5.67. Musée des Cultures Guyanaises—90.8.9 (77 cm.). Photo by Pierre Buirette (1997).

5.68. Musée des Cultures Guyanaises—90.8.1 (23 cm.). Photo by Pierre Buirette (1997).

5.69. Collection of Richard and Sally Price—W95.7 (25 cm.). Photo by Pierre Buirette (1997).

5.70. American Museum of Natural History, New York—26.239. Photo by American Museum of Natural History.

5.71. *Left*, Rijksmuseum voor Volkenkunde, Leiden—2452-504 (26 cm.); *right*, Fowler Museum of Cultural History, Los Angeles—X71-615 (24 cm). Photo by Antonia Graeber (1980).

5.72. Musée des Cultures Guyanaises—90.8.75 (44 cm.). Photo by Pierre Buirette (1997).

5.73. Collection Jean Hurault, Paris (151, 132, 124, 140, 161 cm.). Photo by Antonia Graeber (1980).

5.74. Tropenmuseum, Amsterdam—H2852 (50 cm.). Photo by Antonia Graeber (1980).

5.75. Museum voor Land- en Volkenkunde, Rotterdam—25596 (29 cm.). Photo by Antonia Graeber (1980).

5.76. Rijksmuseum voor Volkenkunde, Leiden—370-424 (45 cm.). Photo by Antonia Graeber (1980).

5.77. Rijksmuseum voor Volkenkunde, Leiden—399-8 (51 cm.). Photo by Antonia Graeber (1980).

5.78. Tropenmuseum, Amsterdam—H2792 (38 cm.). Photo by Antonia Graeber (1980).

5.79. Surinaams Museum, Paramaribo—1042 (57 cm.). Photo by Antonia Graeber (1980).

5.80. Musée de l'Homme, Paris—01.26.2 (65 cm.). Photo by Antonia Graeber (1980).

5.81. Musée de l'Homme, Paris—39.25.581 (41 cm.). Photo by Antonia Graeber (1980).

5.82. Sammlung Herskovits 1930, Hamburgisches Museum für Völkerkunde—30.51.177 (60 cm.). Photo by Antonia Graeber (1980).

5.83. Musée de l'Homme, Paris—81.107.21 (67 cm.). Photo by Antonia Graeber (1980).

5.84. American Museum of Natural History, New York—26.354 (55 cm.). Photo by Antonia Graeber (1980).

5.85. American Museum of Natural History, New York—26.350 (84 cm.). Photo by Antonia Graeber (1980).

5.86. Musée de l'Homme, Paris—99.43.1 (29 cm.). Photo by Antonia Graeber (1980).

5.87. Collection of Richard and Sally Price—W68.6 (16 cm.). Photo by Antonia Graeber (1980).

5.88. Collection of Richard and Sally Price—W68.7 (17 cm.). Photo by Antonia Graeber (1980).

5.89. Royal Museum of Central Africa, Tervuren, Belgium—R.G. 48.42.4 (25 cm.). Photo by Antonia Graeber (1980).

5.90. American Museum of Natural History, New York—26.703 (34 cm.). Photo by Antonia Graeber (1980).

5.91. Musée de l'Homme, Paris—39.25.547 (30 cm.). Photo by Antonia Graeber (1980).

5.92. Melville J. and Frances S. Herskovits Collection—S 32, Schomburg Center for Research in Black Culture (40 cm.). Photo by Antonia Graeber (1980).

5.93. Surinaams Museum, Paramaribo—H331 (36 cm.). Photo by Antonia Graeber (1980).

5.94. Tropenmuseum, Amsterdam—2345-187 (36 cm.). Photo by Antonia Graeber (1980).

5.95. Surinaams Museum, Paramaribo—H155 (39 cm.). Photo by Antonia Graeber (1980).

5.96. Musée de l'Homme, Paris—01.26.4 (38 cm.). Photo by Antonia Graeber (1980).

5.97. American Museum of Natural History, New York—26.203. Photo by American Museum of Natural History.

5.98. Musée de l'Homme, Paris—39.25.538 (31 cm.). Photo by Antonia Graeber (1980).

5.99. Tropenmuseum, Amsterdam—H2509 (41 cm.). Photo by Antonia Graeber (1980).

5.100. Melville J. and Frances S. Herskovits Collection—S 102, Schomburg Center for Research in Black Culture (53 cm.). Photo by Antonia Graeber (1980).

5.101. Surinaams Museum, Paramaribo—H1078 (97 cm.). Photo by Antonia Graeber (1980).

5.102. Collection of Silvia W. de Groot, Amsterdam (56 cm). Photo by Antonia Graeber (1980).

5.103. Surinaams Museum, Paramaribo—H136 (53 cm.). Photo by Antonia Graeber (1980).

5.104. Rijksmuseum voor Volkenkunde, Leiden—399-1 (32 cm.). Photo by Antonia Graeber (1980).

5.105. American Museum of Natural History, New York—26.154 (37 cm.).

Photo by Antonia Graeber (1980).

5.106. Fowler Museum of Cultural History, Los Angeles—X71-632 (102 cm.). Photo by Antonia Graeber (1980).

5.107. Borrowed from the carver for the day by Richard and Sally Price, 5 June 1997 (31 cm.). Photo by Pierre Buirette.

5.108. Musée des Cultures Guyanaises—90.9.4 (37 cm.). Photo by Pierre Buirette (1997).

5.109. Musée des Cultures Guyanaises—90.8.244 (149 cm.). Photo by Pierre Buirette (1997).

Chapter 5, note 1. Drawing by Margaret Falk, after (*left*) a sketch by Sally Price and (*right*) Roth 1924:fig. 81AA.

6.1. From Dark 1954: fig. 51b (also on the cover of his book). Collected in the Saramaka village of Ganzee in the late 1920s (24 cm.).

6.2. Photo by Sally Price (1978).

6.3. Photo by Sally Price (Asindoopo, 1978).

6.4. Photo by Richard Price (Dangogo, 1968).

6.5. Photo by Sally Price (Dangogo, 1968).

6.6. Musée de l'Homme, Paris—78.32.185. Photo by the Photothèque, Musée de l'Homme (negative no. D.80.597.493).

6.7. Rijksmuseum voor Volkenkunde, Leiden—360-1602 (32 cm.). Photo by Rijksmuseum voor Volkenkunde.

6.8. *Left and right rear* (lid and base of a single container): collected before 1887, Tropenmuseum, Amsterdam—A6113c (14 cm.); *front*: collected before 1874, Tropenmuseum, Amsterdam—H2555 (11 cm.). Photo by Antonia Graeber (1980).

6.9. Rijksmuseum voor Volkenkunde, Leiden—1817-250 (22 cm.). Photo by Antonia Graeber (1980).

6.10. Musée de l'Homme, Paris—81.34.6. Photo by the Photothèque, Musée de l'Homme (negative no. D.80.596.493).

6.11. Tropenmuseum, Amsterdam—1556/2 (15 cm.). Photo by Antonia Graeber (1980).

6.12. Collection of Richard and Sally Price—K78.62 (18 cm.). Photo by Antonia Graeber (1980).

6.13. Tropenmuseum, Amsterdam—798/2a,b (42 cm.); carved by Kekeete (Asindoopo), collection of Richard and Sally Price—K76.27 (19 cm.). Photo by Antonia Graeber (1980).

6.14. American Museum of Natural History, New York—26.237a,b (51 cm.). Photo by Antonia Graeber (1980).

6.15. Tropenmuseum, Amsterdam—H2559 (20 cm.). Photo by Antonia Graeber (1980).

6.16. *Left*, collection of Richard and Sally Price—K76.18 (13 cm.), photo by

Antonia Graeber (1980); *right*, collection of Richard and Sally Price—K90.21 (15 cm.), photo by Hans Lorenz (1997).

6.17. Surinaams Museum, Paramaribo—H1066 (18 cm.). Photo by Antonia Graeber (1980).

6.18. *Left*, carved by Keekete (Asindoopo) before 1978, collection of Richard and Sally Price—K78.11 (19 cm.); *right*, carved by Keekete (Asindoopo), 1960s, collection of Richard and Sally Price—K68.2 (23 cm.); *foreground*, carved 1970s in Pempe, collection of Richard and Sally Price—K76.26 (15 cm.). Photos by Antonia Graeber (1980).

6.19. Musée des Cultures Guyanaises—*rear*, 90.8.27 (20 cm.); *foreground, left to right*: 90.8.33 (13 cm.), 90.8.25 (13 cm.), 90.8.22 (14 cm.). Photo by Pierre Buirette (1997).

6.20. *Left to right*: collection of Richard and Sally Price—K76.182 (14 cm.), photo by Antonia Graeber (1980); Surinaams Museum, Paramaribo—T63 (113 cm.), photo by Antonia Graeber (1980); photo by Richard Price (Asindoopo, 1978).

6.21. *Left*, Musée de l'Homme, Paris—35.72.74 (20 cm.); *right*, Surinaams Museum, Paramaribo—T82 (112 cm.). Photos by Antonia Graeber (1980).

6.22. *Left*, American Museum of Natural History, New York—26.380, photo by American Museum of Natural History; *right*, Tropenmuseum, Amsterdam—3290-237 (108 cm.), photo by Antonia Graeber (1980).

6.23. *Left*, collection of Richard and Sally Price—K76.229 (18 cm.), photo by Antonia Graeber (1980); *right*, photo by Richard Price (Dangogo, 1968).

6.24. *Left*, Tropenmuseum, Amsterdam—722/1c (15 cm.); *right*, collection of John C. Walsh, Boston (61 cm.). Photos by Antonia Graeber (1980).

6.25. *Left*, collection of John D. Lenoir (17 cm.); *right*, detail of figure 5.94. Photos by Antonia Graeber (1980).

6.26. *Left*, collection of Richard and Sally Price—K91.1 (26 cm.), photo by Karen McCluney (1997); *right*, detail of S. and R. Price 1980:fig. 204d.

6.27. *Left*, collection of Richard and Sally Price—K68.5 (17 cm.), photo by Antonia Graeber (1980); *right*, photo by Sally Price (Dangogo, 1968).

6.28.
A. Collection of Richard and Sally Price—K90.20 (20 cm.). Photo by Hans Lorenz (1997).
B. Musée des Cultures Guyanaises—90.8.34 (16 cm.). Photo by Pierre Buirette (1997).
C. Collection of Richard and Sally Price—K78.40 (18 cm.). Photo by Antonia Graeber (1980).
D. Musée des Cultures Guyanaises—90.8.55 (20 cm.). Photo by Pierre

Buirette (1997).

E. Musée des Cultures Guyanaises—90.8.21 (16 cm.). Photo by Pierre Buirette (1997).

F. Musée des Cultures Guyanaises—89.2.102(?). Photo by Pierre Buirette (1997).

G. Musée de l'Homme, Paris—35.72.85 (13 cm.). Photo by Antonia Graeber (1980).

H. Musée des Cultures Guyanaises—90.8.162 (25 cm.). Photo by Pierre Buirette (1997).

I. Musée de l'Homme, Paris—39.25.599. Photo by the Photothèque, Musée de l'Homme (negative no. D.80.598.493).

J. Musée des Cultures Guyanaises—90.8.56 (23 cm.). Photo by Pierre Buirette (1997).

6.29.

A. Musée de l'Homme, Paris—81.107.10 (25 cm.). Photo by Antonia Graeber (1980).

B. American Museum of Natural History, New York. From Dark 1954:fig. 50B.

C. Musée de l'Homme, Paris—47.14.39 (21 cm.). Photo by Antonia Graeber (1980).

D. Surinaams Museum, Paramaribo—H1087. Photo by Antonia Graeber (1980).

E. Collection of Richard and Sally Price—K91.3 (24 cm.). Photo by Pierre Buirette (1997).

F. Musée des Cultures Guyanaises—91.8.105 (21 cm.). Photo by Pierre Buirette (1997).

G. Musée des Cultures Guyanaises—91.8.19 (19 cm.). Photo by Pierre Buirette (1997).

H. Musée des Cultures Guyanaises—90.8.100 (22 cm.). Photo by Pierre Buirette (1997).

I. Collection of Richard and Sally Price—K91.2 (25 cm.). Photo by Pierre Buirette (1997).

J. Musée des Cultures Guyanaises—90.8.24 (25 cm.). Photo by Pierre Buirette (1997).

6.30.

A. Collection of Richard and Sally Price—K91.4 (26 cm.). Photo by Pierre Buirette (1997).

B. Musée des Cultures Guyanaises—91.10.13. Photo by Pierre Buirette (1997).

C. University Museum of Archaeology and Anthropology, Cambridge, England—66.181I. Photo by University Museum of Archaeology and

Anthropology.

D. Musée des Cultures Guyanaises—91.10.4. Photo by Pierre Buirette (1997).

E. Collection of Richard and Sally Price—K91.5 (22 cm.). Photo by Pierre Buirette (1997).

F. University Museum of Archaeology and Anthropology, Cambridge, England—66.181A (25 cm.). Photo by University Museum of Archaeology and Anthropology.

G. Collection of John D. Lenoir (19 cm.). Photo by Antonia Graeber (1980).

H. Musée des Cultures Guyanaises—90.10.5 (16 cm.). Photo by Pierre Buirette (1997).

I. Collection of Richard and Sally Price (gift of John D. Lenoir)—K74.3 (24 cm.). Photo by Antonia Graeber (1980).

J. Collection of John D. Lenoir (16 cm.). Photo by Antonia Graeber (1980).

6.31.

A. Collection of Richard and Sally Price—K78.24 (13 cm.). Photo by Sally Price (1978).

B. American Museum of Natural History, New York—26.83 (17 cm.). Photo by American Museum of Natural History.

C. Musée des Cultures Guyanaises—91.9.150. Photo by Pierre Buirette (1997).

D. Collection of Richard and Sally Price—K78.50 (16 cm.). Photo by Antonia Graeber (1980).

E. Collection of Richard and Sally Price—K79.11 (19 cm.). Photo by Sally Price (1982).

F. Collection of Richard and Sally Price—K78.60 (24 cm.). Photo by Antonia Graeber (1980).

G. Musée des Cultures Guyanaises—91.9.95 (22 cm.). Photo by Pierre Buirette (1997).

H. American Museum of Natural History, New York—26.273 (26 cm.) Photo by Antonia Graeber (1980).

I. Collection of Richard and Sally Price—K78.44 (25 cm.). Photo by Antonia Graeber (1980).

J. Collection of Richard and Sally Price—K76.204 (22 cm.). Photo by Antonia Graeber (1980).

7.1. Danish Royal Museum of Fine Arts, Copenhagen—Oil on canvas (58 x 46 cm.). Photo by Danish Royal Museum of Fine Arts.

7.2. Wood decorated with solutions of kaolin (white), soot (black), and berry juice from the annatto plant (red), with agouti hair and jaguar skin. Collection of Richard and Sally Price—M68.17 (33 cm.). Photo by David Porter (1978).

7.3. Photos by Silvia W. de Groot (Godo, 1961).

7.4. *Left*, photo of Asabosi by Richard Price (Dangogo, 1968); *right*, photo by Terry Agerkop (1970s).

7.5. Seed pods (*Thevetia peruviana* Schum.) attached to bands made from commercial cotton twine, collected 1979 in Santigoon. In the past, Maroons bought such anklets from Amerindians who live on the upper Marowijne River, but since these people have stopped producing them, Maroons have been making them for themselves. Fowler Museum of Cultural History, Los Angeles—X79-496 (76 cm. circumference). Photo by Antonia Graeber (1980).

7.6. Photo by Wilhelmina van Wetering (Diitabiki, 1962).

7.7. Photo by Wilhelmina van Wetering (Diitabiki, 1962).

7.8. American Museum of Natural History, New York—26.544 (44 cm.). Photo by Antonia Graeber (1980).

7.9. Drawing by Margaret Falk, after a sketch by Sally Price.

7.10. From Hurault 1970:plate 42. Photo by Jean Hurault.

7.11. Sammlung Herskovits 1930, Hamburgisches Museum für Völkerkunde—30.51.60 (50 cm.). Photo by Antonia Graeber (1980).

7.12. Some of these instruments were collected by Stedman in Suriname— see R. and S. Price 1979.

7.13. Collected in Maripasoula. Musée des Cultures Guyanaises—88.1.15 (47 cm.). From Bilby 1989:64.

7.14. Rijksmuseum voor Volkenkunde, Leiden—360-5696 (82 cm.). Photo by Antonia Graeber (1980).

7.15. Photo by Kenneth Bilby.

page 276. Saramaka comb, early twentieth century. Collection of Richard and Sally Price (gift of Dianne Nevel)—W81.1 (46 cm.). Photo by Hans Lorenz (1998).

8.1. From Thompson 1970:18.

8.2. From Fagg 1952:fig. 7 (after W. D. Webster, Ethnographical Catalogue No. 31, Item No. 167).

8.3. From Thompson 1983:plates 137, 138.

8.4. *Left*, Musée des Arts et Traditions Populaires, Paris—70.97.1, photo by Richard Price; *right*, collection of John C. Walsh, Boston (61 cm.), photo by Antonia Graeber (1980). We are grateful to William C. Sturtevant for bringing the Alsatian chair to our attention.

8.5. *Left*, Musée de l'Homme, Paris—14.5.103, photo by the Photothèque, Musée de l'Homme (negative no. E.79.1451.493); *right*, collection of Richard and Sally Price—K76.186. (19 cm.), photo by David Porter.

8.6. Sammlung Herskovits 1930, Hamburgisches Museum für Völkerkunde—30.51.141 (101 cm.). Photo by Hamburgisches Museum für Völkerkunde.

8.7. Collection of John C. Walsh, Boston (74 cm.). Photo by Antonia Graeber (1980).

8.8. Drawing by Margaret Falk, after (*from top to bottom*) Roth 1924:275Q, V and Stedman 1796:plate 40.

8.9. Drawing by Margaret Falk, after (*from left to right*) Stedman 1796:plate 39; Barbot 1732:237; Stedman 1796:plate 22; and Coster 1866:frontispiece.

Acknowledgments

THE ACKNOWLEDGMENTS for our 1980 book on Maroon arts, which served as catalogue for a large traveling exhibition sponsored by the National Endowment for the Humanities, took nearly 2000 words to spell out, and every one of the people and organizations mentioned there deserves another vote of thanks for this one, which stands on its shoulders. To recap briefly: The UCLA Museum of Cultural History, which has since become the Fowler Museum, provided the original impetus, and its staff poured tremendous time, energy, sensitivity, and expertise into every aspect of the project. Museums in Suriname, the United States, the Netherlands, France, Germany, Belgium, and the United Kingdom opened their storerooms and archives to us and made generous loans for the exhibition and catalogue. Friends and colleagues in Suriname, the Netherlands, France, and the United States also contributed both art objects and documentation. And a number of organizations supported our 1960s and 1970s field, museum, and archival research on Maroon arts—the American Council of Learned Societies, the Fulbright-Hays Program, Johns Hopkins University, the National Science Foundation, the Netherlands Institute for Advanced Study, the University of Florida, and especially the National Endowment for the Humanities.

Moving on to subsequent indebtednesses, we have received support for research that has contributed to this book from a number of sources. Sally Price has held relevant fellowships or grants from the American Council of Learned Societies (1985–86), the National Endowment for the Humanities (1985–88), the Wenner-Gren Foundation (1984–86, 1992–93), and the John Simon Guggenheim Foundation (1992–93). Richard Price has held relevant fellowships or grants from the John Simon Guggenheim Foundation (1992–93), the National Endowment for the Humanities (1992-94), and the Wenner-Gren Foundation (1992–93).

We owe special thanks to a number of people and organizations in French Guiana, where our research has been centered over the past dozen years. The Bureau du Patrimoine Ethnologique, which has recently become the Musée des Cultures Guyanaises, stands at the head of the list. Marie-Paule Jean-Louis has steadfastly refused to allow setbacks from local politics, financial crises, or government-dictated downsizing to cut into her determination to see the realization of the museum, and has extended every professional courtesy to us over our decade-long collaboration. We hope that by providing the new museum with a book that may serve as a catalogue for its Maroon holdings, we will have made clear our gratitude for the cooperative support that she and her staff have offered over the years.

During an intensive, tumultuous week of photographic work in Cayenne in 1997, Pierre Buirette went the extra kilometer to provide illustrations of objects from the future museum's collection for this book. His willingness to work cheerfully in a setting of time pressure, tropical heat, and cramped quarters deserves special thanks.

Colleagues have been generous in sharing their knowledge of Maroons and their arts: Bonno Thoden van Velzen and Ineke van Wetering, John Lenoir, Chris de Beet, Miriam Sterman. Henna Malmberg, Jerry Egger, Laddy van Putten, and the late Ben Scholtens.

We are particularly indebted to two friends and colleagues whose research centers on Maroons in French Guiana and who have shared field data, insights, and commentary on work in progress. Ken Bilby, as sensitive an ethnographer as we have known, has captured the remarkable patchwork of tradition and change in Aluku society with an unusual combination of respect and detachment. His generosity in introducing us to the people and places of his own long-term fieldwork in 1990 opened up a key comparative window for us. Diane Vernon, who has moved permanently to the rough-and-tumble border town of St. Laurent, has added considerable depth to our ethnographic understanding of life in Ndyuka villages.

Others in French Guiana who deserve thanks include Mando Amimba, Anne-Marie Bruleaux, Annie-Claude Clovis, Jean-Claude Conte, Joly Elsol, Angèle Gilormini, Daniel Machine, Alex Miles, Jozef Obentie Ameikan, Arthur Othily, Ronald Pansa, and Peter Redfield.

Adiante Franszoon, who has become a full-time woodcarver in Baltimore, continues to provide an important link for us to changing Saramaka and other Suriname realities.

Ken Bilby and Leah Price provided much appreciated comments on the manuscript. Martha Cooper generously contributed a number of previously unpublished photographs.

We are deeply grateful to the museums and individuals whose collections are visually represented in this book. Their contributions are enumerated in the section entitled "Additional Information on Illustrations."

The College of William and Mary, through the good offices of Provost

Gillian T. Cell, contributed a key subvention toward the publication of this book.

It has, once again, been a pleasure to work closely with the staff at Beacon Press—Margaret Park Bridges, Dan Ochsner, Colleen Lanick, and most especially Deb Chasman, our editor extraordinaire. *Maroon Arts* represents our second consecutive collaboration with book artist Scott-Martin Kosofsky, who has once again realized our design concept with notable imagination and flair.